So I'm a Spider, So What?

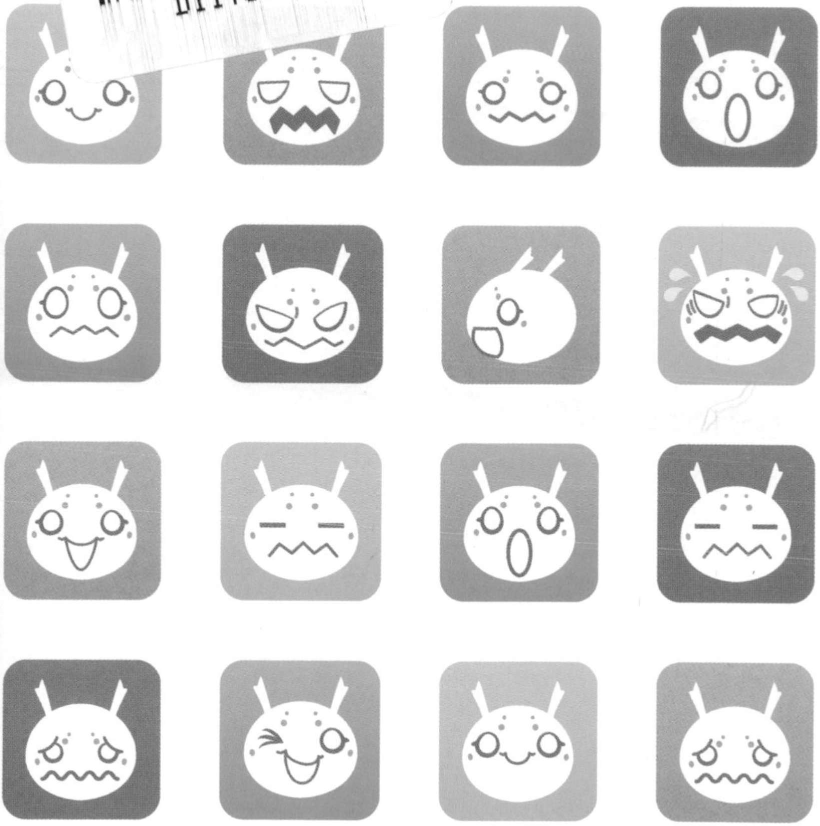

Art:
Asahiro Kakashi

Original Story:
Okina Baba

Character Design:
Tsukasa Kiryu

So I'm a Spider, So What?

CONTENTS

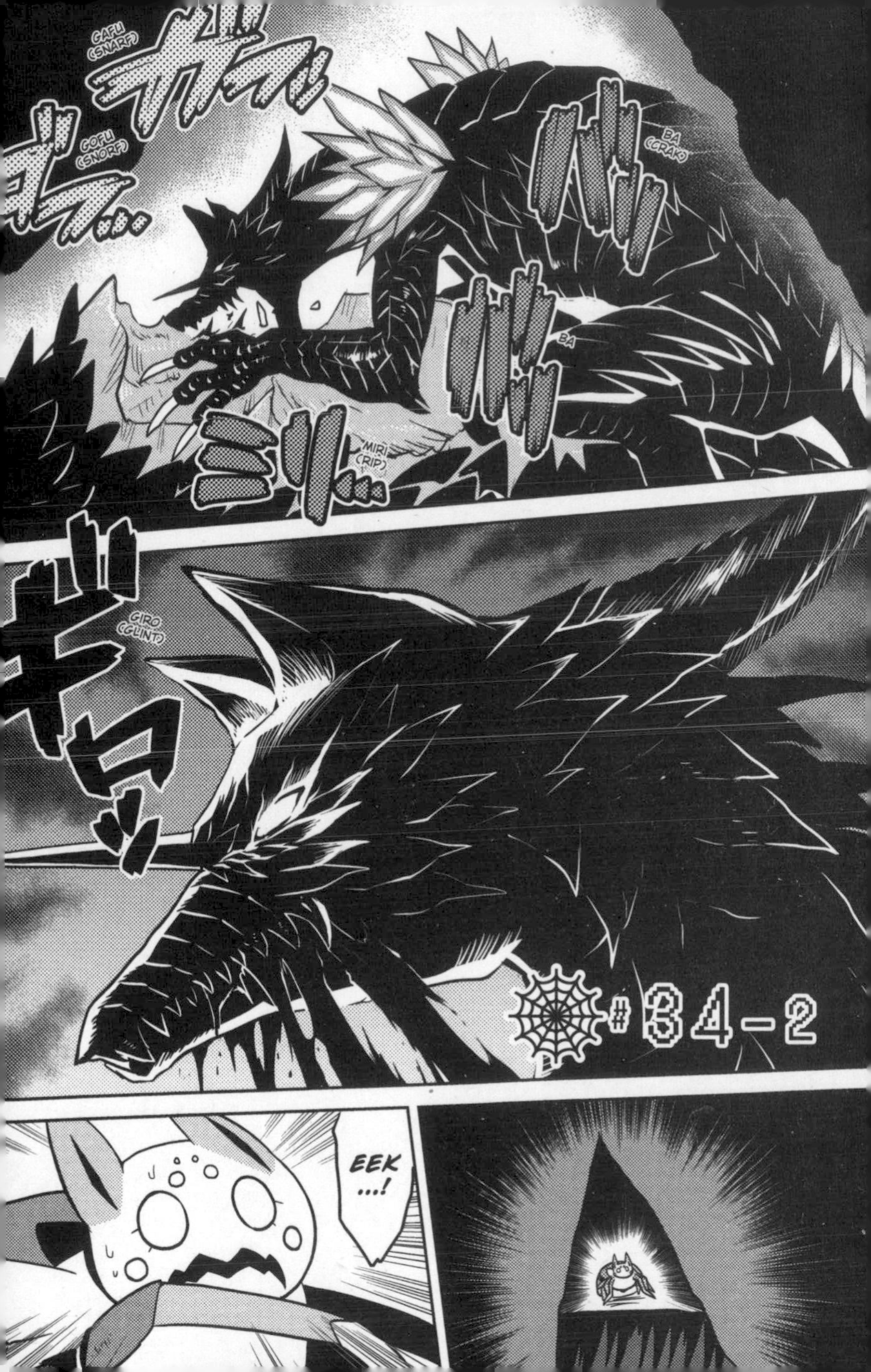
BA (CRAK)
GAFU (SNARF)
GOFU (SNORF)
BA
MIRI (RIP)
#34-2
GIRO (GLINT)
EEK ...!

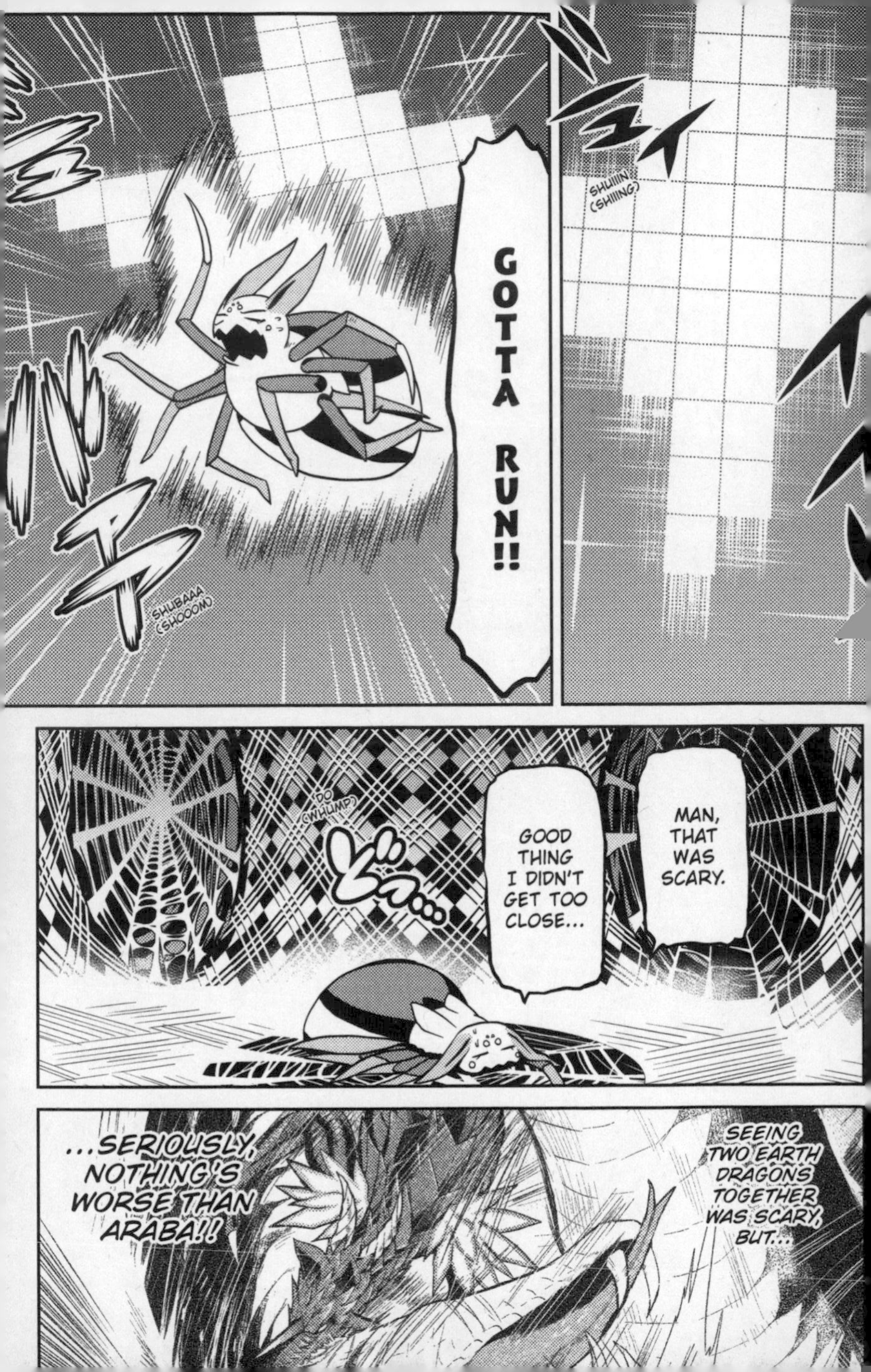
SHUIIN (SHIING)
GOTTA RUN!!
SHUBAAA (SHOOOM)
MAN, THAT WAS SCARY.
GOOD THING I DIDN'T GET TOO CLOSE...
DO (WHUMP)
SEEING TWO EARTH DRAGONS TOGETHER WAS SCARY, BUT...
...SERIOUSLY, NOTHING'S WORSE THAN ARABA!!

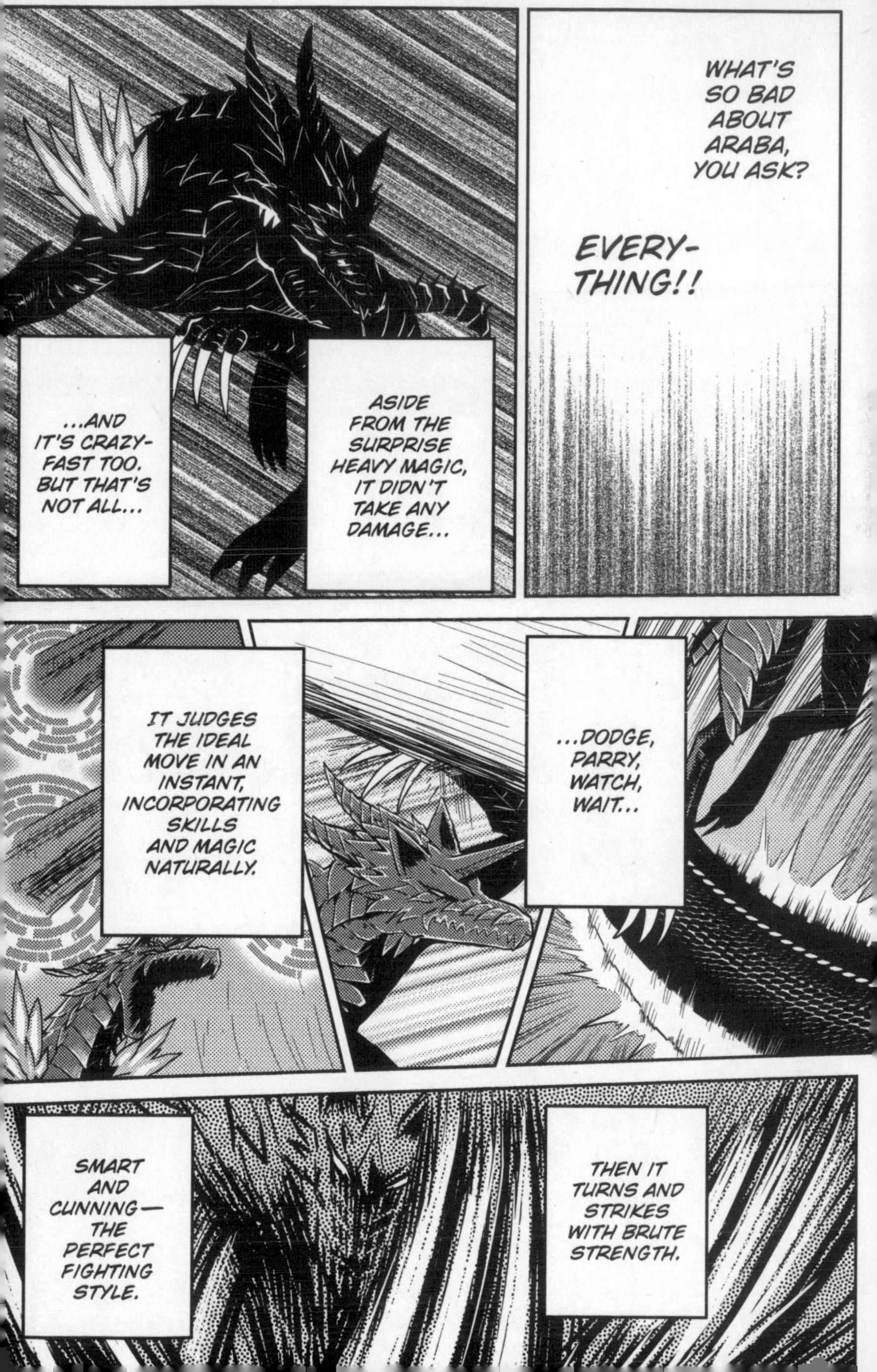
WHAT'S SO BAD ABOUT ARABA, YOU ASK?
EVERY-THING!!
ASIDE FROM THE SURPRISE HEAVY MAGIC, IT DIDN'T TAKE ANY DAMAGE...
...AND IT'S CRAZY-FAST TOO. BUT THAT'S NOT ALL...
...DODGE, PARRY, WATCH, WAIT...
IT JUDGES THE IDEAL MOVE IN AN INSTANT, INCORPORATING SKILLS AND MAGIC NATURALLY.
THEN IT TURNS AND STRIKES WITH BRUTE STRENGTH.
SMART AND CUNNING—THE PERFECT FIGHTING STYLE.

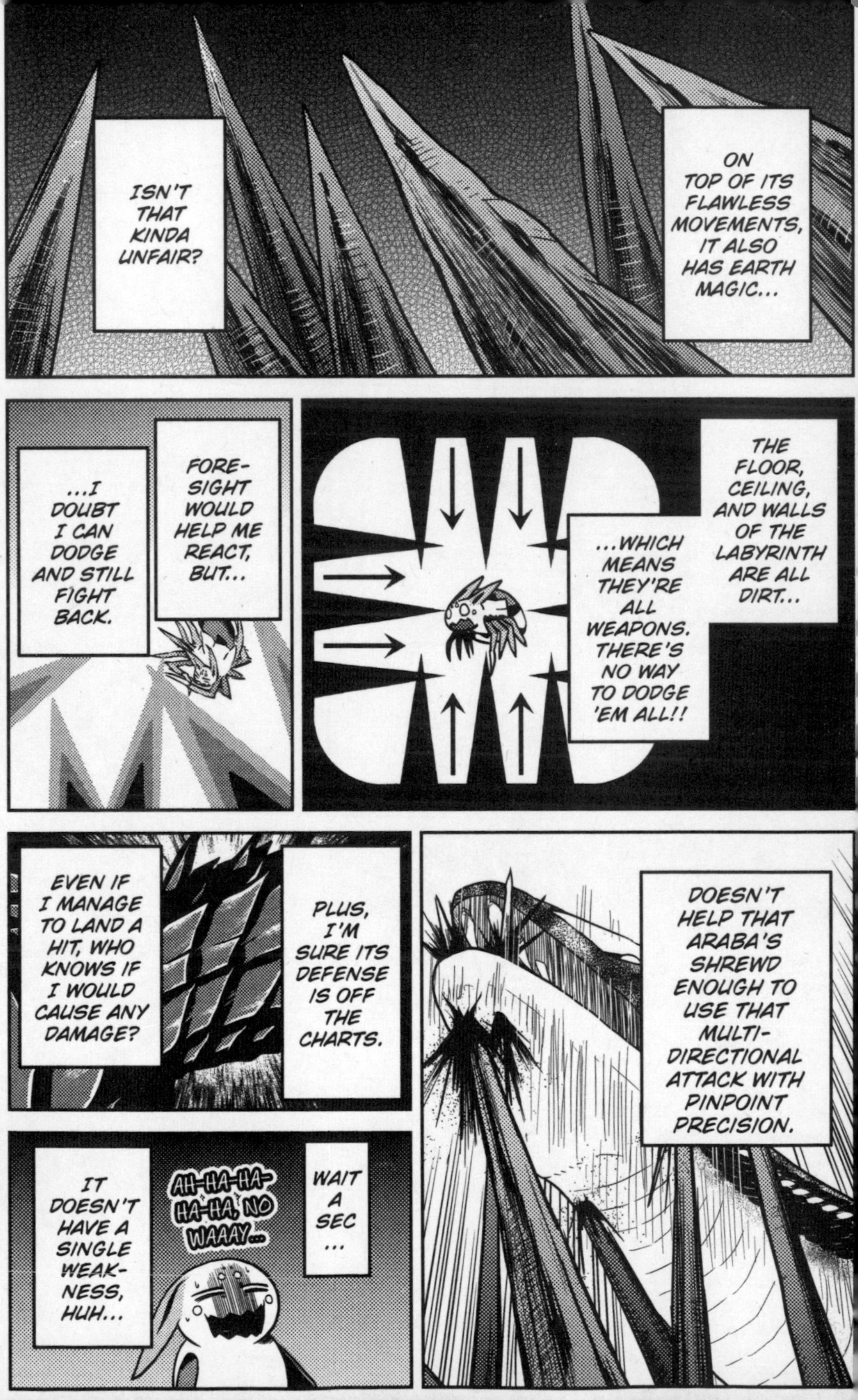
ON TOP OF ITS FLAWLESS MOVEMENTS, IT ALSO HAS EARTH MAGIC...
ISN'T THAT KINDA UNFAIR?
THE FLOOR, CEILING, AND WALLS OF THE LABYRINTH ARE ALL DIRT...
...WHICH MEANS THEY'RE ALL WEAPONS. THERE'S NO WAY TO DODGE 'EM ALL!!
FORE-SIGHT WOULD HELP ME REACT, BUT...
...I DOUBT I CAN DODGE AND STILL FIGHT BACK.
DOESN'T HELP THAT ARABA'S SHREWD ENOUGH TO USE THAT MULTI-DIRECTIONAL ATTACK WITH PINPOINT PRECISION.
PLUS, I'M SURE ITS DEFENSE IS OFF THE CHARTS.
EVEN IF I MANAGE TO LAND A HIT, WHO KNOWS IF I WOULD CAUSE ANY DAMAGE?
WAIT A SEC...
AH-HA-HA-HA-HA, NO WAAAY...
IT DOESN'T HAVE A SINGLE WEAK-NESS, HUH...

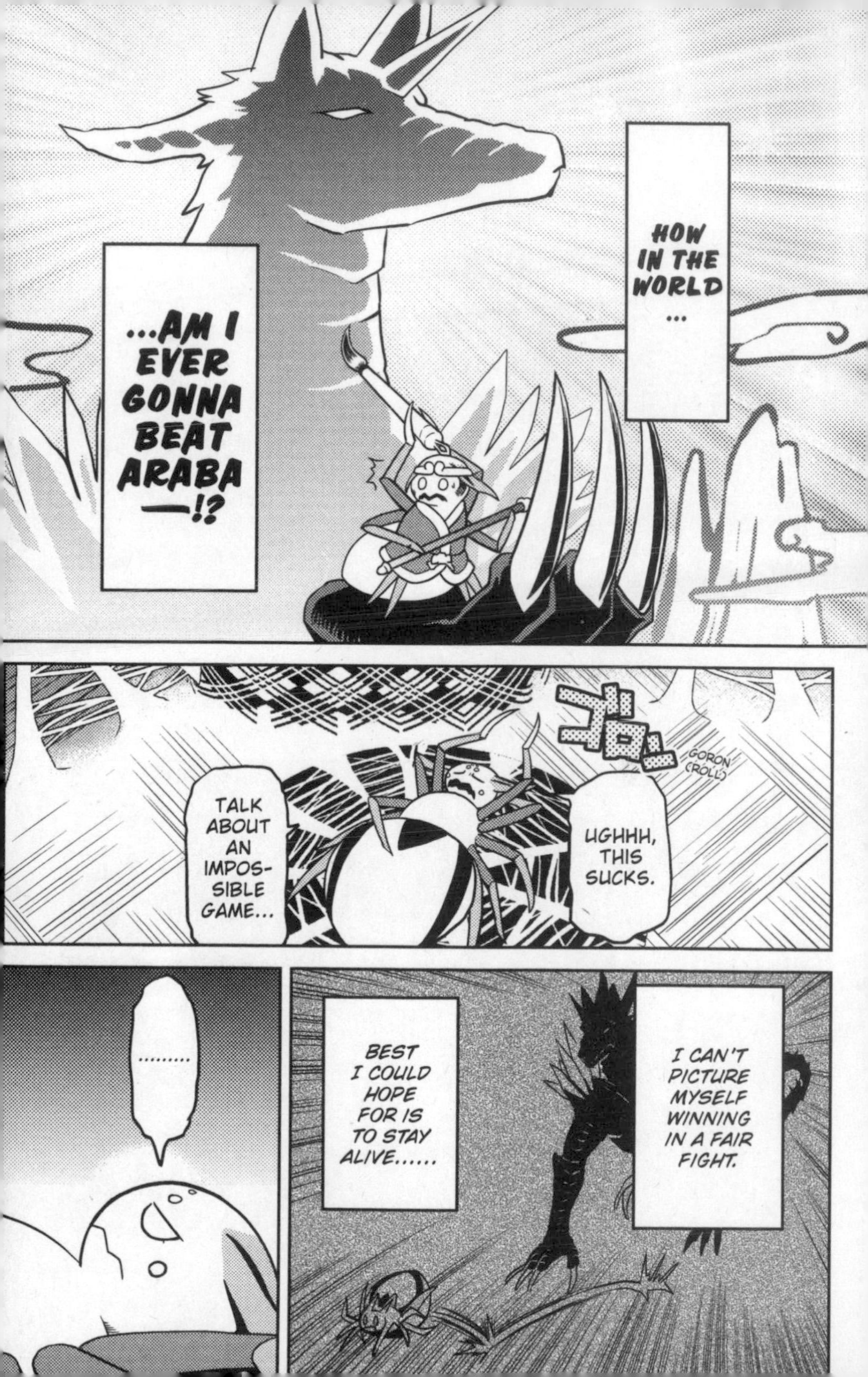
HOW IN THE WORLD ...
...AM I EVER GONNA BEAT ARABA—!?
GORON (ROLL)
UGHHH, THIS SUCKS.
TALK ABOUT AN IMPOSSIBLE GAME...
I CAN'T PICTURE MYSELF WINNING IN A FAIR FIGHT.
BEST I COULD HOPE FOR IS TO STAY ALIVE......
....

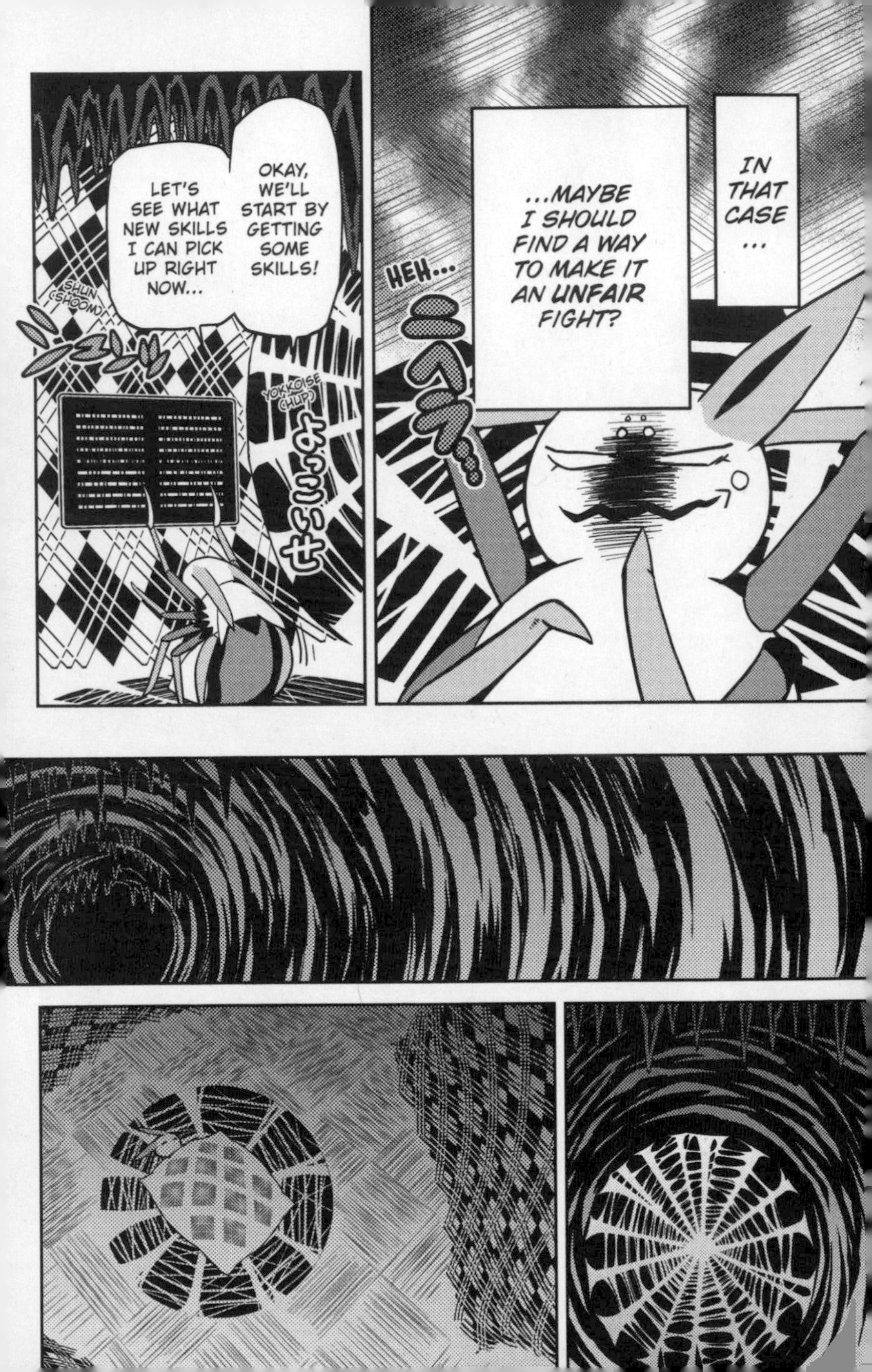
IN THAT CASE...
...MAYBE I SHOULD FIND A WAY TO MAKE IT AN UNFAIR FIGHT?
HEH...
OKAY, WE'LL START BY GETTING SOME SKILLS!
LET'S SEE WHAT NEW SKILLS I CAN PICK UP RIGHT NOW...
YOKKOISE (HUP)
よっこいせ
SHUN (SHOOM)

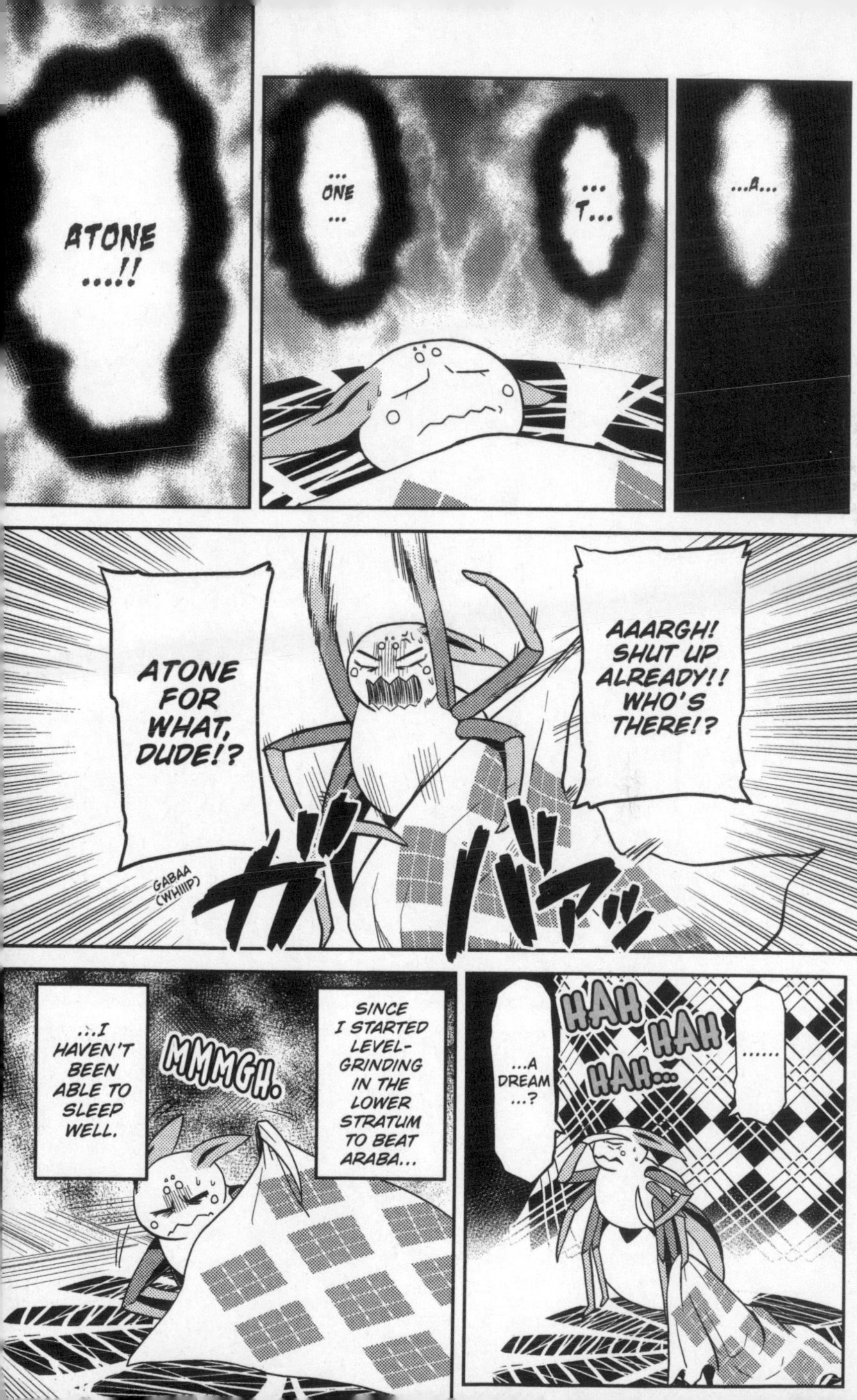
...A...
... T...
... ONE ...
ATONE ....!!
AAARGH! SHUT UP ALREADY!! WHO'S THERE!?
ATONE FOR WHAT, DUDE!?
GABAA (WHIIIP)
......
HAH HAH HAH...
...A DREAM ...?
SINCE I STARTED LEVEL-GRINDING IN THE LOWER STRATUM TO BEAT ARABA...
MMMGH.
...I HAVEN'T BEEN ABLE TO SLEEP WELL.

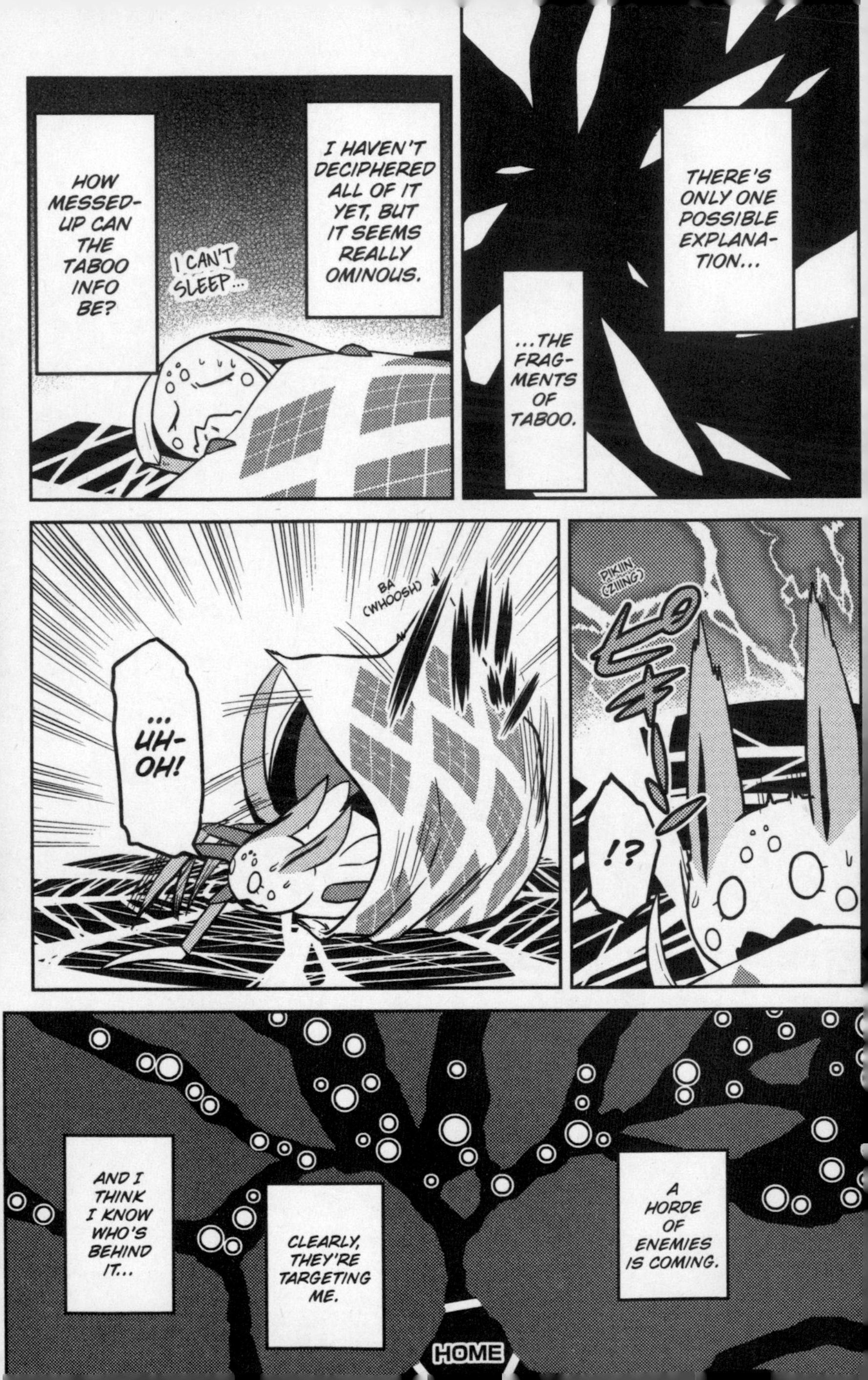
THERE'S ONLY ONE POSSIBLE EXPLANATION...
...THE FRAGMENTS OF TABOO.
I HAVEN'T DECIPHERED ALL OF IT YET, BUT IT SEEMS REALLY OMINOUS.
I CAN'T SLEEP...
HOW MESSED-UP CAN THE TABOO INFO BE?
PIKIIN (ZIIING)
!?
BA (WHOOSH)
...UH-OH!
A HORDE OF ENEMIES IS COMING.
CLEARLY, THEY'RE TARGETING ME.
AND I THINK I KNOW WHO'S BEHIND IT...
HOME

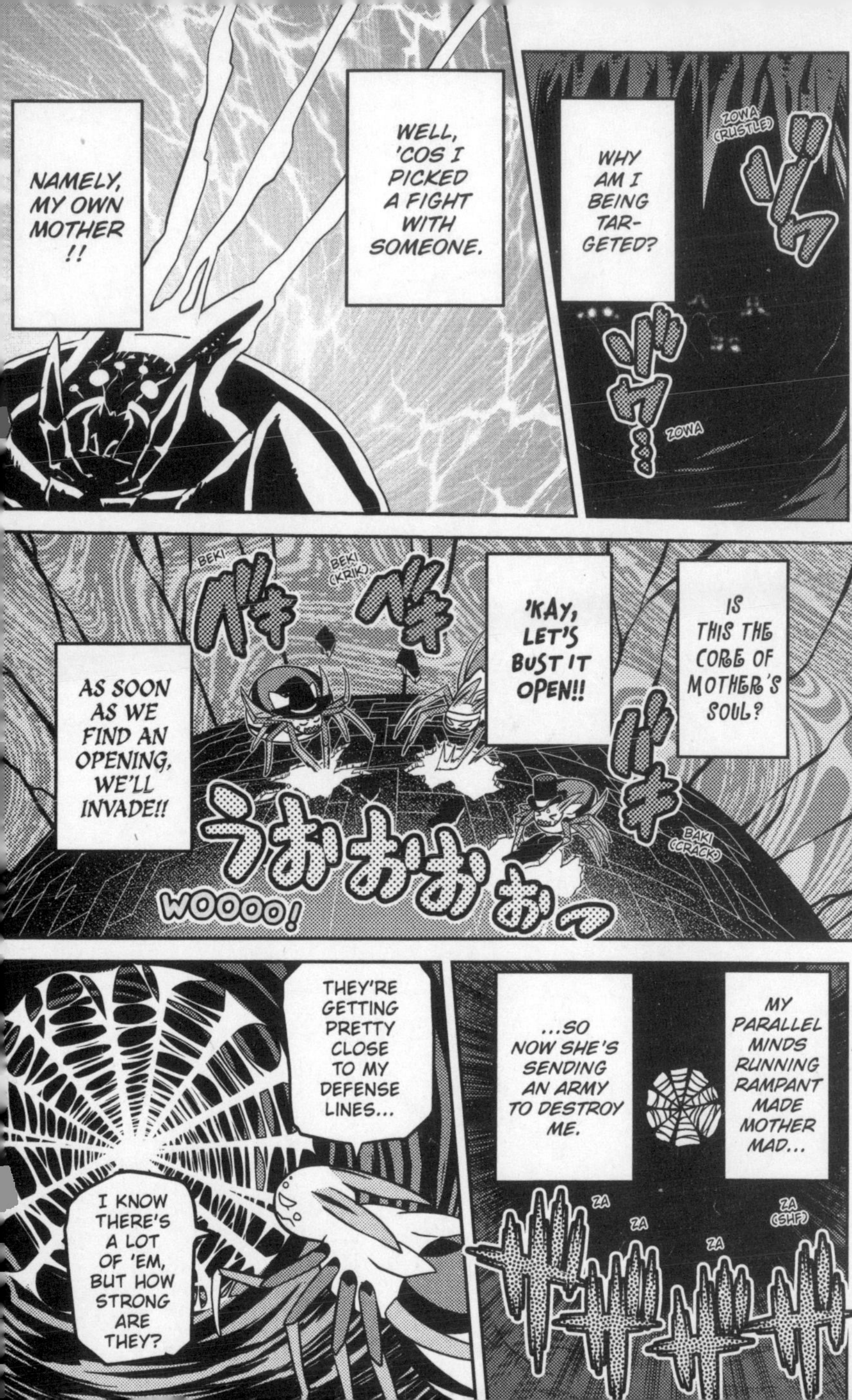
WHY AM I BEING TAR-GETED?
ZOWA (RUSTLE)
ZOWA
WELL, 'COS I PICKED A FIGHT WITH SOMEONE.
NAMELY, MY OWN MOTHER!!
IS THIS THE CORE OF MOTHER'S SOUL?
BAKI (CRACK)
'KAY, LET'S BUST IT OPEN!!
BEKI (KRIK)
BEKI
AS SOON AS WE FIND AN OPENING, WE'LL INVADE!!
WOOOO!
MY PARALLEL MINDS RUNNING RAMPANT MADE MOTHER MAD...
...SO NOW SHE'S SENDING AN ARMY TO DESTROY ME.
ZA (SHF)
ZA
ZA
ZA
THEY'RE GETTING PRETTY CLOSE TO MY DEFENSE LINES...
I KNOW THERE'S A LOT OF 'EM, BUT HOW STRONG ARE THEY?

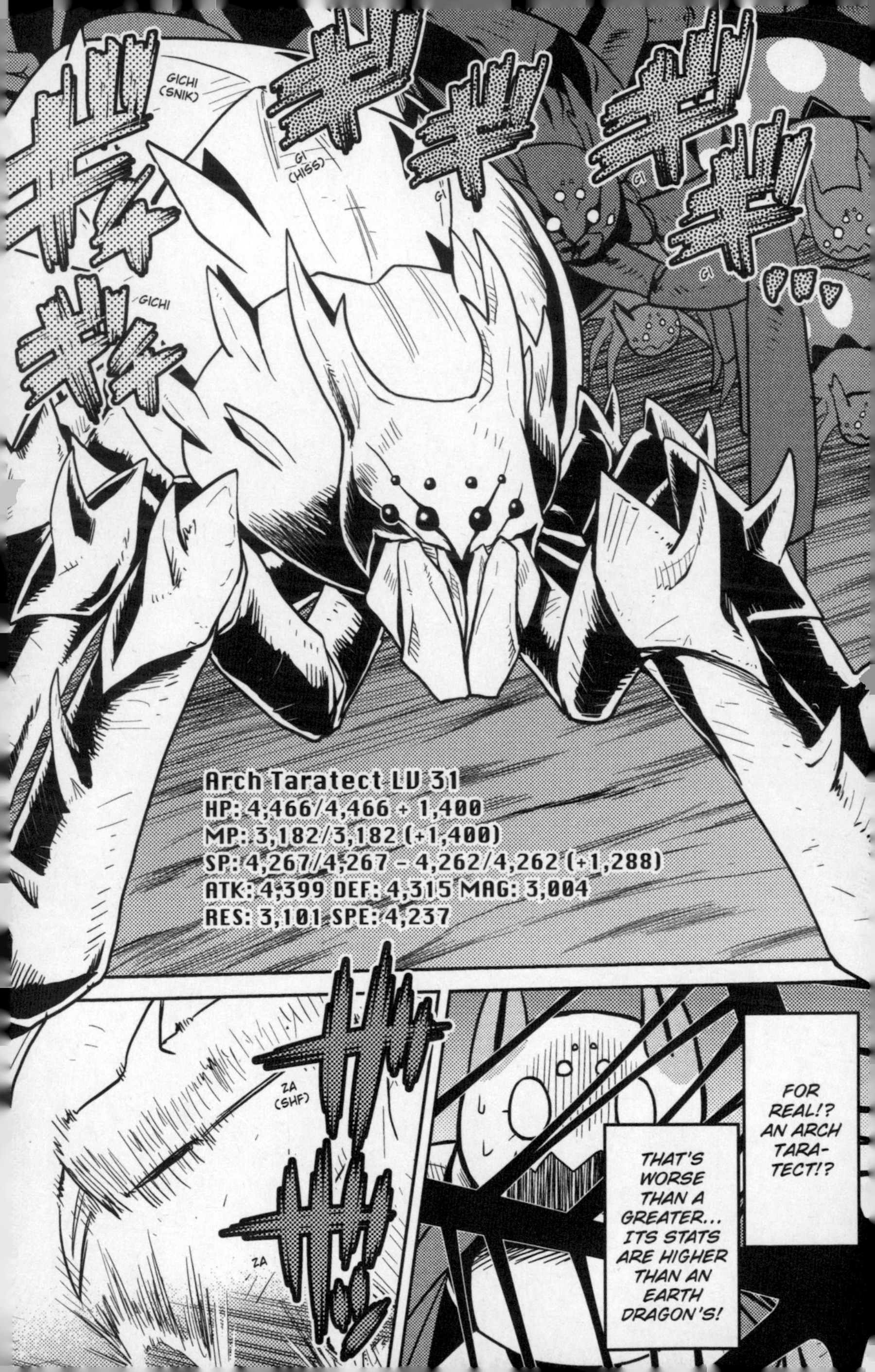
GI
GI
GI
GI
(HISS)
GICHI
(SNIK)
GICHI
Arch Taratect LV 31
HP: 4,466/4,466 + 1,400
MP: 3,182/3,182 (+1,400)
SP: 4,267/4,267 - 4,262/4,262 (+1,288)
ATK: 4,399 DEF: 4,315 MAG: 3,004
RES: 3,101 SPE: 4,237
FOR REAL!? AN ARCH TARATECT!?
THAT'S WORSE THAN A GREATER... ITS STATS ARE HIGHER THAN AN EARTH DRAGON'S!
ZA
(SHF)
ZA

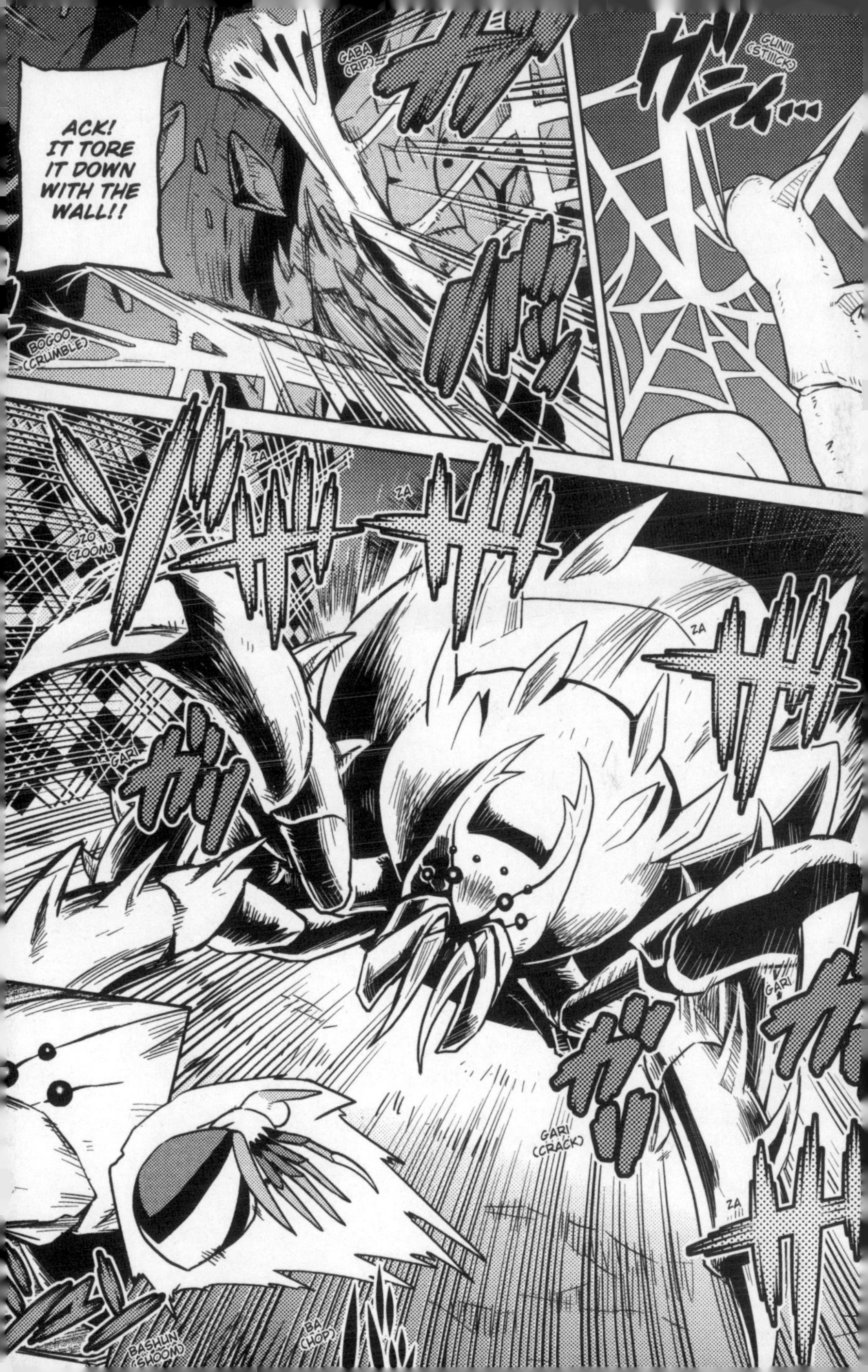
GUNII (STIIICK)
GABA (RIP)
ACK! IT TORE IT DOWN WITH THE WALL!!
BOGOO (CRUMBLE)
ZA
ZA
ZA
ZO (ZOOM)
GARI
GARI (CRACK)
GARI
ZA
BA (HOP)
BASHUN (SHOOM)

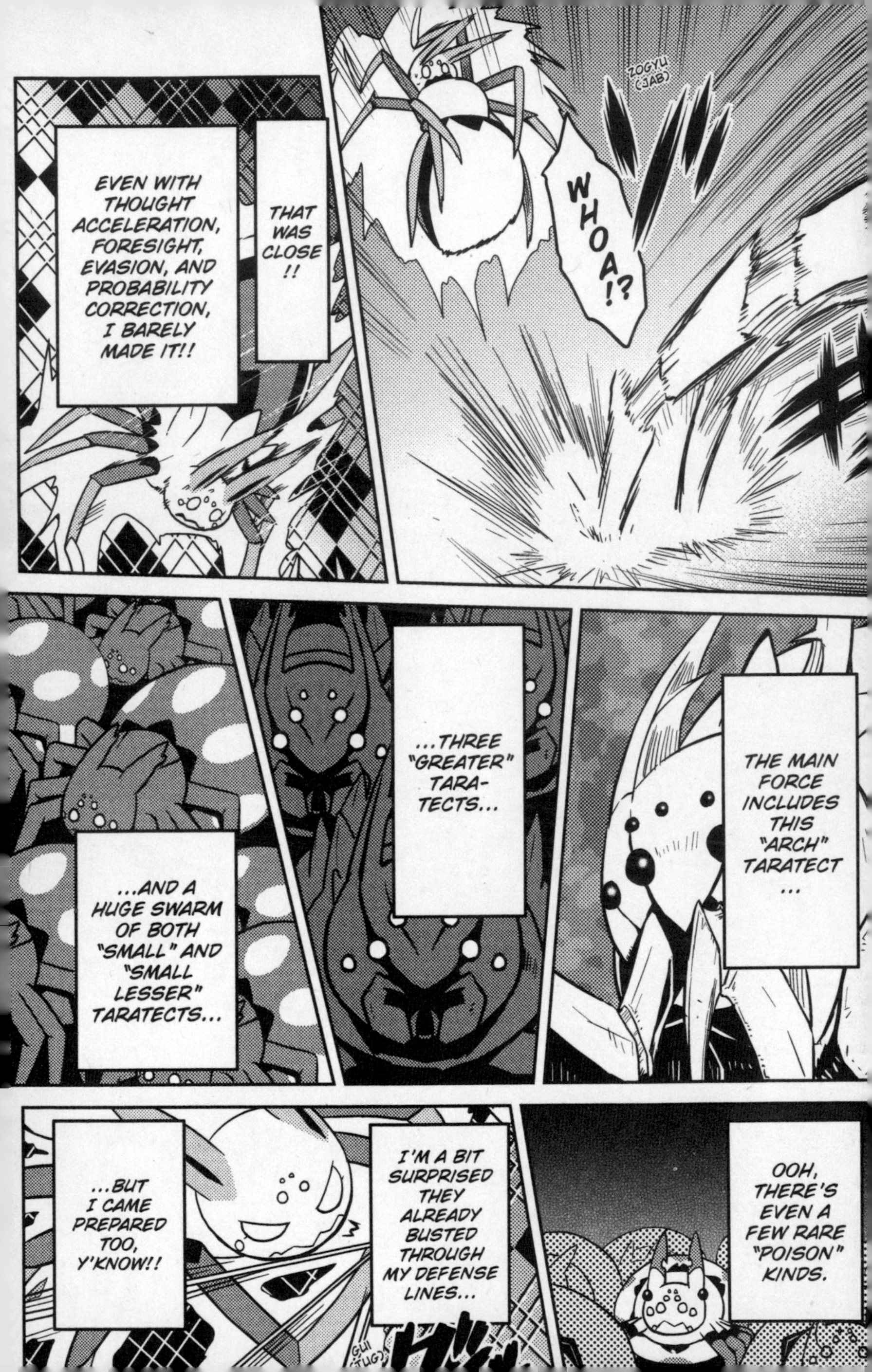
ZOGYU (JAB)
WHOA!?
THAT WAS CLOSE!!
EVEN WITH THOUGHT ACCELERATION, FORESIGHT, EVASION, AND PROBABILITY CORRECTION, I BARELY MADE IT!!
THE MAIN FORCE INCLUDES THIS "ARCH" TARATECT...
...THREE "GREATER" TARA-TECTS...
...AND A HUGE SWARM OF BOTH "SMALL" AND "SMALL LESSER" TARATECTS...
OOH, THERE'S EVEN A FEW RARE "POISON" KINDS.
I'M A BIT SURPRISED THEY ALREADY BUSTED THROUGH MY DEFENSE LINES...
...BUT I CAME PREPARED TOO, Y'KNOW!!
GUI (TUG)

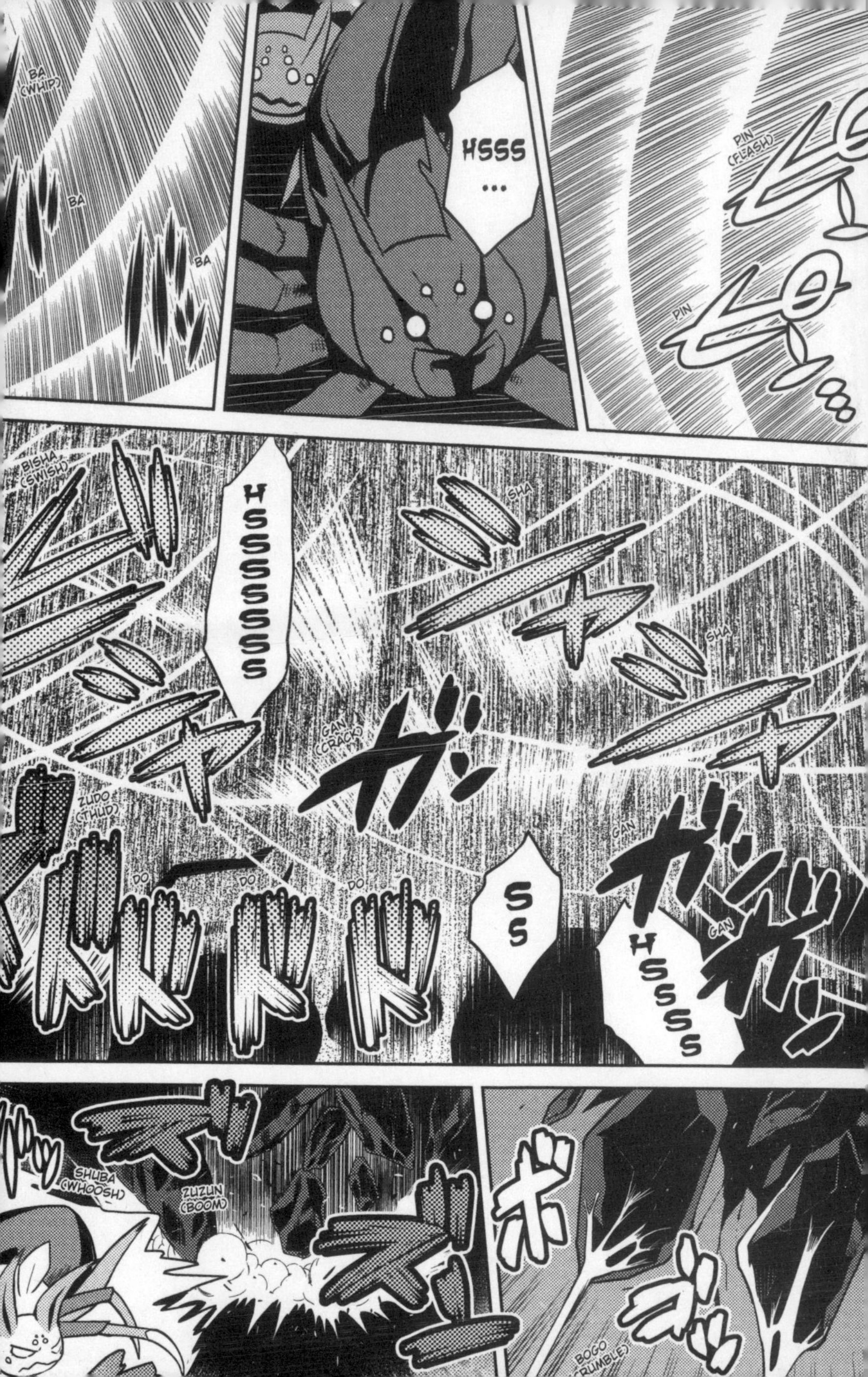
PIN (FLASH)
PIN
HSSS ...
BA (WHIP)
BA
BA
SHA
SHA
GAN
GAN
HSSSS
SS
HSSSSSSSS
BISHA (SWISH)
GAN (CRACK)
ZUDO (THUD)
DO
DO
DO
BOGO (RUMBLE)
ZUZUN (BOOM)
SHUBA (WHOOSH)

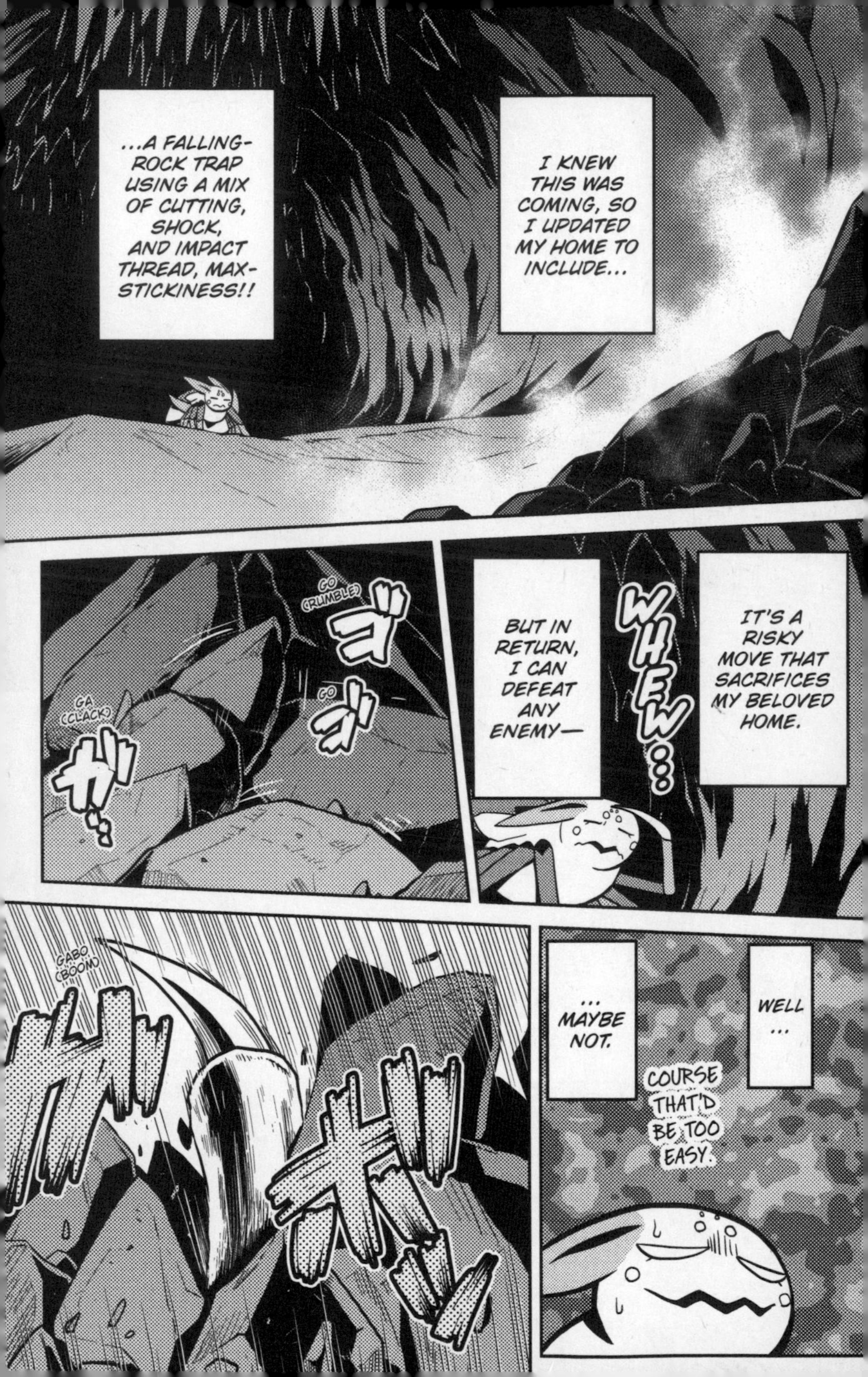
I KNEW THIS WAS COMING, SO I UPDATED MY HOME TO INCLUDE...
...A FALLING-ROCK TRAP USING A MIX OF CUTTING, SHOCK, AND IMPACT THREAD, MAX-STICKINESS!!
IT'S A RISKY MOVE THAT SACRIFICES MY BELOVED HOME.
WHEW...
BUT IN RETURN, I CAN DEFEAT ANY ENEMY—
GO (RUMBLE)
GO
GA (CLACK)
WELL...
...MAYBE NOT.
COURSE THAT'D BE TOO EASY.
GABO (BOOM)

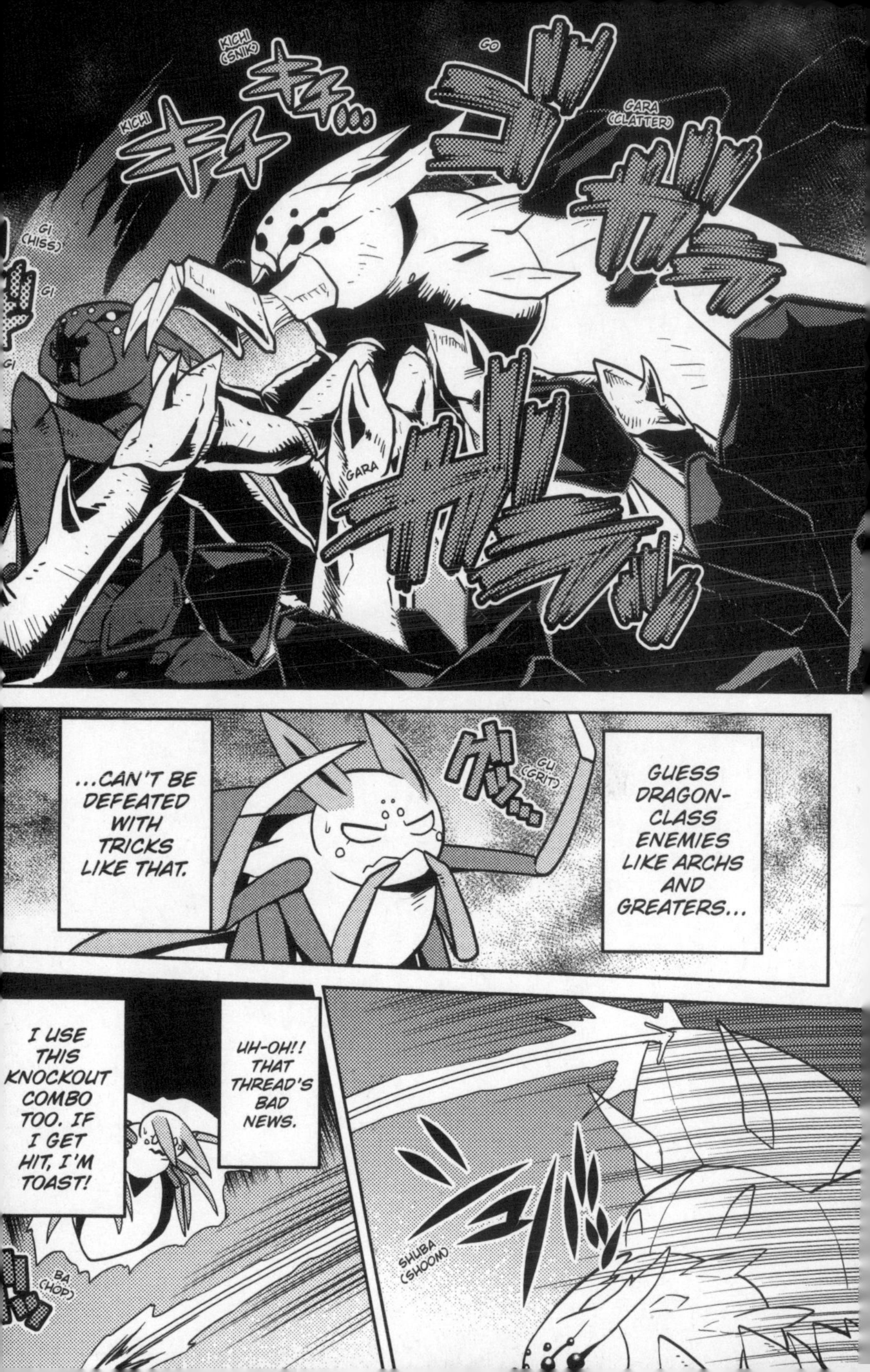
GO
GARA (CLATTER)
KICHI (SNIK)
KICHI
GI (HISS)
GI
GI
GARA
GUESS DRAGON-CLASS ENEMIES LIKE ARCHS AND GREATERS...
GU (GRIT)
...CAN'T BE DEFEATED WITH TRICKS LIKE THAT.
SHUBA (SHOOM)
UH-OH!! THAT THREAD'S BAD NEWS.
I USE THIS KNOCKOUT COMBO TOO. IF I GET HIT, I'M TOAST!
BA (HOP)

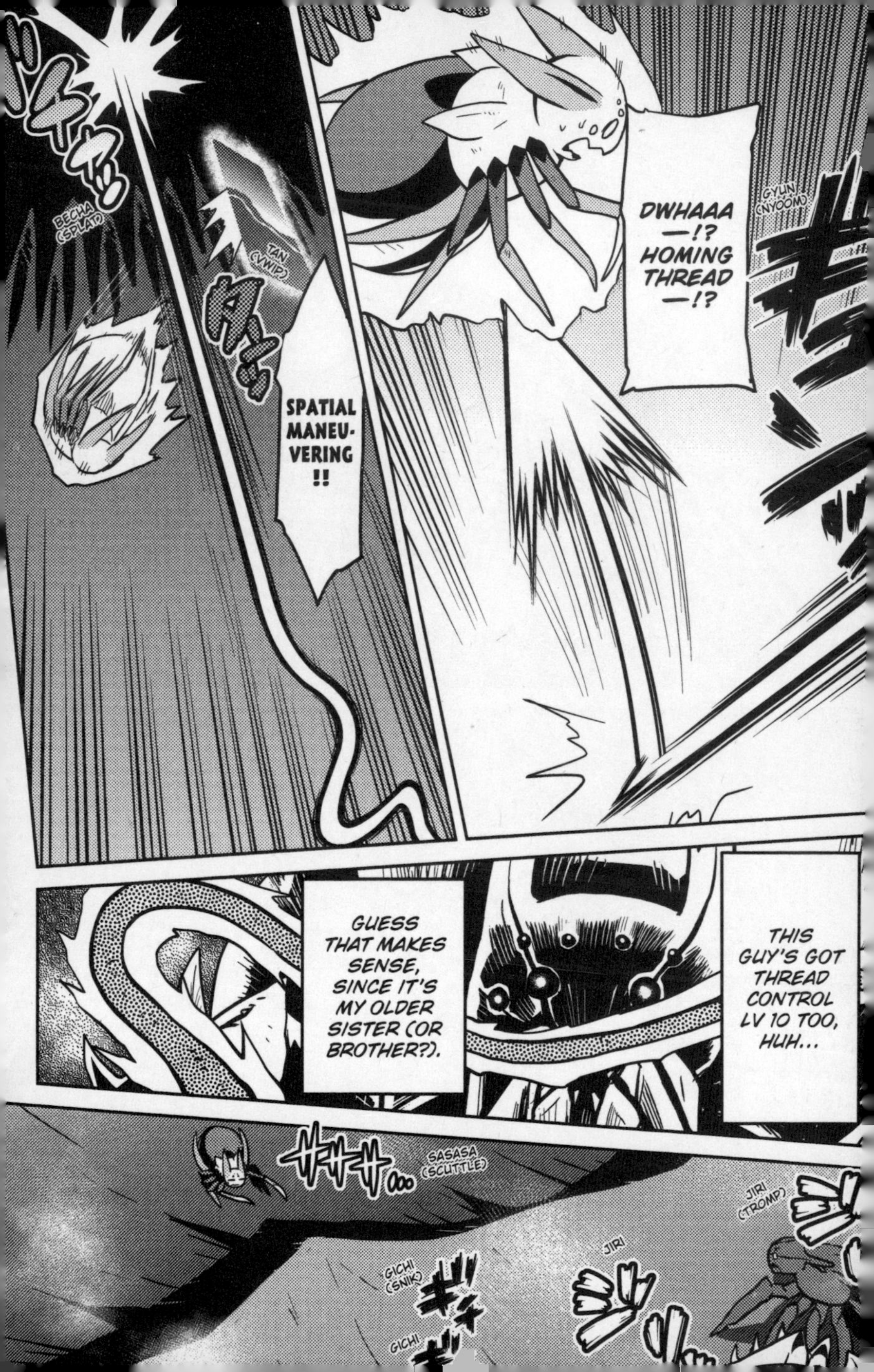
GYLUN (NYOOM)
DWHAAA—!? HOMING THREAD—!?
SPATIAL MANEU-VERING!!
TAN (VWIP)
BECHA (SPLAT)
THIS GUY'S GOT THREAD CONTROL LV 10 TOO, HUH...
GUESS THAT MAKES SENSE, SINCE IT'S MY OLDER SISTER (OR BROTHER?).
JIRI (TROMP)
SASASA (SCUTTLE)
JIRI
GICHI (SNIK)
GICHI

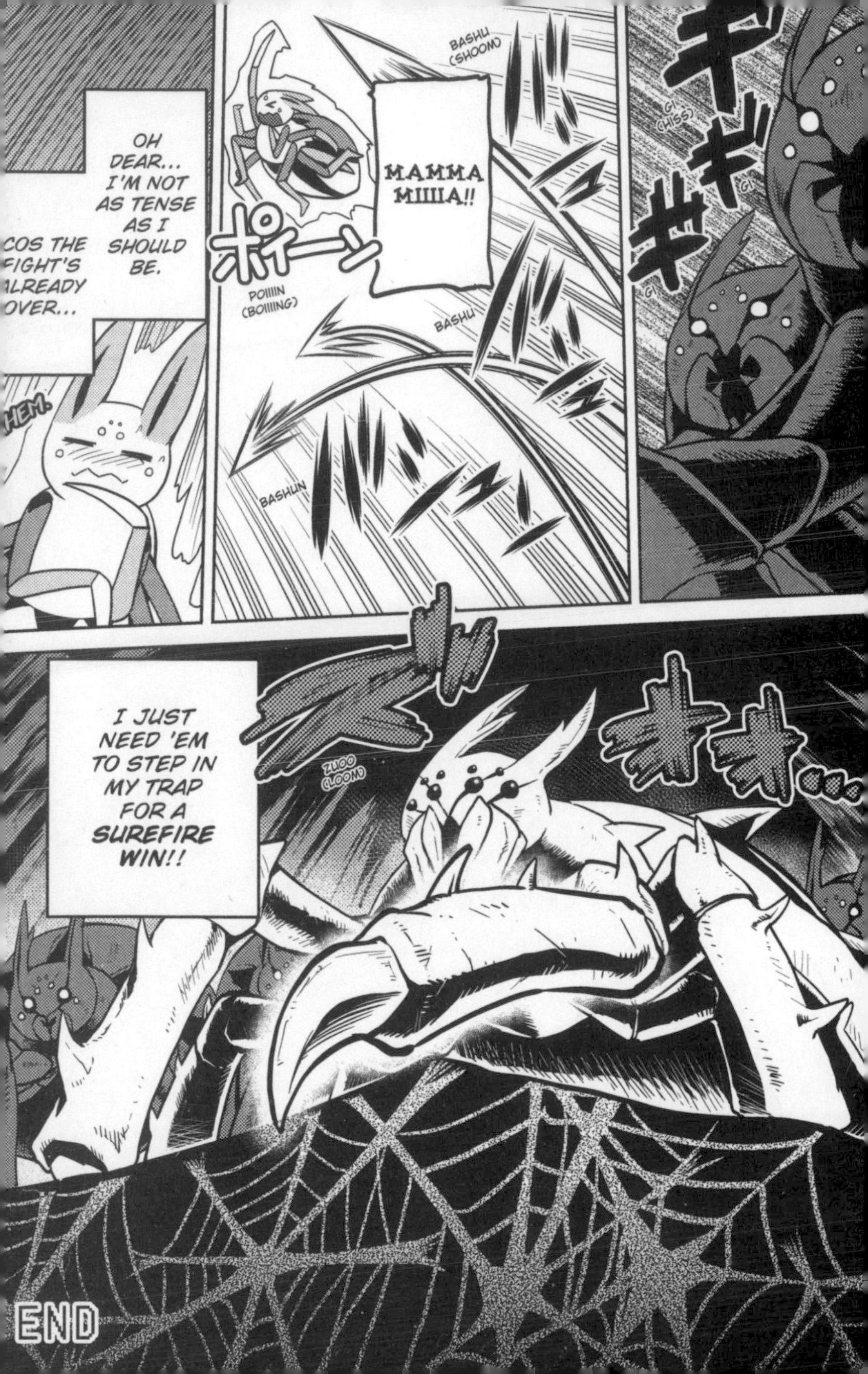

GI (HISS)
GI
GI
BASHU (SHOOM)
MAMMA MIIIIA!!
ポイーン
POIIIIN (BOIIIING)
BASHU
BASHUN
OH DEAR... I'M NOT AS TENSE AS I SHOULD BE.
COS THE FIGHT'S ALREADY OVER...
HEM.
I JUST NEED 'EM TO STEP IN MY TRAP FOR A SUREFIRE WIN!!
ZUOO (LOOM)
END

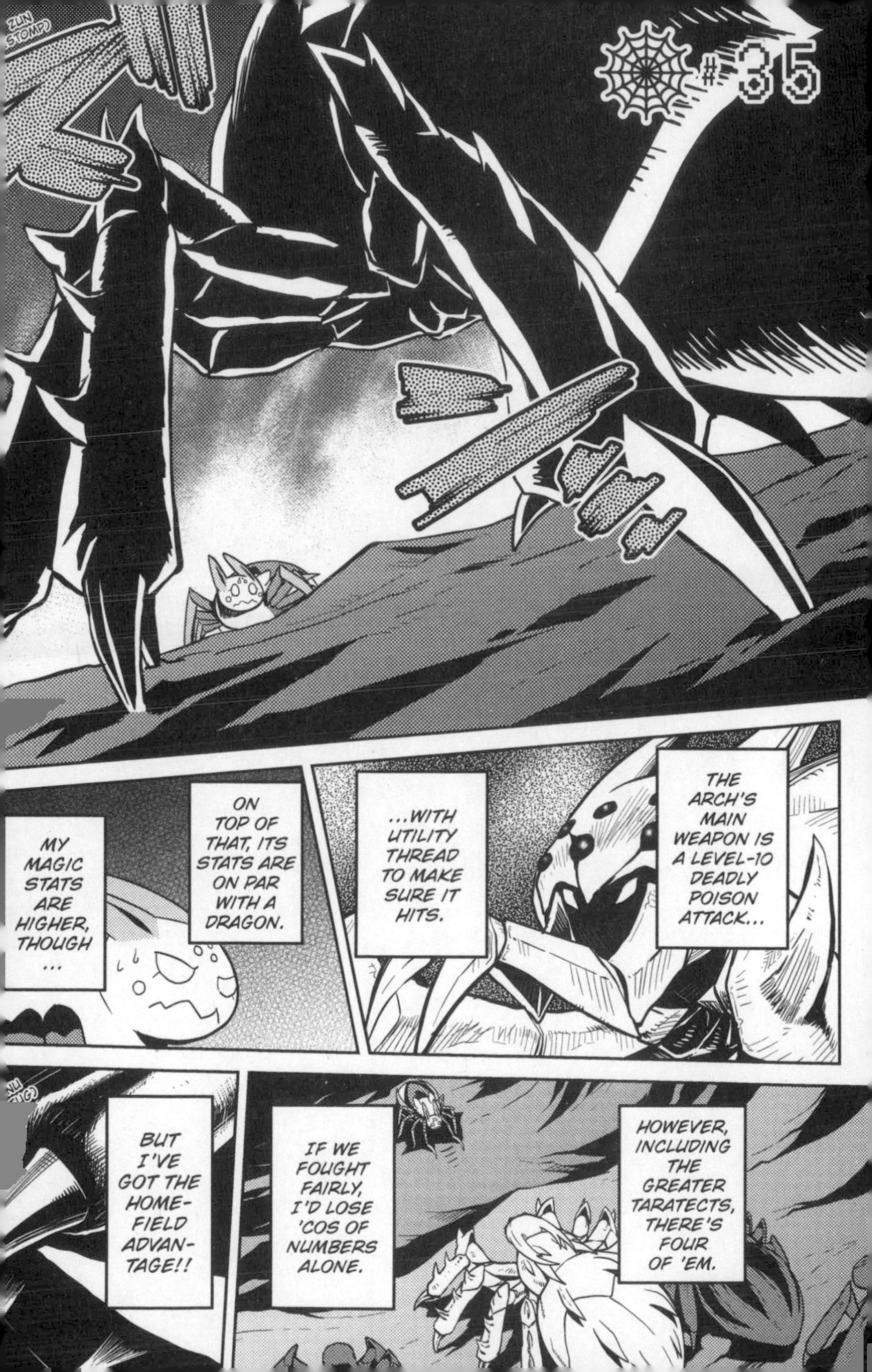
#35
ZUN (STOMP)
THE ARCH'S MAIN WEAPON IS A LEVEL-10 DEADLY POISON ATTACK...
...WITH UTILITY THREAD TO MAKE SURE IT HITS.
ON TOP OF THAT, ITS STATS ARE ON PAR WITH A DRAGON.
MY MAGIC STATS ARE HIGHER, THOUGH...
HOWEVER, INCLUDING THE GREATER TARATECTS, THERE'S FOUR OF 'EM.
IF WE FOUGHT FAIRLY, I'D LOSE 'COS OF NUMBERS ALONE.
BUT I'VE GOT THE HOME-FIELD ADVANTAGE!!

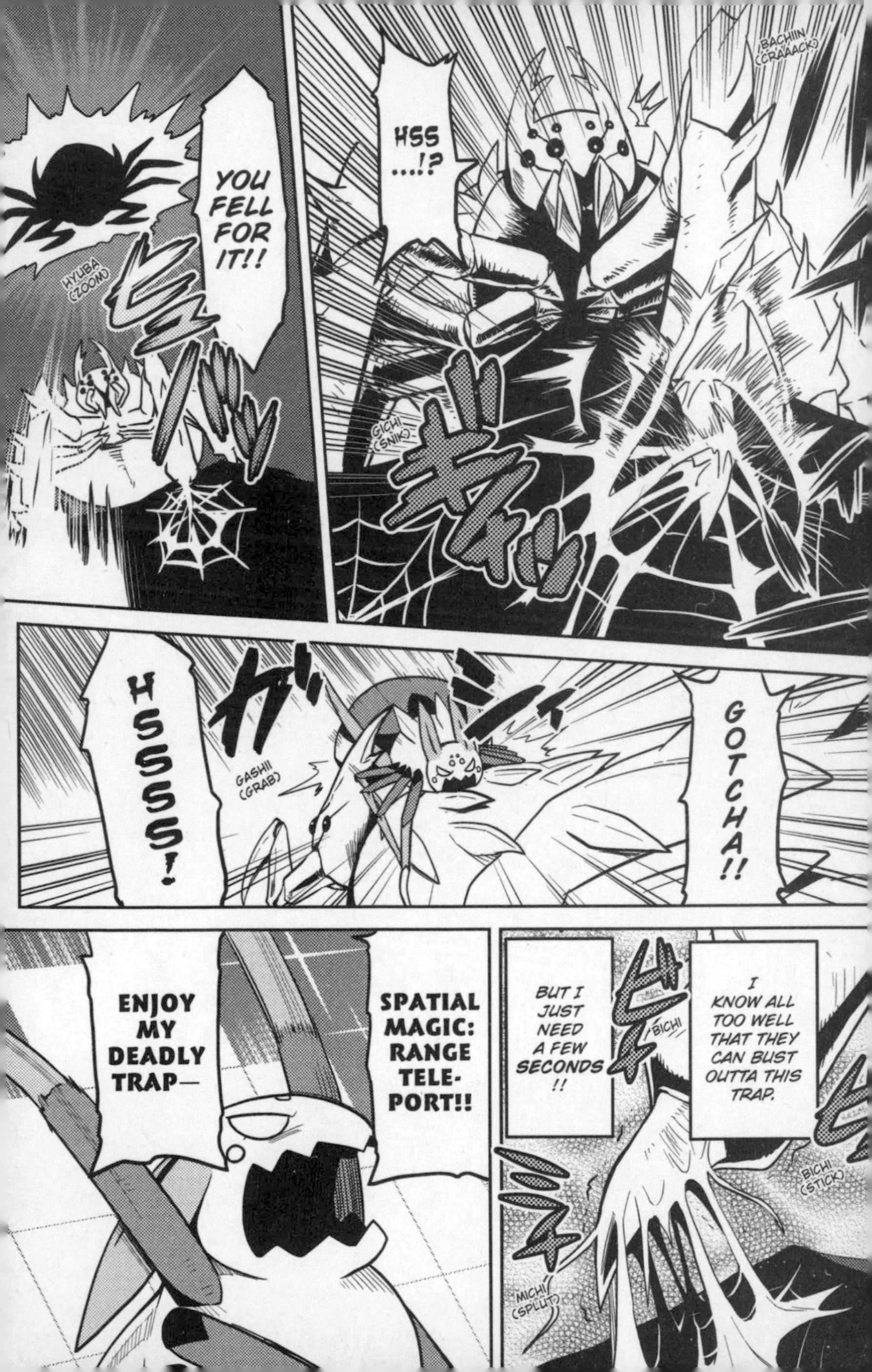
BACHIIN (CRAAACK)
HSS ....!?
GICHI (SNIK)
YOU FELL FOR IT!!
HYUBA (ZOOM)
GOTCHA!!
GASHII (GRAB)
HSSSSS!
I KNOW ALL TOO WELL THAT THEY CAN BUST OUTTA THIS TRAP.
BUT I JUST NEED A FEW SECONDS!!
BICHI
BICHI (STICK)
MICHI (SPLUT)
SPATIAL MAGIC: RANGE TELE-PORT!!
ENJOY MY DEADLY TRAP—

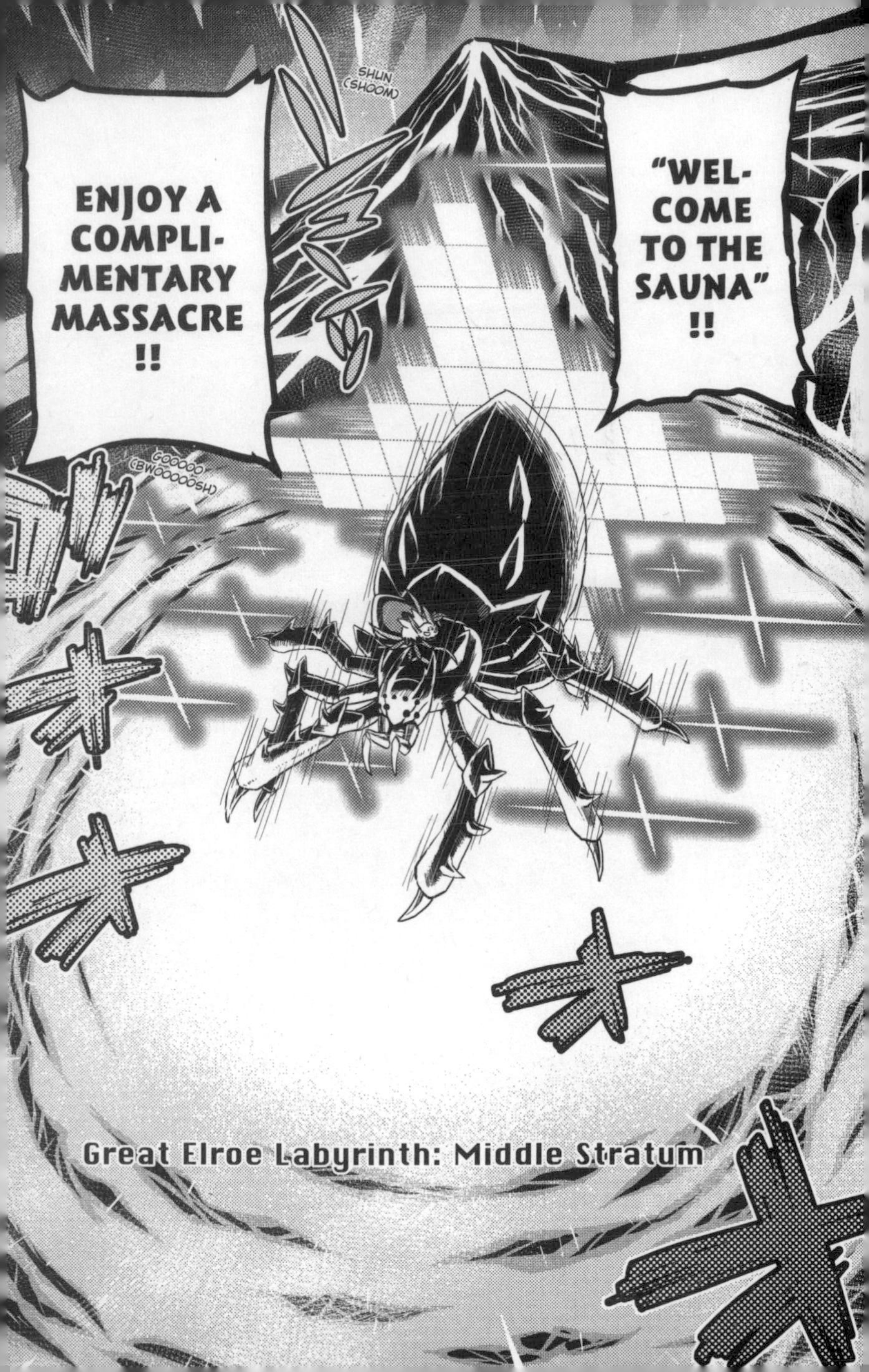
"WEL-COME TO THE SAUNA"!!
SHUN (SHOOM)
ENJOY A COMPLI-MENTARY MASSACRE!!
GOOOOO (BWOOOOOSH)
Great Elroe Labyrinth: Middle Stratum

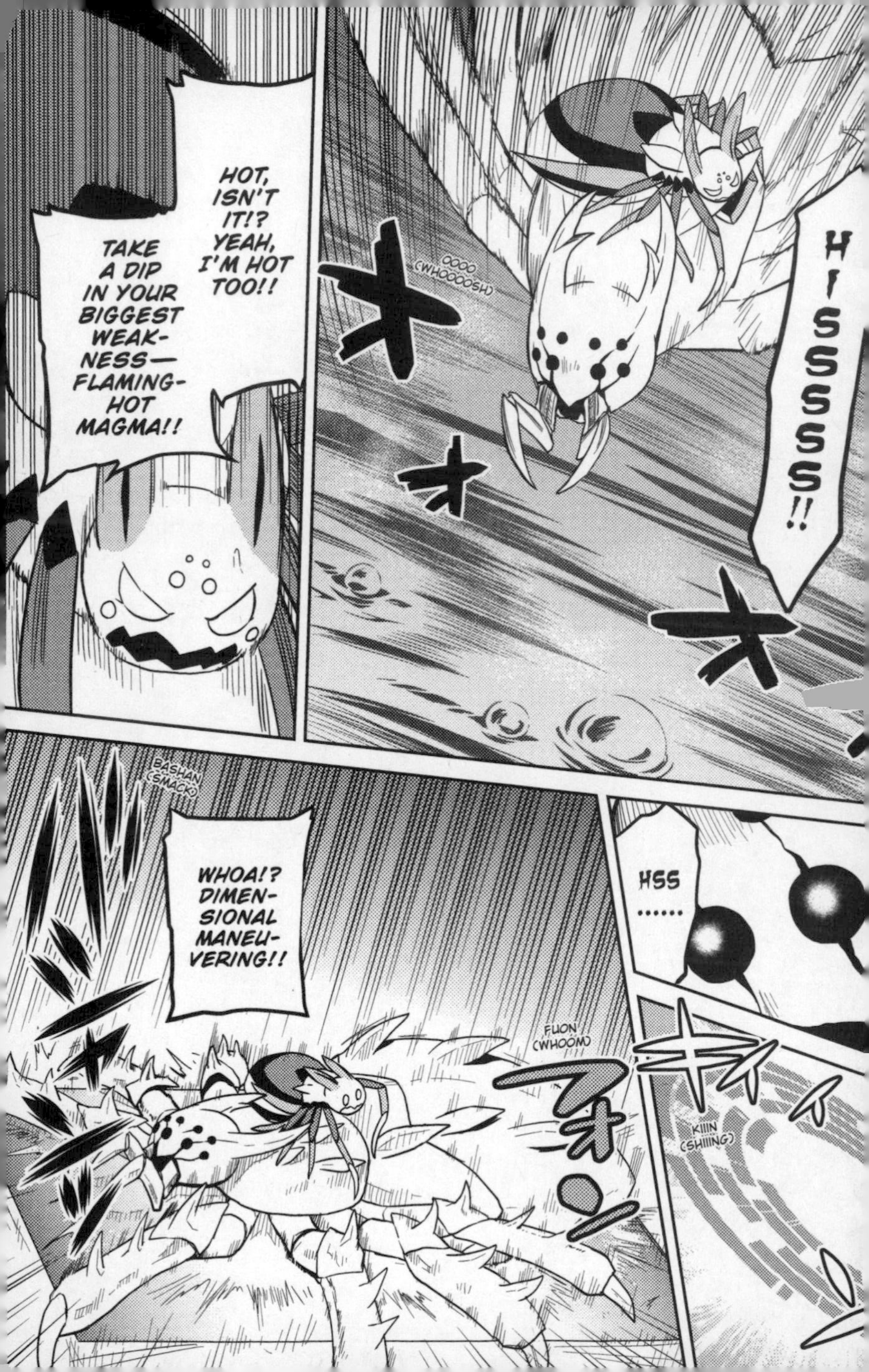
OOOO (WHOOOOSH)
HISSSSSS!!
HOT, ISN'T IT!? YEAH, I'M HOT TOO!!
TAKE A DIP IN YOUR BIGGEST WEAK-NESS—FLAMING-HOT MAGMA!!
HSS ......
KIIIN (SHIIING)
BASHAN (SMACK)
WHOA!? DIMEN-SIONAL MANEU-VERING!!
FUON (WHOOM)

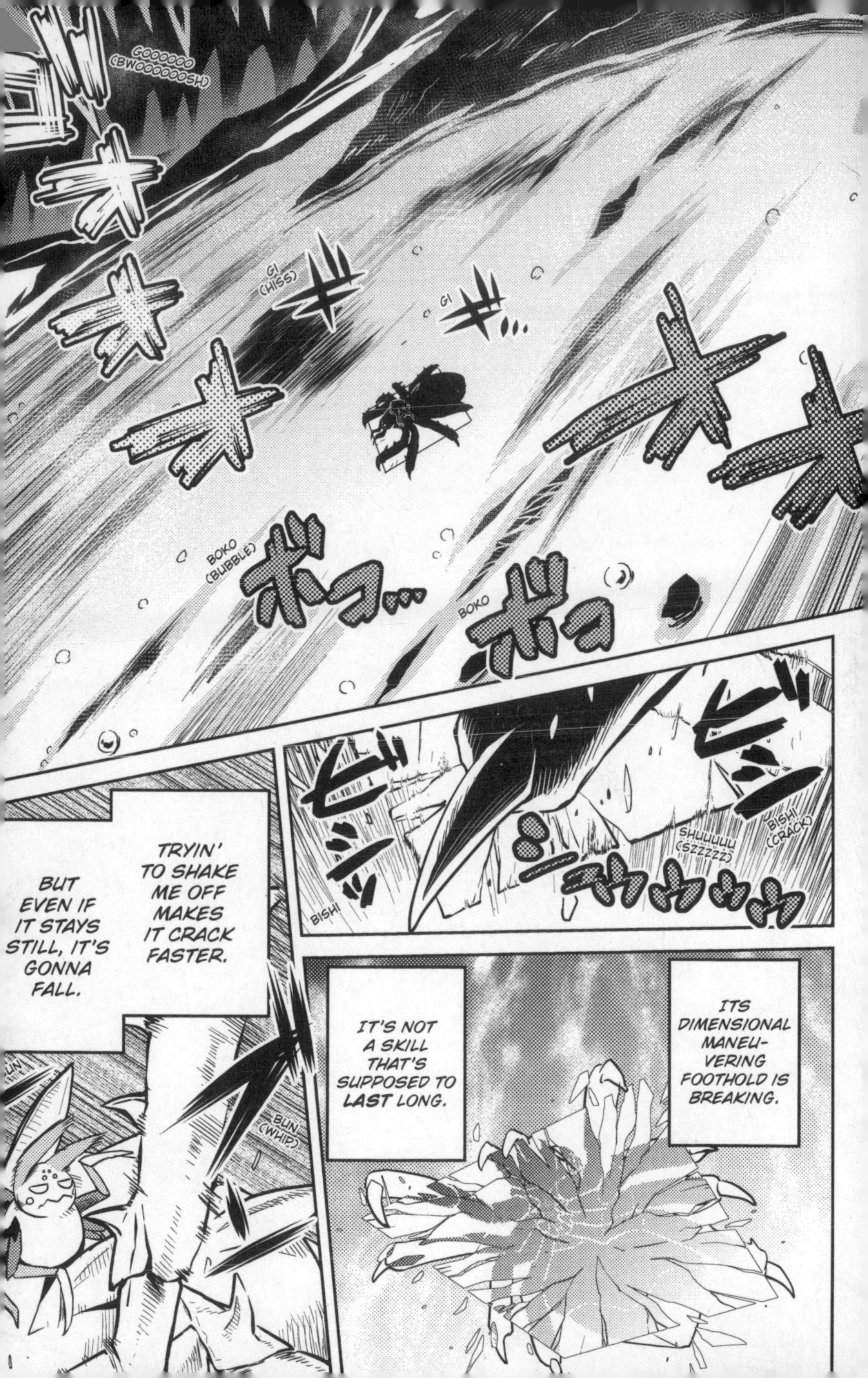
GOOOOOO (BWOOOOOOSH)
GI
GI (HISS)
BOKO
BOKO (BUBBLE)
BISHI (CRACK)
SHUUUUU (SZZZZZ)
BISHI
ITS DIMENSIONAL MANEU-VERING FOOTHOLD IS BREAKING.
IT'S NOT A SKILL THAT'S SUPPOSED TO LAST LONG.
TRYIN' TO SHAKE ME OFF MAKES IT CRACK FASTER.
BUT EVEN IF IT STAYS STILL, IT'S GONNA FALL.
BUN (WHIP)

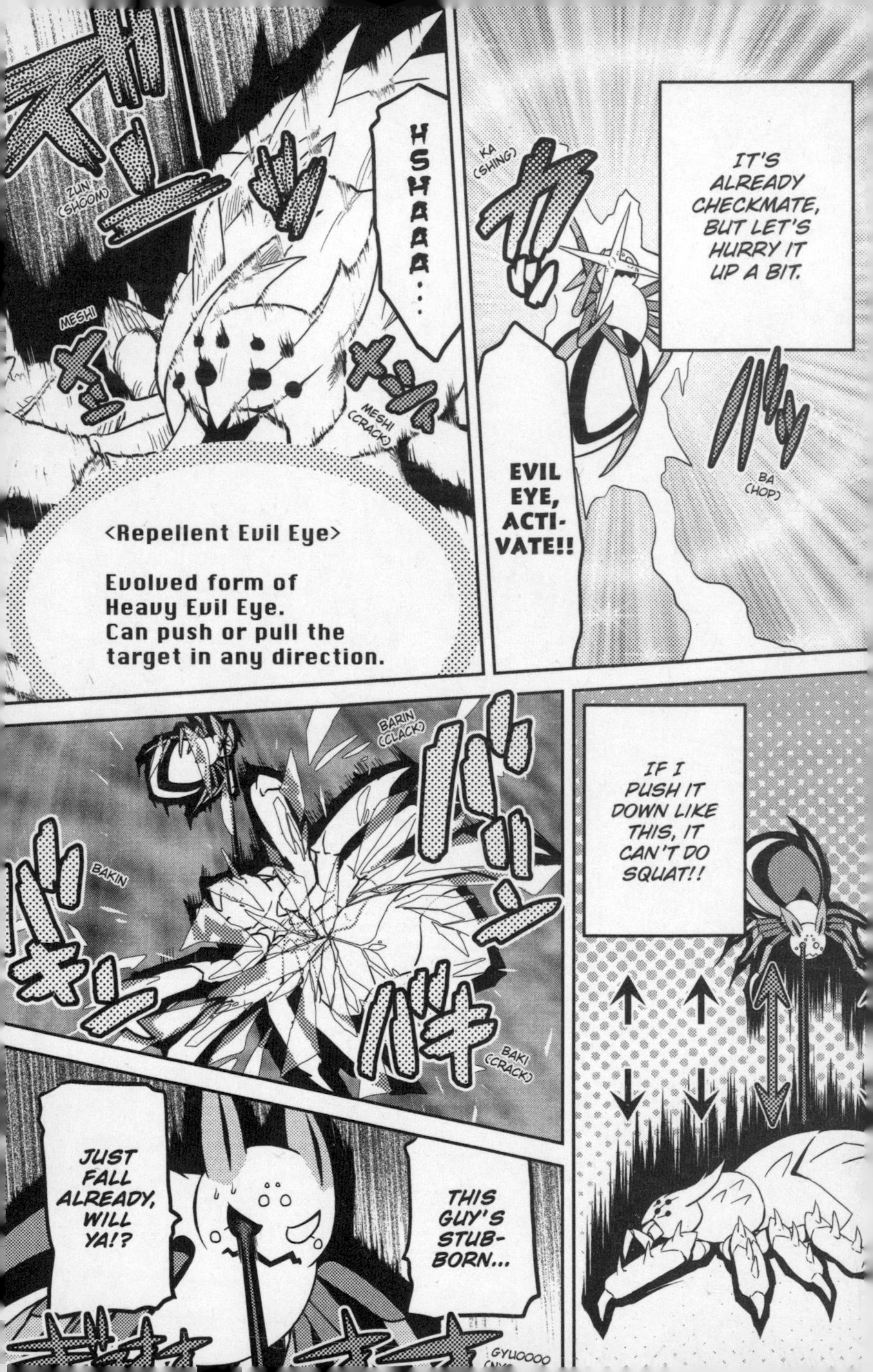
IT'S ALREADY CHECKMATE, BUT LET'S HURRY IT UP A BIT.
KA (SHING)
BA (HOP)
EVIL EYE, ACTIVATE!!
HSHAAA...
ZUN (SHOOM)
MESHI
MESHI (CRACK)
<Repellent Evil Eye>
Evolved form of Heavy Evil Eye. Can push or pull the target in any direction.
IF I PUSH IT DOWN LIKE THIS, IT CAN'T DO SQUAT!!
BARIN (CLACK)
BAKIN
BAKI (CRACK)
THIS GUY'S STUBBORN...
JUST FALL ALREADY, WILL YA!?
GYUOOOO

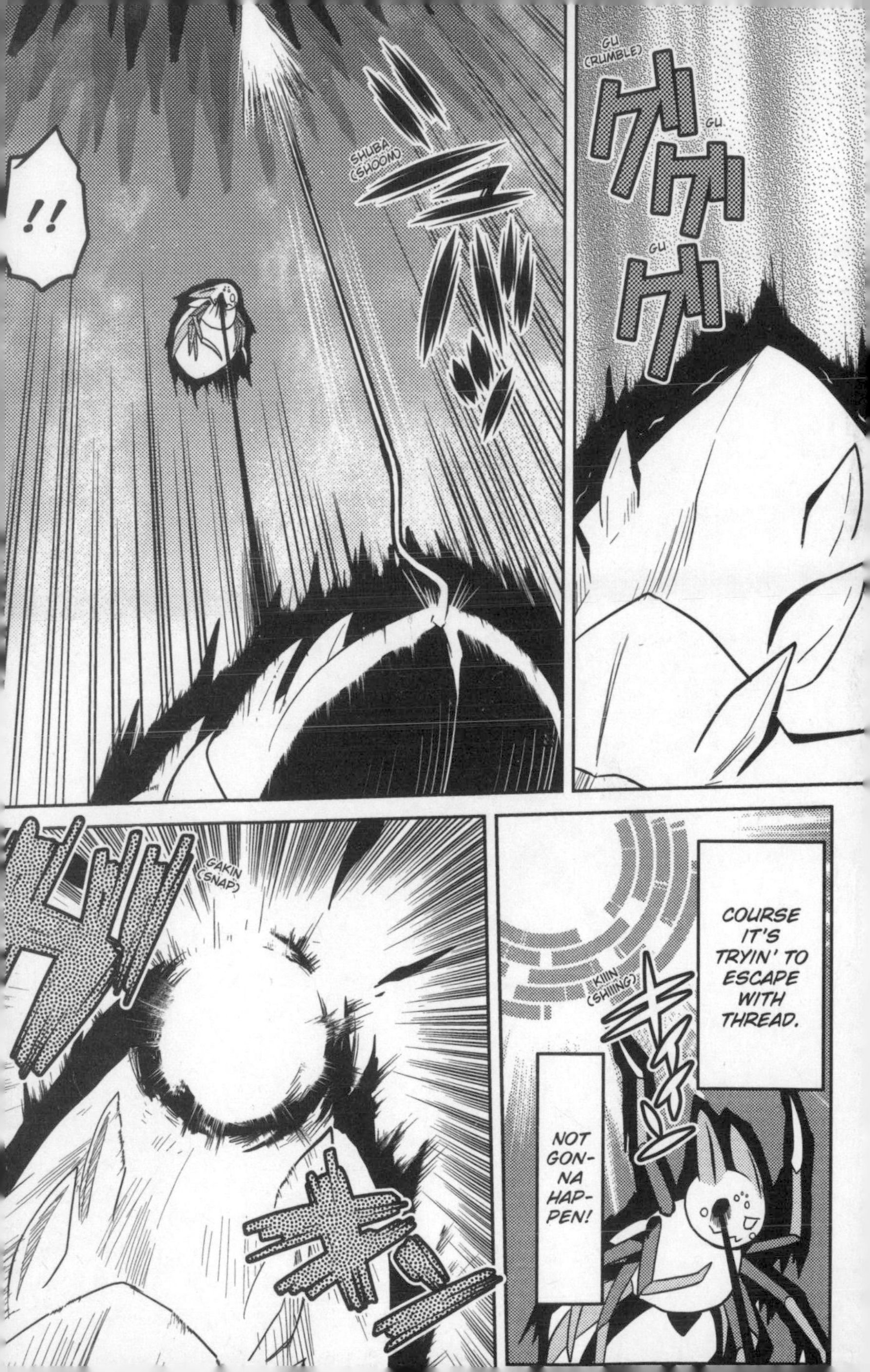
GU (RUMBLE)
GU
GU
SHUBA (SHOOM)
!!
COURSE IT'S TRYIN' TO ESCAPE WITH THREAD.
KIIN (SHIIING)
NOT GON-NA HAP-PEN!
GAKIN (SNAP)

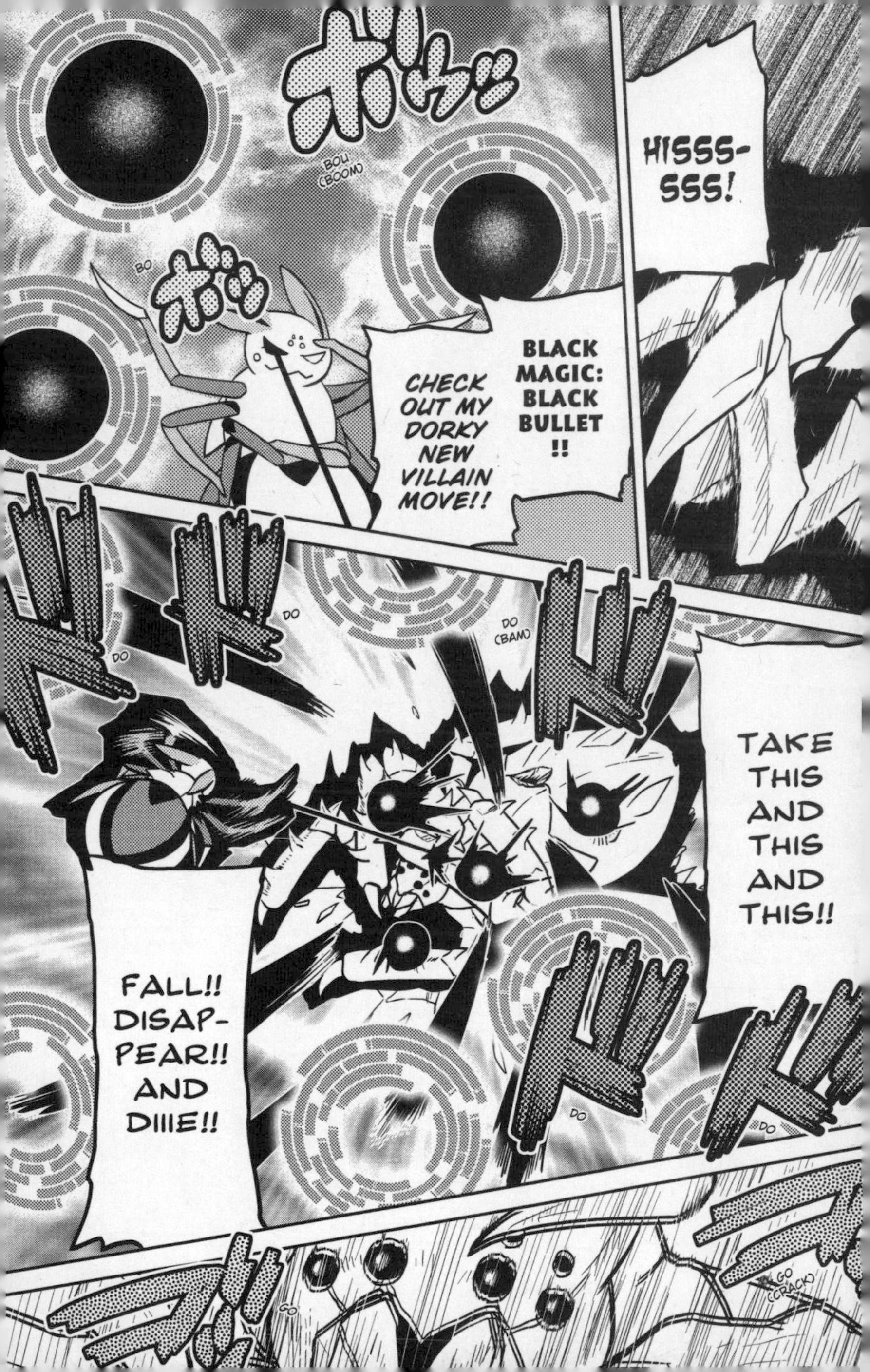
HISSS-SSS!
BOU (BOOM)
BO
BLACK MAGIC: BLACK BULLET!!
CHECK OUT MY DORKY NEW VILLAIN MOVE!!
DO (BAM)
DO
DO
TAKE THIS AND THIS AND THIS!!
FALL!! DISAP-PEAR!! AND DIIIE!!
DO
DO
GO (CRACK)
GO

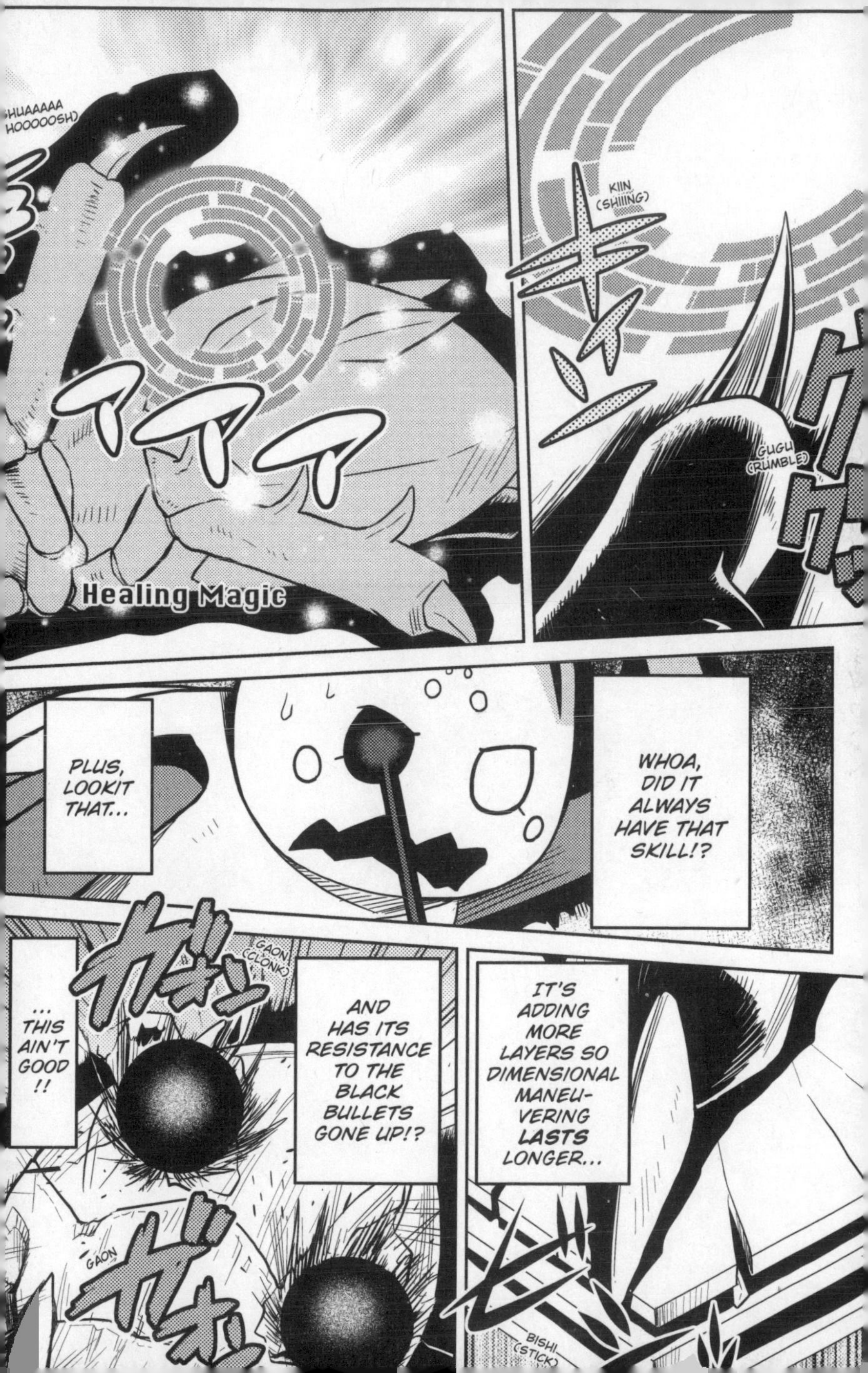
KIIN (SHIIING)
GUGU (RUMBLE)
SHUAAAAA HOOOOOSH)
Healing Magic
WHOA, DID IT ALWAYS HAVE THAT SKILL!?
PLUS, LOOKIT THAT...
IT'S ADDING MORE LAYERS SO DIMENSIONAL MANEU-VERING LASTS LONGER...
BISHI (STICK)
GAON (CLONK)
AND HAS ITS RESISTANCE TO THE BLACK BULLETS GONE UP!?
... THIS AIN'T GOOD!!
GAON

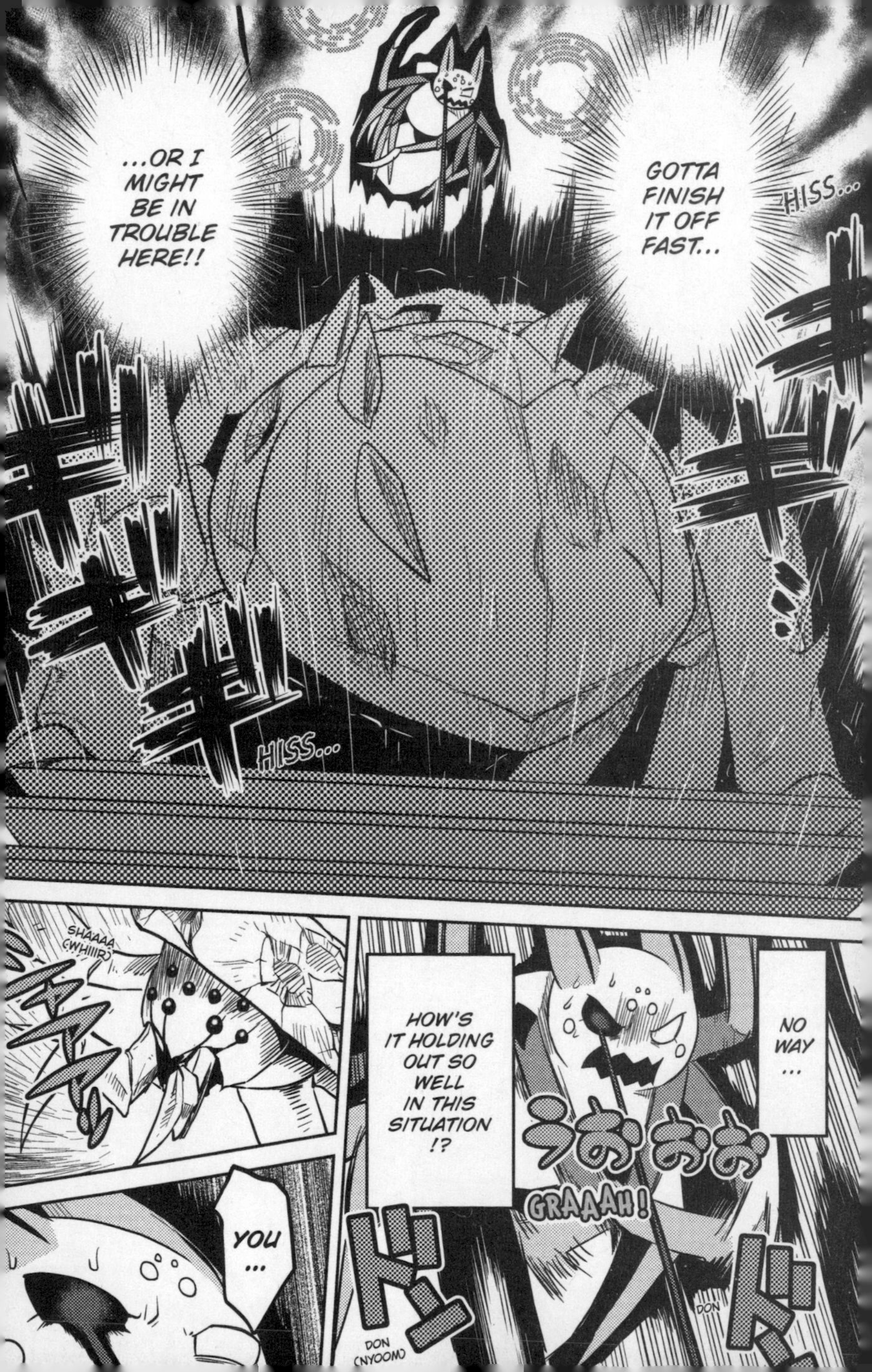
HISS...
GOTTA FINISH IT OFF FAST...
...OR I MIGHT BE IN TROUBLE HERE!!
HISS...
NO WAY ...
HOW'S IT HOLDING OUT SO WELL IN THIS SITUATION !?
うおおお
GRAAAH!
ド
DON
ド
DON (NYOOM)
SHAAAA (WHIIIR)
YOU ...

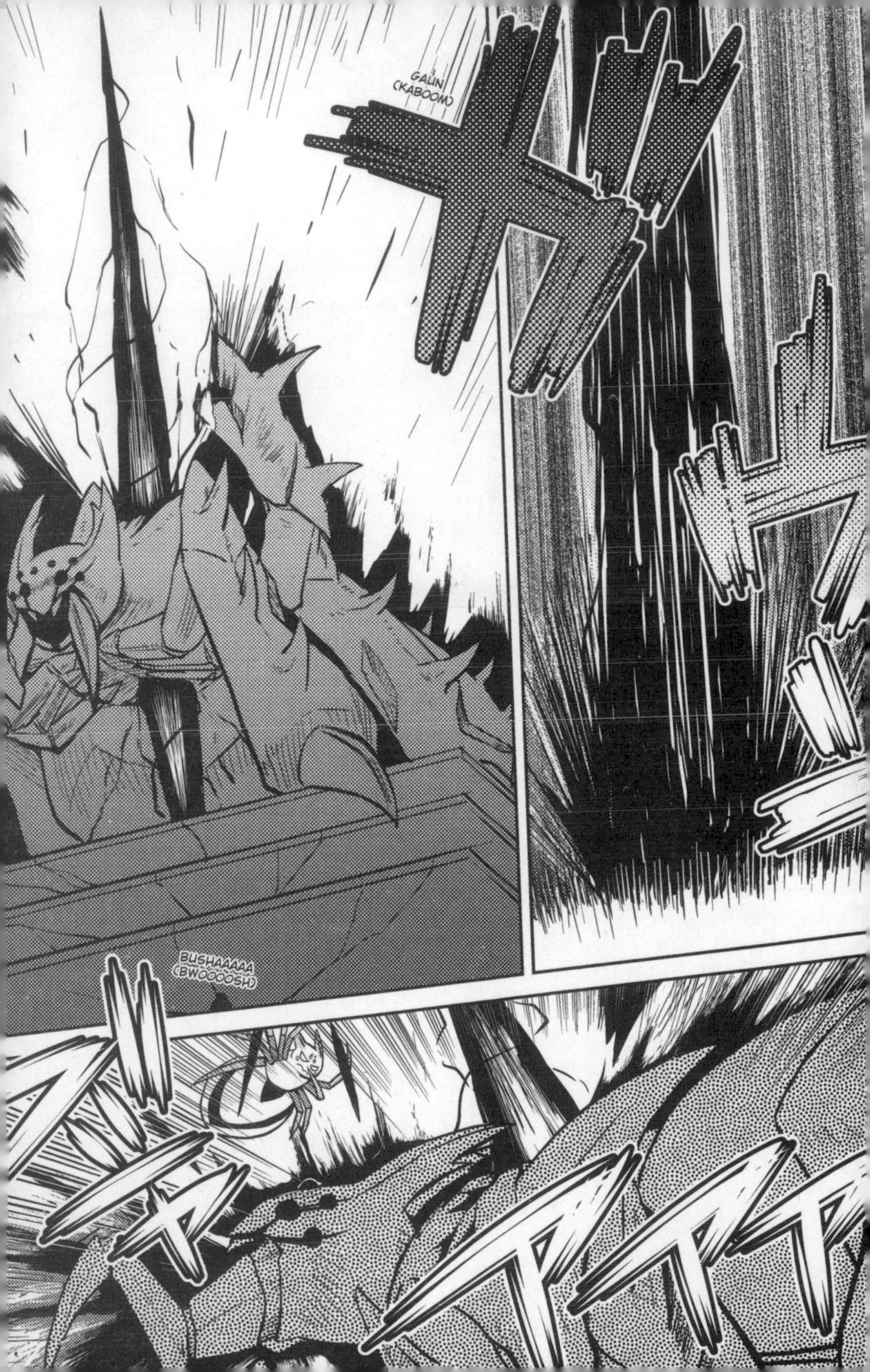
GALIN
(KABOOM)
BUSHAAAAAA
(BWOOOOOSH)

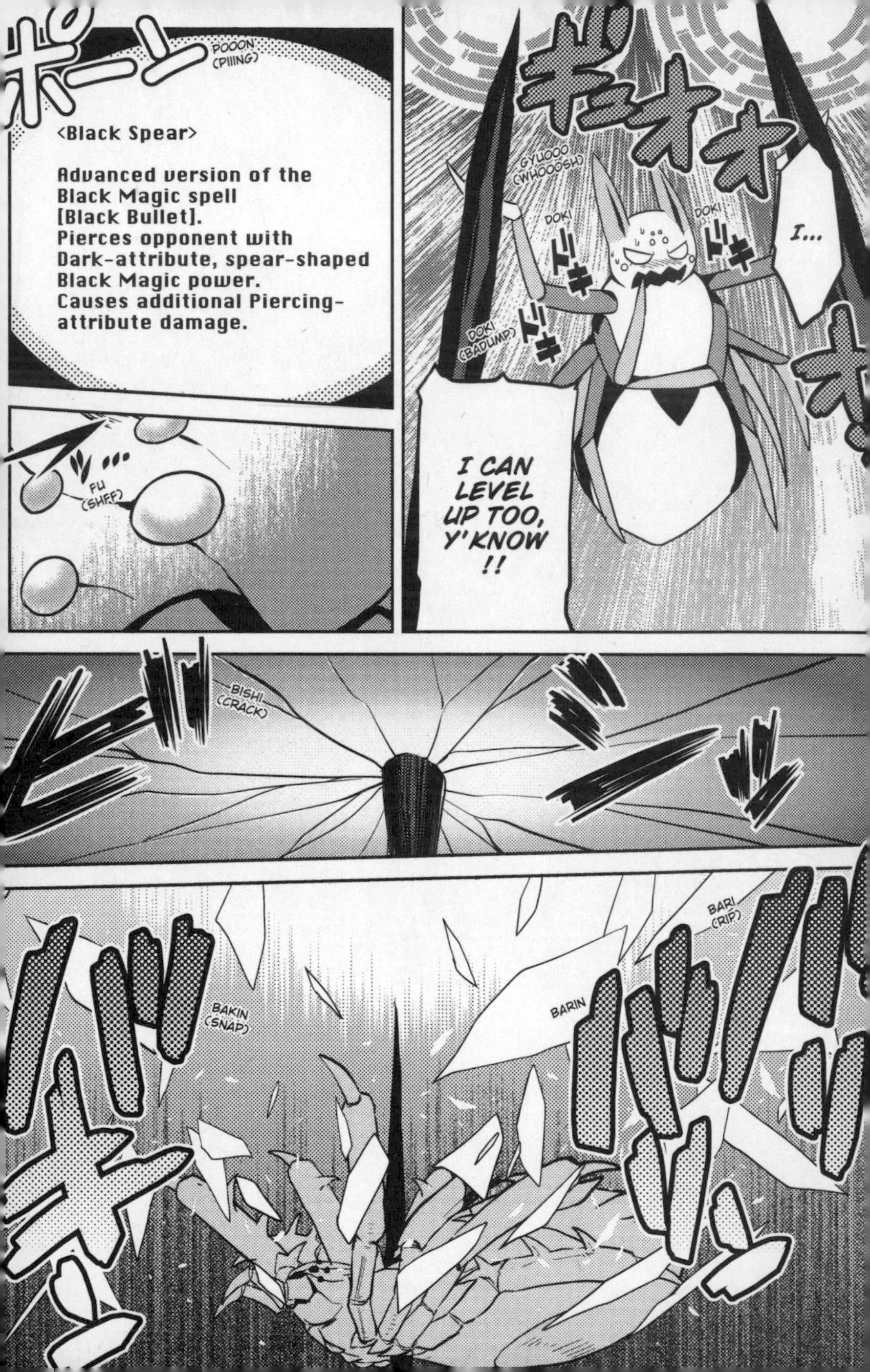
GYUOOO (WHOOOSH)
I...
DOKI
DOKI
DOKI (BADUMP)
I CAN LEVEL UP TOO, Y'KNOW !!
POOON (PIIING)
<Black Spear>
Advanced version of the Black Magic spell [Black Bullet].
Pierces opponent with Dark-attribute, spear-shaped Black Magic power.
Causes additional Piercing-attribute damage.
FU (SHFF)
BISHI (CRACK)
BARI (RIP)
BARIN
BAKIN (SNAP)

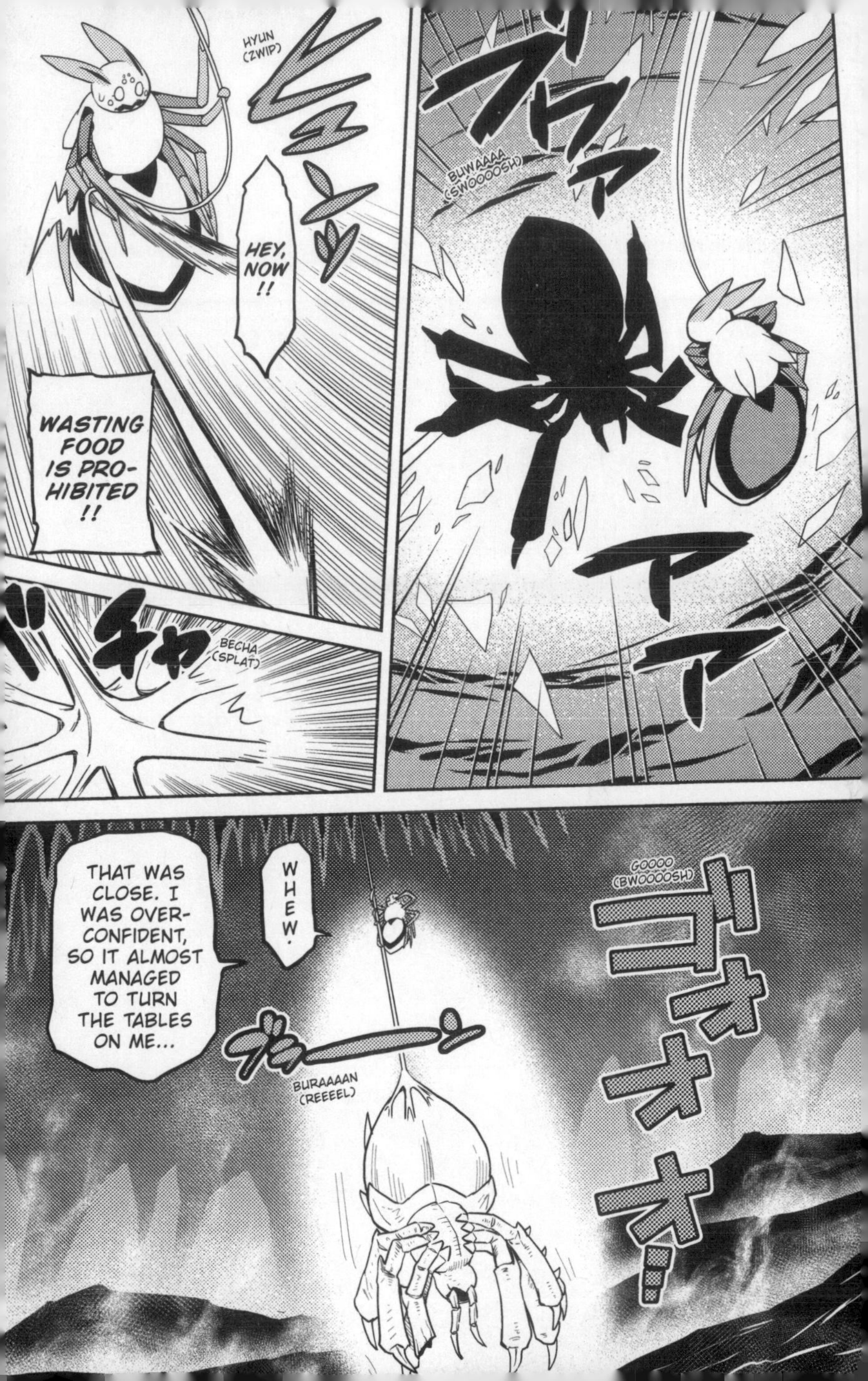
BUWAAAA (SWOOOOSH)
HYUN (ZWIP)
HEY, NOW!!
WASTING FOOD IS PRO-HIBITED!!
BECHA (SPLAT)
GOOOO (BWOOOOSH)
WHEW.
THAT WAS CLOSE. I WAS OVER-CONFIDENT, SO IT ALMOST MANAGED TO TURN THE TABLES ON ME...
BURAAAAN (REEEEL)

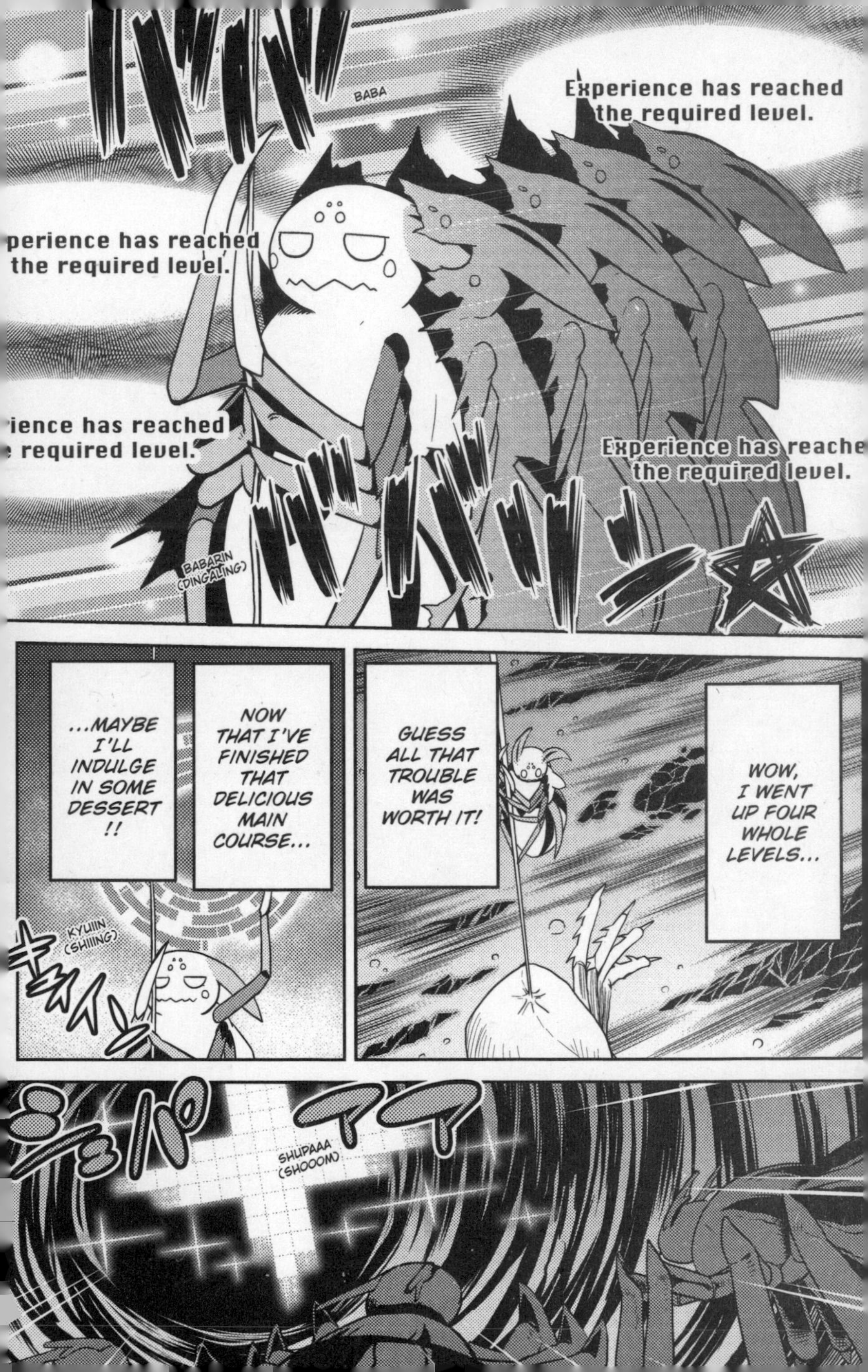
BABA
Experience has reached the required level.
perience has reached the required level.
Experience has reache the required level.
rience has reached e required level.
BABARIN (DINGALING)
WOW, I WENT UP FOUR WHOLE LEVELS...
GUESS ALL THAT TROUBLE WAS WORTH IT!
NOW THAT I'VE FINISHED THAT DELICIOUS MAIN COURSE...
...MAYBE I'LL INDULGE IN SOME DESSERT!!
KYUIIN (SHIIING)
SHUPAAA (SHOOOM)

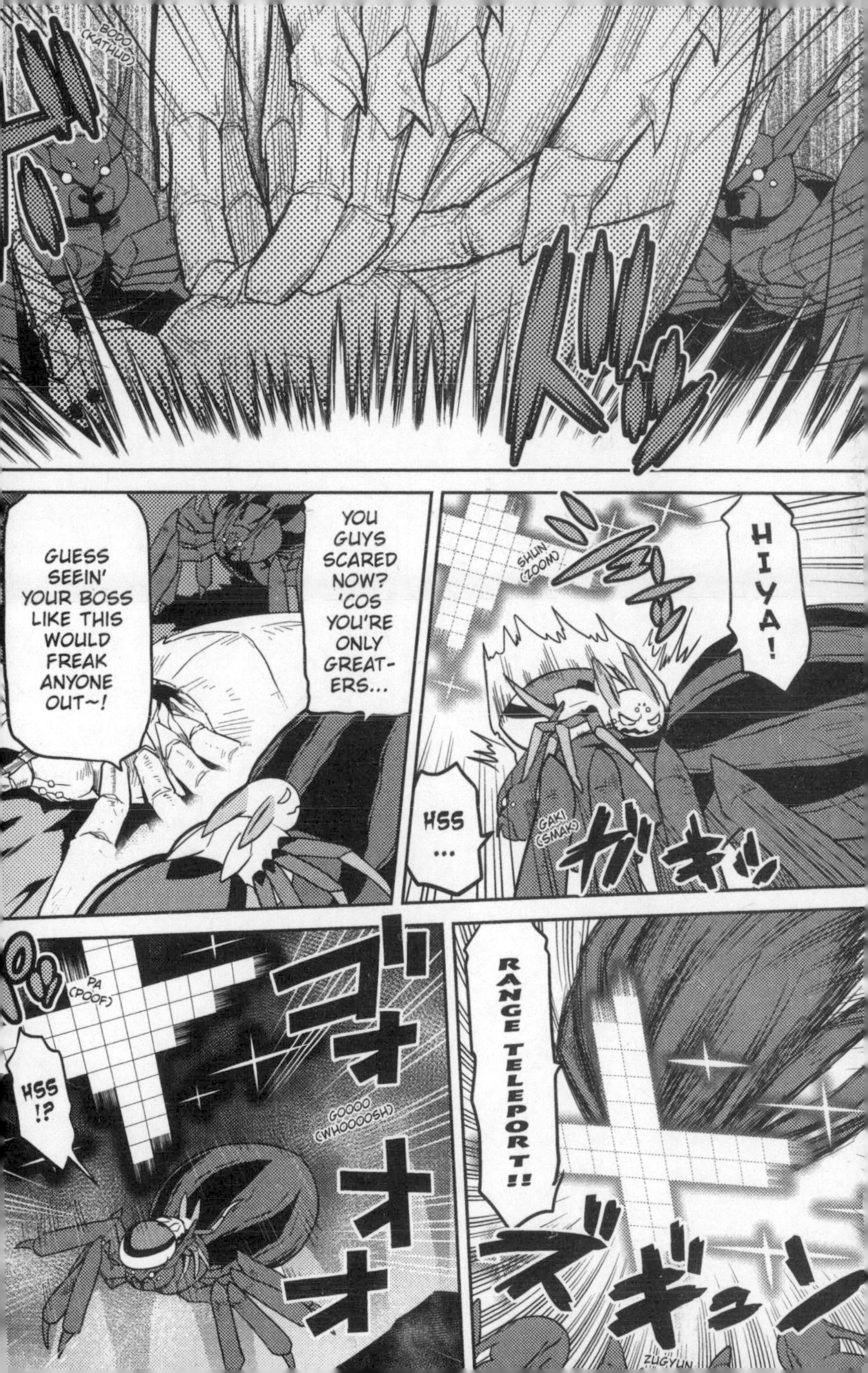
BODO (KATHUD)
HIYA!
SHUN (ZOOM)
HSS...
GAKI (SMAK)
YOU GUYS SCARED NOW? 'COS YOU'RE ONLY GREATERS...
GUESS SEEIN' YOUR BOSS LIKE THIS WOULD FREAK ANYONE OUT~!
RANGE TELEPORT!!
ZUGYUN
GOOOO (WHOOOOSH)
PA (POOF)
HSS !?

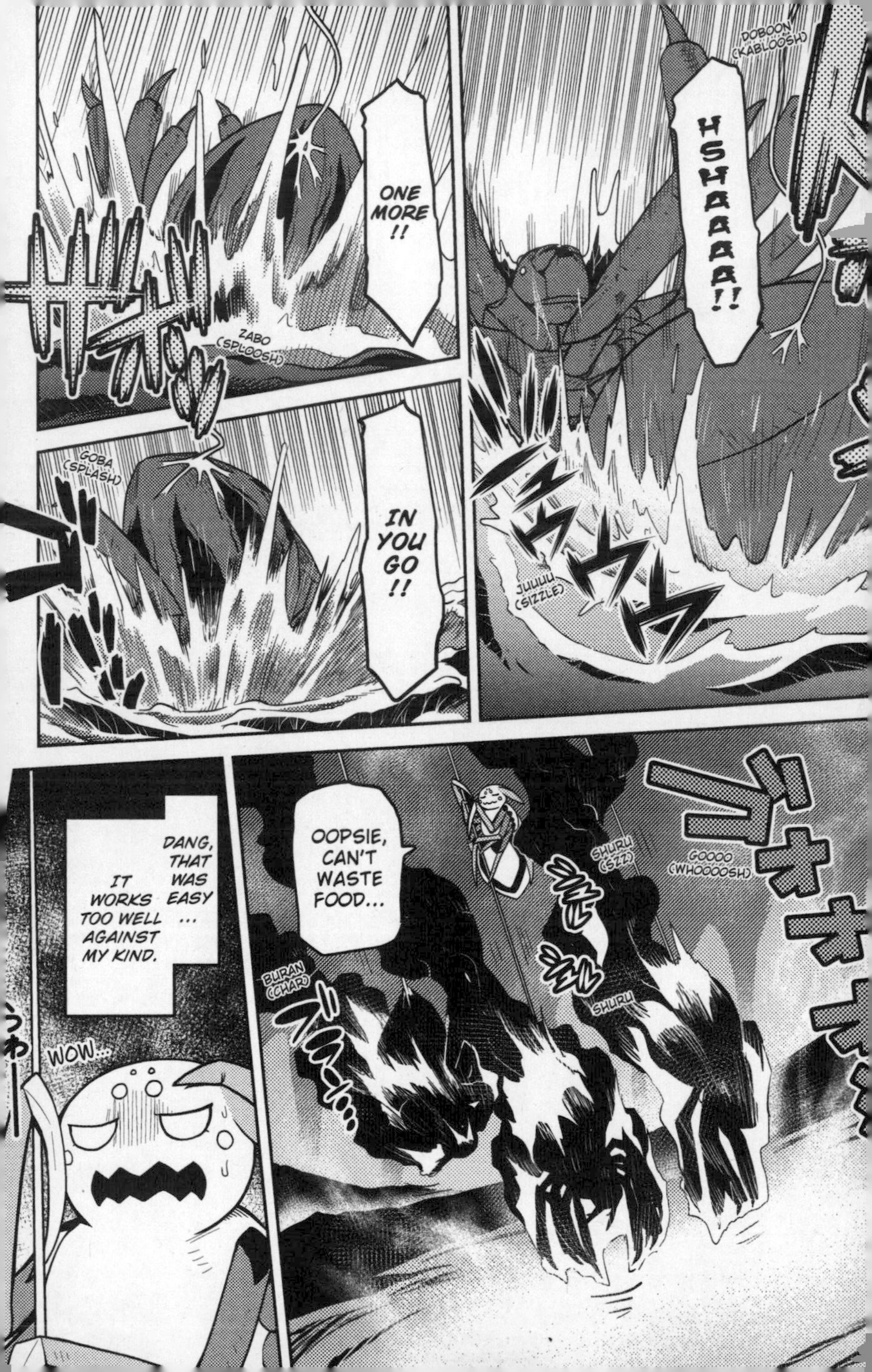
DOBOON (KABLOOSH)
HSHAAAA!!
JUUUU (SIZZLE)
ONE MORE !!
ZABO (SPLOOSH)
IN YOU GO !!
GOBA (SPLASH)
GOOOO (WHOOOOSH)
SHURU (SZZ)
OOPSIE, CAN'T WASTE FOOD...
SHURU
BURAN (CHAR)
DANG, THAT WAS EASY ...
IT WORKS TOO WELL AGAINST MY KIND.
うわー
WOW...

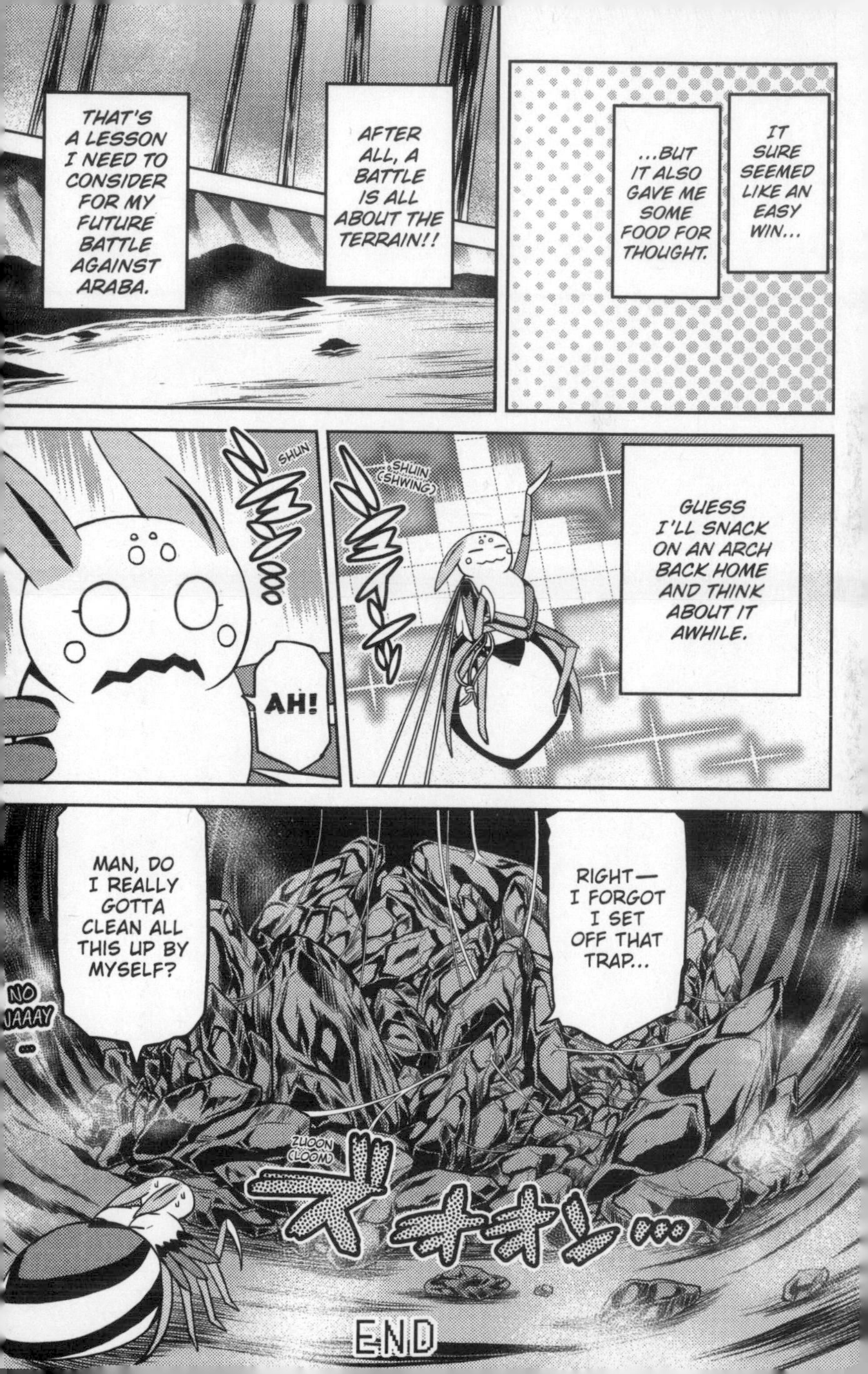
IT SURE SEEMED LIKE AN EASY WIN...
...BUT IT ALSO GAVE ME SOME FOOD FOR THOUGHT.
AFTER ALL, A BATTLE IS ALL ABOUT THE TERRAIN!!
THAT'S A LESSON I NEED TO CONSIDER FOR MY FUTURE BATTLE AGAINST ARABA.
GUESS I'LL SNACK ON AN ARCH BACK HOME AND THINK ABOUT IT AWHILE.
SHUIN (SHWING)
SHUN
AH!
RIGHT— I FORGOT I SET OFF THAT TRAP...
MAN, DO I REALLY GOTTA CLEAN ALL THIS UP BY MYSELF?
NO
ZUOON (LOOM)
END

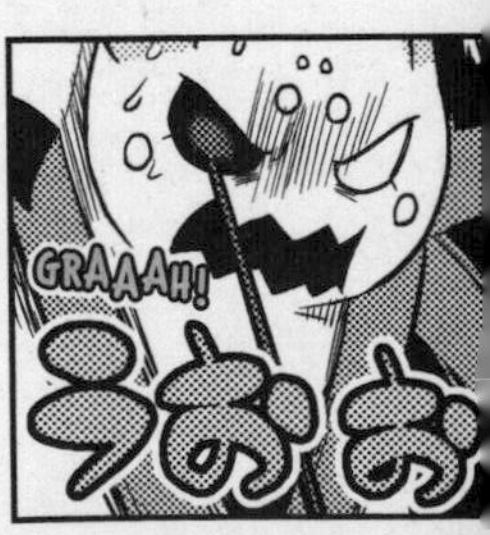
GRAAAH!
うおお

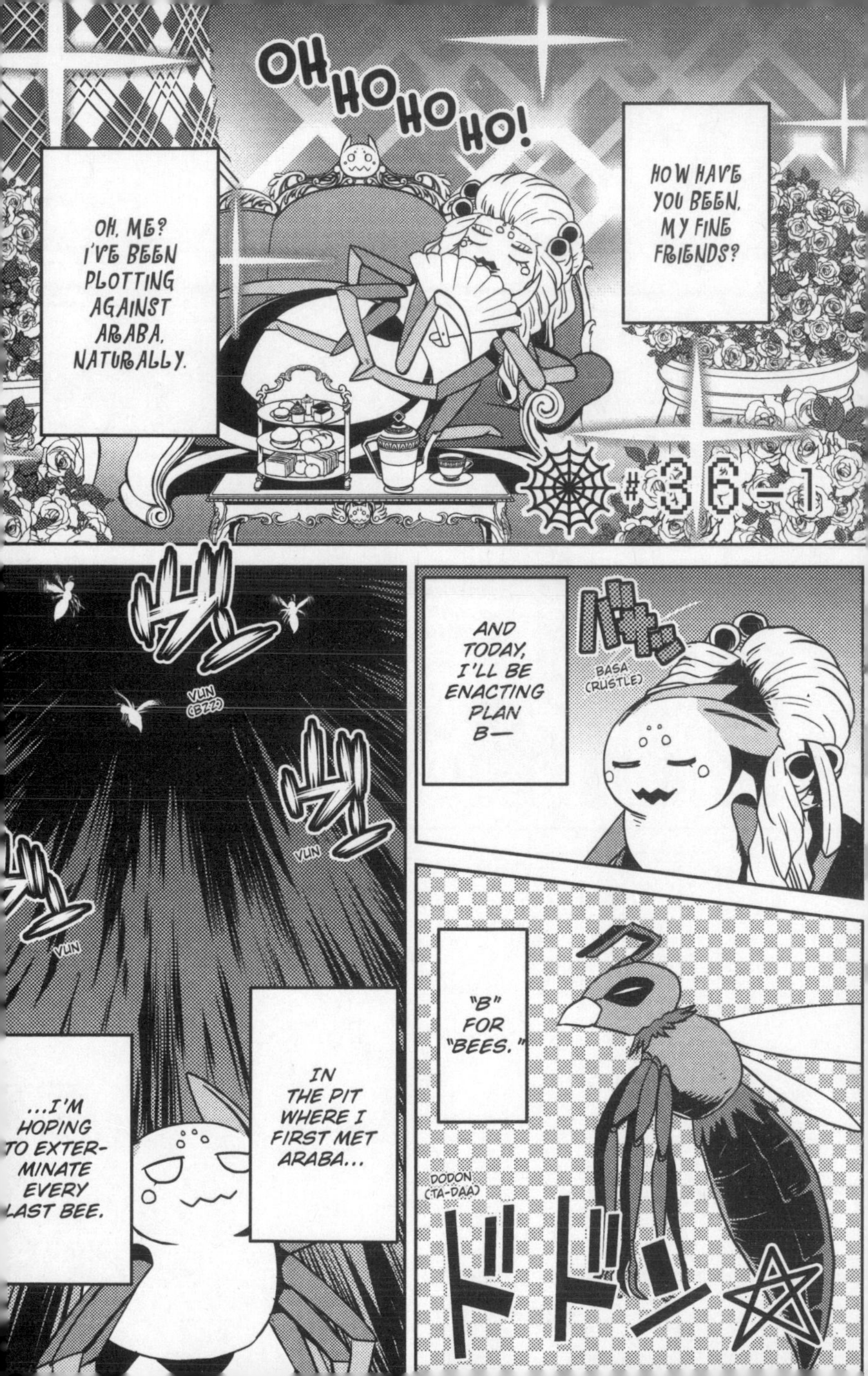
OH HO HO HO!
HOW HAVE YOU BEEN, MY FINE FRIENDS?
OH, ME? I'VE BEEN PLOTTING AGAINST ARABA, NATURALLY.
#36-1
AND TODAY, I'LL BE ENACTING PLAN B—
BASA (RUSTLE)
"B" FOR "BEES."
DODON (TA-DAA)
VUN (BZZ)
VUN
VUN
IN THE PIT WHERE I FIRST MET ARABA...
...I'M HOPING TO EXTER-MINATE EVERY LAST BEE.

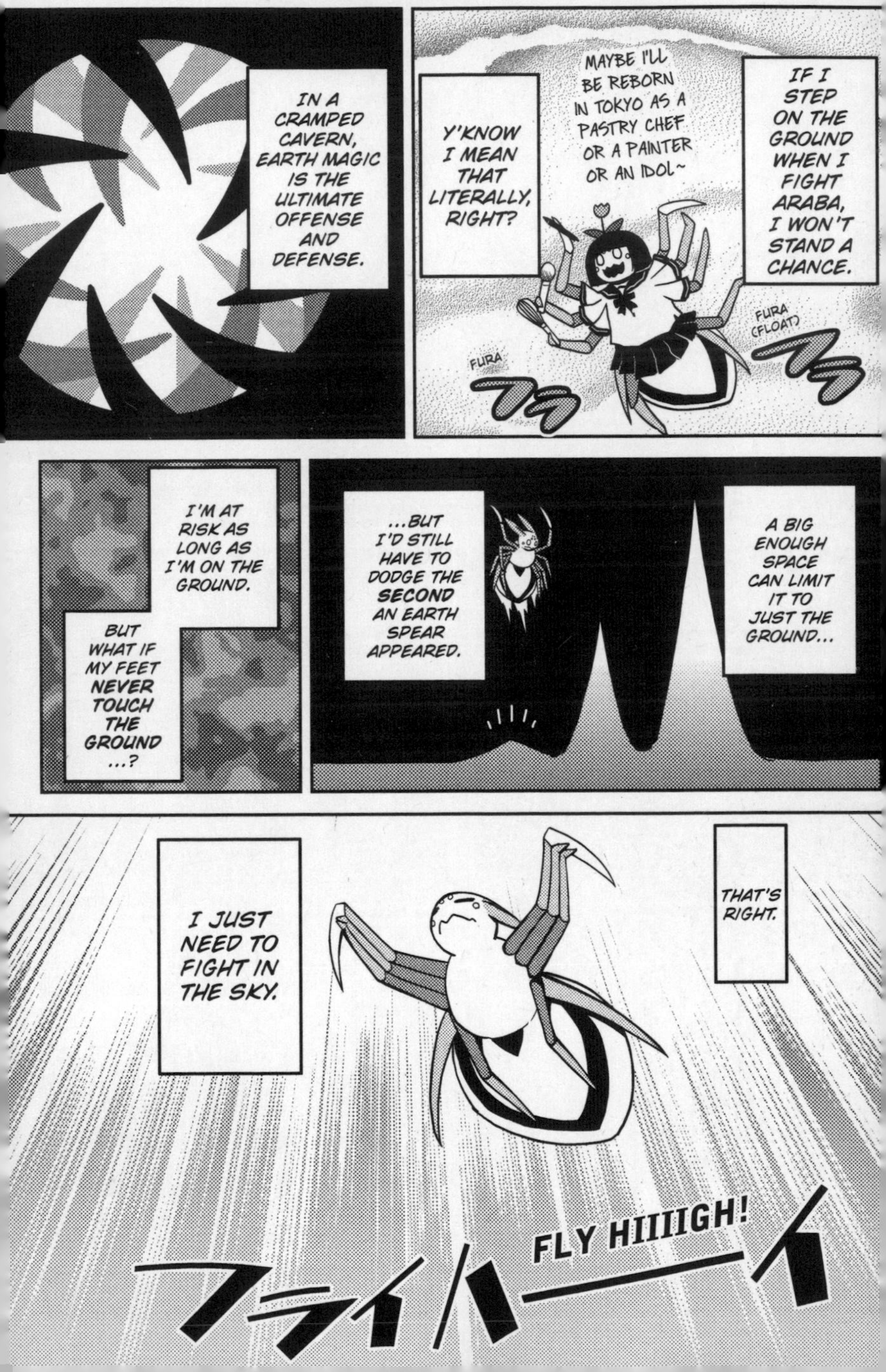
IF I STEP ON THE GROUND WHEN I FIGHT ARABA, I WON'T STAND A CHANCE.
MAYBE I'LL BE REBORN IN TOKYO AS A PASTRY CHEF OR A PAINTER OR AN IDOL~
Y'KNOW I MEAN THAT LITERALLY, RIGHT?
FURA (FLOAT)
FURA
IN A CRAMPED CAVERN, EARTH MAGIC IS THE ULTIMATE OFFENSE AND DEFENSE.
A BIG ENOUGH SPACE CAN LIMIT IT TO JUST THE GROUND...
...BUT I'D STILL HAVE TO DODGE THE SECOND AN EARTH SPEAR APPEARED.
I'M AT RISK AS LONG AS I'M ON THE GROUND.
BUT WHAT IF MY FEET NEVER TOUCH THE GROUND ...?
THAT'S RIGHT.
I JUST NEED TO FIGHT IN THE SKY.
FLY HIIIIGH!
フライハーイ

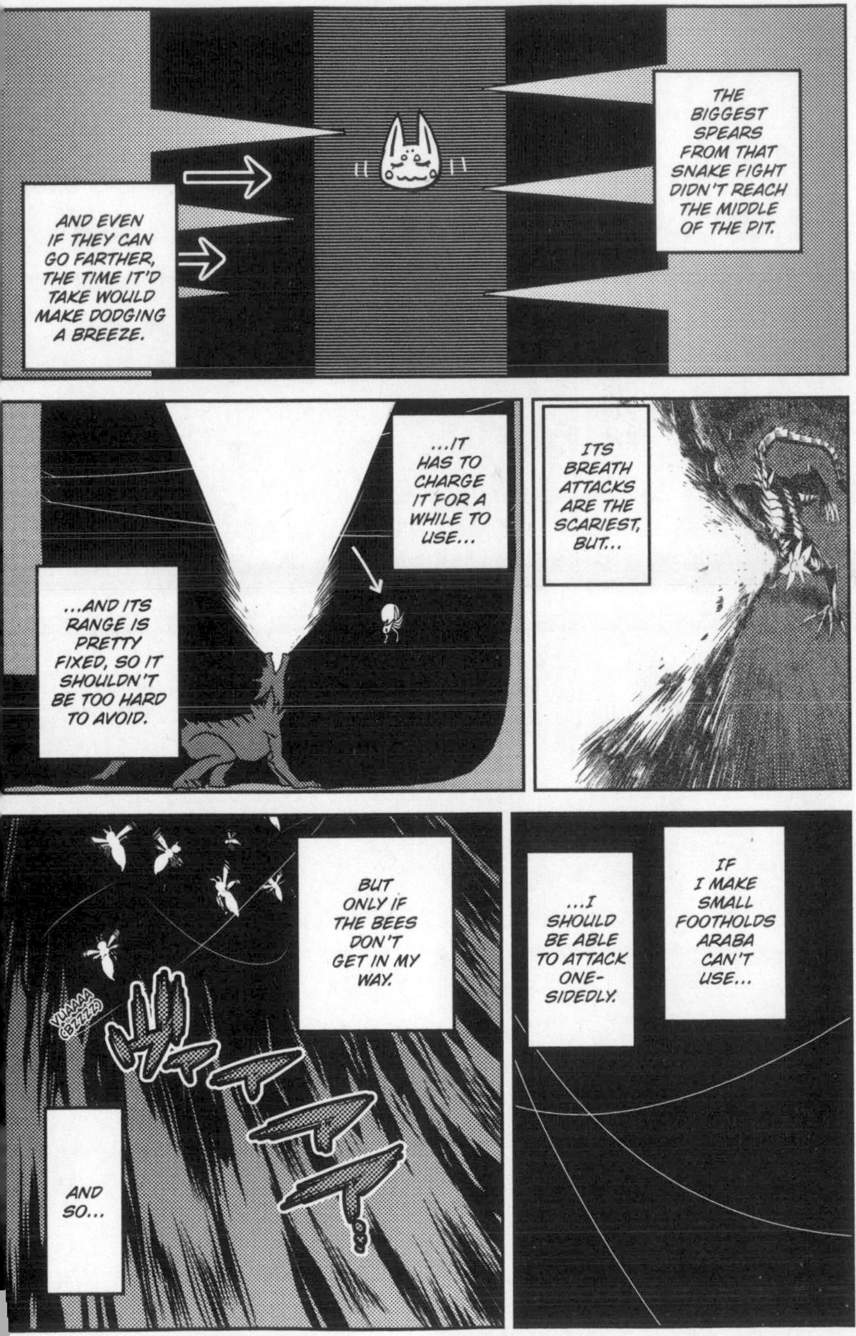
THE BIGGEST SPEARS FROM THAT SNAKE FIGHT DIDN'T REACH THE MIDDLE OF THE PIT.
AND EVEN IF THEY CAN GO FARTHER, THE TIME IT'D TAKE WOULD MAKE DODGING A BREEZE.
ITS BREATH ATTACKS ARE THE SCARIEST, BUT...
...IT HAS TO CHARGE IT FOR A WHILE TO USE...
...AND ITS RANGE IS PRETTY FIXED, SO IT SHOULDN'T BE TOO HARD TO AVOID.
IF I MAKE SMALL FOOTHOLDS ARABA CAN'T USE...
...I SHOULD BE ABLE TO ATTACK ONE-SIDEDLY.
BUT ONLY IF THE BEES DON'T GET IN MY WAY.
VUAAAA (BZZZZ)
AND SO...

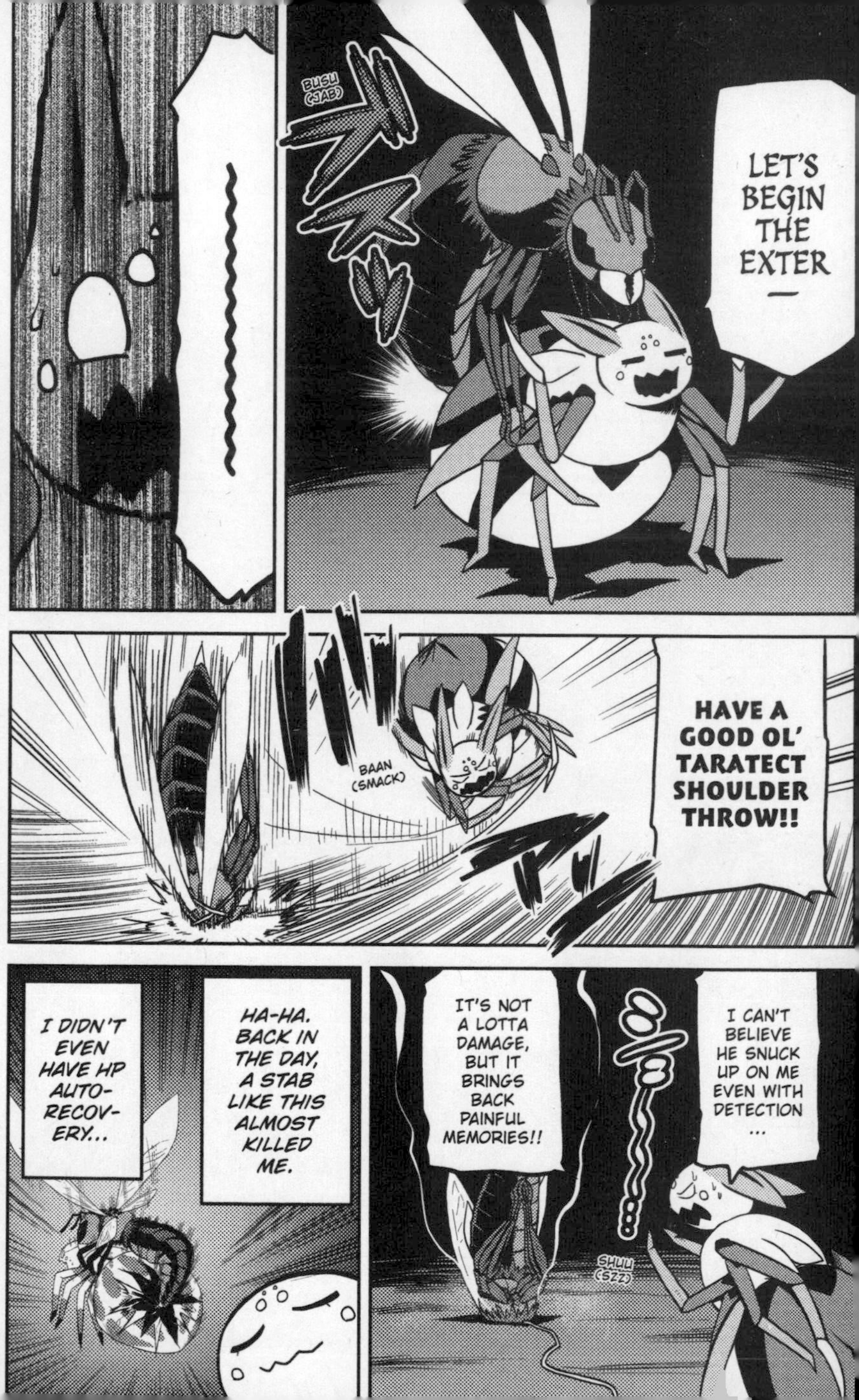
LET'S BEGIN THE EXTER—
BUSU (JAB)
HAVE A GOOD OL' TARATECT SHOULDER THROW!!
BAAN (SMACK)
I CAN'T BELIEVE HE SNUCK UP ON ME EVEN WITH DETECTION...
IT'S NOT A LOTTA DAMAGE, BUT IT BRINGS BACK PAINFUL MEMORIES!!
SHUU (SZZ)
HA-HA. BACK IN THE DAY, A STAB LIKE THIS ALMOST KILLED ME.
I DIDN'T EVEN HAVE HP AUTO-RECOVERY...

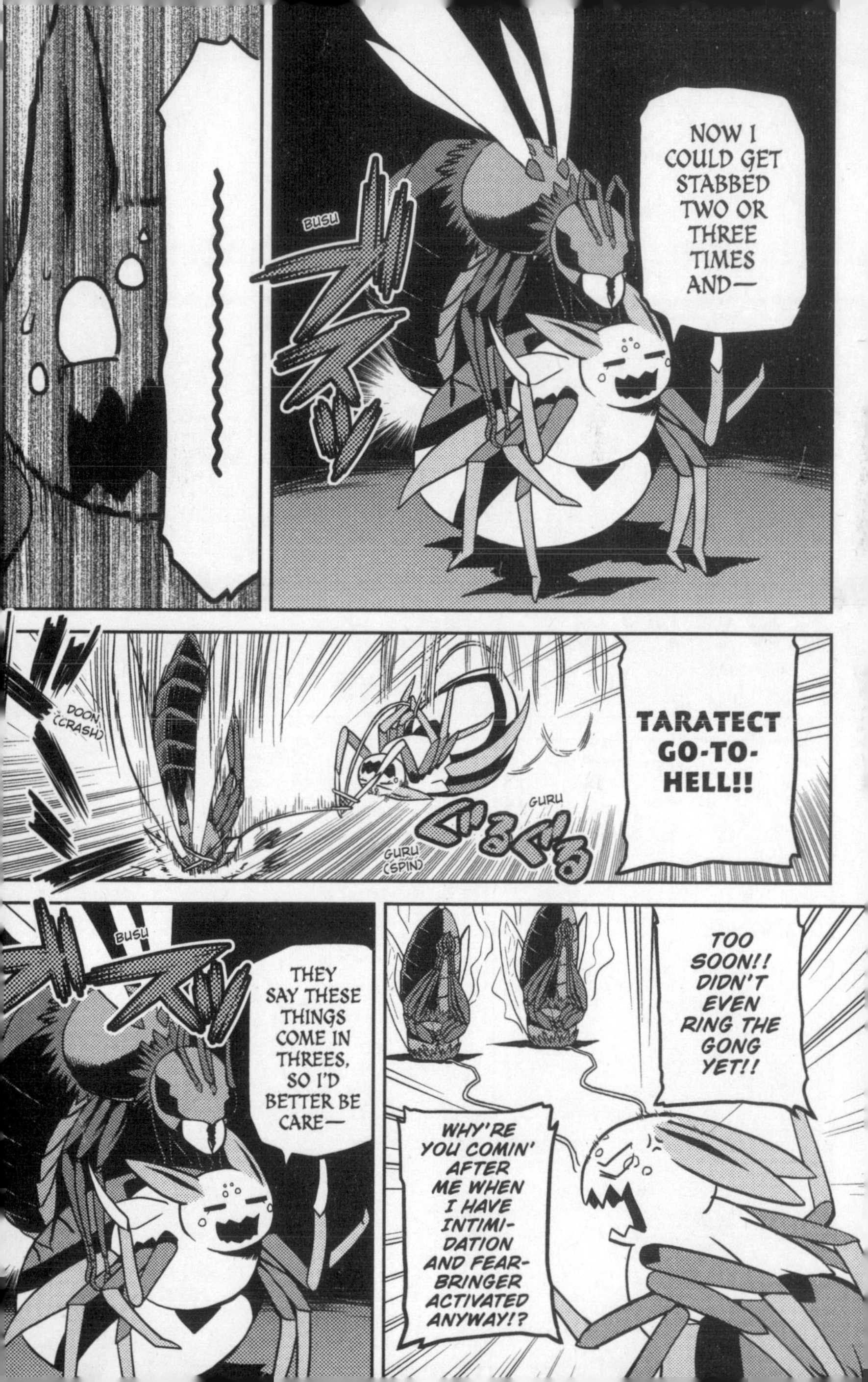
NOW I COULD GET STABBED TWO OR THREE TIMES AND—
BUSU
TARATECT GO-TO-HELL!!
GURU
GURU (SPIN)
DOON (CRASH)
TOO SOON!! DIDN'T EVEN RING THE GONG YET!!
WHY'RE YOU COMIN' AFTER ME WHEN I HAVE INTIMI-DATION AND FEAR-BRINGER ACTIVATED ANYWAY!?
BUSU
THEY SAY THESE THINGS COME IN THREES, SO I'D BETTER BE CARE—

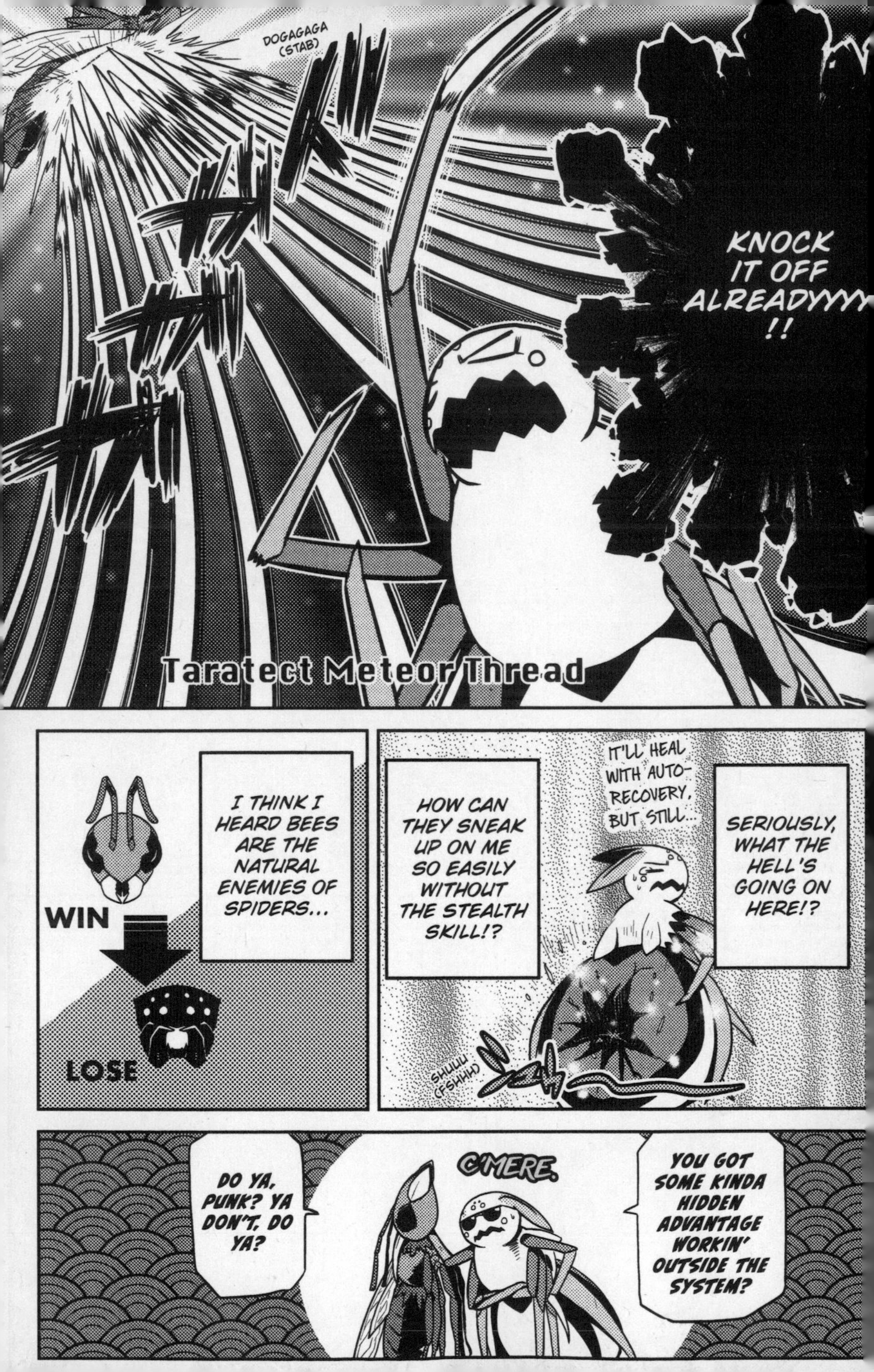

KNOCK IT OFF ALREADYYYY!!
DOGAGAGA (STAB)
Taratect Meteor Thread
SERIOUSLY, WHAT THE HELL'S GOING ON HERE!?
IT'LL HEAL WITH AUTO-RECOVERY, BUT STILL...
HOW CAN THEY SNEAK UP ON ME SO EASILY WITHOUT THE STEALTH SKILL!?
SHUUU (FSHHH)
I THINK I HEARD BEES ARE THE NATURAL ENEMIES OF SPIDERS...
WIN
LOSE
YOU GOT SOME KINDA HIDDEN ADVANTAGE WORKIN' OUTSIDE THE SYSTEM?
C'MERE.
DO YA, PUNK? YA DON'T, DO YA?

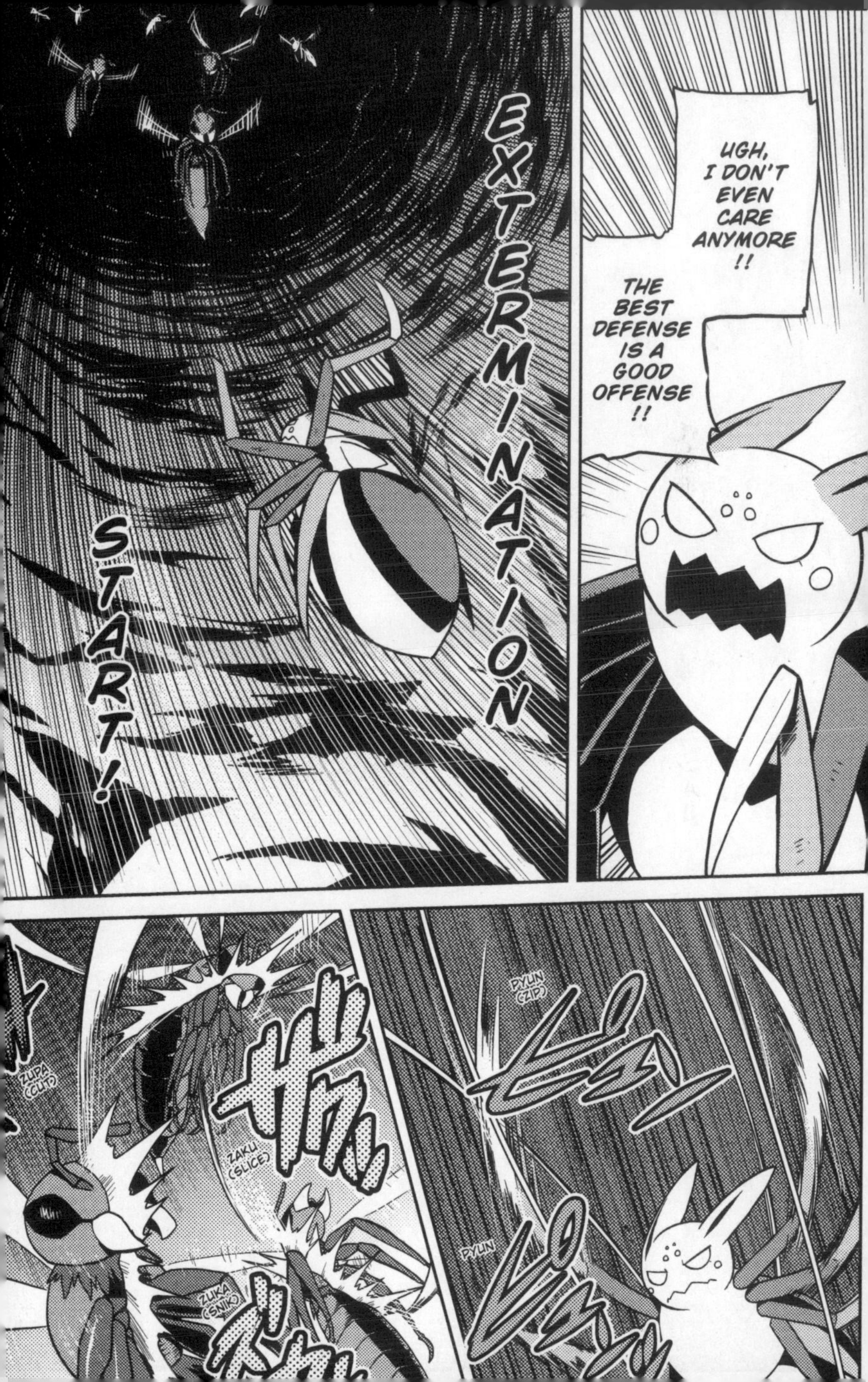
UGH, I DON'T EVEN CARE ANYMORE !!
THE BEST DEFENSE IS A GOOD OFFENSE !!
EXTERMINATION
START!
PYUN (ZIP)
PYUN
ZUPA (CUT)
ZAKU (SLICE)
ZUKA (SNIK)

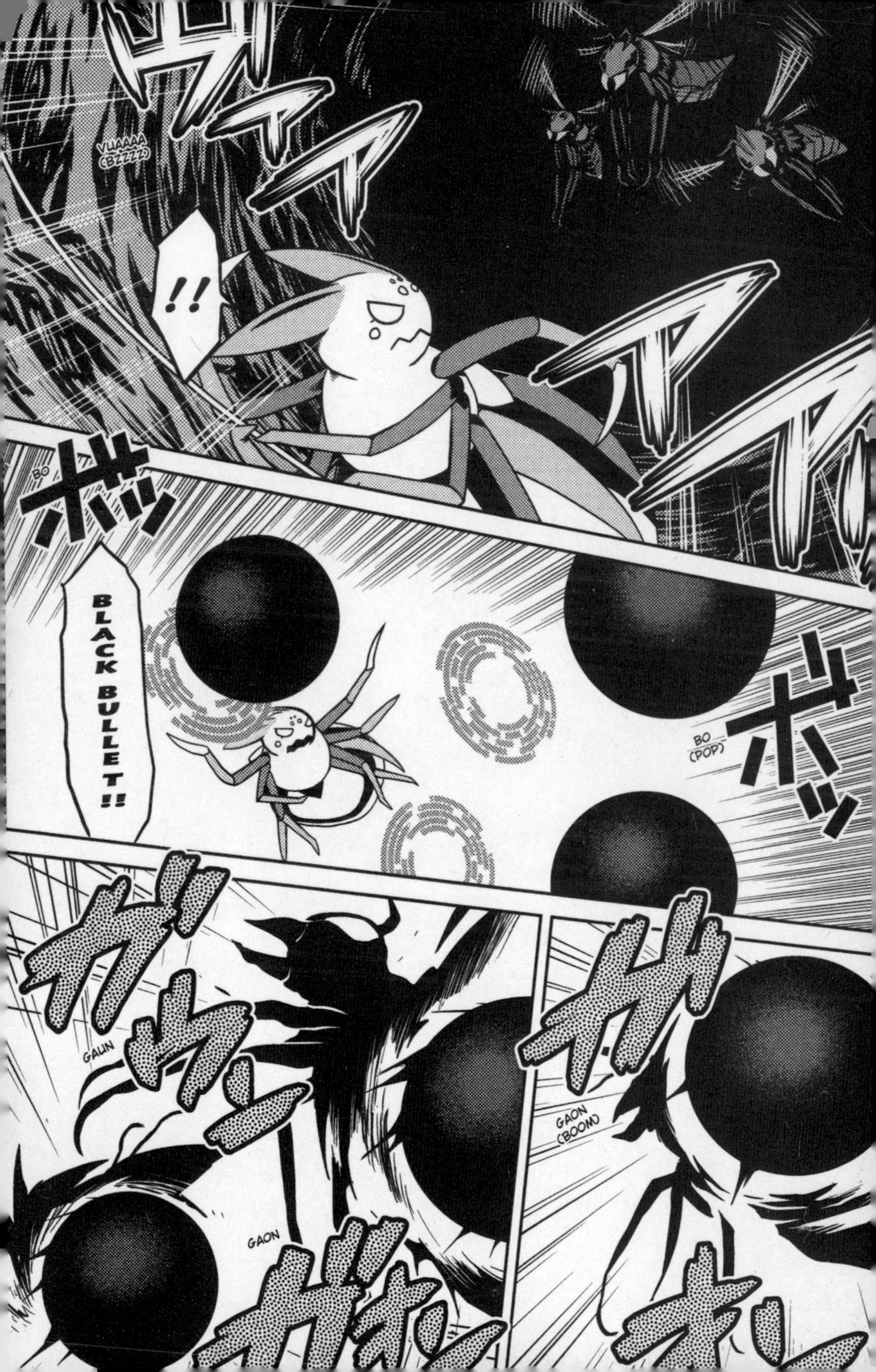
VIJAAAA (BZZZZ)
!!
BO (POP)
BLACK BULLET!!
BO
GAON (BOOM)
GAUN
GAON

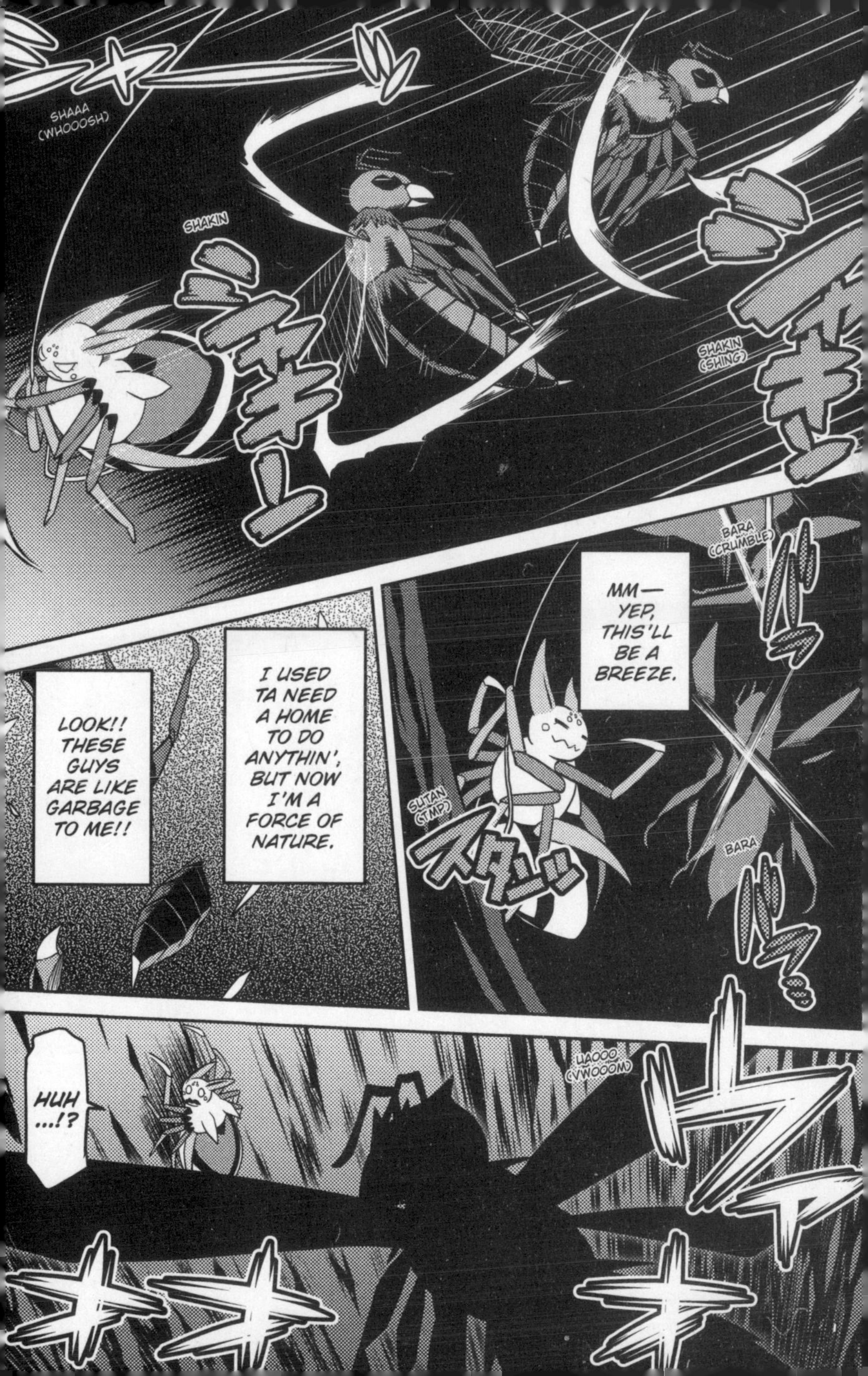
SHAKIN (SHING)
SHAKIN
SHAAA (WHOOOSH)
BARA (CRUMBLE)
MM— YEP, THIS'LL BE A BREEZE.
SUTAN (STMP)
BARA
I USED TA NEED A HOME TO DO ANYTHIN', BUT NOW I'M A FORCE OF NATURE.
LOOK!! THESE GUYS ARE LIKE GARBAGE TO ME!!
UAOOO (VWOOOM)
HUH ...!?

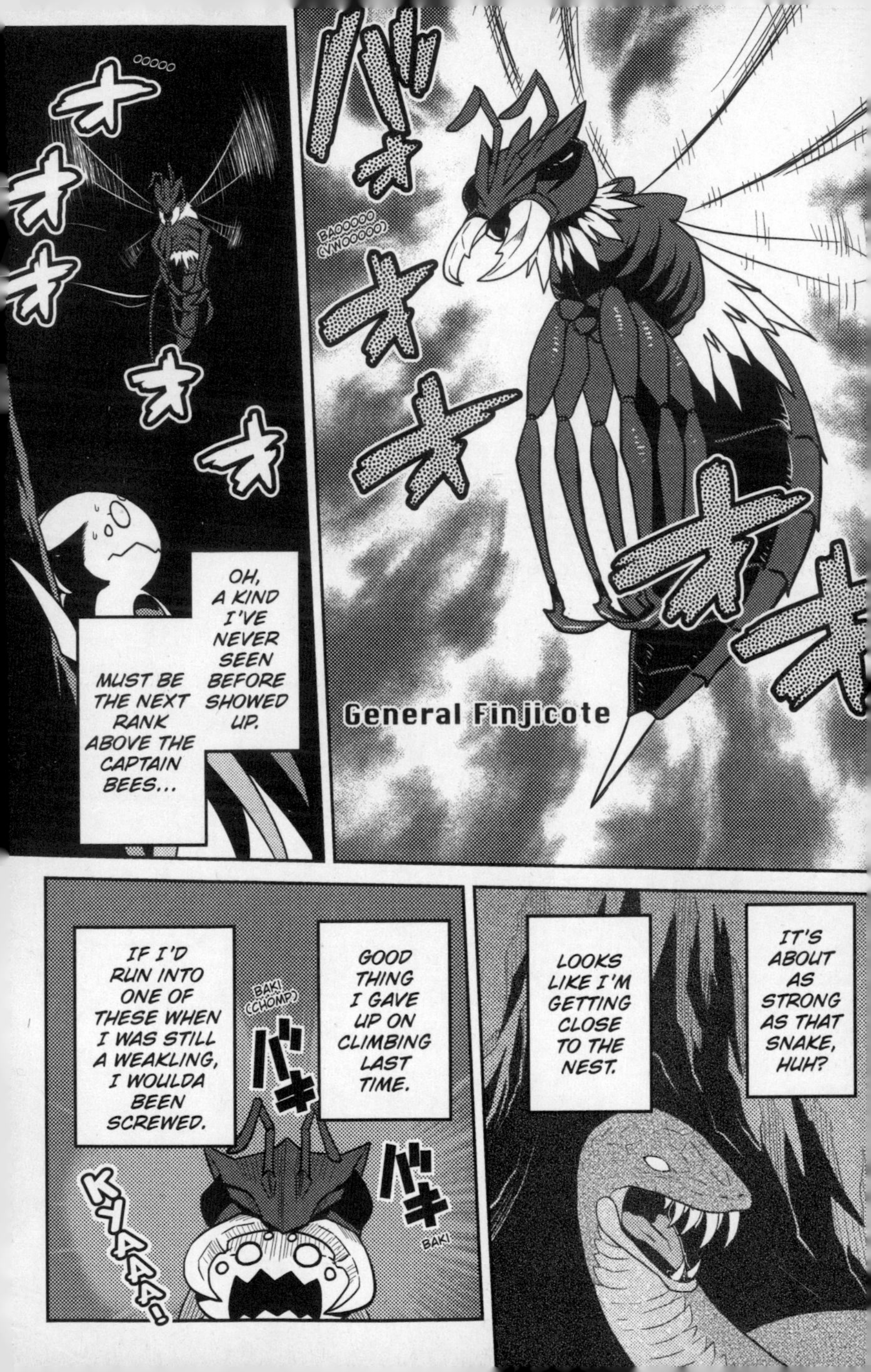

BAOOOOO (VWOOOOO)
General Finjicote
OOOOO
OH, A KIND I'VE NEVER SEEN BEFORE SHOWED UP.
MUST BE THE NEXT RANK ABOVE THE CAPTAIN BEES...
IT'S ABOUT AS STRONG AS THAT SNAKE, HUH?
LOOKS LIKE I'M GETTING CLOSE TO THE NEST.
GOOD THING I GAVE UP ON CLIMBING LAST TIME.
IF I'D RUN INTO ONE OF THESE WHEN I WAS STILL A WEAKLING, I WOULDA BEEN SCREWED.
BAKI (CHOMP)
BAKI
KYAAA!

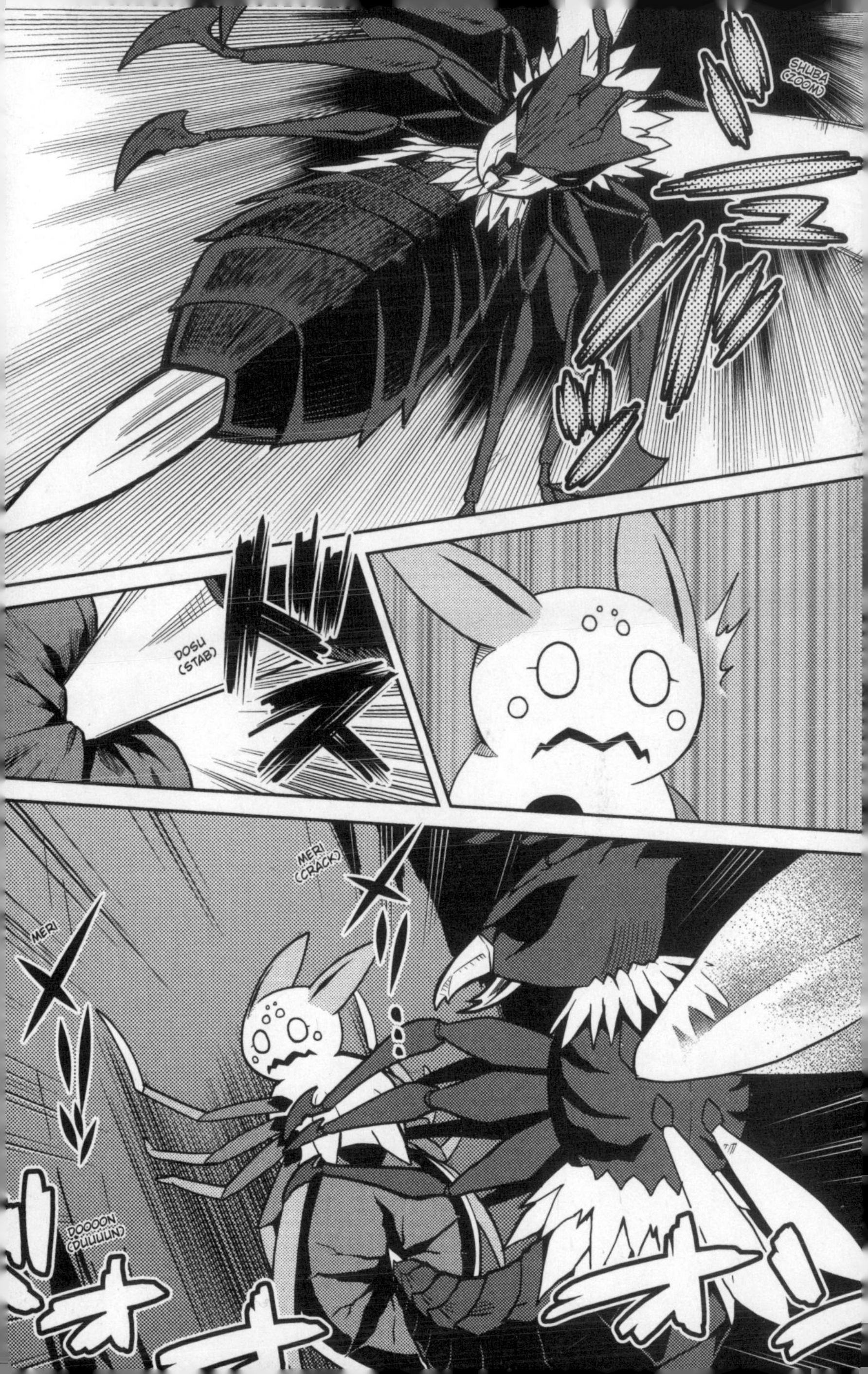
SHUBA (ZOOM)
DOSU (STAB)
MERI (CRACK)
MERI
DOOOON (DUUUUN)

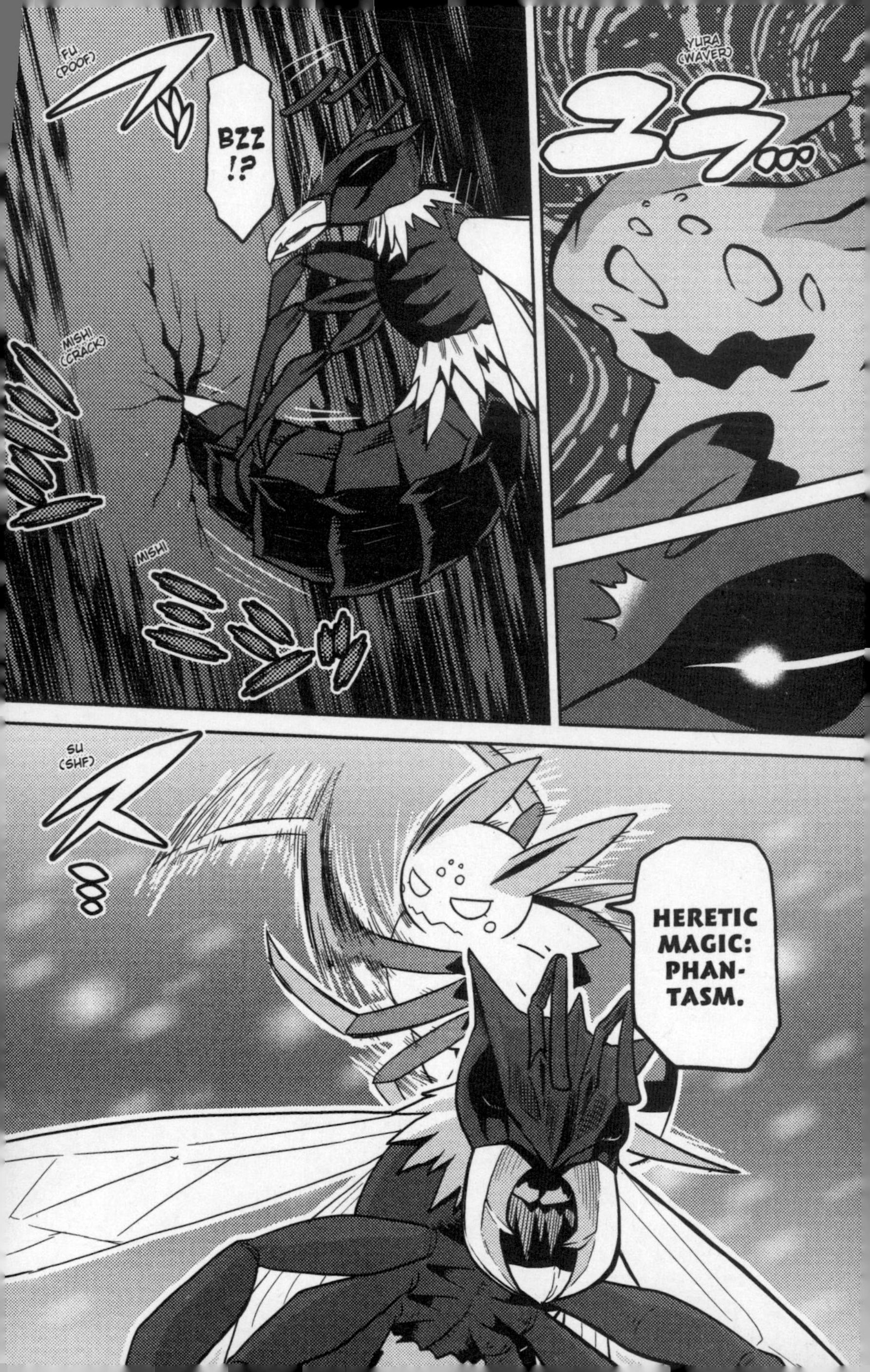
YURA
(WAVER)
FU
(POOF)
BZZ
!?
MISHI
(CRACK)
MISHI
SU
(SHF)
HERETIC MAGIC: PHAN-TASM.

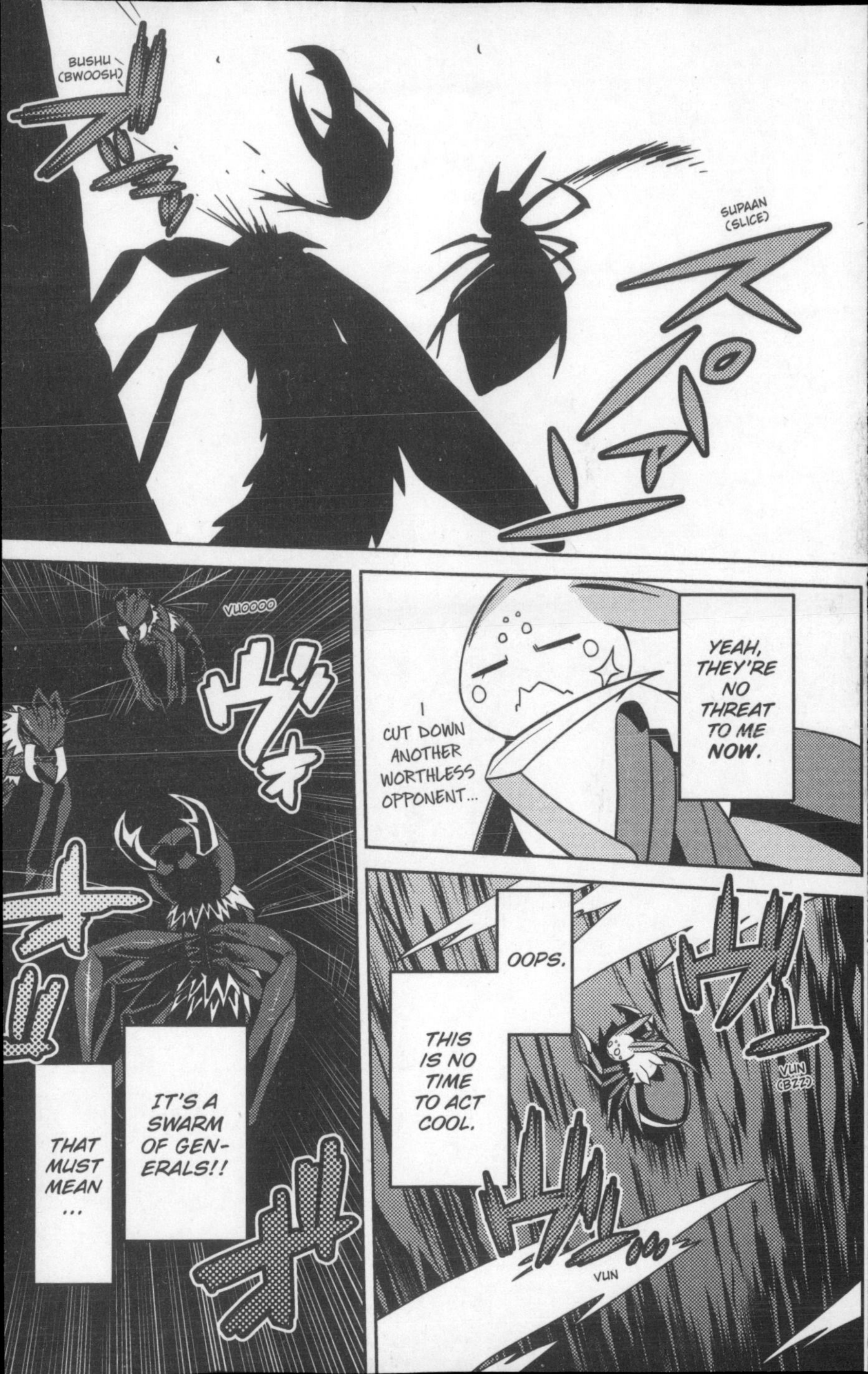
SUPAAN (SLICE)
BUSHU (BWOOSH)
YEAH, THEY'RE NO THREAT TO ME NOW.
I CUT DOWN ANOTHER WORTHLESS OPPONENT...
OOPS.
THIS IS NO TIME TO ACT COOL.
VUN (BZZ)
VUN
VUOOOO
IT'S A SWARM OF GEN-ERALS!!
THAT MUST MEAN ...

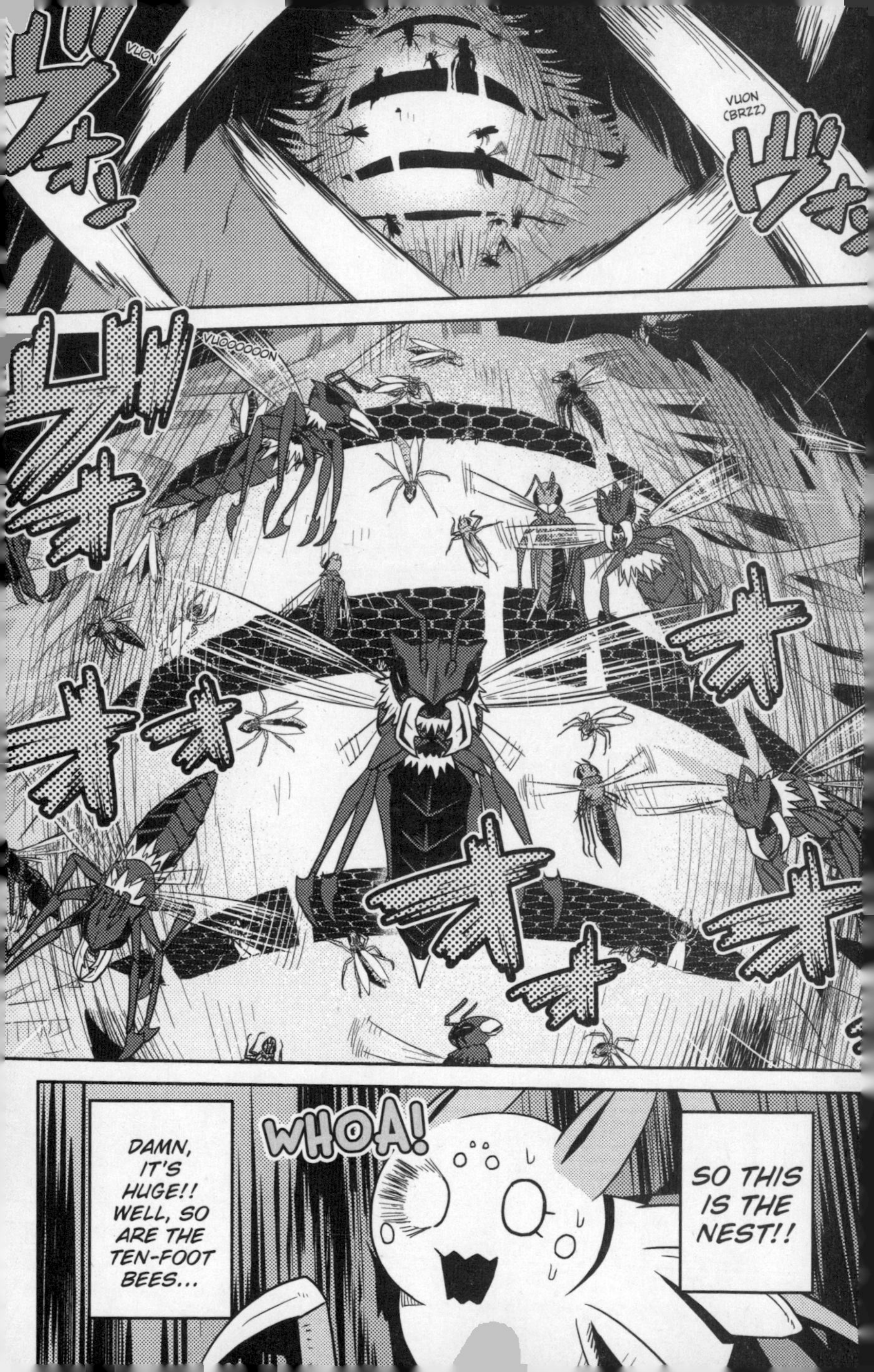
VUON (BRZZ)
VUON
VUOOOOOON
SO THIS IS THE NEST!!
WHOA!
DAMN, IT'S HUGE!! WELL, SO ARE THE TEN-FOOT BEES...

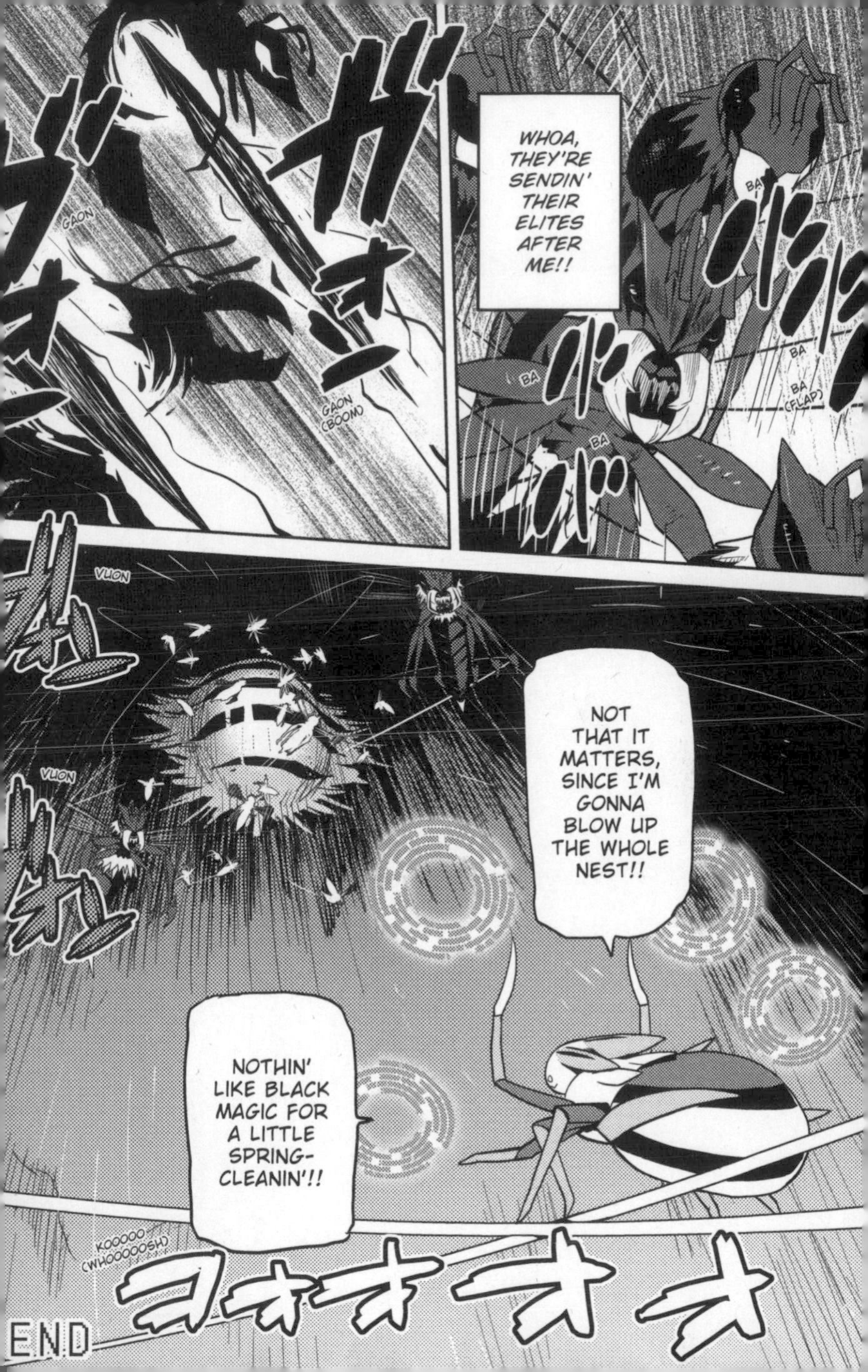

WHOA, THEY'RE SENDIN' THEIR ELITES AFTER ME!!
BA
BA
BA
BA (FLAP)
BA
GAON
GAON (BOOM)
NOT THAT IT MATTERS, SINCE I'M GONNA BLOW UP THE WHOLE NEST!!
VUON
VUON
NOTHIN' LIKE BLACK MAGIC FOR A LITTLE SPRING-CLEANIN'!!
KOOOOO (WHOOOOOSH)
END

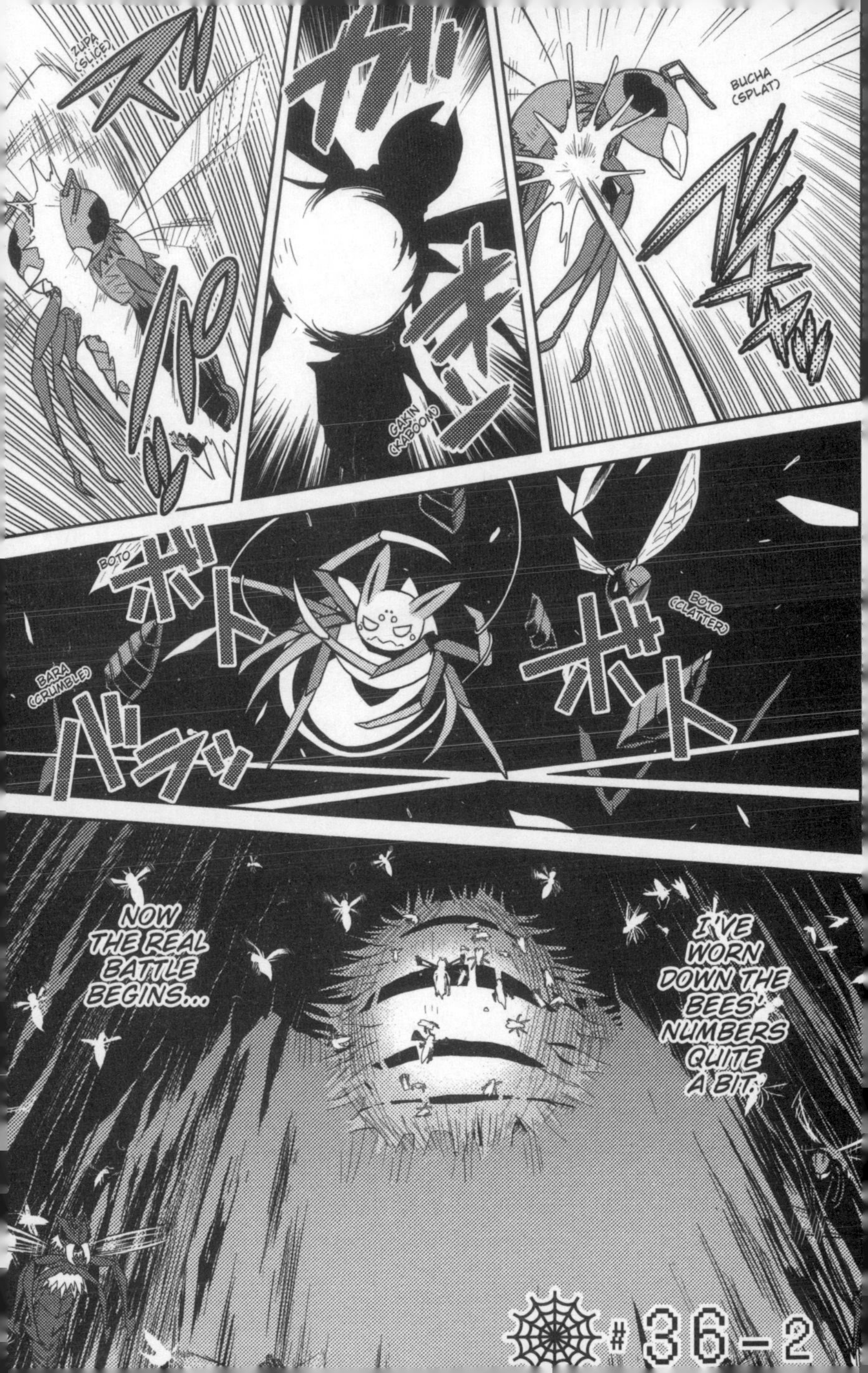
BUCHA (SPLAT)
GAKIN (KABOOM)
ZUPA (SLICE)
BOTO (CLATTER)
BOTO
BARA (CRUMBLE)
I'VE WORN DOWN THE BEES' NUMBERS QUITE A BIT.
NOW THE REAL BATTLE BEGINS...
#36-2

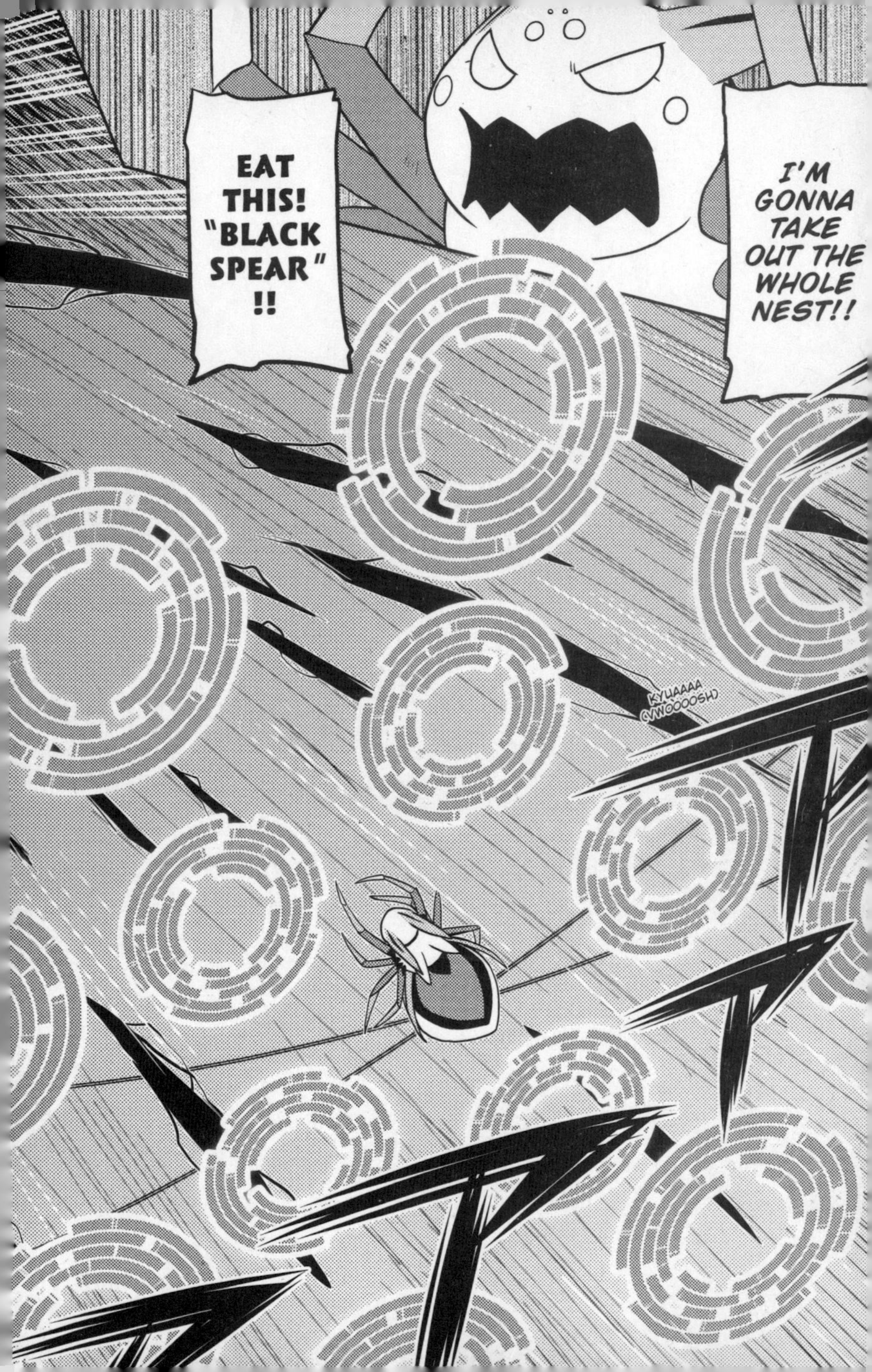
I'M GONNA TAKE OUT THE WHOLE NEST!!
EAT THIS! "BLACK SPEAR" !!
KYUAAAA (VWOOOOSH)

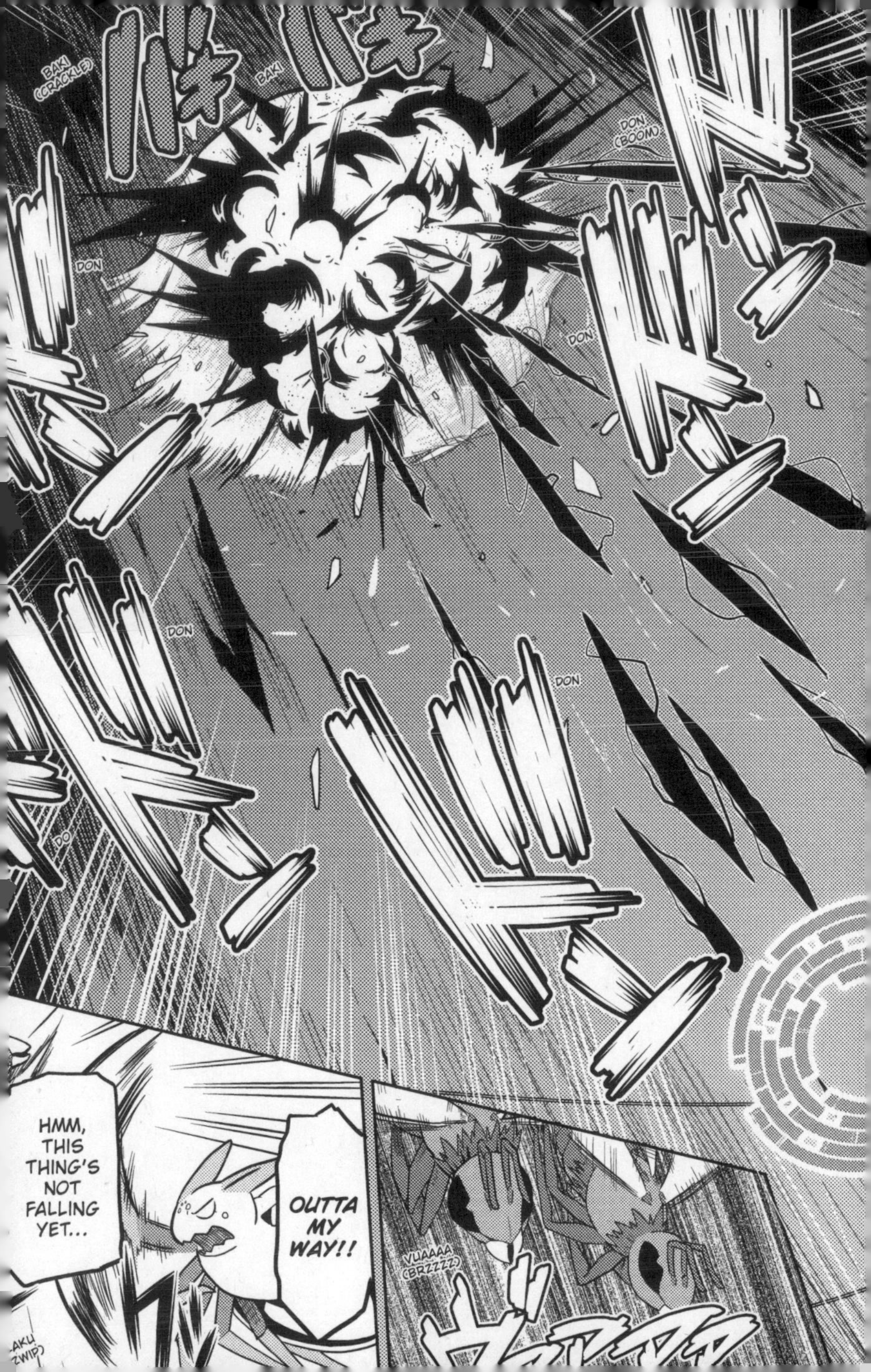
DON (BOOM)
BAKI
BAKI (CRACKLE)
DON
DON
DON
DON
DO
VUAAAA (BRZZZZ)
HMM, THIS THING'S NOT FALLING YET...
OUTTA MY WAY!!

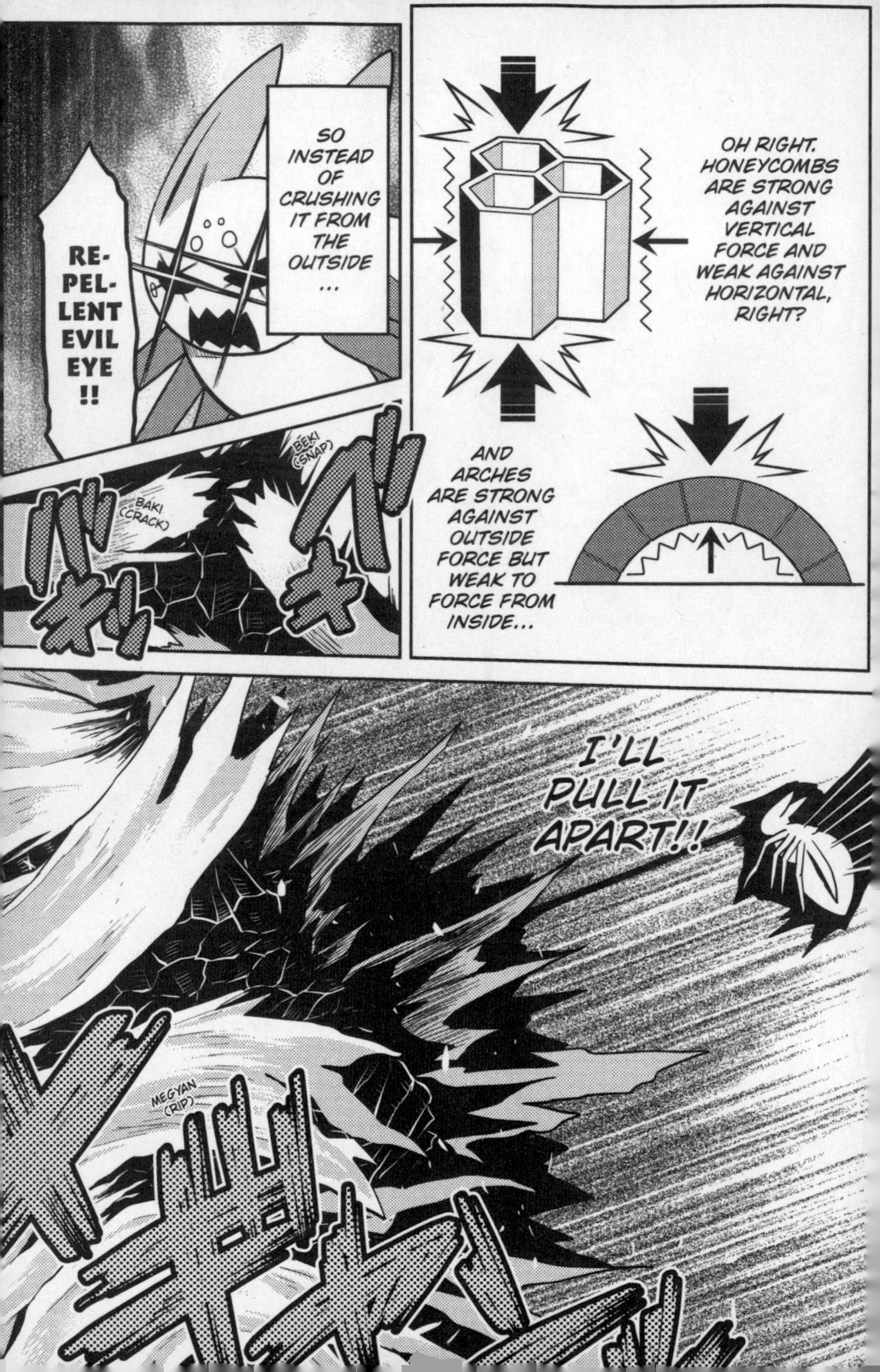
OH RIGHT. HONEYCOMBS ARE STRONG AGAINST VERTICAL FORCE AND WEAK AGAINST HORIZONTAL, RIGHT?
AND ARCHES ARE STRONG AGAINST OUTSIDE FORCE BUT WEAK TO FORCE FROM INSIDE...
SO INSTEAD OF CRUSHING IT FROM THE OUTSIDE ...
REPELLENT EVIL EYE!!
BEKI (SNAP)
BAKI (CRACK)
I'LL PULL IT APART!!
MEGYAN (RIP)

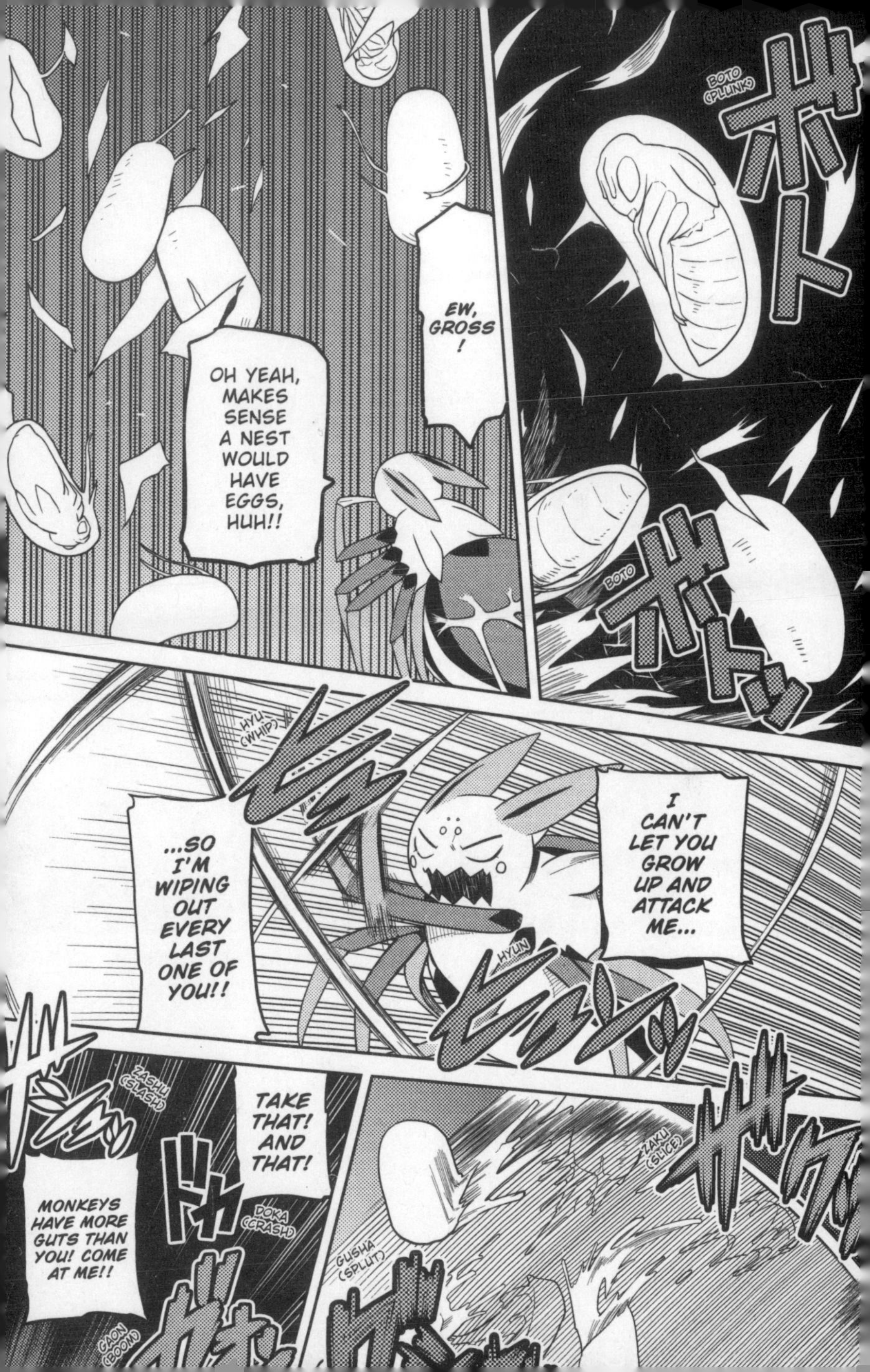
BOTO (PLUNK)
BOTO
EW, GROSS!
OH YEAH, MAKES SENSE A NEST WOULD HAVE EGGS, HUH!!
I CAN'T LET YOU GROW UP AND ATTACK ME...
HYU (WHIP)
...SO I'M WIPING OUT EVERY LAST ONE OF YOU!!
HYUN
ZAKU (SLICE)
GUSHA (SPLUT)
TAKE THAT! AND THAT!
ZASHU (SLASH)
DOKA (CRASH)
MONKEYS HAVE MORE GUTS THAN YOU! COME AT ME!!
GAON (BOOM)

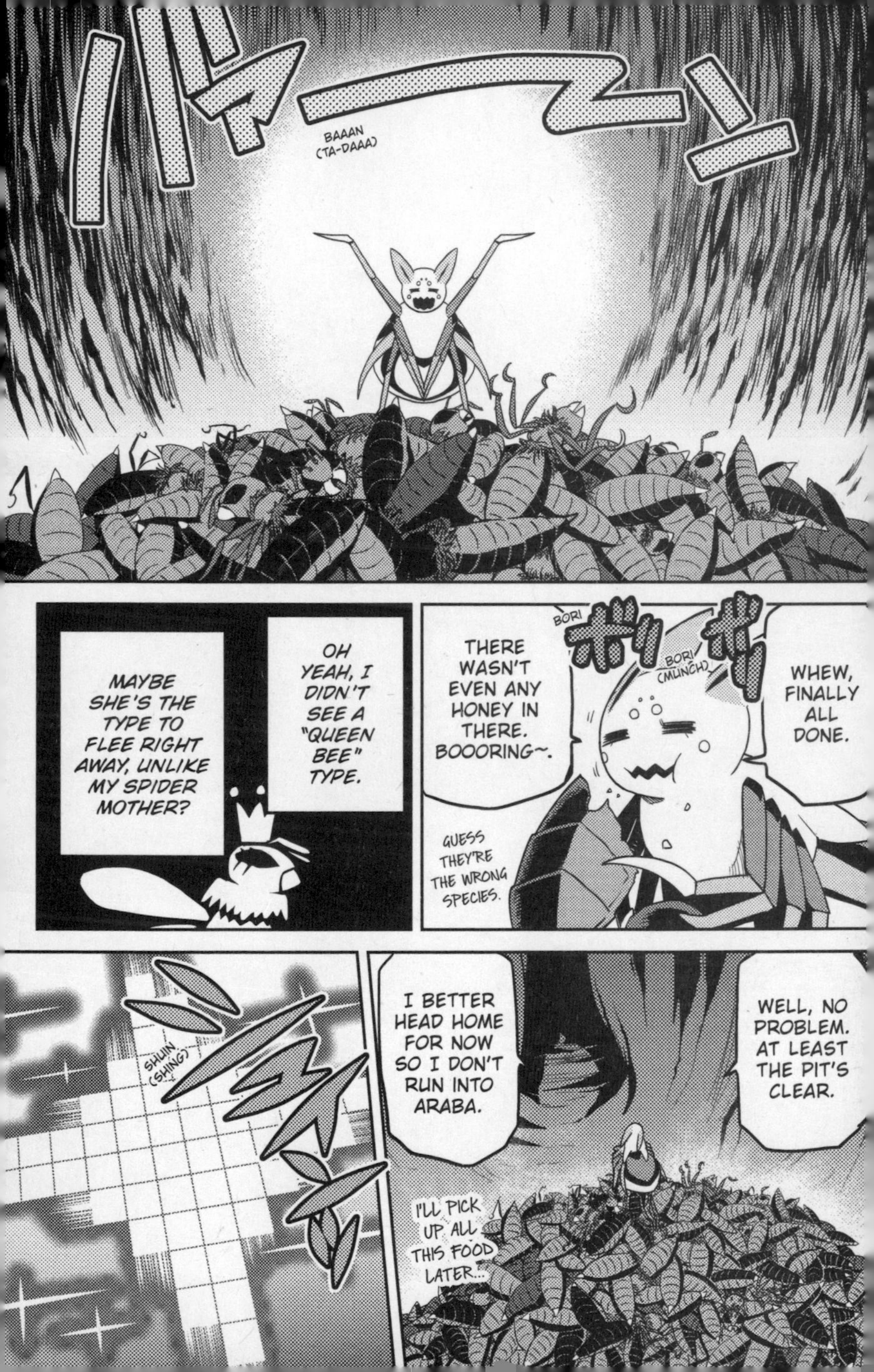
BAAAN (TA-DAAA)
WHEW, FINALLY ALL DONE.
BORI BORI (MUNCH)
THERE WASN'T EVEN ANY HONEY IN THERE. BOOORING~.
GUESS THEY'RE THE WRONG SPECIES.
OH YEAH, I DIDN'T SEE A "QUEEN BEE" TYPE.
MAYBE SHE'S THE TYPE TO FLEE RIGHT AWAY, UNLIKE MY SPIDER MOTHER?
WELL, NO PROBLEM. AT LEAST THE PIT'S CLEAR.
I BETTER HEAD HOME FOR NOW SO I DON'T RUN INTO ARABA.
I'LL PICK UP ALL THIS FOOD LATER...
SHUIN (SHING)

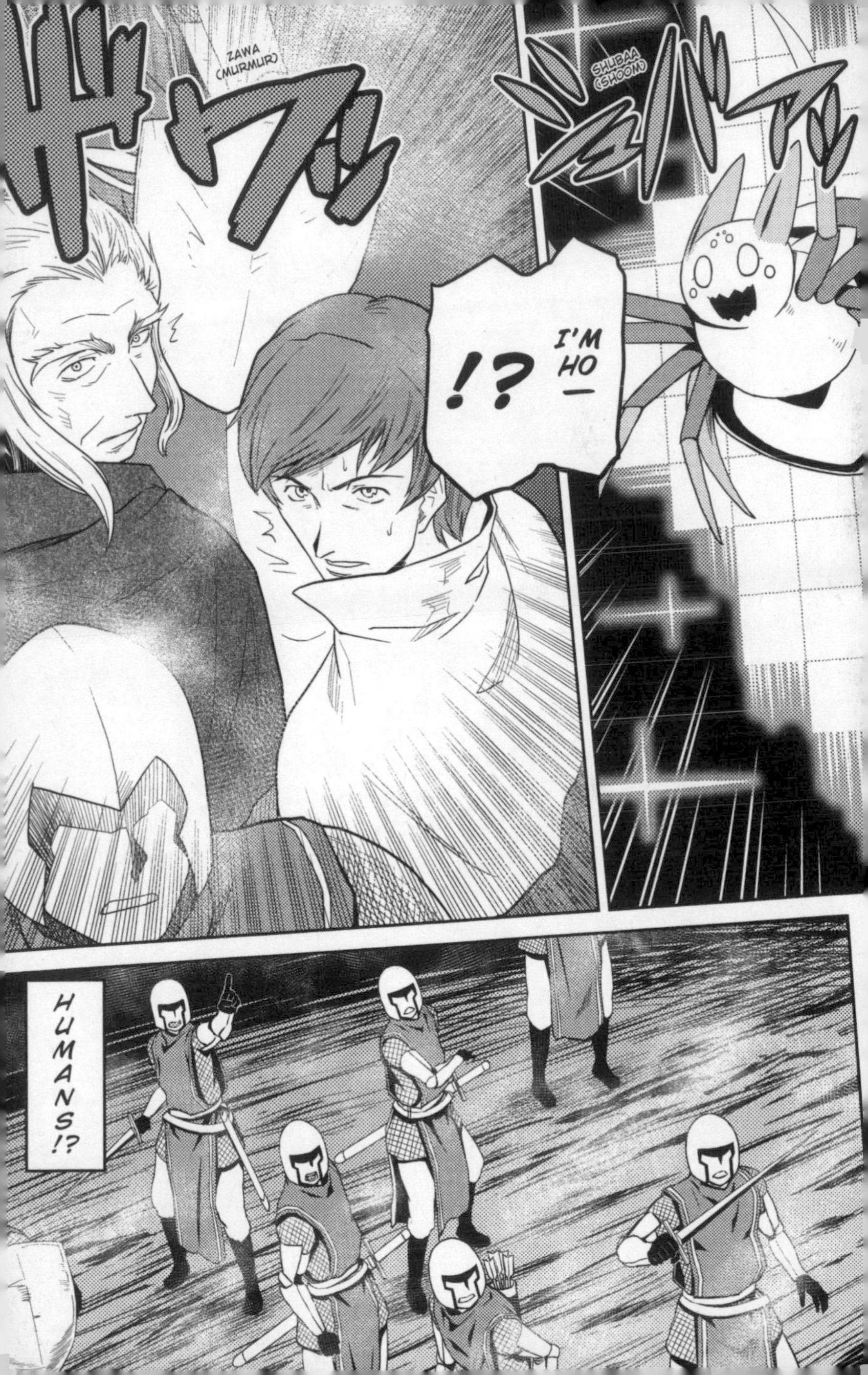
SHUBAA (SHOOM)
I'M HO—
ZAWA (MURMUR)
!?
HUMANS!?

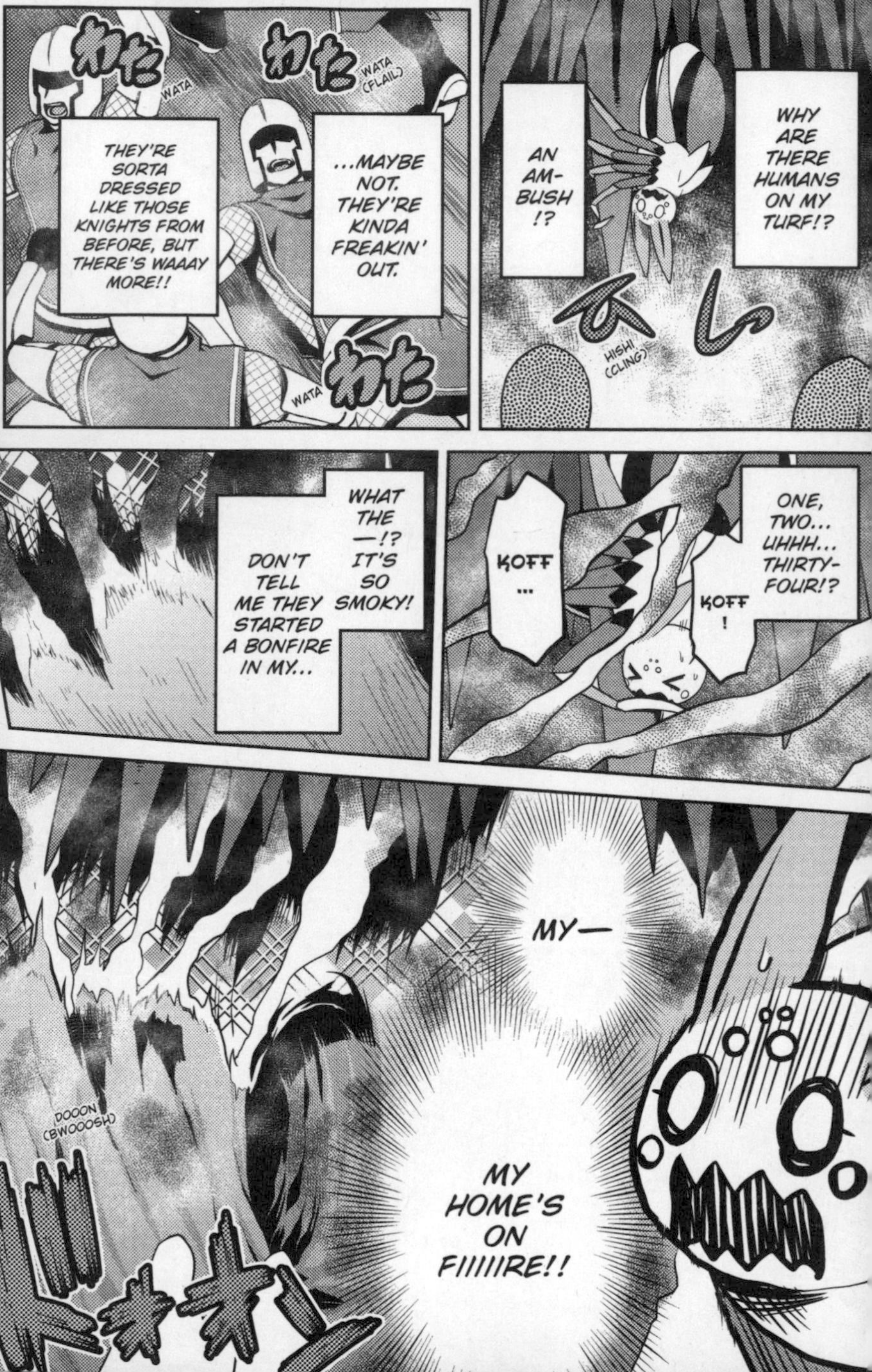
WHY ARE THERE HUMANS ON MY TURF!?
AN AMBUSH!?
HISHI (CLING)
WATA (FLAIL)
...MAYBE NOT. THEY'RE KINDA FREAKIN' OUT.
WATA
THEY'RE SORTA DRESSED LIKE THOSE KNIGHTS FROM BEFORE, BUT THERE'S WAAAY MORE!!
WATA
ONE, TWO... UHHH... THIRTY-FOUR!?
KOFF!
KOFF...
WHAT THE—!? IT'S SO SMOKY!
DON'T TELL ME THEY STARTED A BONFIRE IN MY...
MY—
DOOON (BWOOOSH)
MY HOME'S ON FIIIIIRE!!

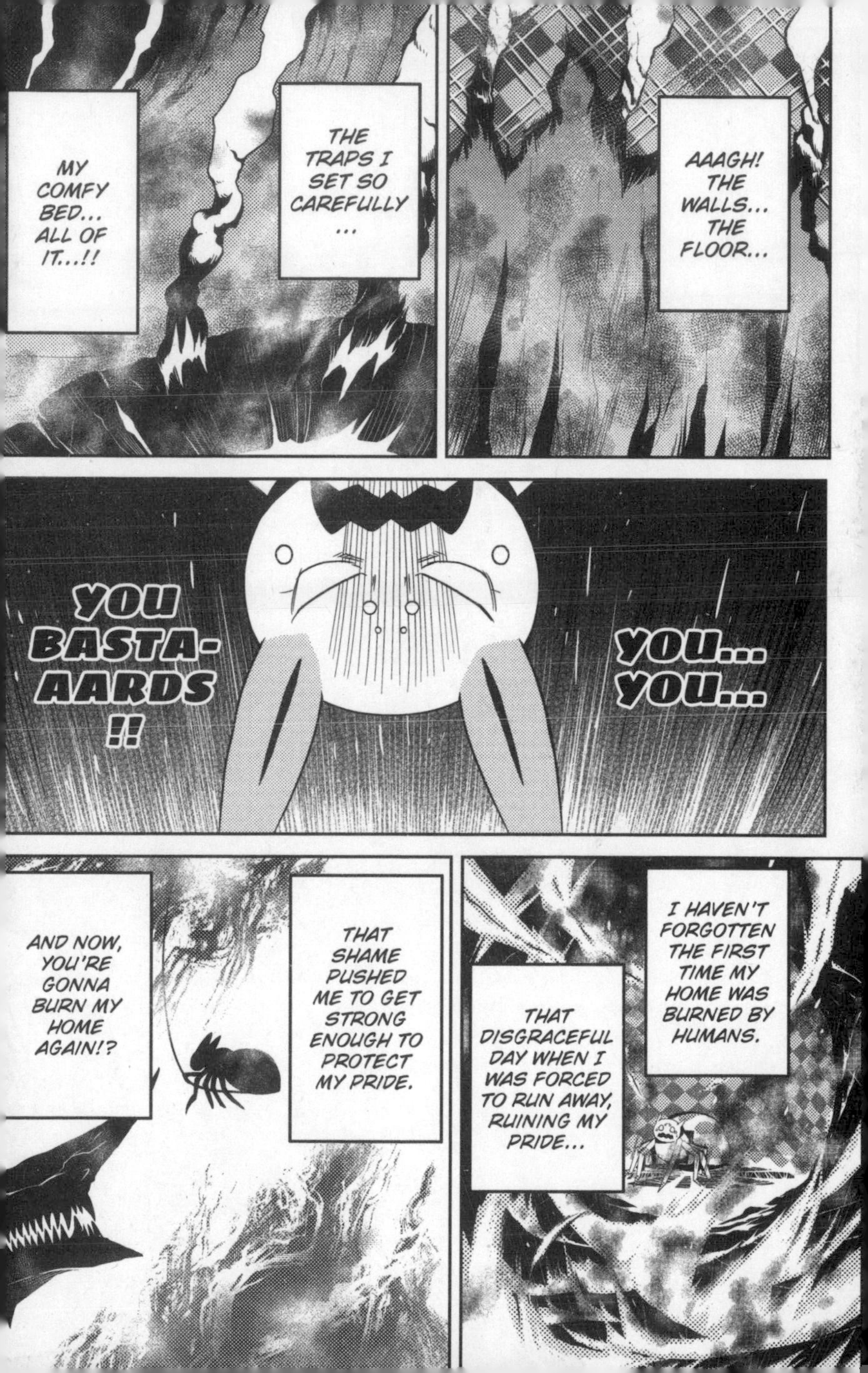
AAAGH! THE WALLS... THE FLOOR...
THE TRAPS I SET SO CAREFULLY...
MY COMFY BED... ALL OF IT...!!
YOU... YOU...
YOU BASTA-AARDS!!
I HAVEN'T FORGOTTEN THE FIRST TIME MY HOME WAS BURNED BY HUMANS.
THAT DISGRACEFUL DAY WHEN I WAS FORCED TO RUN AWAY, RUINING MY PRIDE...
THAT SHAME PUSHED ME TO GET STRONG ENOUGH TO PROTECT MY PRIDE.
AND NOW, YOU'RE GONNA BURN MY HOME AGAIN!?

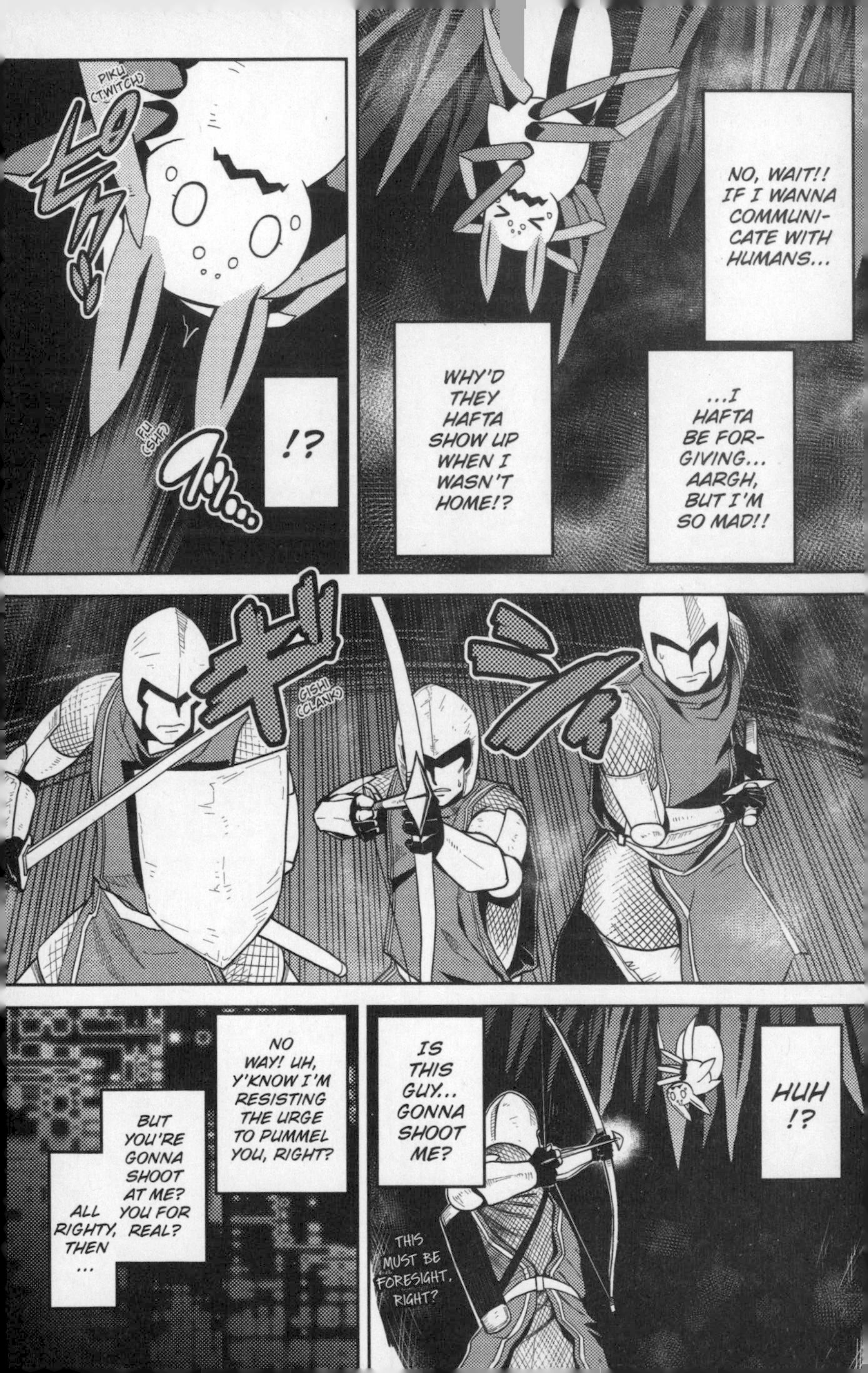
NO, WAIT!! IF I WANNA COMMUNICATE WITH HUMANS...
...I HAFTA BE FORGIVING... AARGH, BUT I'M SO MAD!!
WHY'D THEY HAFTA SHOW UP WHEN I WASN'T HOME!?
PIKU (TWITCH)
!?
FU (SH)
GISHI (CLANK)
HUH !?
IS THIS GUY... GONNA SHOOT ME?
THIS MUST BE FORESIGHT, RIGHT?
NO WAY! UH, Y'KNOW I'M RESISTING THE URGE TO PUMMEL YOU, RIGHT?
BUT YOU'RE GONNA SHOOT AT ME? YOU FOR REAL?
ALL RIGHTY, THEN ...

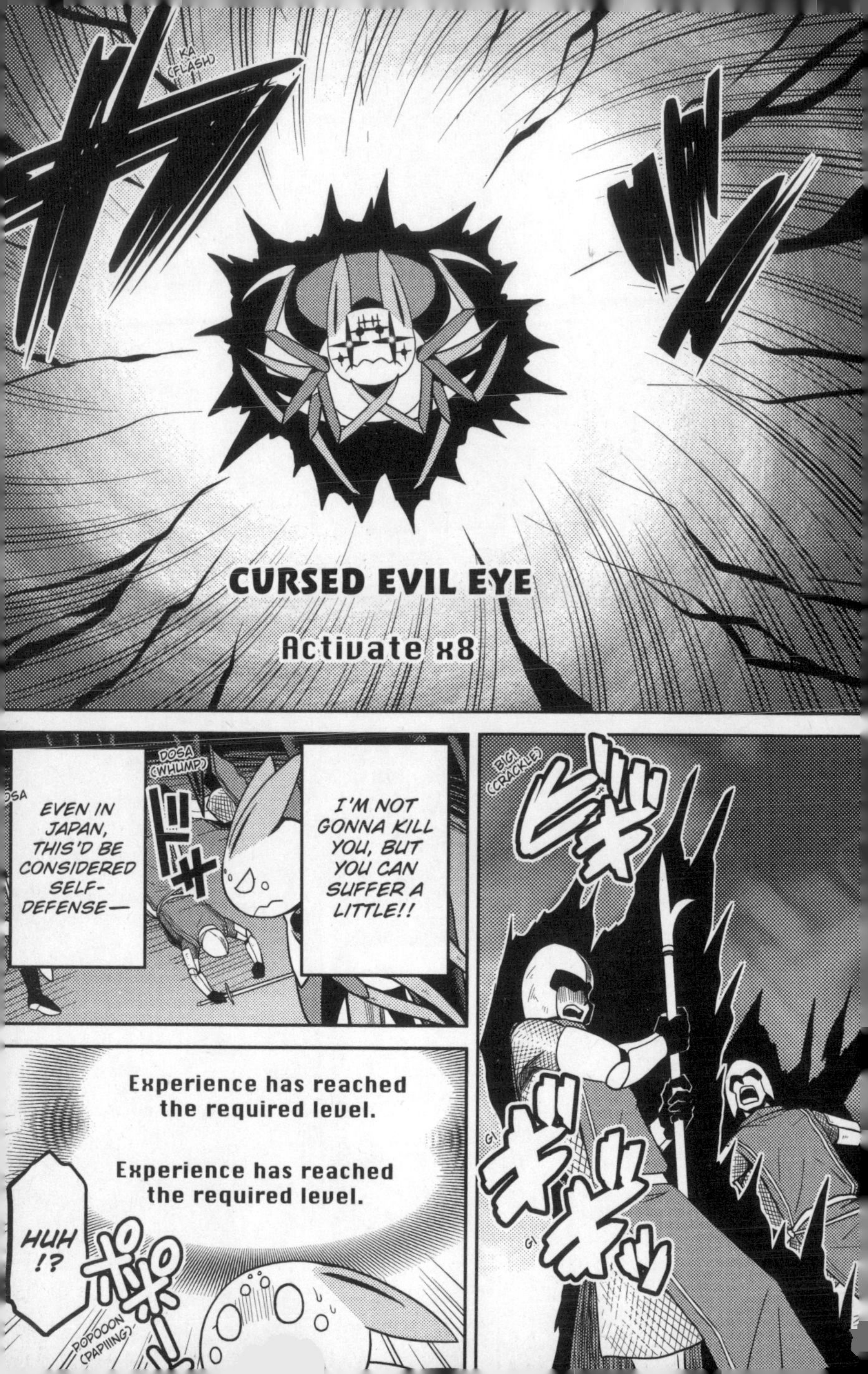
KA (FLASH)
CURSED EVIL EYE
Activate x8
BIGI (CRACKLE)
GI
GI
DOSA (WHUMP)
I'M NOT GONNA KILL YOU, BUT YOU CAN SUFFER A LITTLE!!
EVEN IN JAPAN, THIS'D BE CONSIDERED SELF-DEFENSE—
DOSA
Experience has reached the required level.
Experience has reached the required level.
HUH!?
POPOOON (PAPIING)

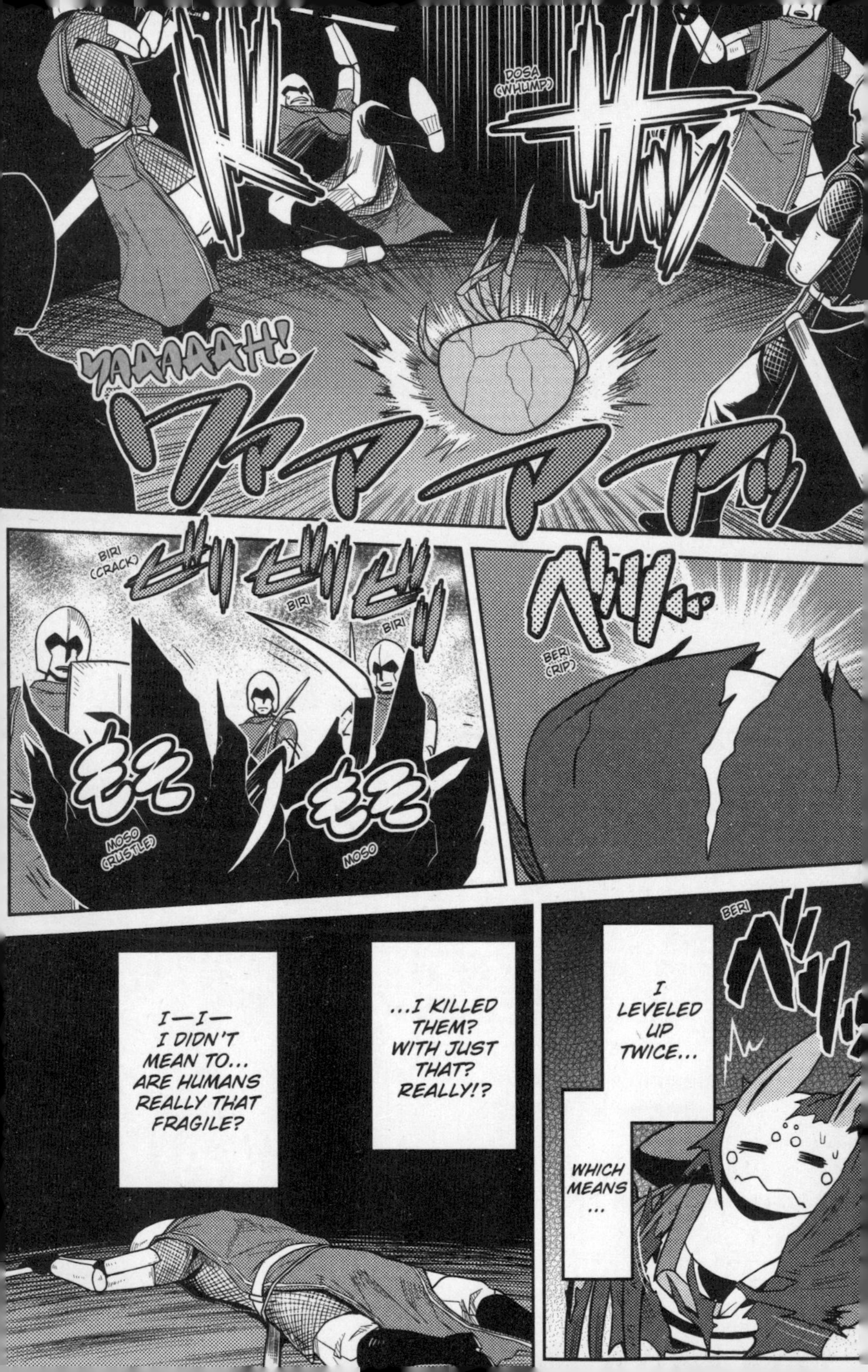
DOSA (WHUMP)
YAAAAAH!
BERI (RIP)
BIRI (CRACK)
BIRI
BIRI
MOSO (RUSTLE)
MOSO
BERI
I LEVELED UP TWICE...
WHICH MEANS...
...I KILLED THEM? WITH JUST THAT? REALLY!?
I—I— I DIDN'T MEAN TO... ARE HUMANS REALLY THAT FRAGILE?

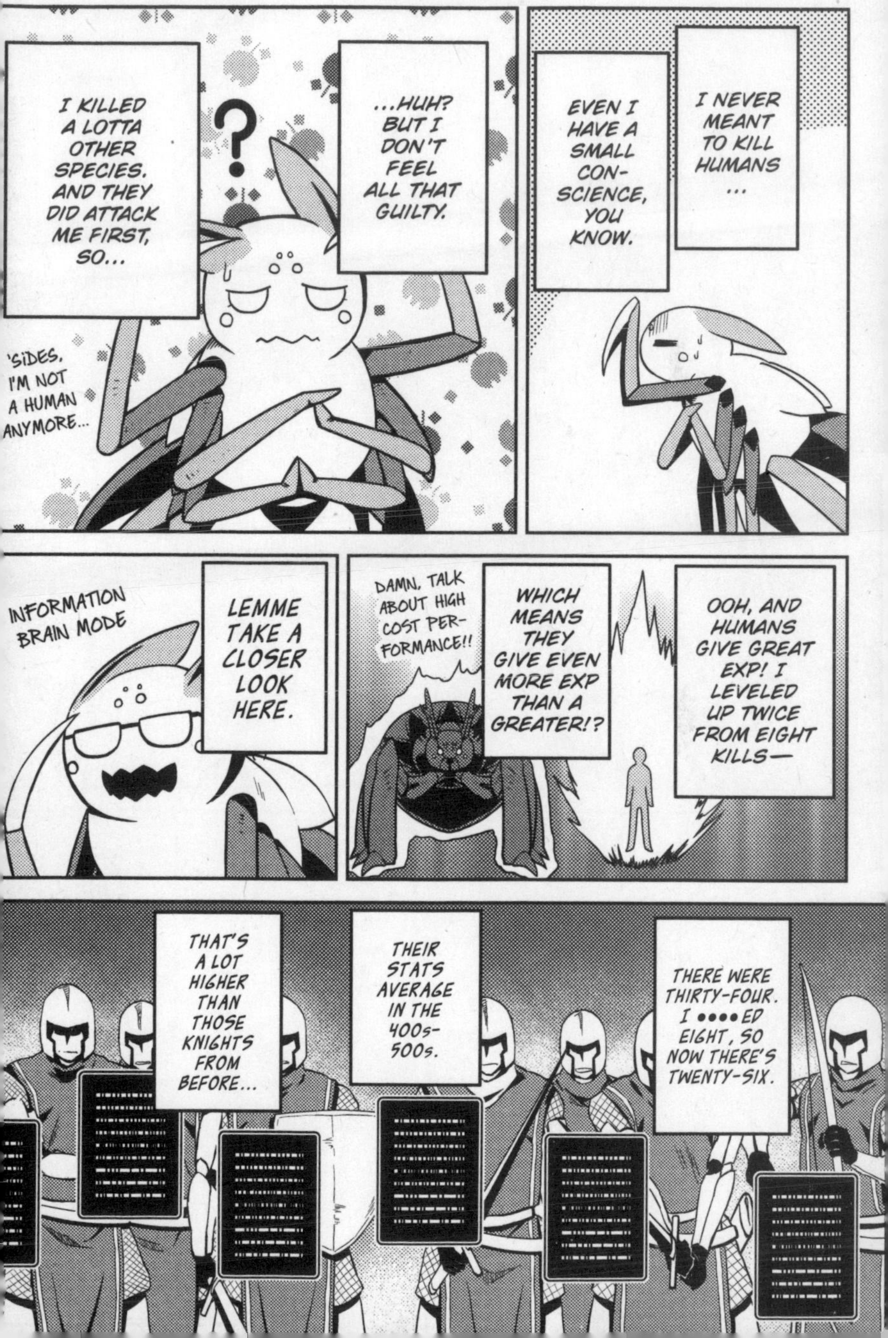
I NEVER MEANT TO KILL HUMANS...
EVEN I HAVE A SMALL CON-SCIENCE, YOU KNOW.
...HUH? BUT I DON'T FEEL ALL THAT GUILTY.
I KILLED A LOTTA OTHER SPECIES. AND THEY DID ATTACK ME FIRST, SO...
'SIDES, I'M NOT A HUMAN ANYMORE...
OOH, AND HUMANS GIVE GREAT EXP! I LEVELED UP TWICE FROM EIGHT KILLS—
WHICH MEANS THEY GIVE EVEN MORE EXP THAN A GREATER!?
DAMN, TALK ABOUT HIGH COST PER-FORMANCE!!
LEMME TAKE A CLOSER LOOK HERE.
INFORMATION BRAIN MODE
THERE WERE THIRTY-FOUR. I ●●●●ED EIGHT, SO NOW THERE'S TWENTY-SIX.
THEIR STATS AVERAGE IN THE 400s-500s.
THAT'S A LOT HIGHER THAN THOSE KNIGHTS FROM BEFORE...

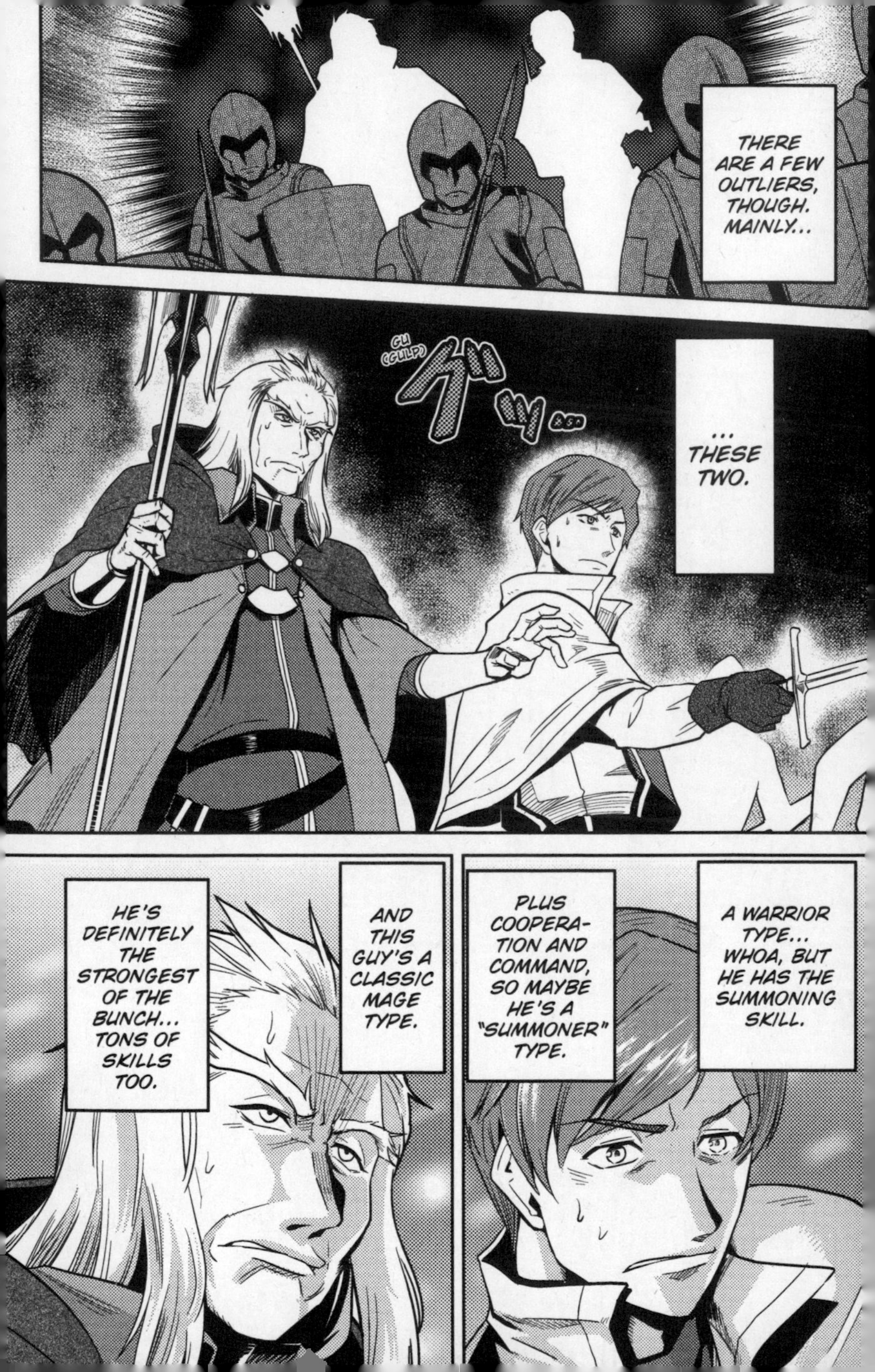
THERE ARE A FEW OUTLIERS, THOUGH. MAINLY...
GU (GULP)
... THESE TWO.
A WARRIOR TYPE... WHOA, BUT HE HAS THE SUMMONING SKILL.
PLUS COOPERATION AND COMMAND, SO MAYBE HE'S A "SUMMONER" TYPE.
AND THIS GUY'S A CLASSIC MAGE TYPE.
HE'S DEFINITELY THE STRONGEST OF THE BUNCH... TONS OF SKILLS TOO.

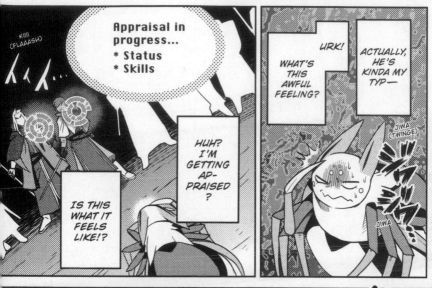

ACTUALLY, HE'S KINDA MY TYP—
URK! WHAT'S THIS AWFUL FEELING?
JIWA (TWINGE)
JIWA
Appraisal in progress...
* Status
* Skills
KIIII (FLAAASH)
HUH? I'M GETTING AP-PRAISED?
IS THIS WHAT IT FEELS LIKE!?
NOOOO~
WHAT'RE YOU LOOKIN' AT!? GROSS!! YOU PERVS!!
I'M GONNA USE MY "RULER'S AUTHORITY"!! BLOCK APPRAISAL!!
BAKIIIIN (CRAAACK)
[Ruler's Authority] use approved.
[Appraisal] skill effects blocked.

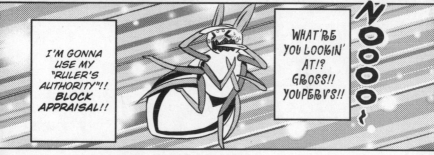

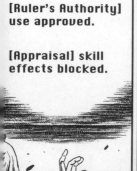

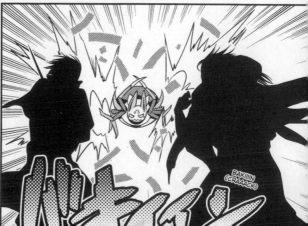

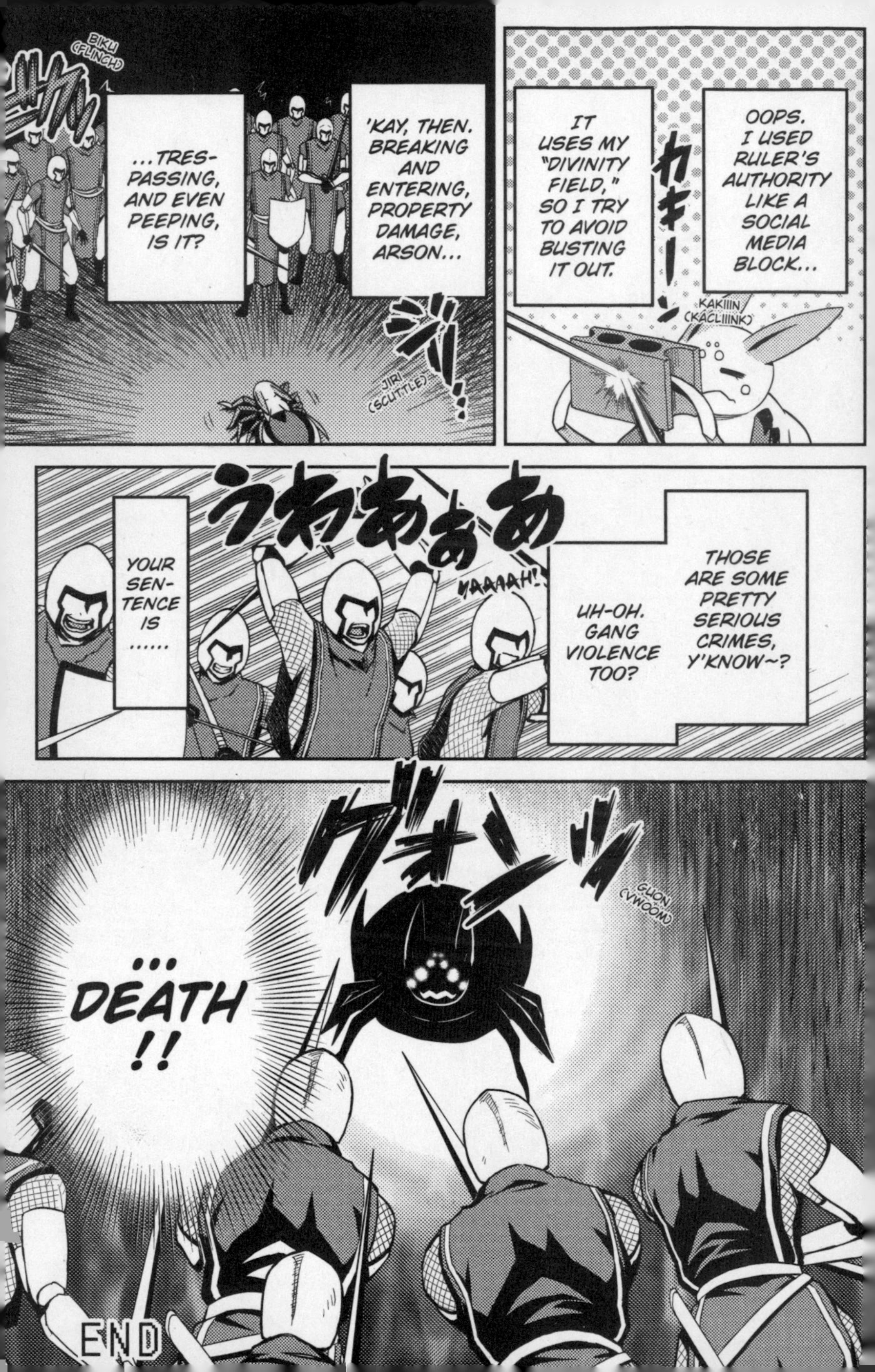
OOPS. I USED RULER'S AUTHORITY LIKE A SOCIAL MEDIA BLOCK...
IT USES MY "DIVINITY FIELD," SO I TRY TO AVOID BUSTING IT OUT.
KAKIIN (KACLIIINK)
'KAY, THEN. BREAKING AND ENTERING, PROPERTY DAMAGE, ARSON...
BIKU (FLINCH)
...TRES-PASSING, AND EVEN PEEPING, IS IT?
JIRI (SCUTTLE)
THOSE ARE SOME PRETTY SERIOUS CRIMES, Y'KNOW~?
UH-OH. GANG VIOLENCE TOO?
YAAAAH!
うわあぁあ
YOUR SEN-TENCE IS ......
GUON (VWOOM)
...DEATH !!
END

So I'm a Spider, So What?

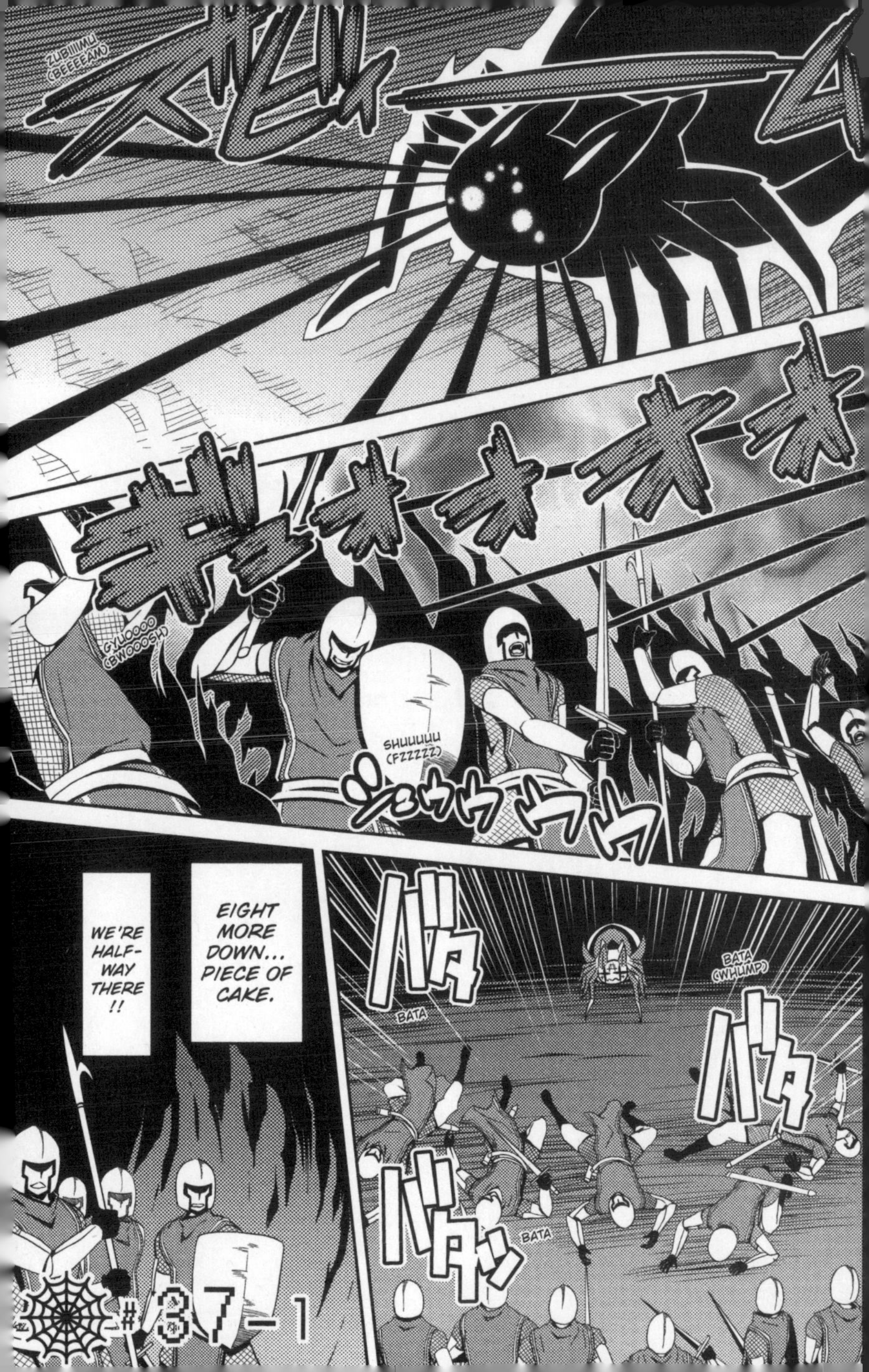
ZUBIIIIMU
(BEEEEEAM)
GYUOOOO
(BWOOOSH)
SHUUUUU
(FZZZZZ)
BATA
(WHUMP)
BATA
BATA
EIGHT MORE DOWN... PIECE OF CAKE.
WE'RE HALF-WAY THERE!!
#37-1

WOW.

THEY'RE STILL COMING, EVEN THOUGH I KILLED HALF THEIR FRIENDS?

BURU

BURU (TREMBLE)

YAAAAH!

DA (DASH)

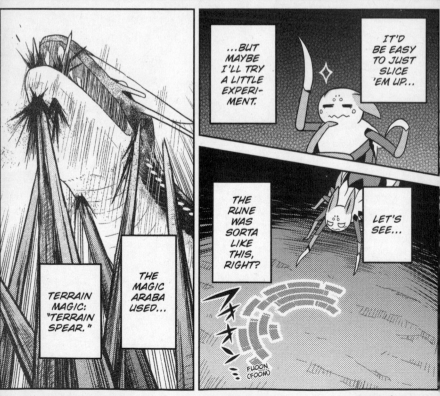

IT'D BE EASY TO JUST SLICE 'EM UP...

...BUT MAYBE I'LL TRY A LITTLE EXPERIMENT.

LET'S SEE...

THE RUNE WAS SORTA LIKE THIS, RIGHT?

THE MAGIC ARABA USED...

TERRAIN MAGIC: "TERRAIN SPEAR."

FUOON (FOOM)

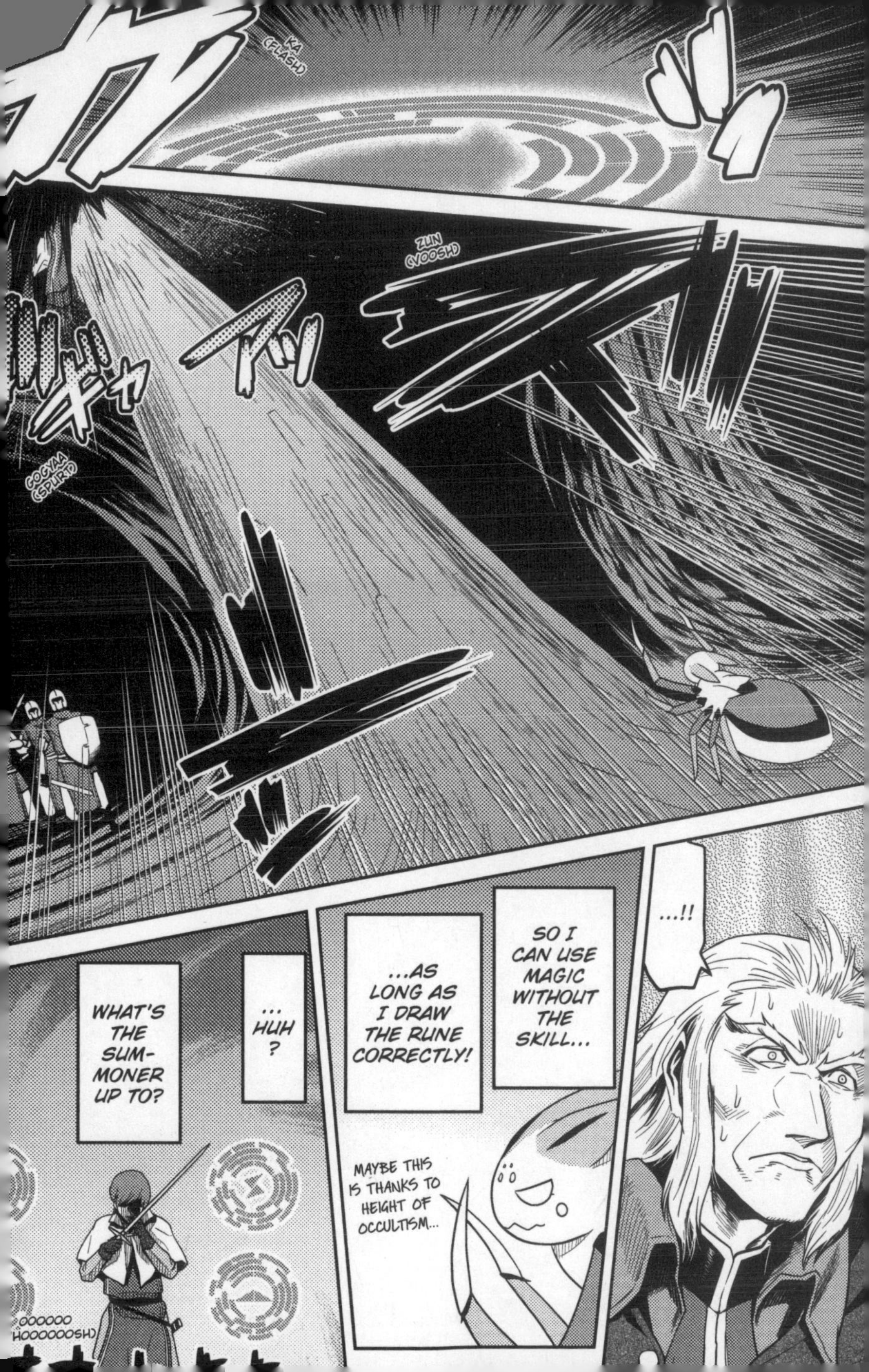
KA (FLASH)
ZUN (VOOSH)
GOGYAA (SPURT)
...!!
SO I CAN USE MAGIC WITHOUT THE SKILL...
...AS LONG AS I DRAW THE RUNE CORRECTLY!
MAYBE THIS IS THANKS TO HEIGHT OF OCCULTISM...
...HUH?
WHAT'S THE SUMMONER UP TO?
OOOOOO HOOOOOOSH)

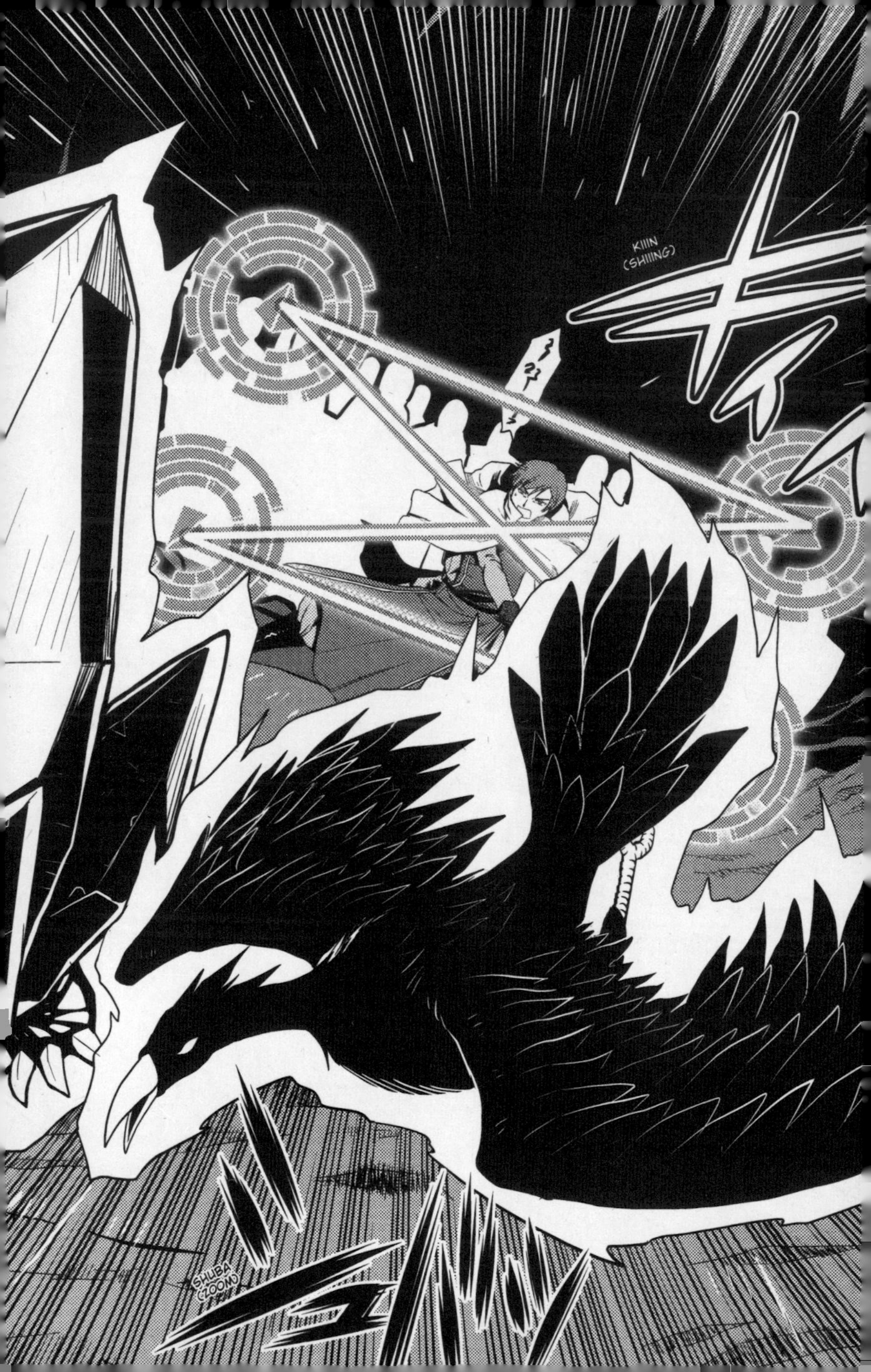
KIIIN
(SHIIING)
SHUBA
(ZOOM)

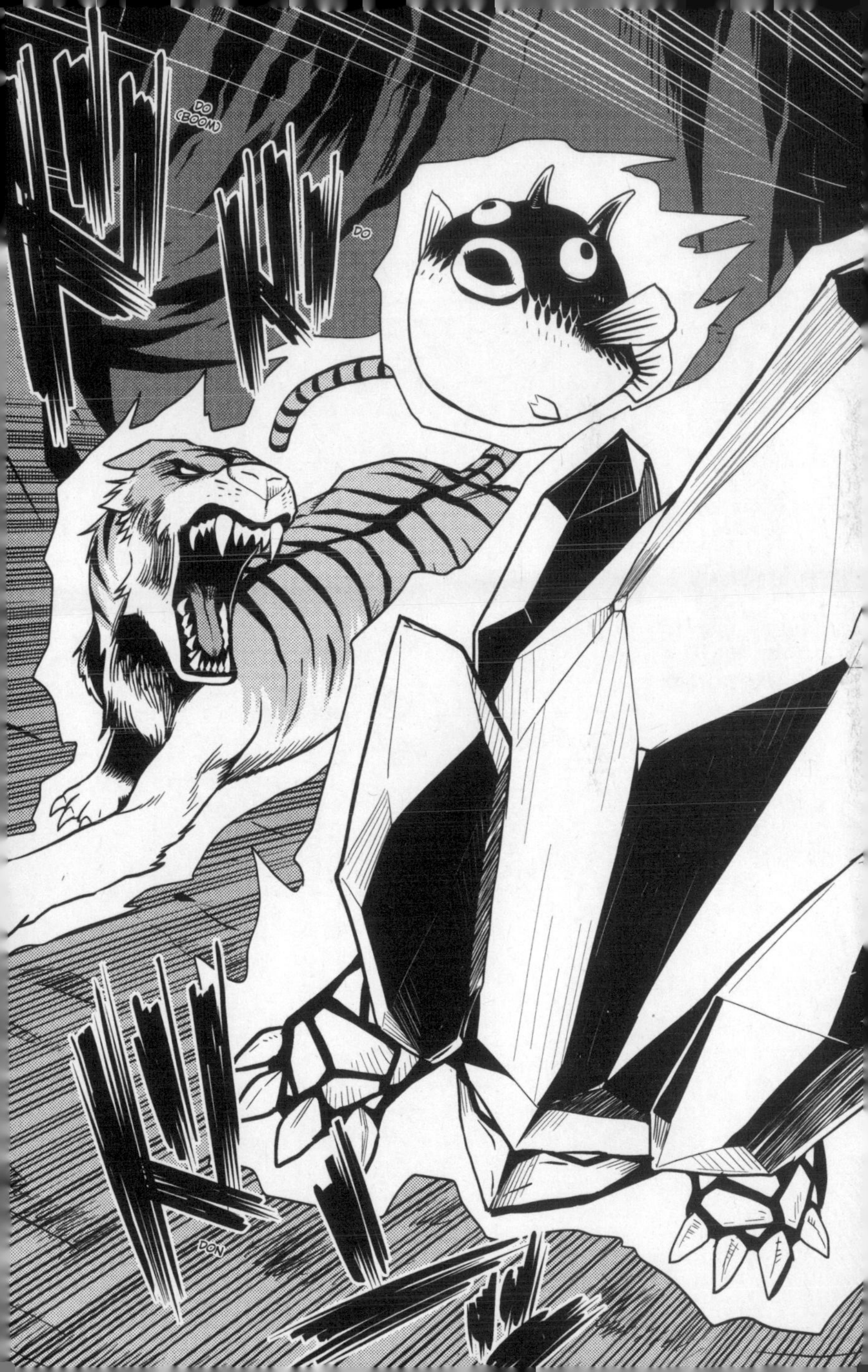
DO (BOOM)
DO
DON

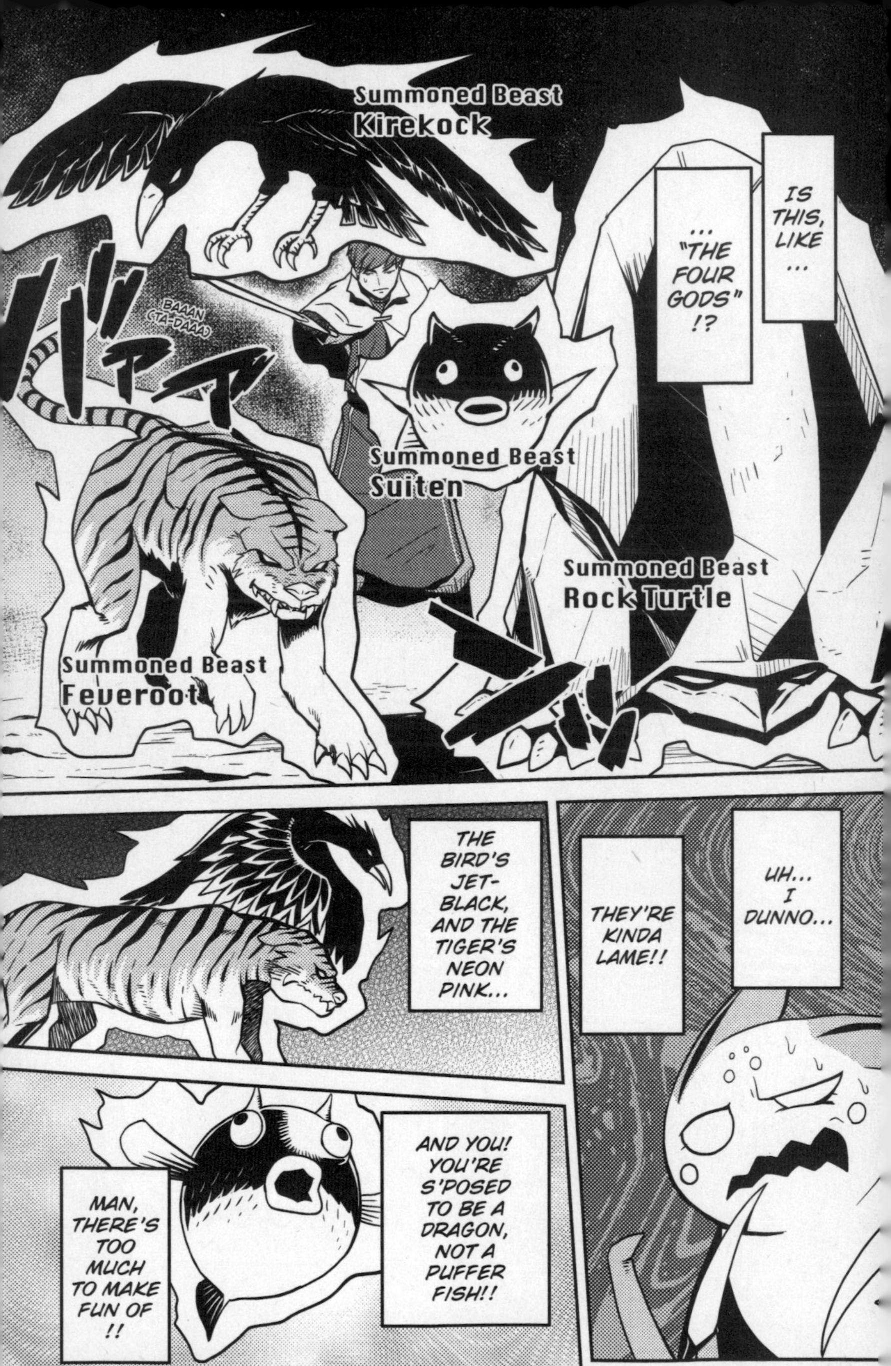
IS THIS, LIKE...
..."THE FOUR GODS"!?
Summoned Beast Kirekock
BAAAN (TA-DAAA)
Summoned Beast Suiten
Summoned Beast Rock Turtle
Summoned Beast Feveroot
UH... I DUNNO...
THEY'RE KINDA LAME!!
THE BIRD'S JET-BLACK, AND THE TIGER'S NEON PINK...
AND YOU! YOU'RE S'POSED TO BE A DRAGON, NOT A PUFFER FISH!!
MAN, THERE'S TOO MUCH TO MAKE FUN OF!!

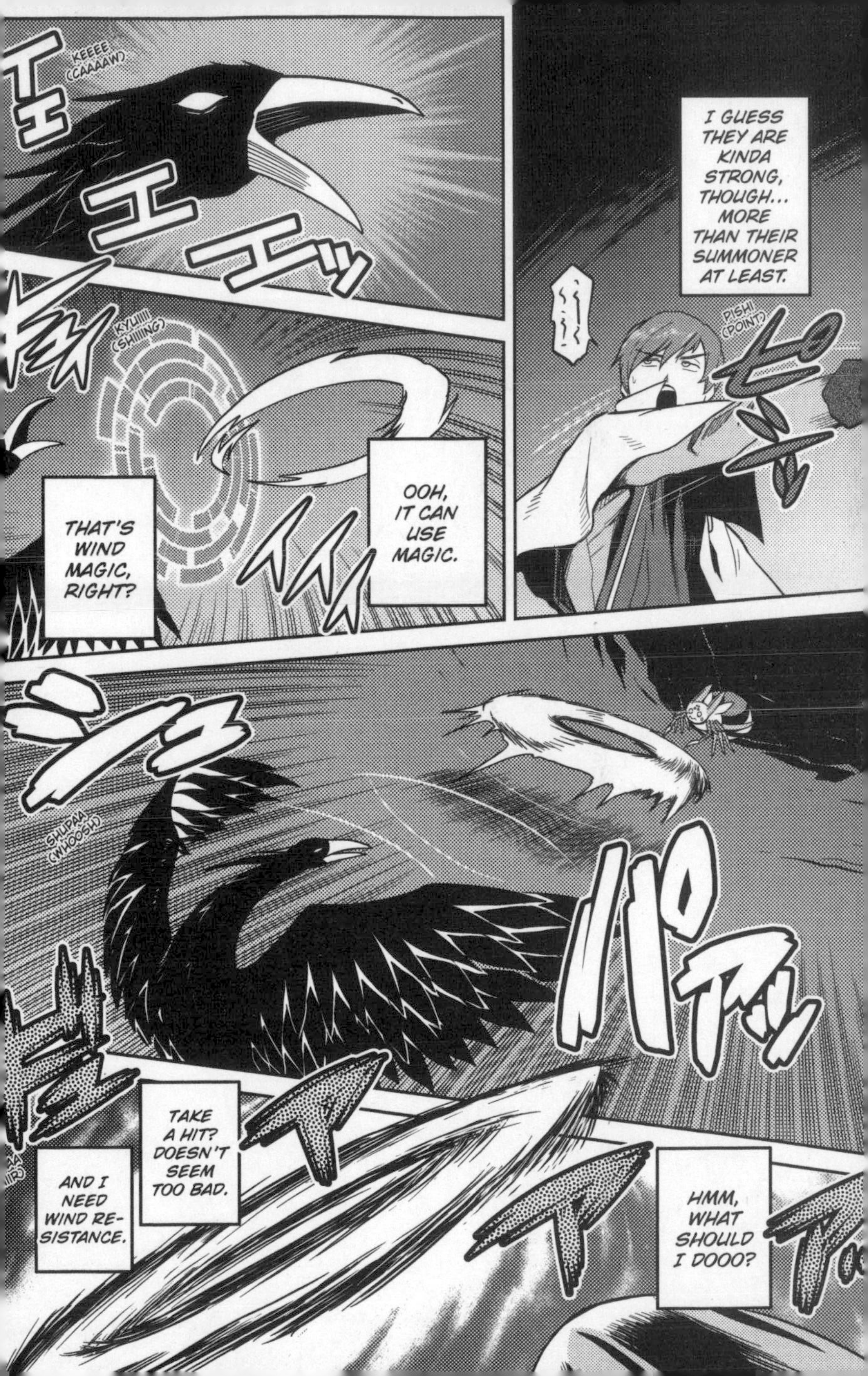
I GUESS THEY ARE KINDA STRONG, THOUGH... MORE THAN THEIR SUMMONER AT LEAST.
PISHI (POINT)
KEEEE (CAAAAW)
KYUIIII (SHIIIING)
OOH, IT CAN USE MAGIC.
THAT'S WIND MAGIC, RIGHT?
SHUPAA (WHOOSH)
HMM, WHAT SHOULD I DOOO?
TAKE A HIT? DOESN'T SEEM TOO BAD.
AND I NEED WIND RESISTANCE.

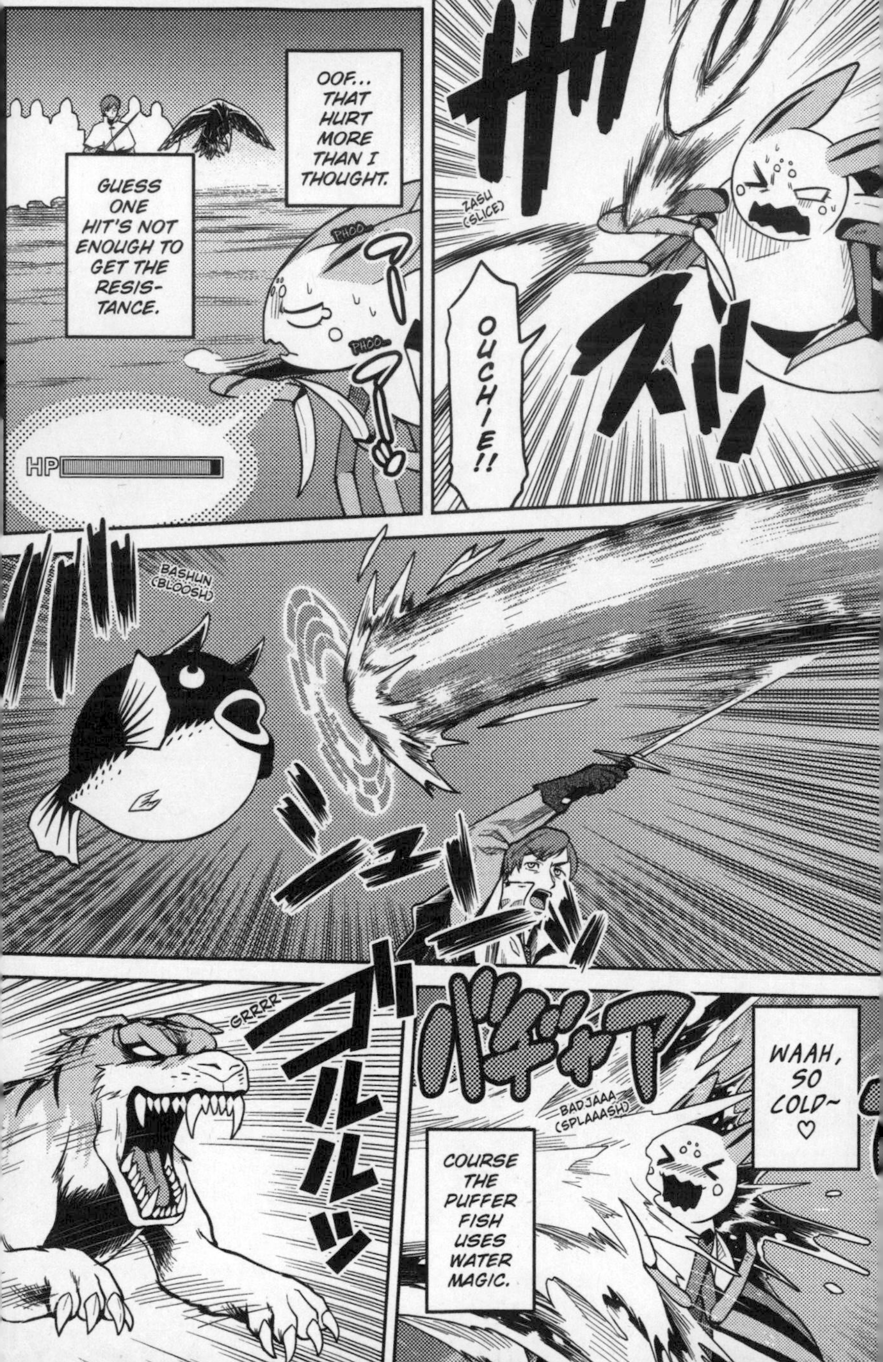
ZASU (SLICE)
OUCHIE!!
OOF... THAT HURT MORE THAN I THOUGHT.
GUESS ONE HIT'S NOT ENOUGH TO GET THE RESIS-TANCE.
PHOO...
PHOO...
HP
BASHUN (BLOOSH)
WAAH, SO COLD~ ♡
BADJAAA (SPLAAASH)
COURSE THE PUFFER FISH USES WATER MAGIC.
GRRRR

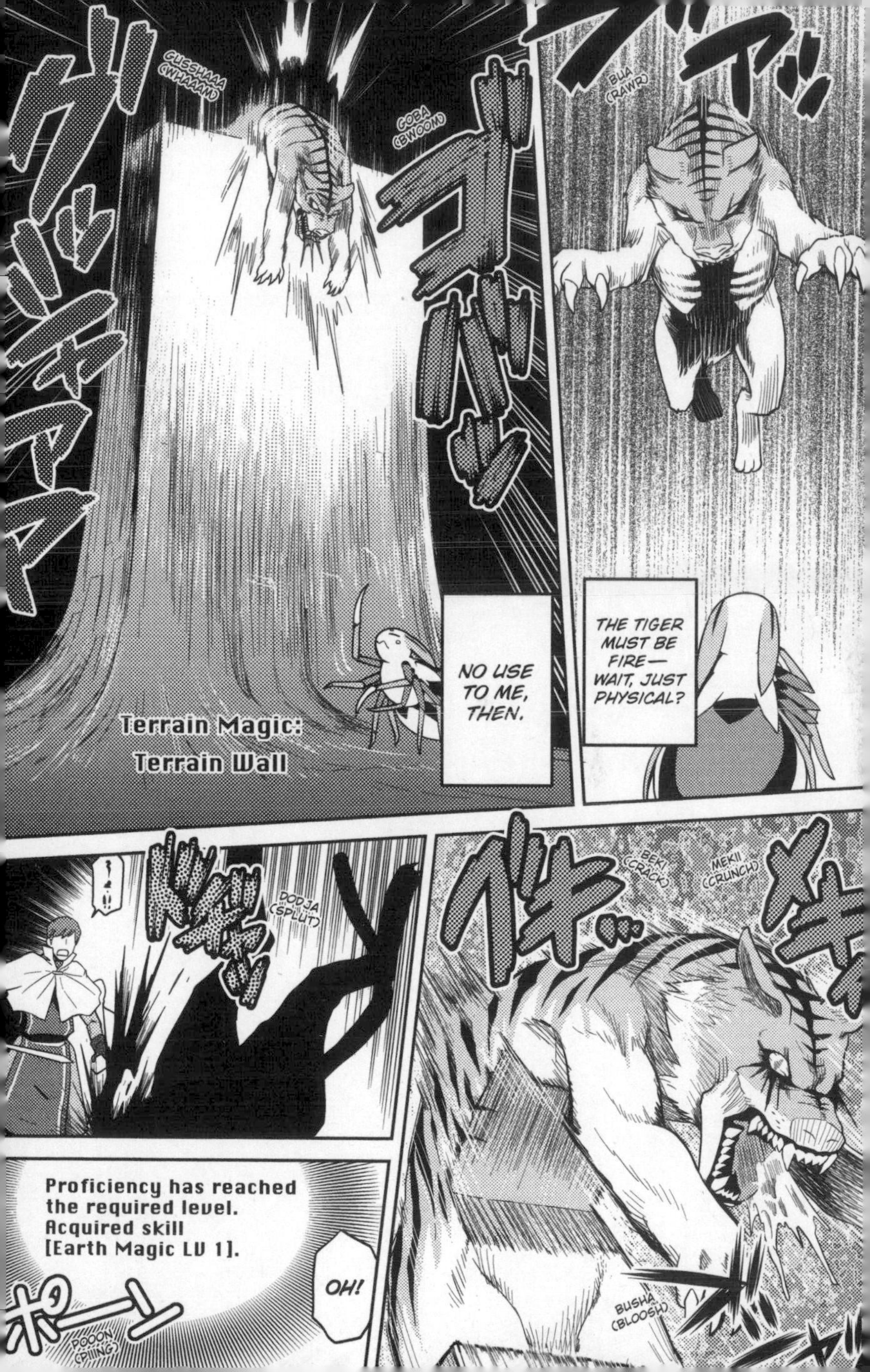
BUA (RAWR)
THE TIGER MUST BE FIRE— WAIT, JUST PHYSICAL?
NO USE TO ME, THEN.
GOBA (BWOOM)
GUSSHAAA (WHAAAND)
Terrain Magic: Terrain Wall
MEKII (CRUNCH)
BEKI (CRACK)
BUSHA (BLOOSH)
DODJA (SPLUT)
OH!
Proficiency has reached the required level. Acquired skill [Earth Magic LV 1].
POOON (PIING)

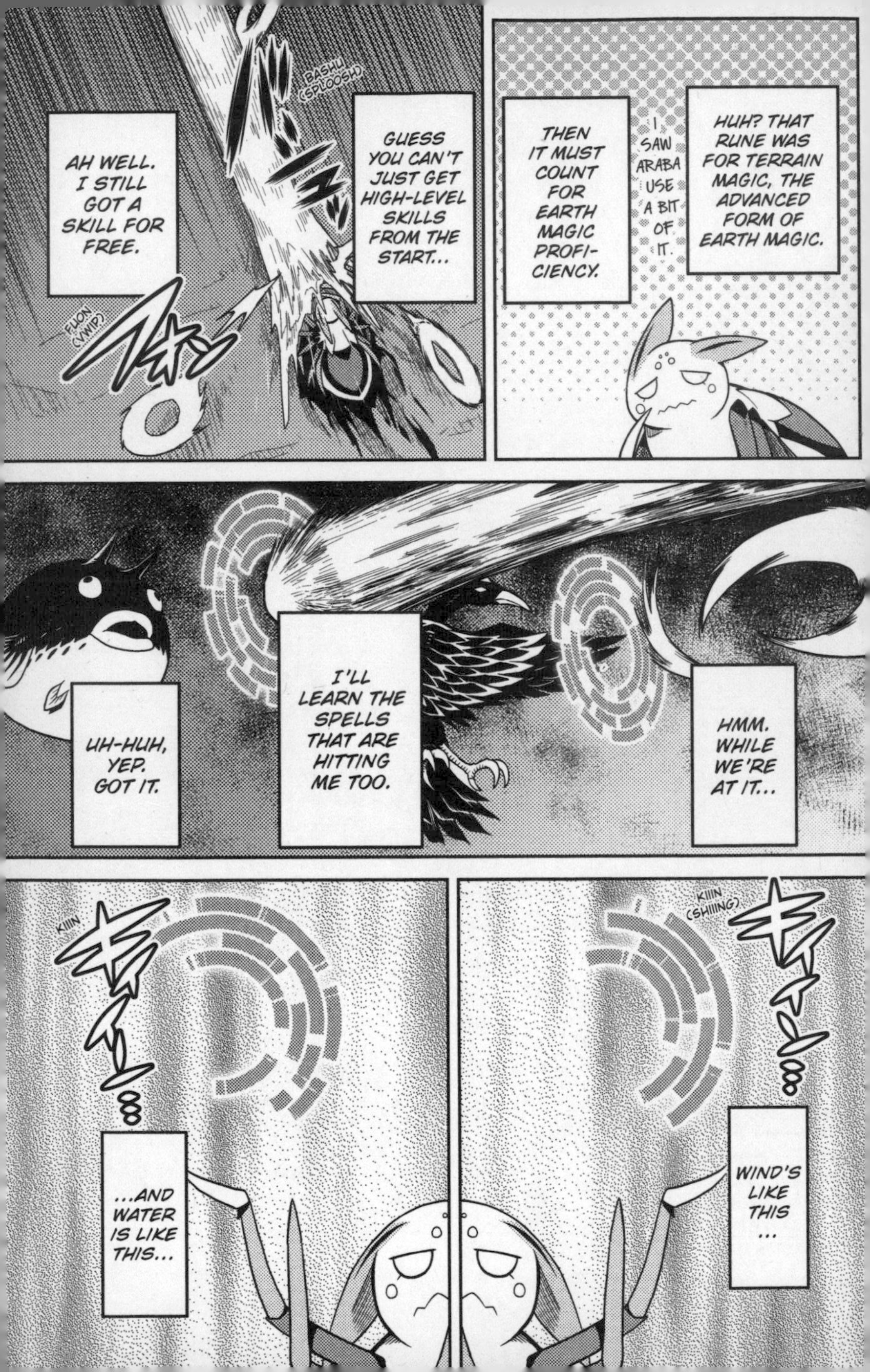
HUH? THAT RUNE WAS FOR TERRAIN MAGIC, THE ADVANCED FORM OF EARTH MAGIC.
I SAW ARABA USE A BIT OF IT.
THEN IT MUST COUNT FOR EARTH MAGIC PROFICIENCY.
BASHU (SPLOOSH)
GUESS YOU CAN'T JUST GET HIGH-LEVEL SKILLS FROM THE START...
AH WELL. I STILL GOT A SKILL FOR FREE.
FUON (VWIP)
HMM. WHILE WE'RE AT IT...
I'LL LEARN THE SPELLS THAT ARE HITTING ME TOO.
UH-HUH, YEP. GOT IT.
KIIIN (SHIIING)
WIND'S LIKE THIS...
KIIIN
...AND WATER IS LIKE THIS...

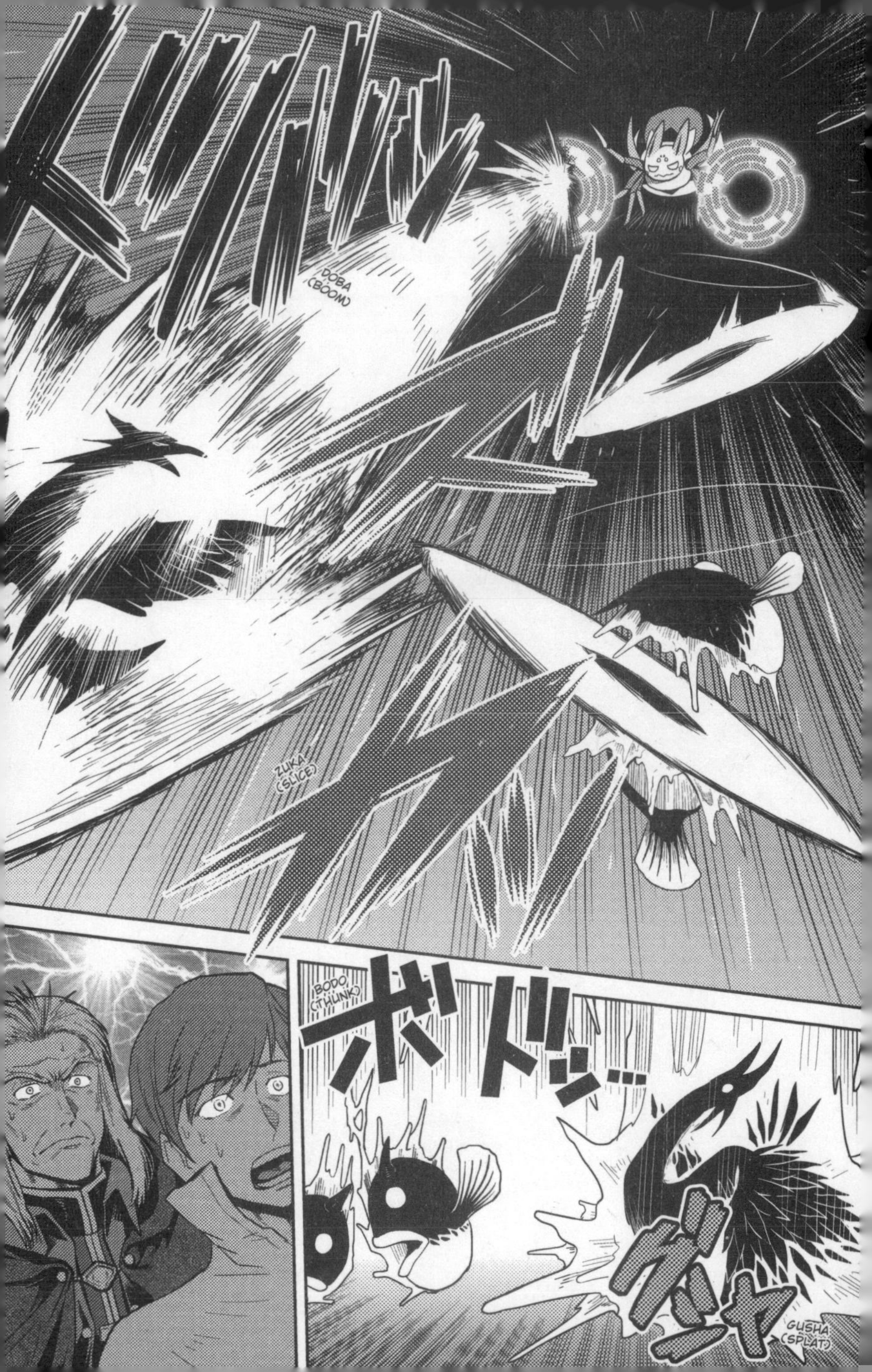
DOBA (BOOM)
ZUKA (SLICE)
ボドッ…
BODO (THUNK)
グシャ
GUSHA (SPLAT)

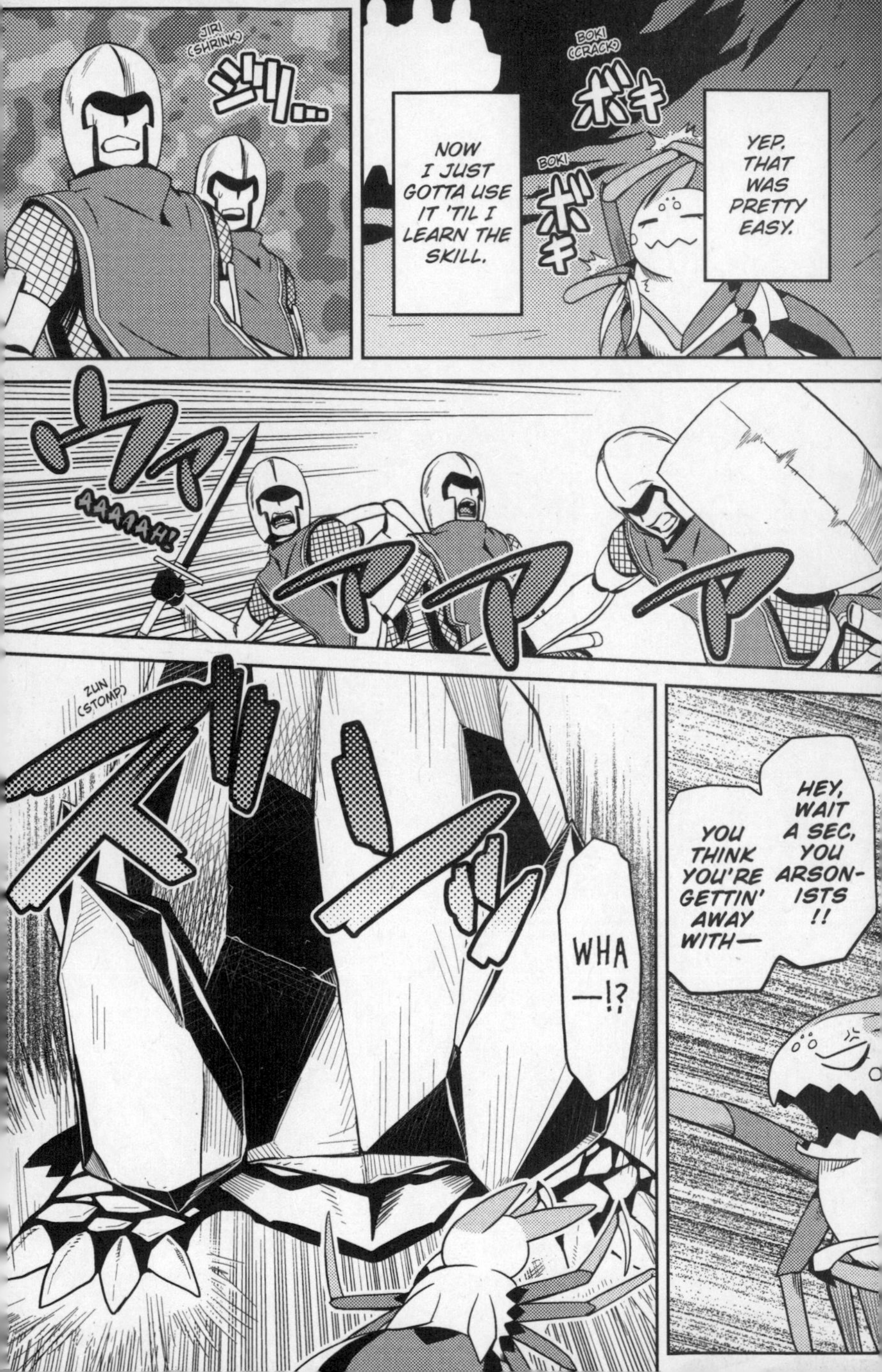

BOKI (CRACK)
ボキ
YEP. THAT WAS PRETTY EASY.
NOW I JUST GOTTA USE IT 'TIL I LEARN THE SKILL.
BOKI
ボキ
JIRI (SHRINK)
ジリ…
AAAAAH!
HEY, WAIT A SEC, YOU ARSONISTS!!
YOU THINK YOU'RE GETTIN' AWAY WITH—
ZUN (STOMP)
WHA—!?

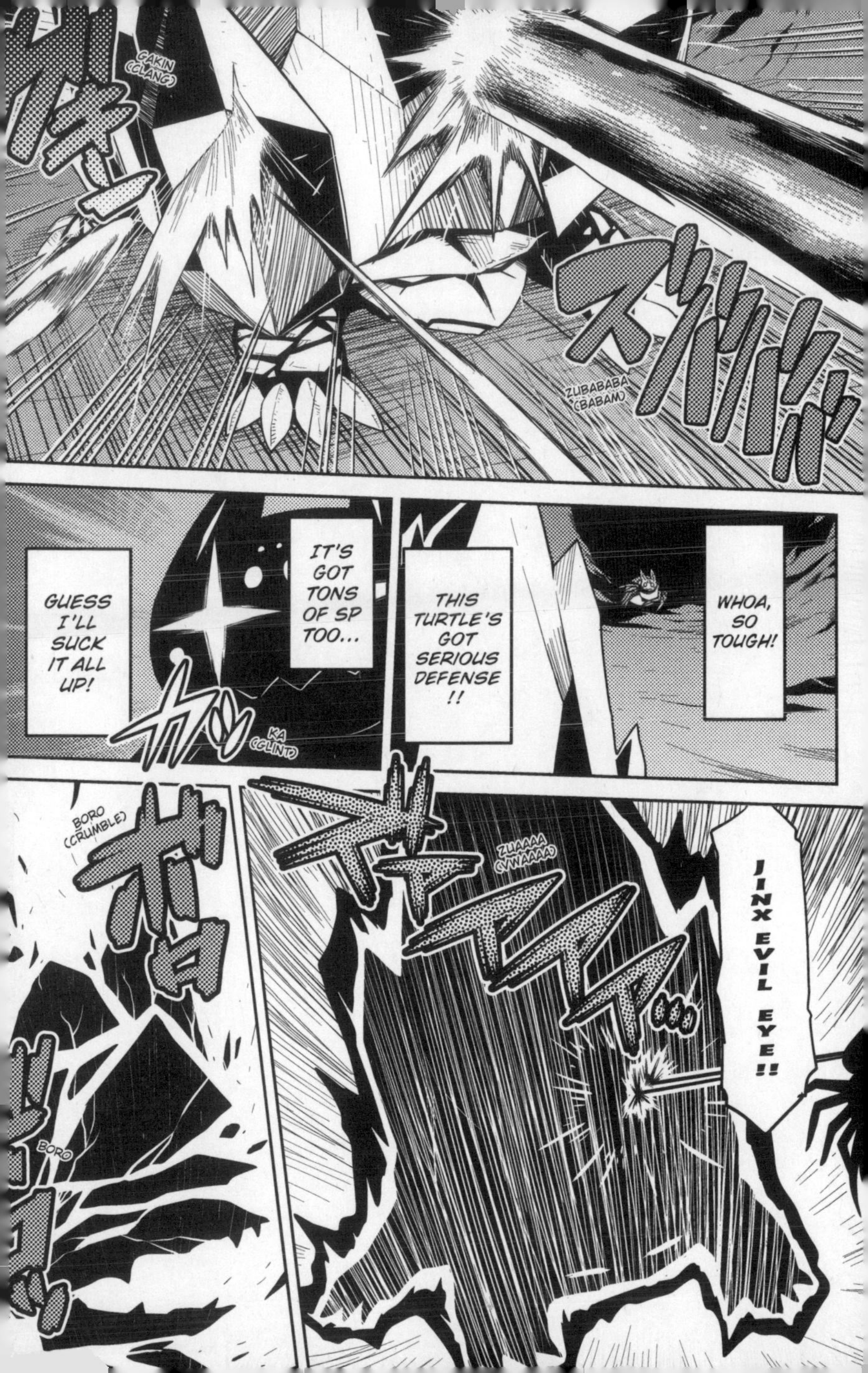
GAKIN (CLANG)
ZUBABABA (BABAM)
WHOA, SO TOUGH!
THIS TURTLE'S GOT SERIOUS DEFENSE!!
IT'S GOT TONS OF SP TOO...
GUESS I'LL SUCK IT ALL UP!
KA (GLINT)
JINX EVIL EYE!!
ZUAAAA (VWAAAA)
BORO (CRUMBLE)
BORO

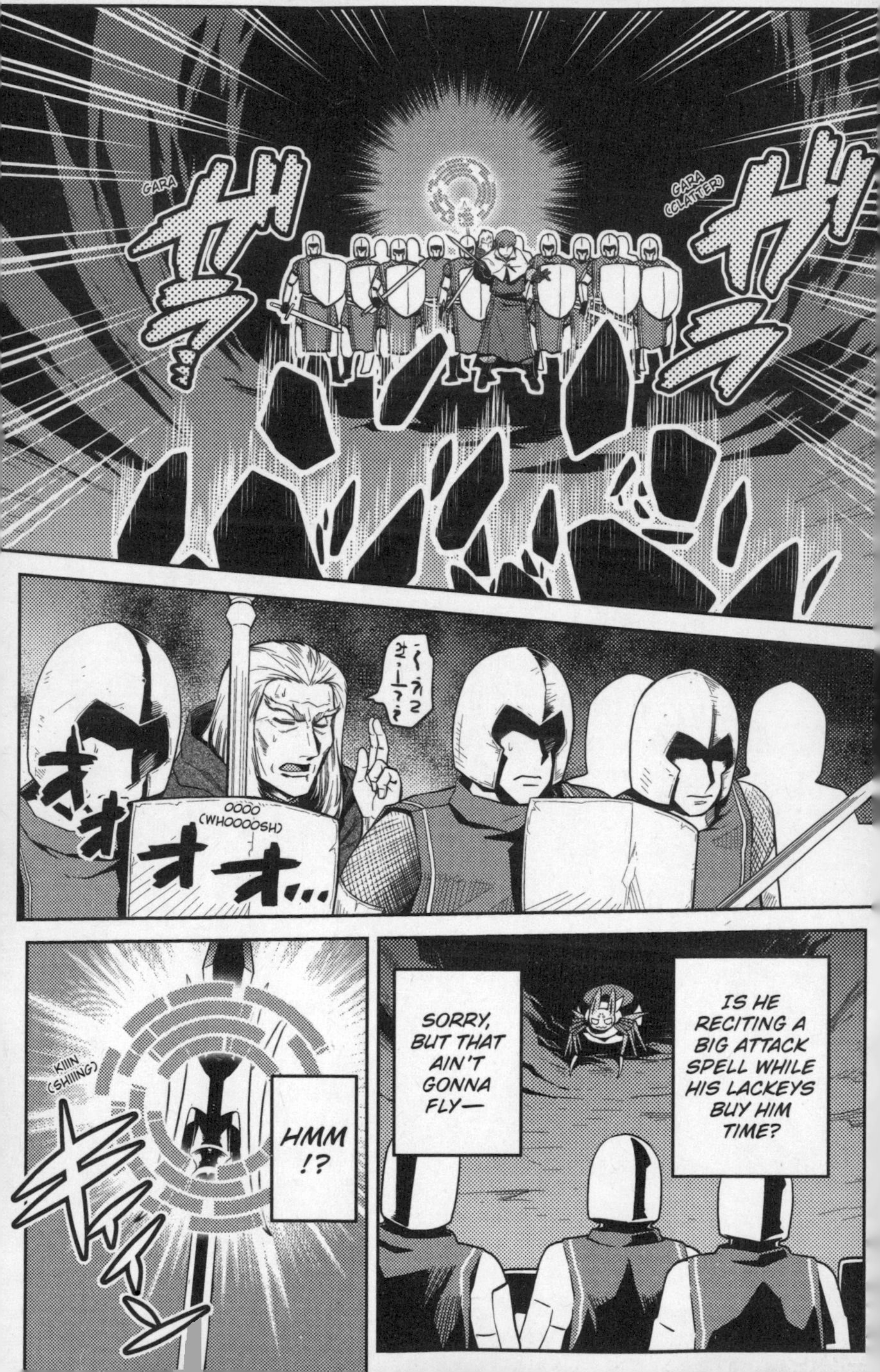
GARA (CLATTER)
GARA
OOOO (WHOOOOSH)
IS HE RECITING A BIG ATTACK SPELL WHILE HIS LACKEYS BUY HIM TIME?
SORRY, BUT THAT AIN'T GONNA FLY—
HMM !?
KIIIN (SHIIING)

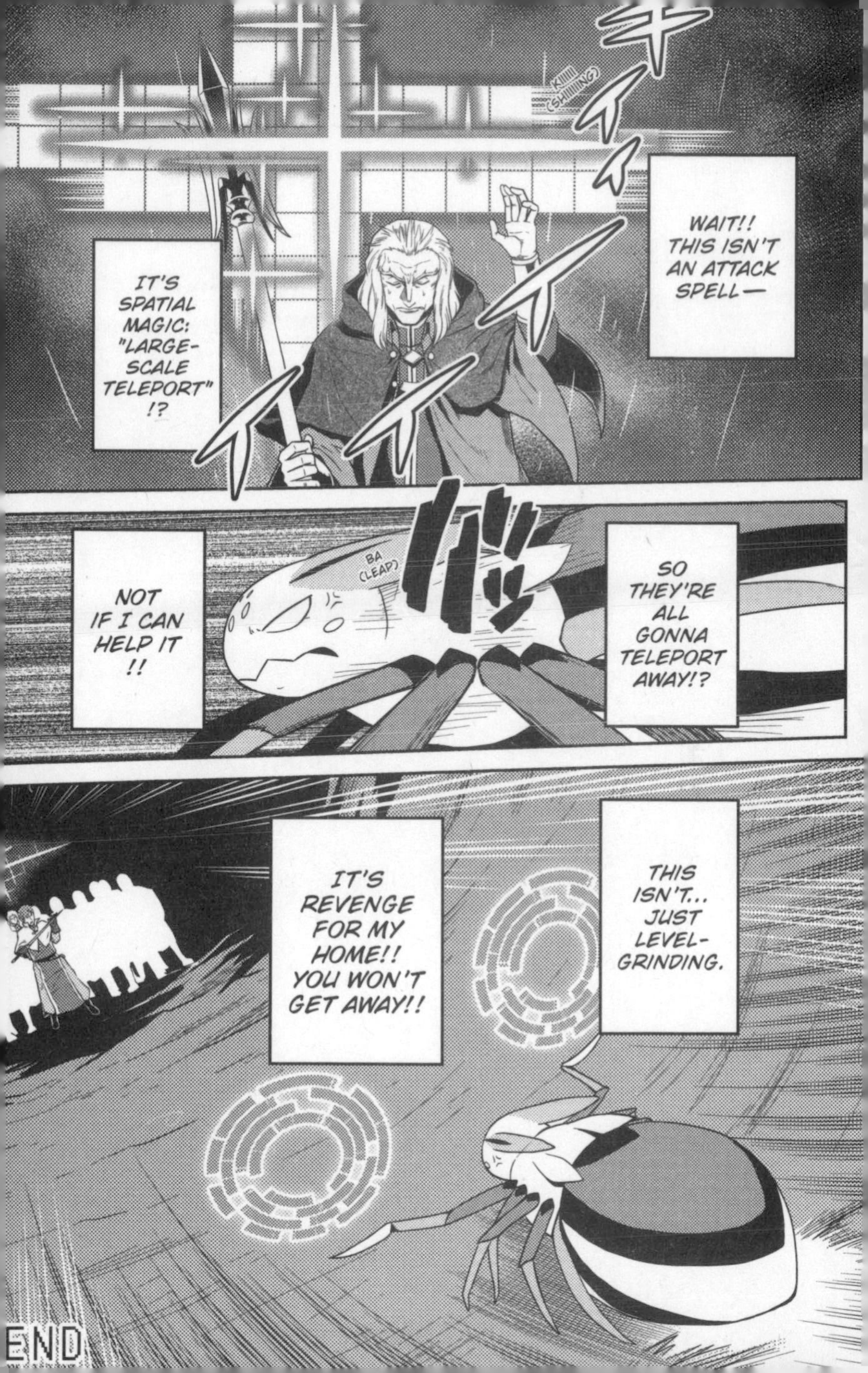
KIIIIIII (SHIIIIING)
WAIT!! THIS ISN'T AN ATTACK SPELL—
IT'S SPATIAL MAGIC: "LARGE-SCALE TELEPORT" !?
SO THEY'RE ALL GONNA TELEPORT AWAY!?
BA (LEAP)
NOT IF I CAN HELP IT !!
THIS ISN'T... JUST LEVEL-GRINDING.
IT'S REVENGE FOR MY HOME!! YOU WON'T GET AWAY!!
END

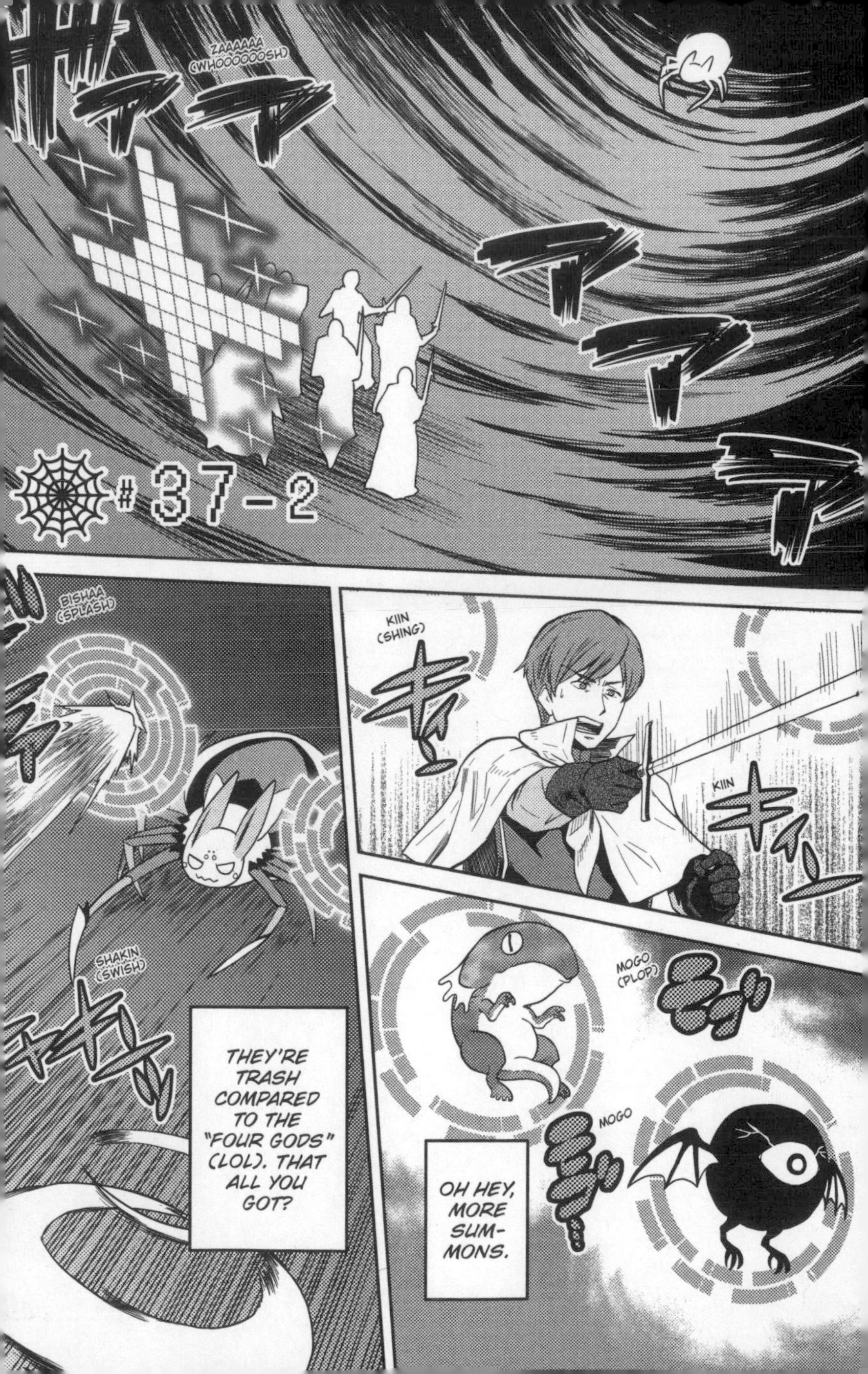
ZAAAAAA
(WHOOOOOOSH)
#37-2
KIIN
(SHING)
KIIN
MOGO
(PLOP)
MOGO
OH HEY, MORE SUM-MONS.
BISHAA
(SPLASH)
SHAKIN
(SWISH)
THEY'RE TRASH COMPARED TO THE "FOUR GODS" (LOL). THAT ALL YOU GOT?

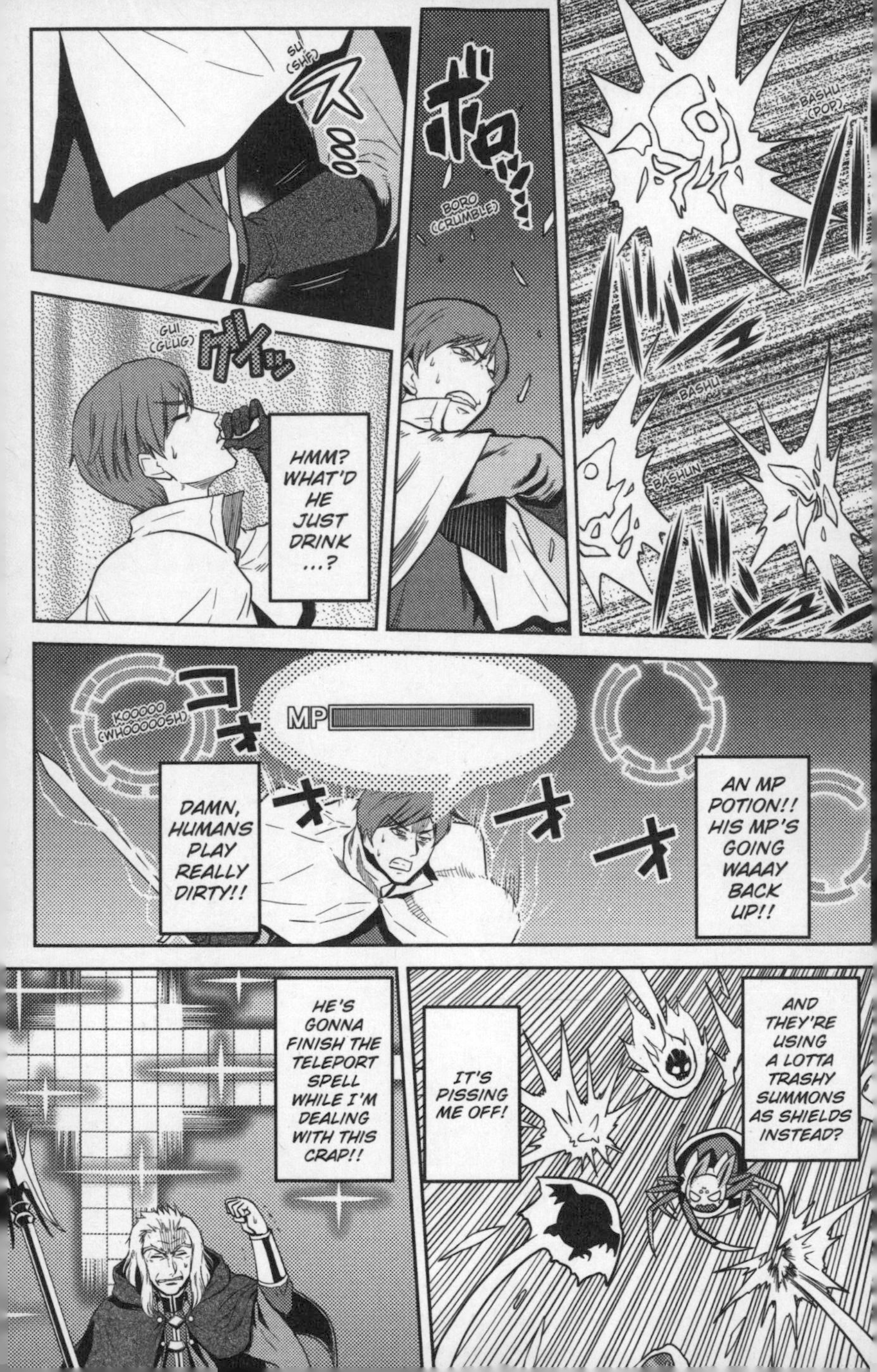
BASHU (POP)
BASHU
BASHUN
BORO (CRUMBLE)
SU (SHF)
GUI (GLUG)
HMM? WHAT'D HE JUST DRINK ...?
KOOOOO (WHOOOOOSH)
MP
AN MP POTION!! HIS MP'S GOING WAAAY BACK UP!!
DAMN, HUMANS PLAY REALLY DIRTY!!
AND THEY'RE USING A LOTTA TRASHY SUMMONS AS SHIELDS INSTEAD?
IT'S PISSING ME OFF!
HE'S GONNA FINISH THE TELEPORT SPELL WHILE I'M DEALING WITH THIS CRAP!!

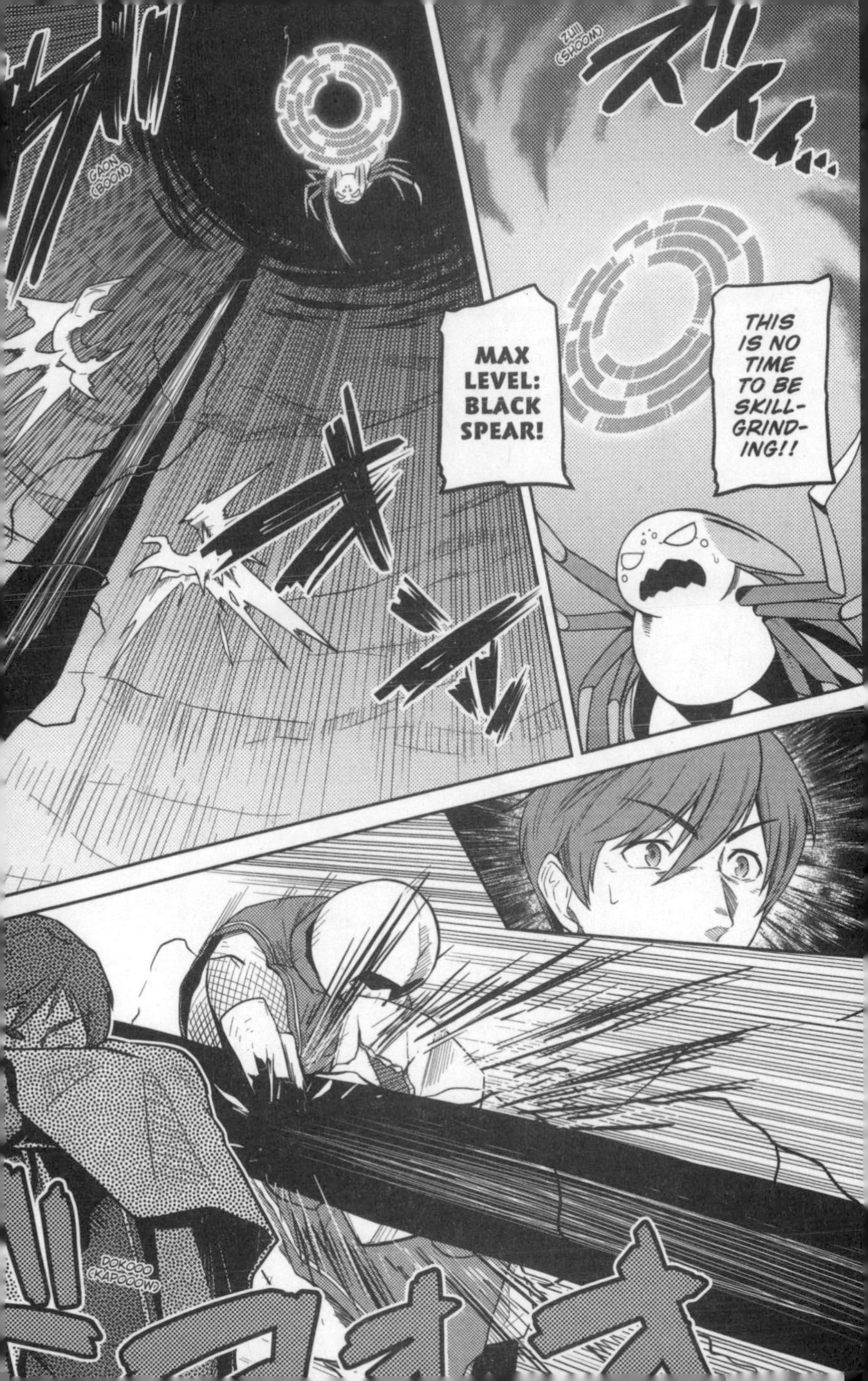
ZUII (SHOOM)
THIS IS NO TIME TO BE SKILL-GRINDING!!
MAX LEVEL: BLACK SPEAR!
GAON (BOOM)
DOKOOO (KAPOOOW)

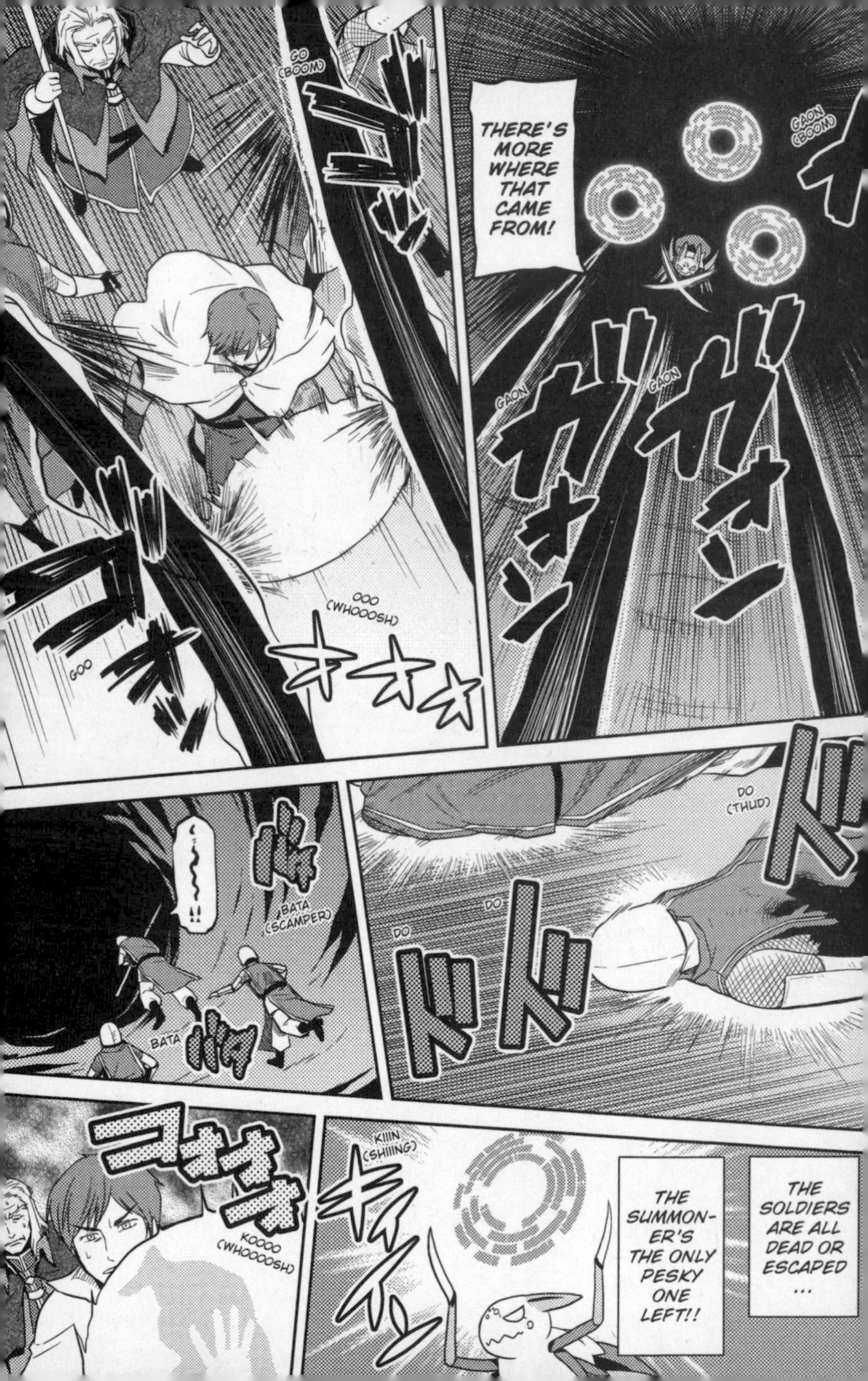

THERE'S MORE WHERE THAT CAME FROM!
GAON (BOOM)
GAON
GAON
GO (BOOM)
GOO
OOO (WHOOOSH)
DO (THUD)
DO
DO
く～～!!
BATA (SCAMPER)
BATA
THE SOLDIERS ARE ALL DEAD OR ESCAPED...
THE SUMMONER'S THE ONLY PESKY ONE LEFT!!
KIIN (SHIIING)
KOOOO (WHOOOOSH)

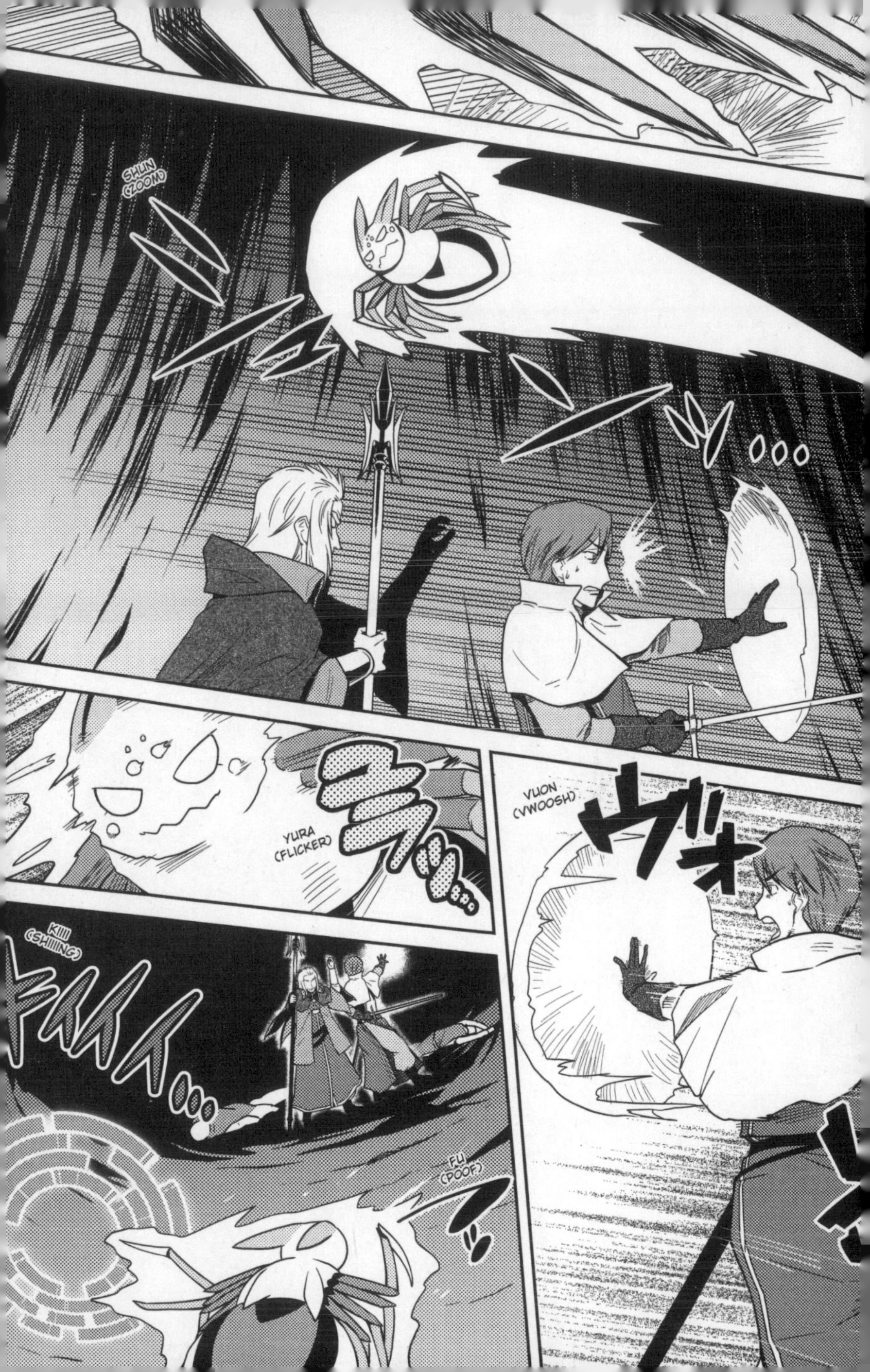
SHUN (ZOOM)
VUON (VWOOSH)
YURA (FLICKER)
KIIII (SHIIIING)
FU (POOF)

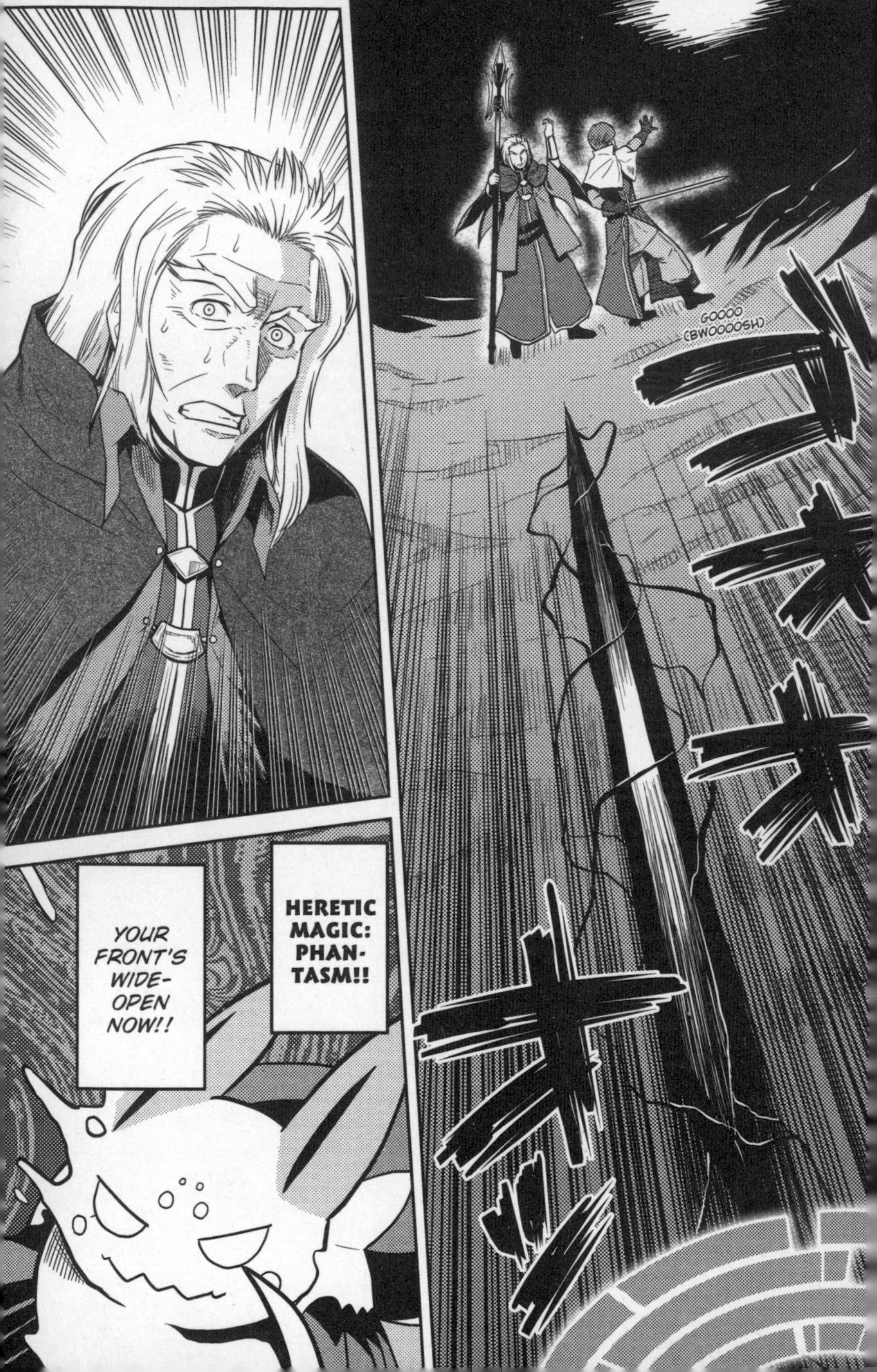
GOOOO
(BWOOOOSH)
HERETIC MAGIC: PHANTASM!!
YOUR FRONT'S WIDE-OPEN NOW!!

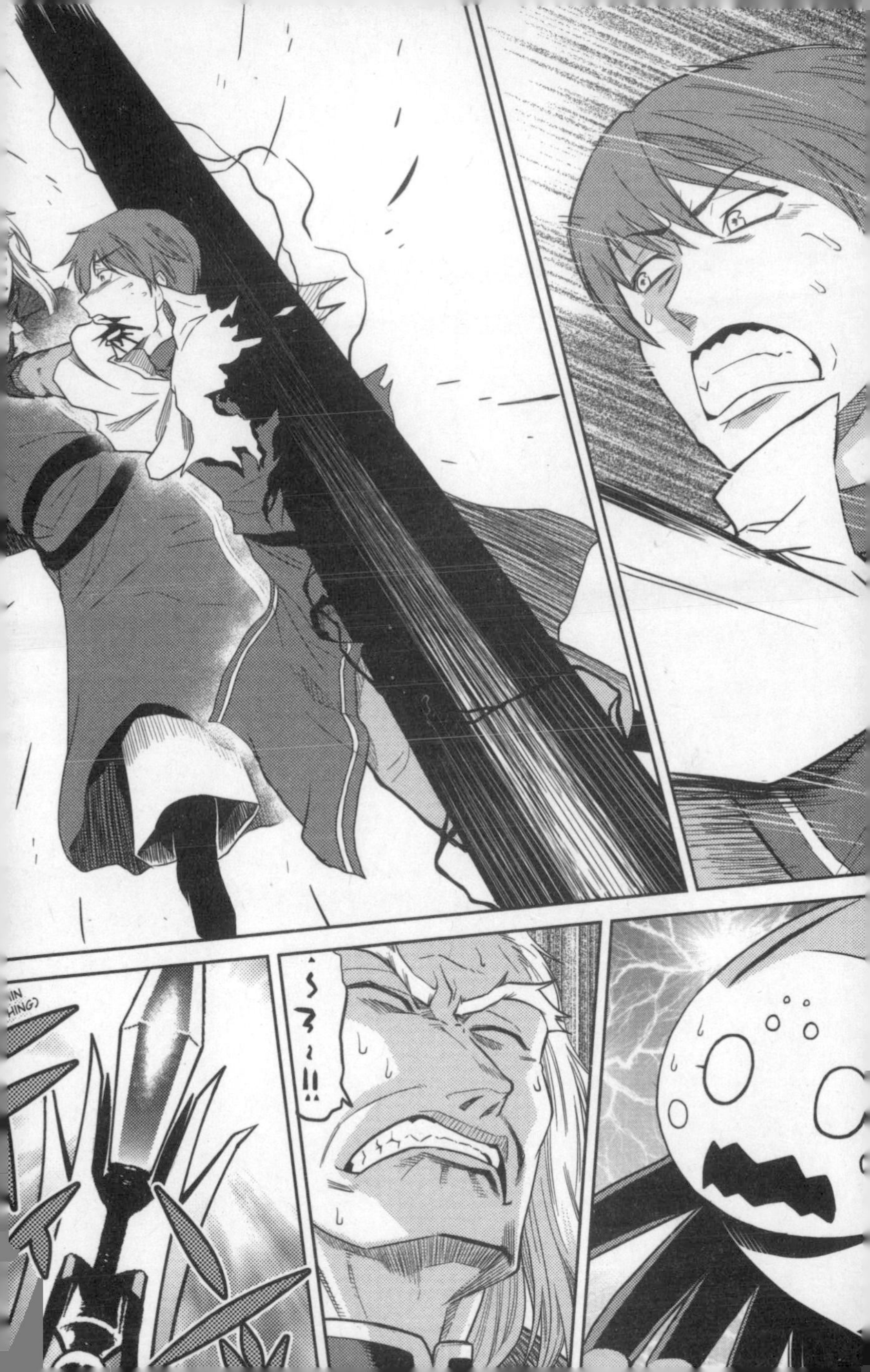

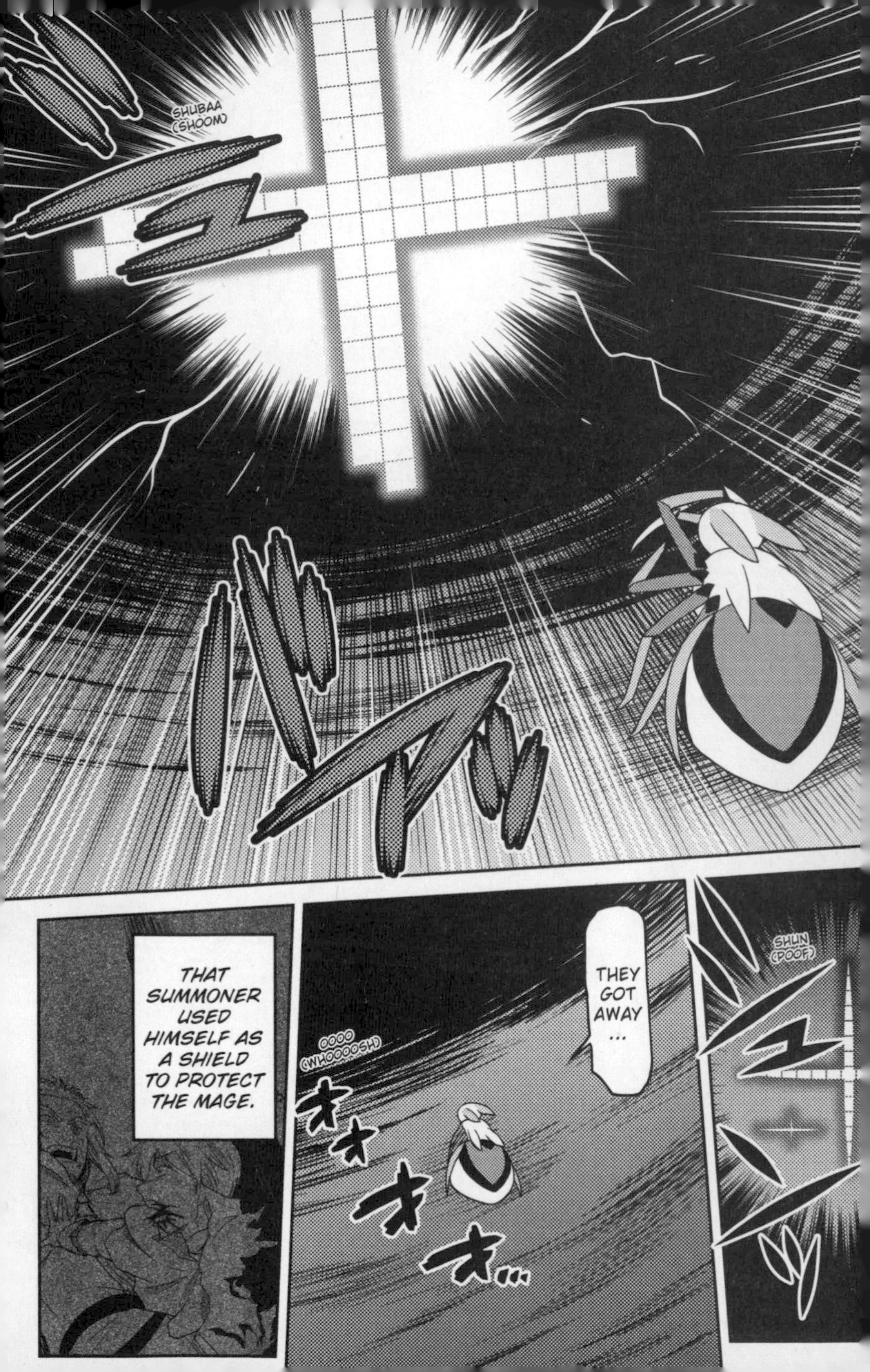
SHUBAA (SHOOM)
SHUN (POOF)
THEY GOT AWAY ...
OOOO (WHOOOOSH)
THAT SUMMONER USED HIMSELF AS A SHIELD TO PROTECT THE MAGE.

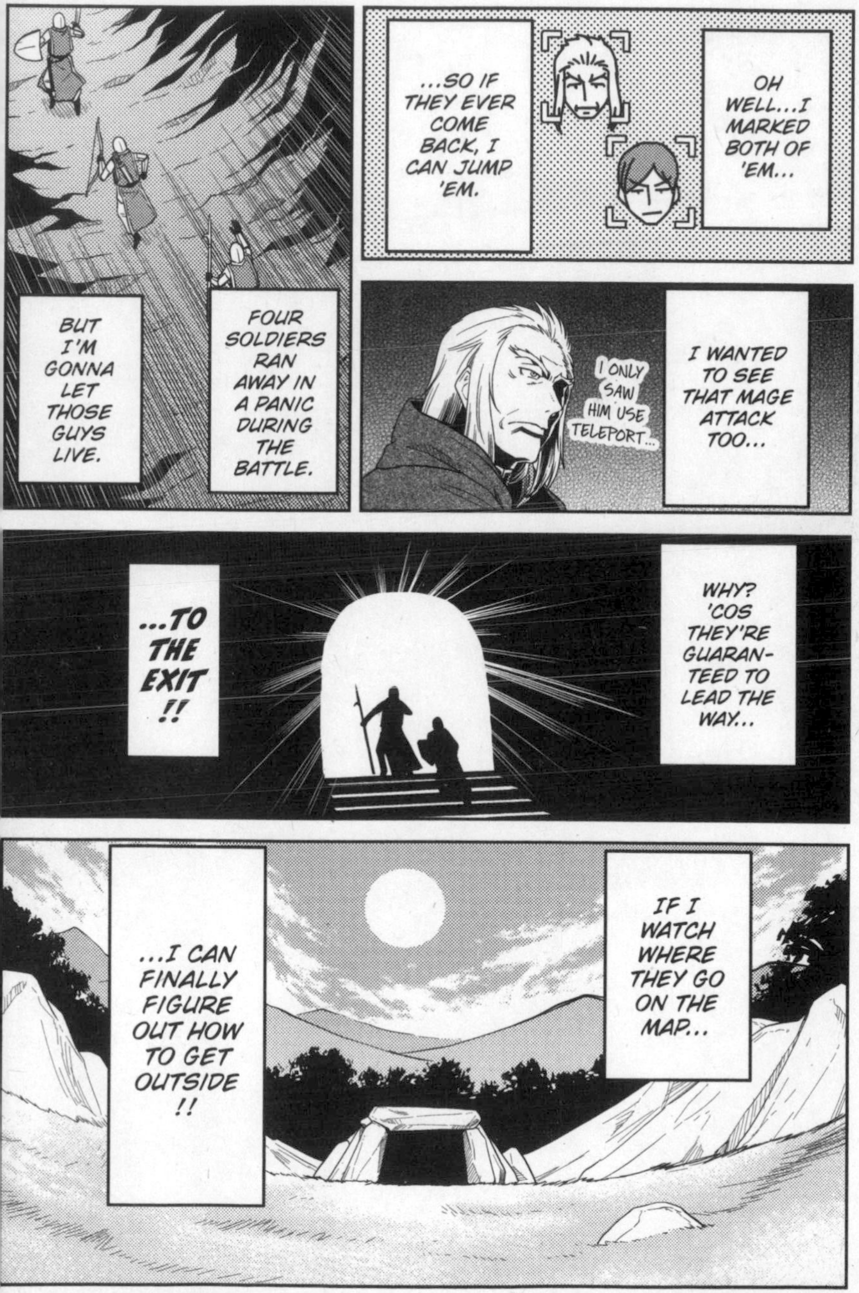
OH WELL...I MARKED BOTH OF 'EM...
...SO IF THEY EVER COME BACK, I CAN JUMP 'EM.
I WANTED TO SEE THAT MAGE ATTACK TOO...
I ONLY SAW HIM USE TELEPORT...
FOUR SOLDIERS RAN AWAY IN A PANIC DURING THE BATTLE.
BUT I'M GONNA LET THOSE GUYS LIVE.
WHY? 'COS THEY'RE GUARAN-TEED TO LEAD THE WAY...
...TO THE EXIT!!
IF I WATCH WHERE THEY GO ON THE MAP...
...I CAN FINALLY FIGURE OUT HOW TO GET OUTSIDE!!

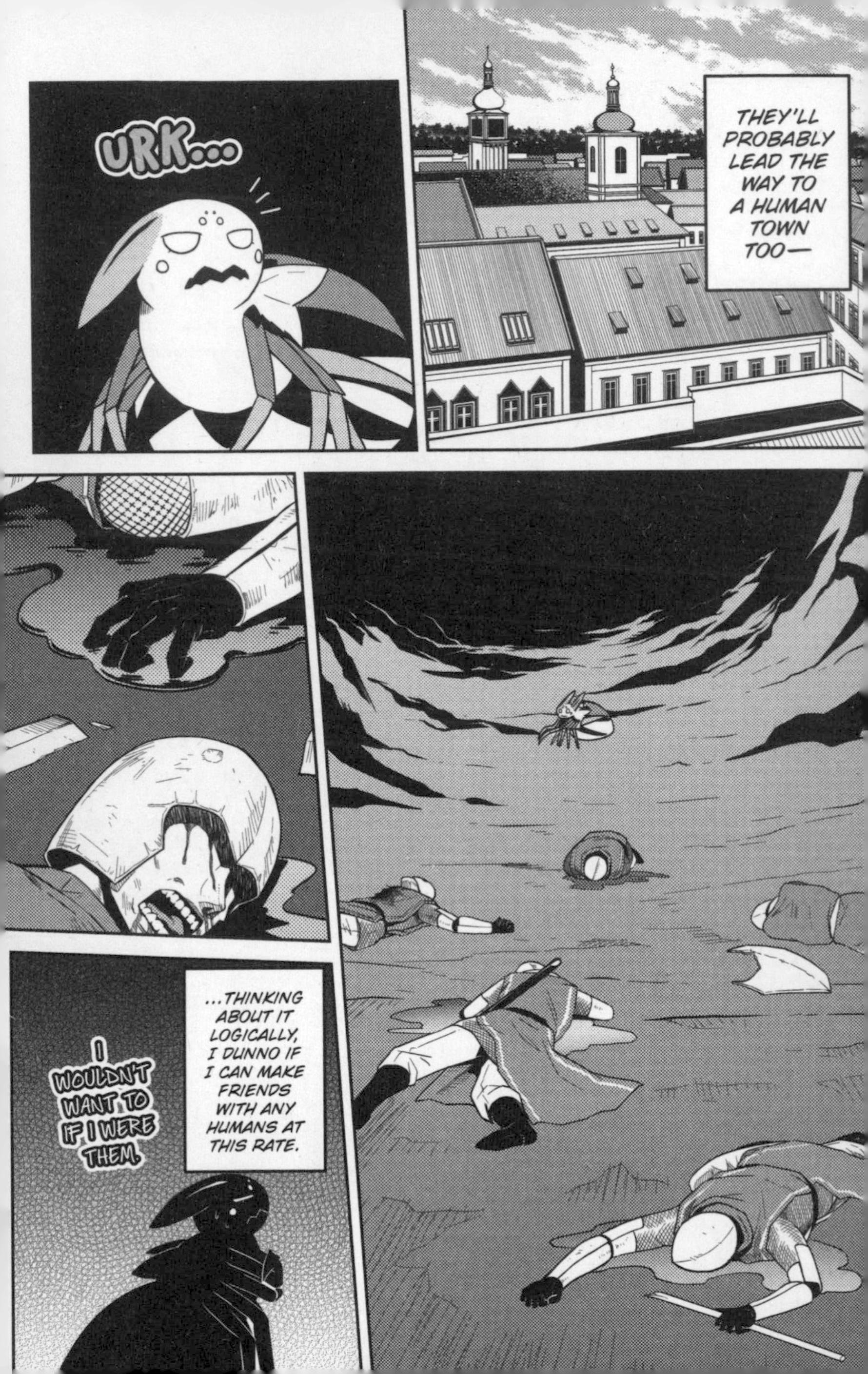
THEY'LL PROBABLY LEAD THE WAY TO A HUMAN TOWN TOO—
URK...
...THINKING ABOUT IT LOGICALLY, I DUNNO IF I CAN MAKE FRIENDS WITH ANY HUMANS AT THIS RATE.
I WOULDN'T WANT TO IF I WERE THEM.

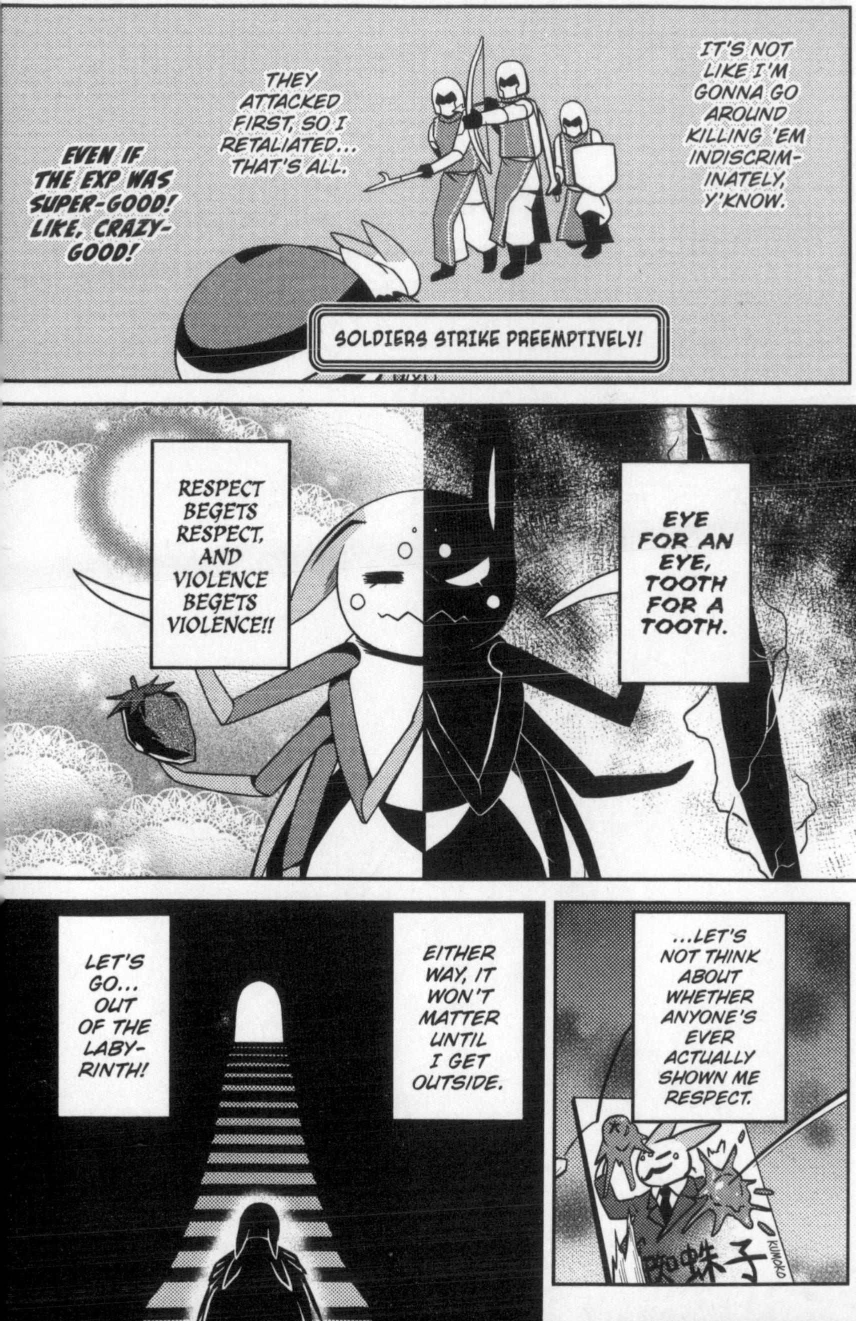
IT'S NOT LIKE I'M GONNA GO AROUND KILLING 'EM INDISCRIM-INATELY, Y'KNOW.
THEY ATTACKED FIRST, SO I RETALIATED... THAT'S ALL.
EVEN IF THE EXP WAS SUPER-GOOD! LIKE, CRAZY-GOOD!
SOLDIERS STRIKE PREEMPTIVELY!
EYE FOR AN EYE, TOOTH FOR A TOOTH.
RESPECT BEGETS RESPECT, AND VIOLENCE BEGETS VIOLENCE!!
...LET'S NOT THINK ABOUT WHETHER ANYONE'S EVER ACTUALLY SHOWN ME RESPECT.
蜘蛛子
KUMOKO
EITHER WAY, IT WON'T MATTER UNTIL I GET OUTSIDE.
LET'S GO... OUT OF THE LABY-RINTH!

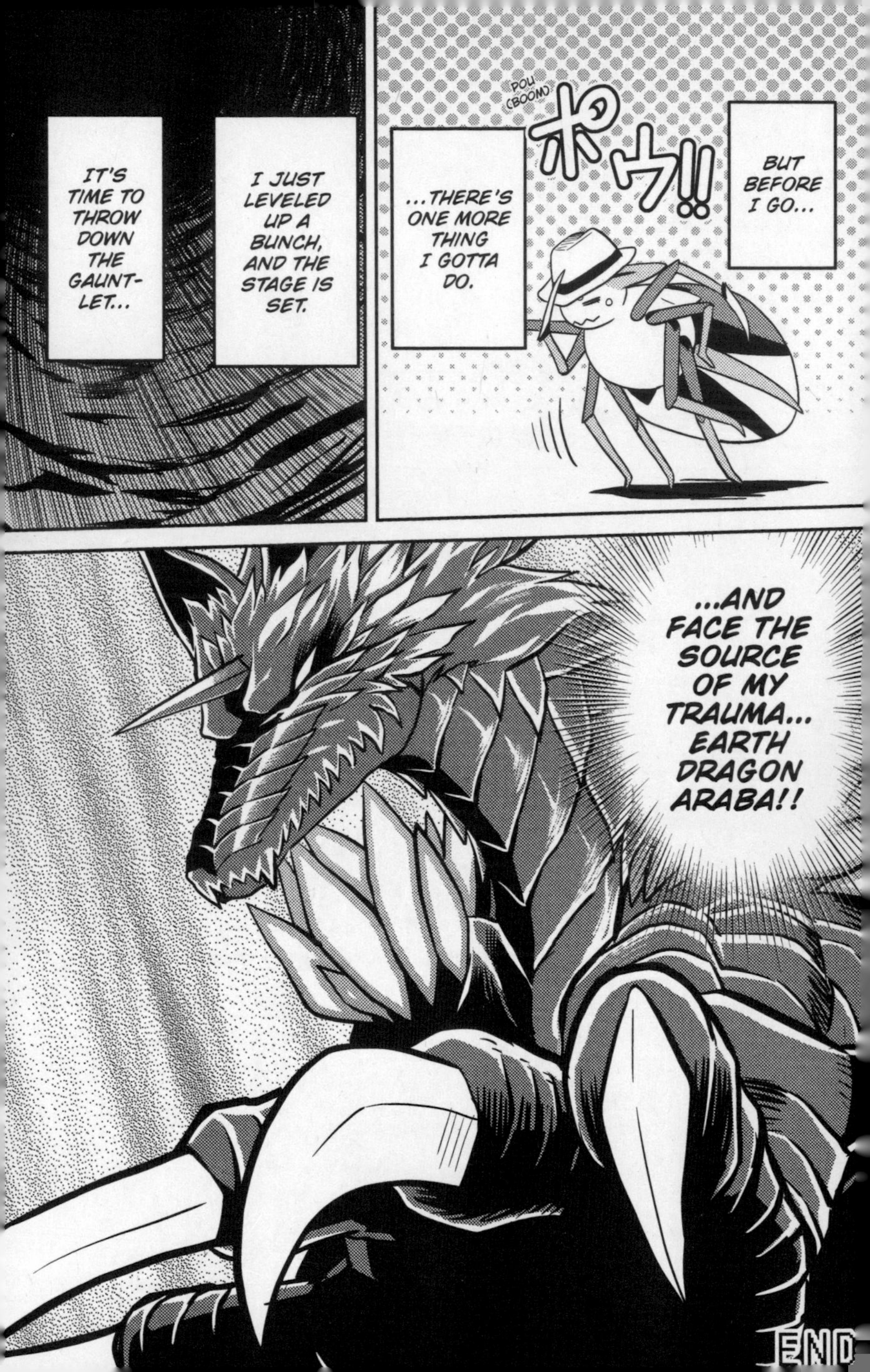
BUT BEFORE I GO...
ポウ!!
POU (BOOM)
...THERE'S ONE MORE THING I GOTTA DO.
I JUST LEVELED UP A BUNCH, AND THE STAGE IS SET.
IT'S TIME TO THROW DOWN THE GAUNT-LET...
...AND FACE THE SOURCE OF MY TRAUMA... EARTH DRAGON ARABA!!
END

So I'm a Spider, So What?

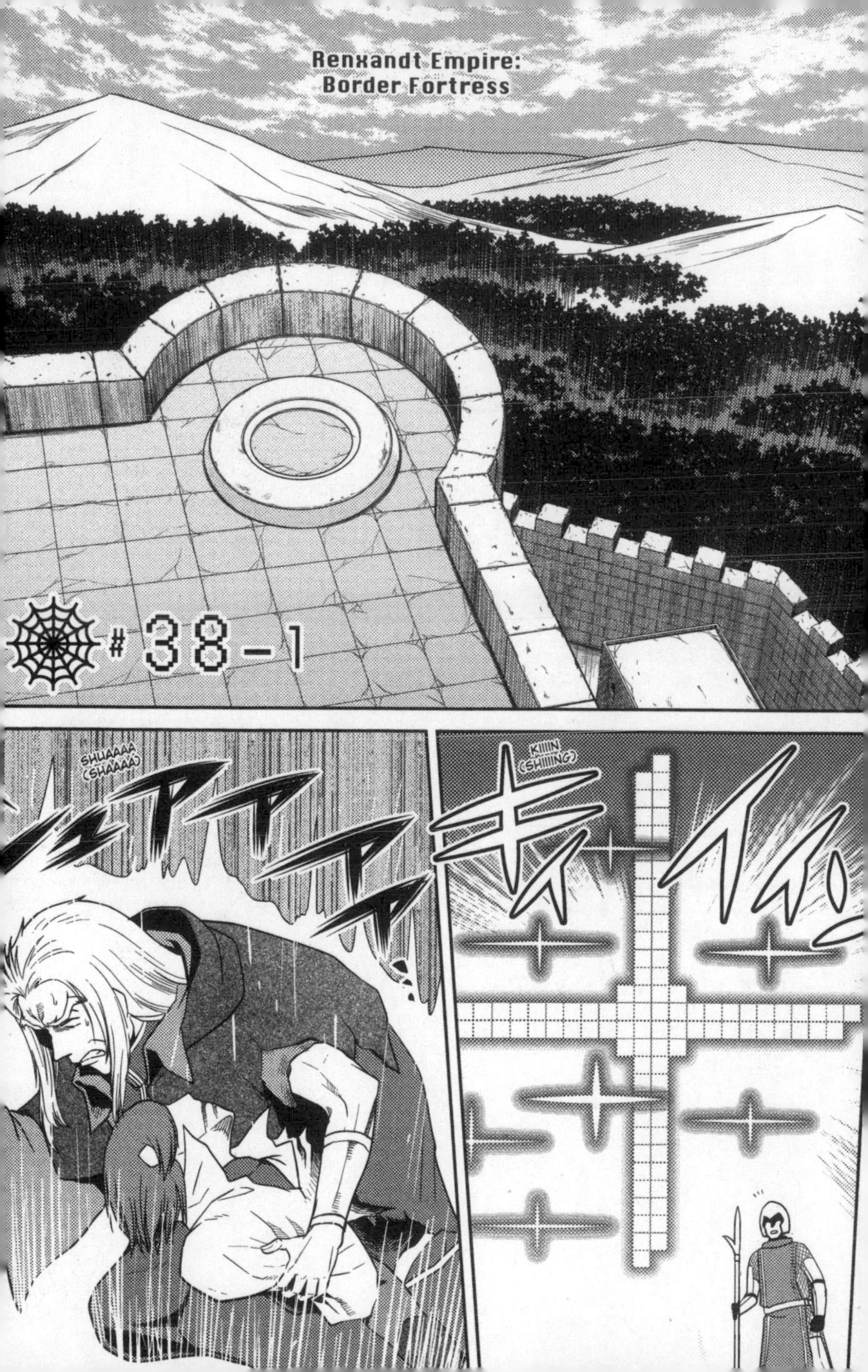
Renxandt Empire:
Border Fortress
#38-1
KIIIIN
(SHIIIING)
SHUAAAA
(SHAAAA)

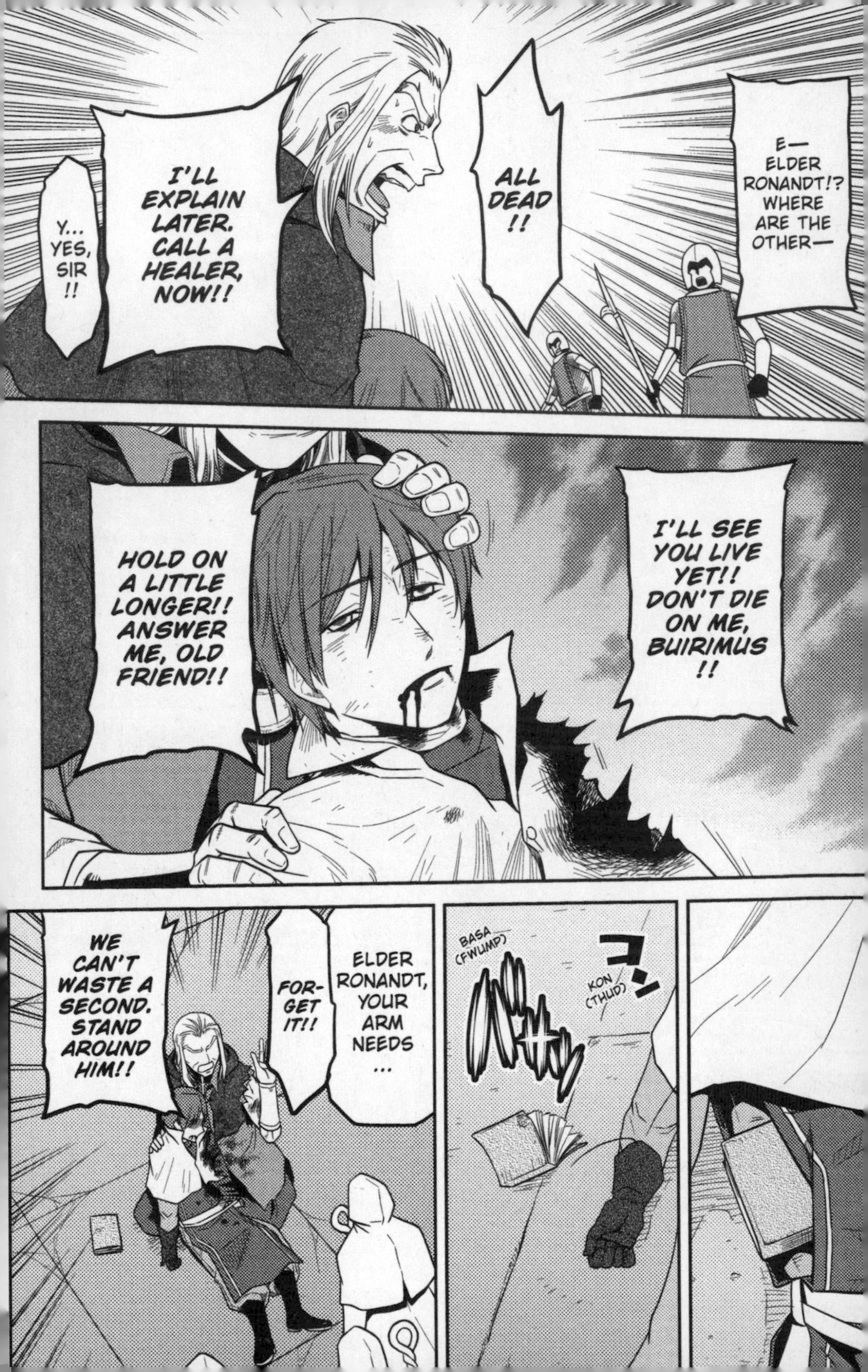

E— ELDER RONANDT!? WHERE ARE THE OTHER—
ALL DEAD!!
I'LL EXPLAIN LATER. CALL A HEALER, NOW!!
Y... YES, SIR!!
I'LL SEE YOU LIVE YET!! DON'T DIE ON ME, BUIRIMUS!!
HOLD ON A LITTLE LONGER!! ANSWER ME, OLD FRIEND!!
KON (THUD)
BASA (FWUMP)
ELDER RONANDT, YOUR ARM NEEDS ...
FOR-GET IT!!
WE CAN'T WASTE A SECOND. STAND AROUND HIM!!

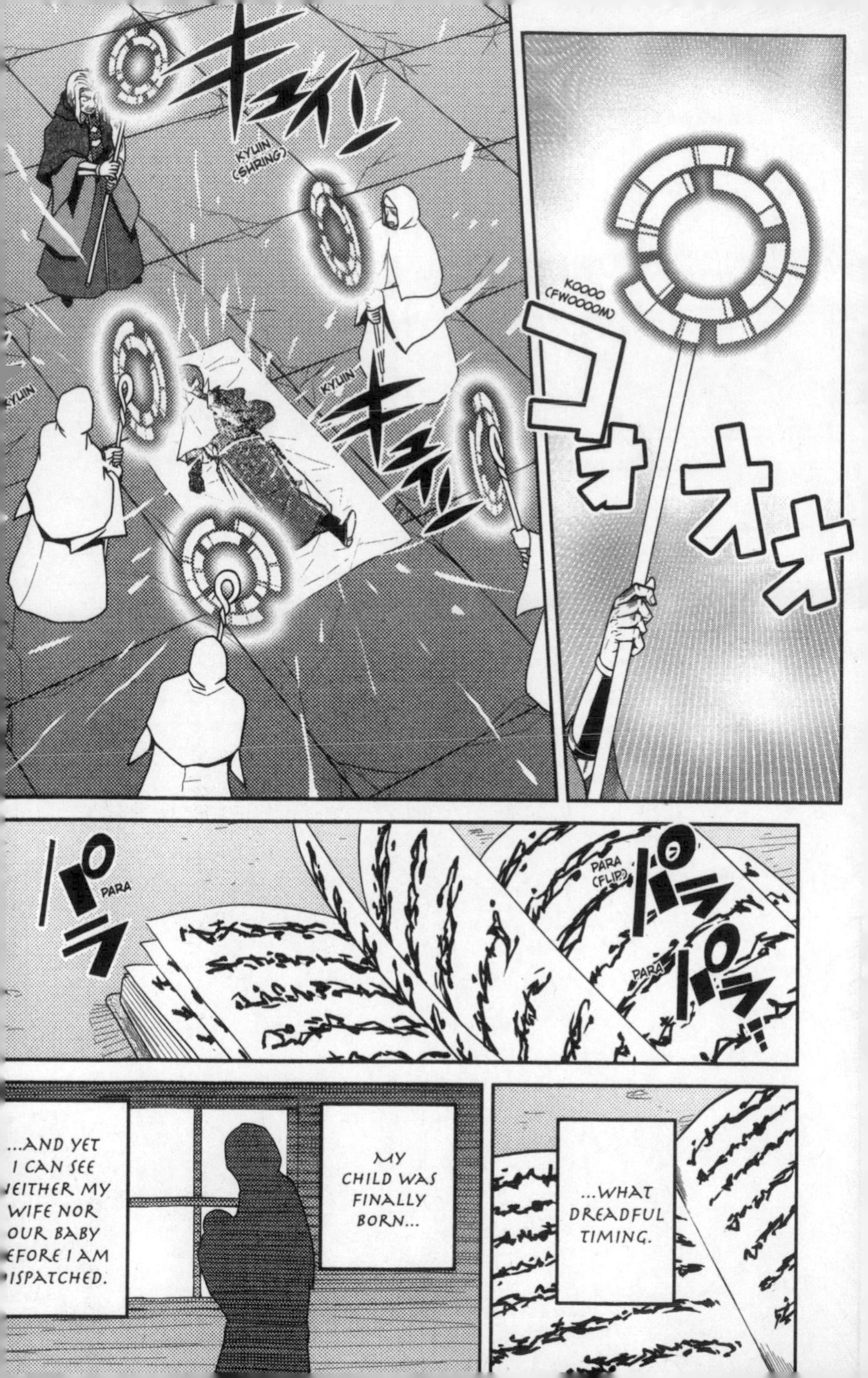

KOOOO (FWOOOOM)
コォオオ
キュイン
KYUIN (SHRING)
KYUIN
キュイン
KYUIN
パラパラ
PARA (FLIP)
PARA
パラ
PARA
...WHAT DREADFUL TIMING.
MY CHILD WAS FINALLY BORN...
...AND YET I CAN SEE
EITHER MY WIFE NOR OUR BABY
EFORE I AM
ISPATCHED.

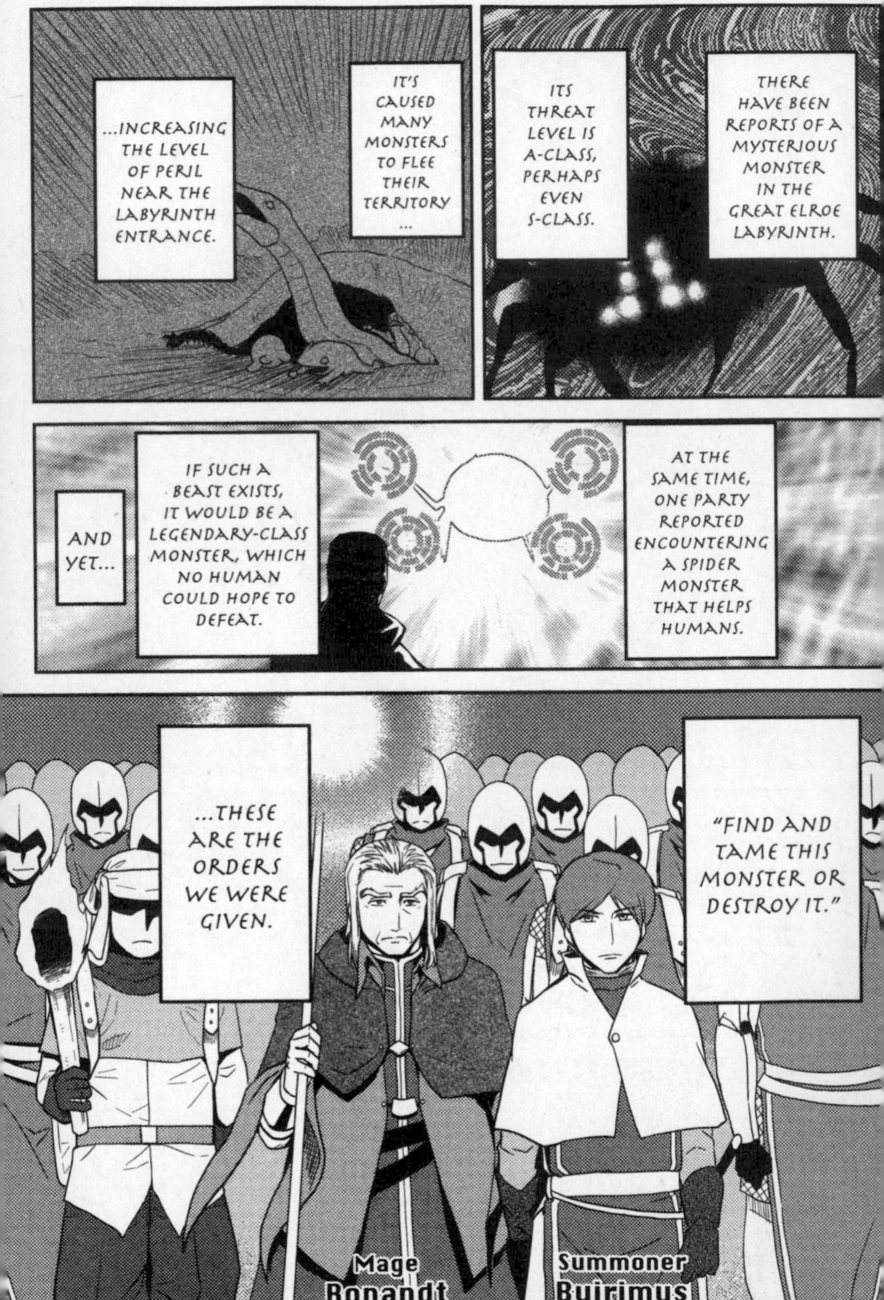
THERE HAVE BEEN REPORTS OF A MYSTERIOUS MONSTER IN THE GREAT ELROE LABYRINTH.
ITS THREAT LEVEL IS A-CLASS, PERHAPS EVEN S-CLASS.
IT'S CAUSED MANY MONSTERS TO FLEE THEIR TERRITORY ...
...INCREASING THE LEVEL OF PERIL NEAR THE LABYRINTH ENTRANCE.
AT THE SAME TIME, ONE PARTY REPORTED ENCOUNTERING A SPIDER MONSTER THAT HELPS HUMANS.
IF SUCH A BEAST EXISTS, IT WOULD BE A LEGENDARY-CLASS MONSTER, WHICH NO HUMAN COULD HOPE TO DEFEAT.
AND YET...
"FIND AND TAME THIS MONSTER OR DESTROY IT."
...THESE ARE THE ORDERS WE WERE GIVEN.
Summoner Buirimus
Mage Ronandt

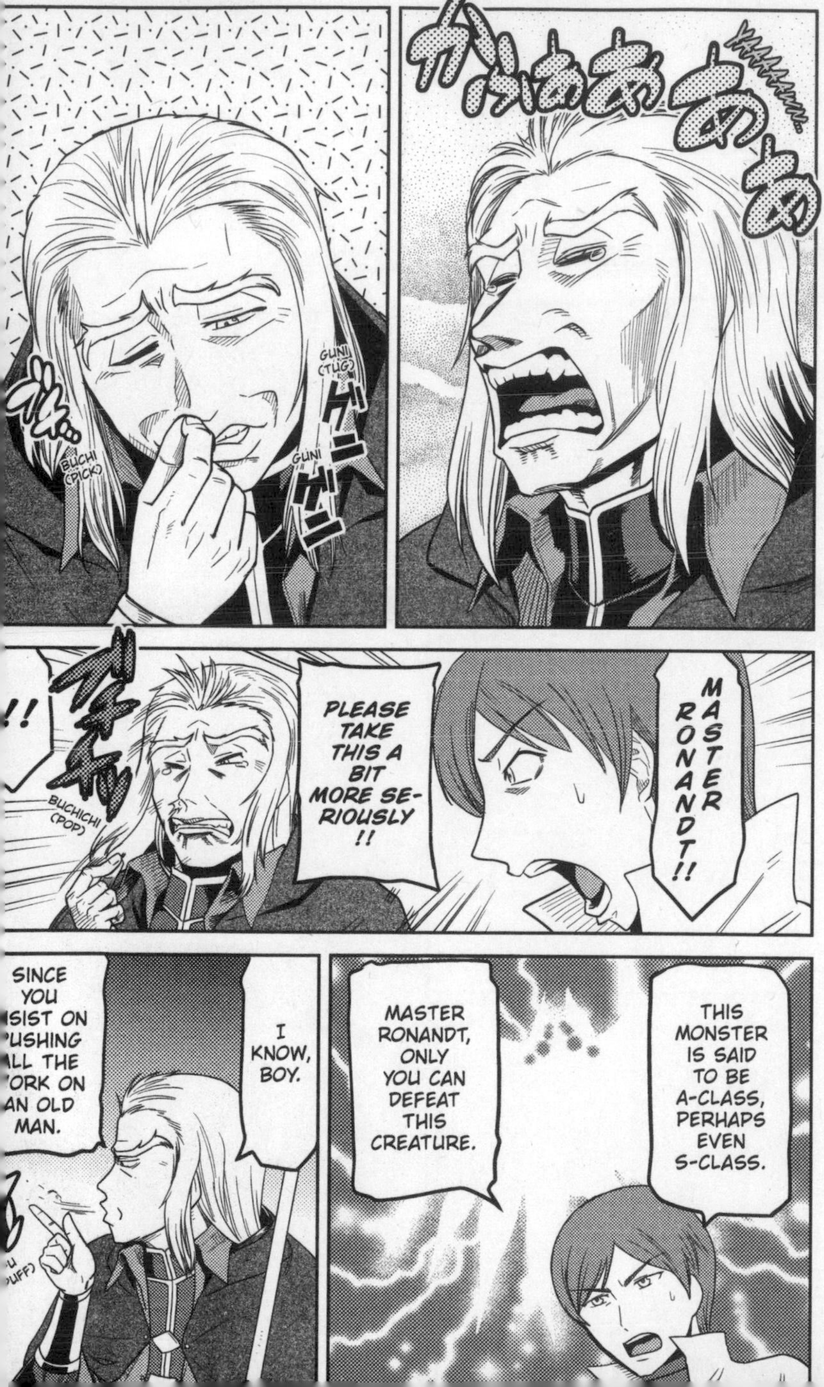
GUNI (TUG)
GUNI
BUCHI (PICK)
MASTER RONANDT!!
PLEASE TAKE THIS A BIT MORE SE-RIOUSLY!!
BUCHICHI (POP)
!!
THIS MONSTER IS SAID TO BE A-CLASS, PERHAPS EVEN S-CLASS.
MASTER RONANDT, ONLY YOU CAN DEFEAT THIS CREATURE.
I KNOW, BOY.
SINCE YOU SIST ON USHING LL THE ORK ON AN OLD MAN.

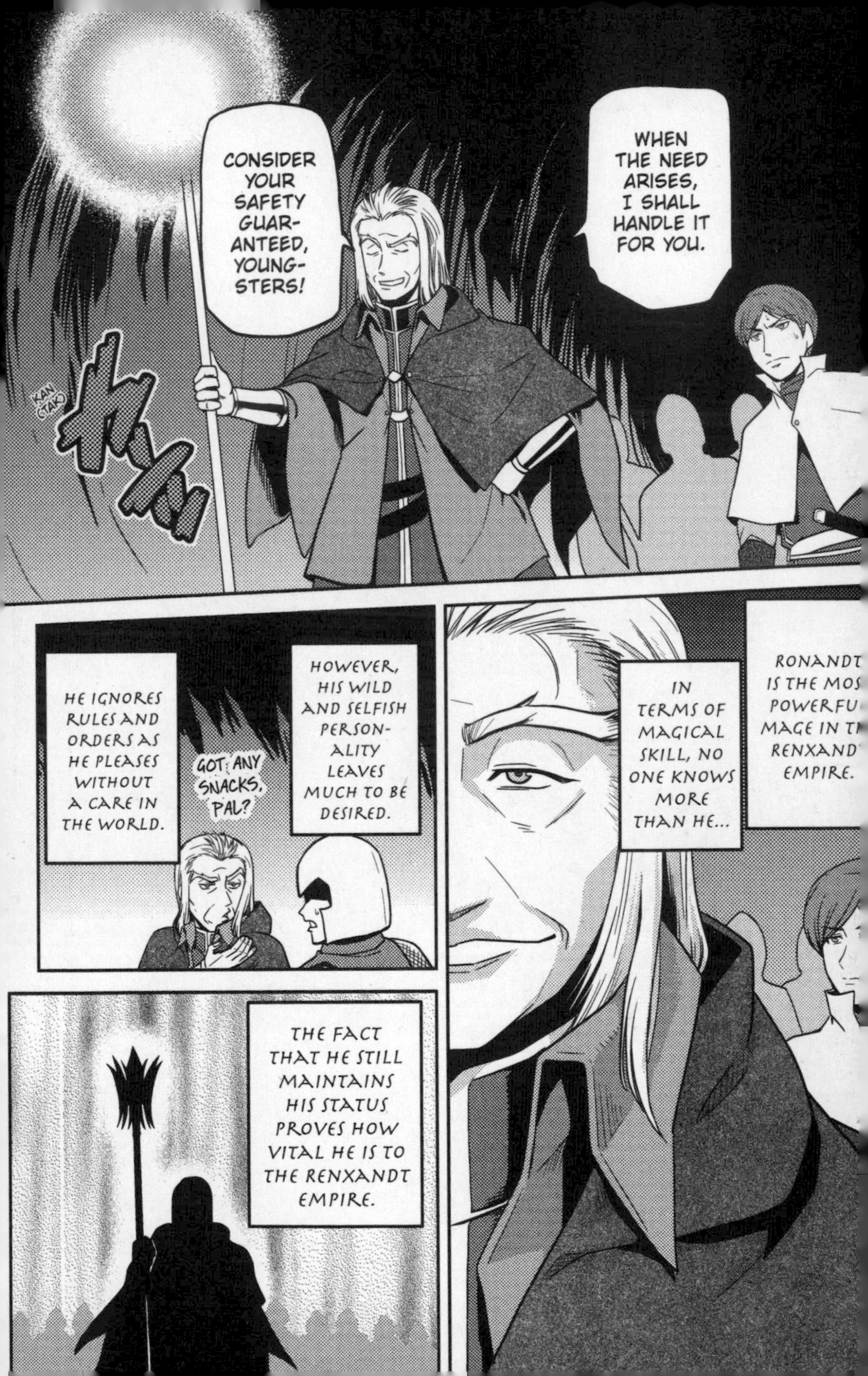
WHEN THE NEED ARISES, I SHALL HANDLE IT FOR YOU.
CONSIDER YOUR SAFETY GUAR-ANTEED, YOUNG-STERS!
KAN (TAK)
RONANDT IS THE MOS POWERFU MAGE IN TH RENXANDT EMPIRE.
IN TERMS OF MAGICAL SKILL, NO ONE KNOWS MORE THAN HE...
HOWEVER, HIS WILD AND SELFISH PERSON-ALITY LEAVES MUCH TO BE DESIRED.
GOT ANY SNACKS, PAL?
HE IGNORES RULES AND ORDERS AS HE PLEASES WITHOUT A CARE IN THE WORLD.
THE FACT THAT HE STILL MAINTAINS HIS STATUS PROVES HOW VITAL HE IS TO THE RENXANDT EMPIRE.

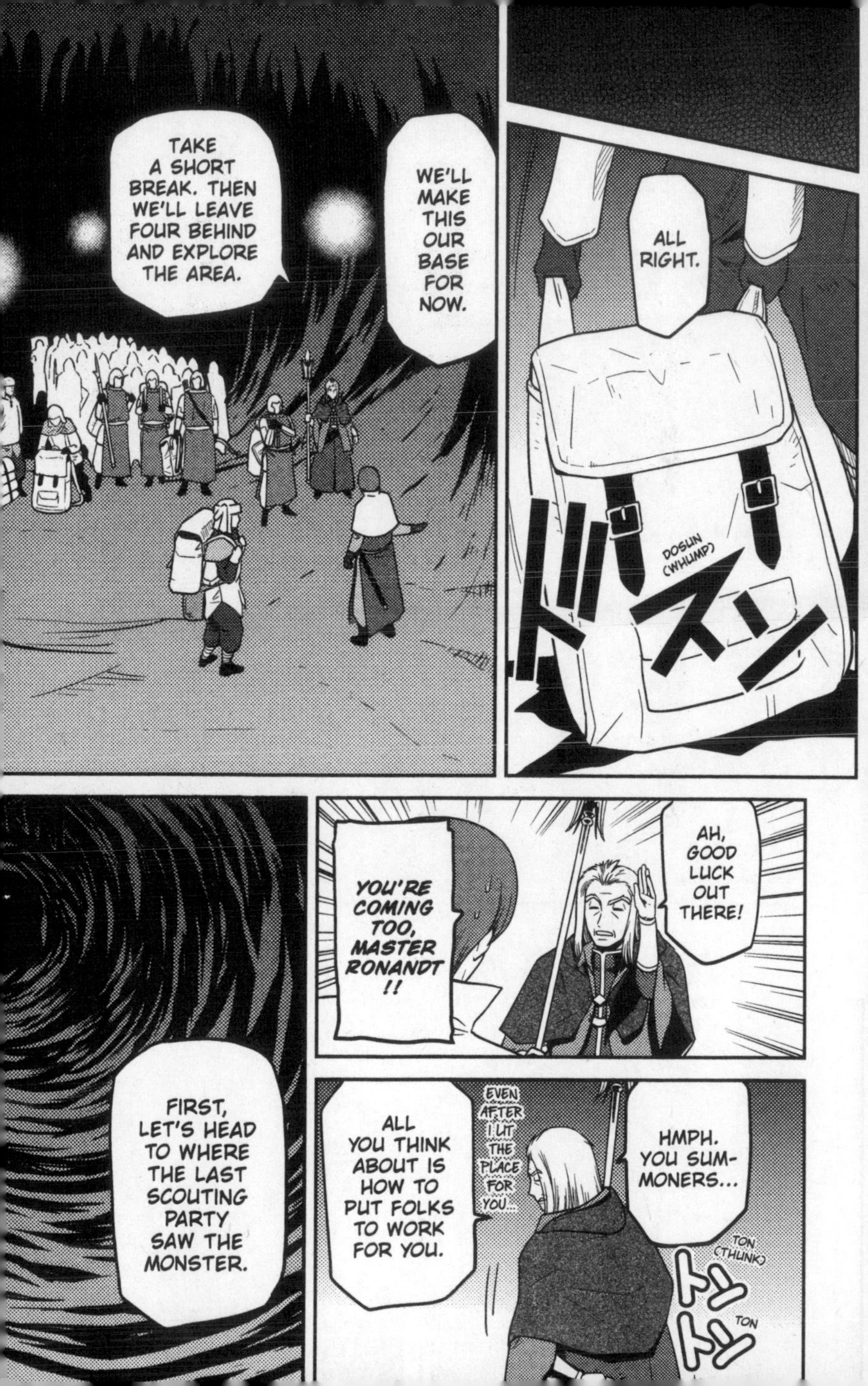
ALL RIGHT.
DOSUN (WHUMP)
WE'LL MAKE THIS OUR BASE FOR NOW.
TAKE A SHORT BREAK. THEN WE'LL LEAVE FOUR BEHIND AND EXPLORE THE AREA.
AH, GOOD LUCK OUT THERE!
YOU'RE COMING TOO, MASTER RONANDT!!
HMPH. YOU SUMMONERS...
EVEN AFTER I LIT THE PLACE FOR YOU...
ALL YOU THINK ABOUT IS HOW TO PUT FOLKS TO WORK FOR YOU.
TON (THUNK)
TON
FIRST, LET'S HEAD TO WHERE THE LAST SCOUTING PARTY SAW THE MONSTER.

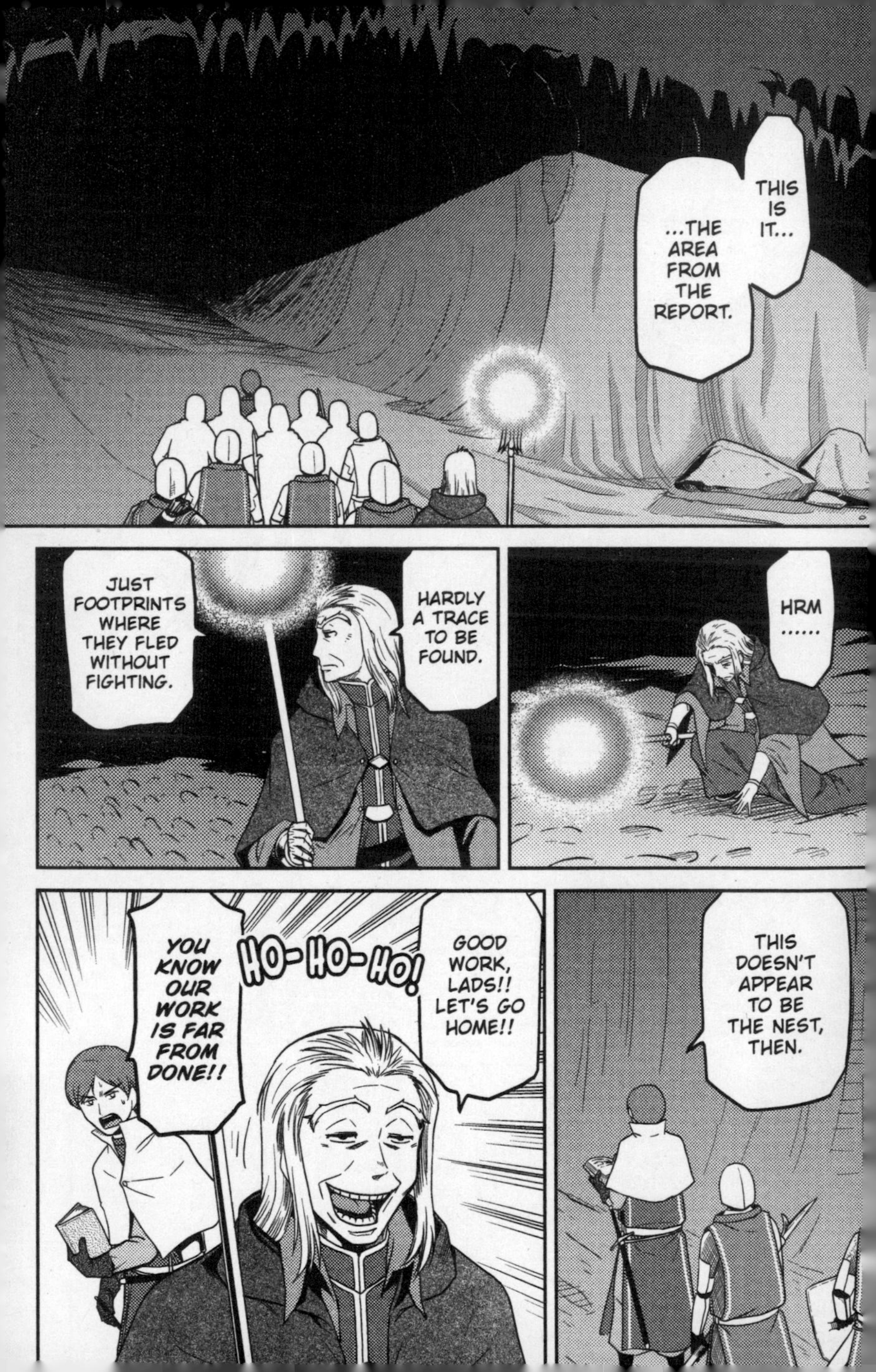
THIS IS IT...
...THE AREA FROM THE REPORT.
HRM ......
HARDLY A TRACE TO BE FOUND.
JUST FOOTPRINTS WHERE THEY FLED WITHOUT FIGHTING.
THIS DOESN'T APPEAR TO BE THE NEST, THEN.
GOOD WORK, LADS!! LET'S GO HOME!!
HO-HO-HO!
YOU KNOW OUR WORK IS FAR FROM DONE!!

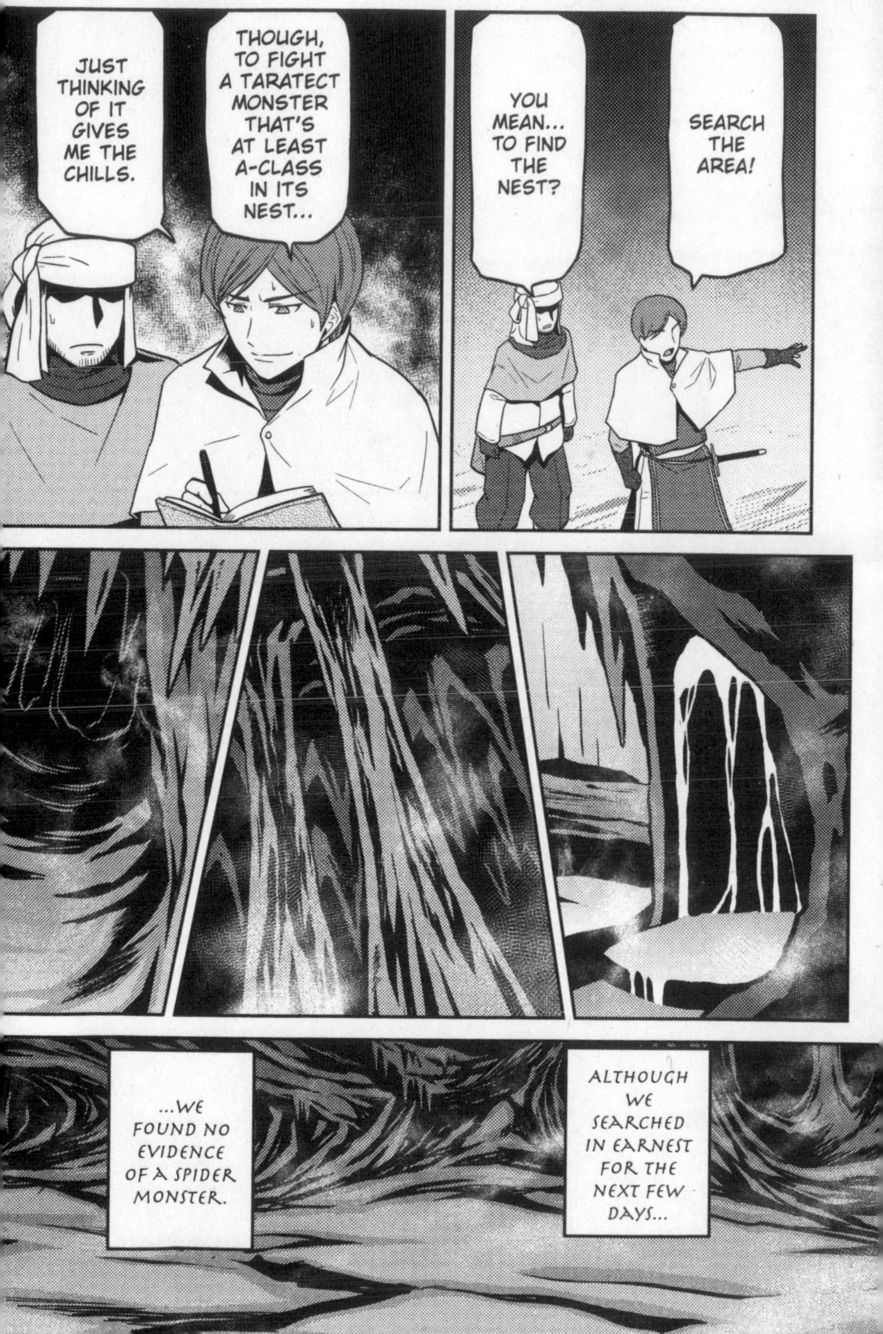
SEARCH THE AREA!
YOU MEAN... TO FIND THE NEST?
THOUGH, TO FIGHT A TARATECT MONSTER THAT'S AT LEAST A-CLASS IN ITS NEST...
JUST THINKING OF IT GIVES ME THE CHILLS.
ALTHOUGH WE SEARCHED IN EARNEST FOR THE NEXT FEW DAYS...
...WE FOUND NO EVIDENCE OF A SPIDER MONSTER.

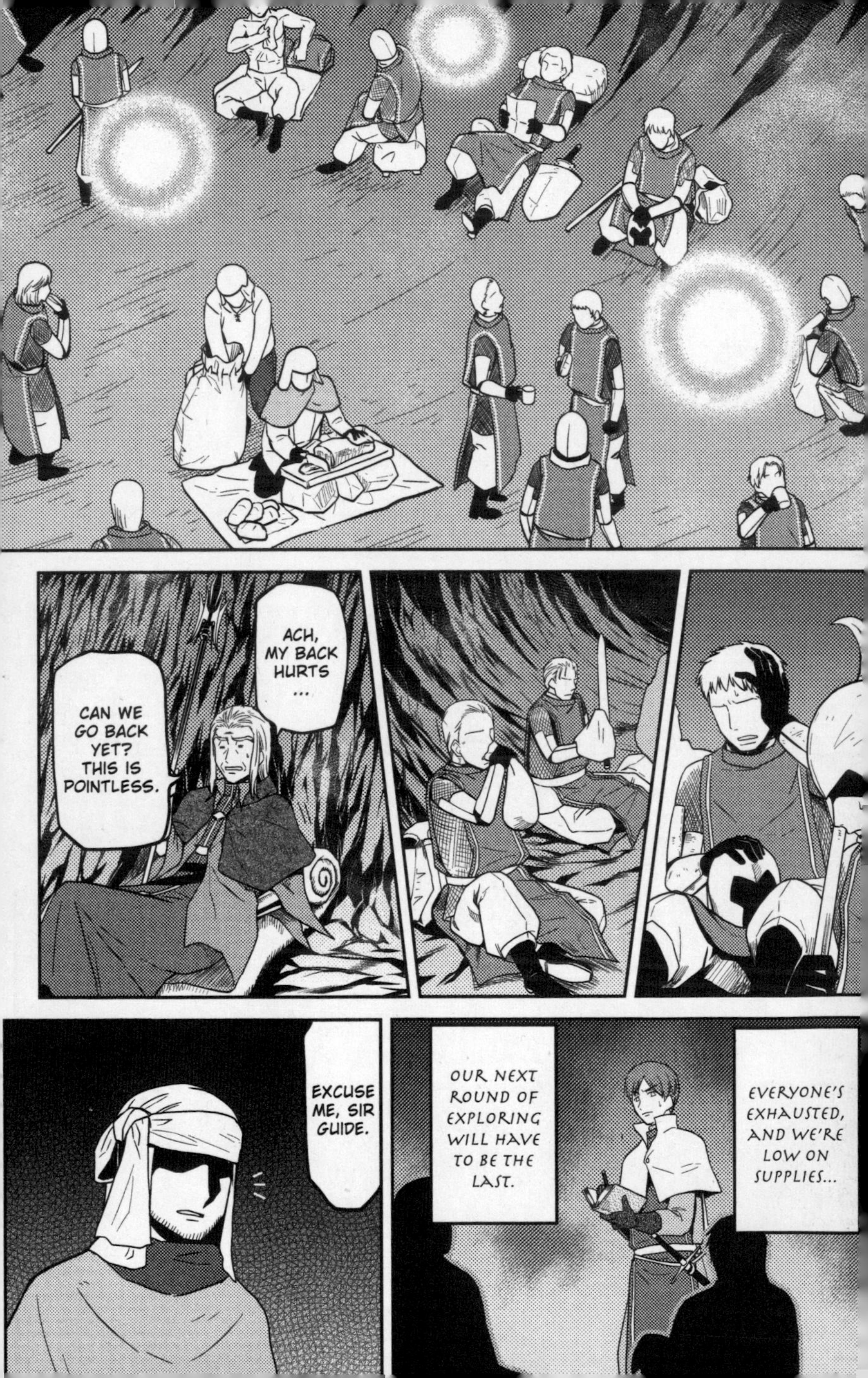
ACH, MY BACK HURTS ...
CAN WE GO BACK YET? THIS IS POINTLESS.
EVERYONE'S EXHAUSTED, AND WE'RE LOW ON SUPPLIES...
OUR NEXT ROUND OF EXPLORING WILL HAVE TO BE THE LAST.
EXCUSE ME, SIR GUIDE.

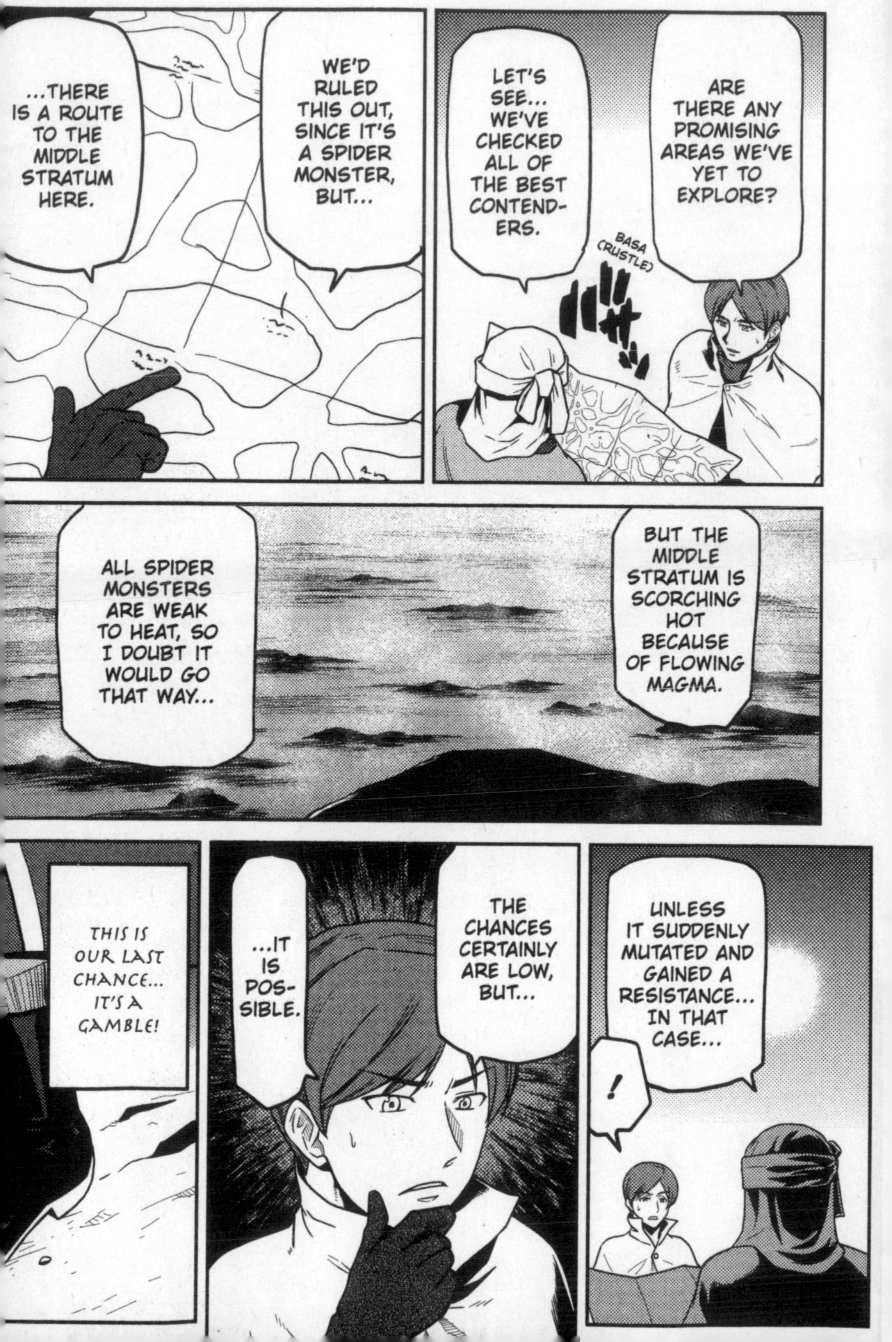
ARE THERE ANY PROMISING AREAS WE'VE YET TO EXPLORE?
LET'S SEE... WE'VE CHECKED ALL OF THE BEST CONTEND-ERS.
BASA (RUSTLE)
WE'D RULED THIS OUT, SINCE IT'S A SPIDER MONSTER, BUT...
...THERE IS A ROUTE TO THE MIDDLE STRATUM HERE.
BUT THE MIDDLE STRATUM IS SCORCHING HOT BECAUSE OF FLOWING MAGMA.
ALL SPIDER MONSTERS ARE WEAK TO HEAT, SO I DOUBT IT WOULD GO THAT WAY...
UNLESS IT SUDDENLY MUTATED AND GAINED A RESISTANCE... IN THAT CASE...
!
THE CHANCES CERTAINLY ARE LOW, BUT...
...IT IS POS-SIBLE.
THIS IS OUR LAST CHANCE... IT'S A GAMBLE!

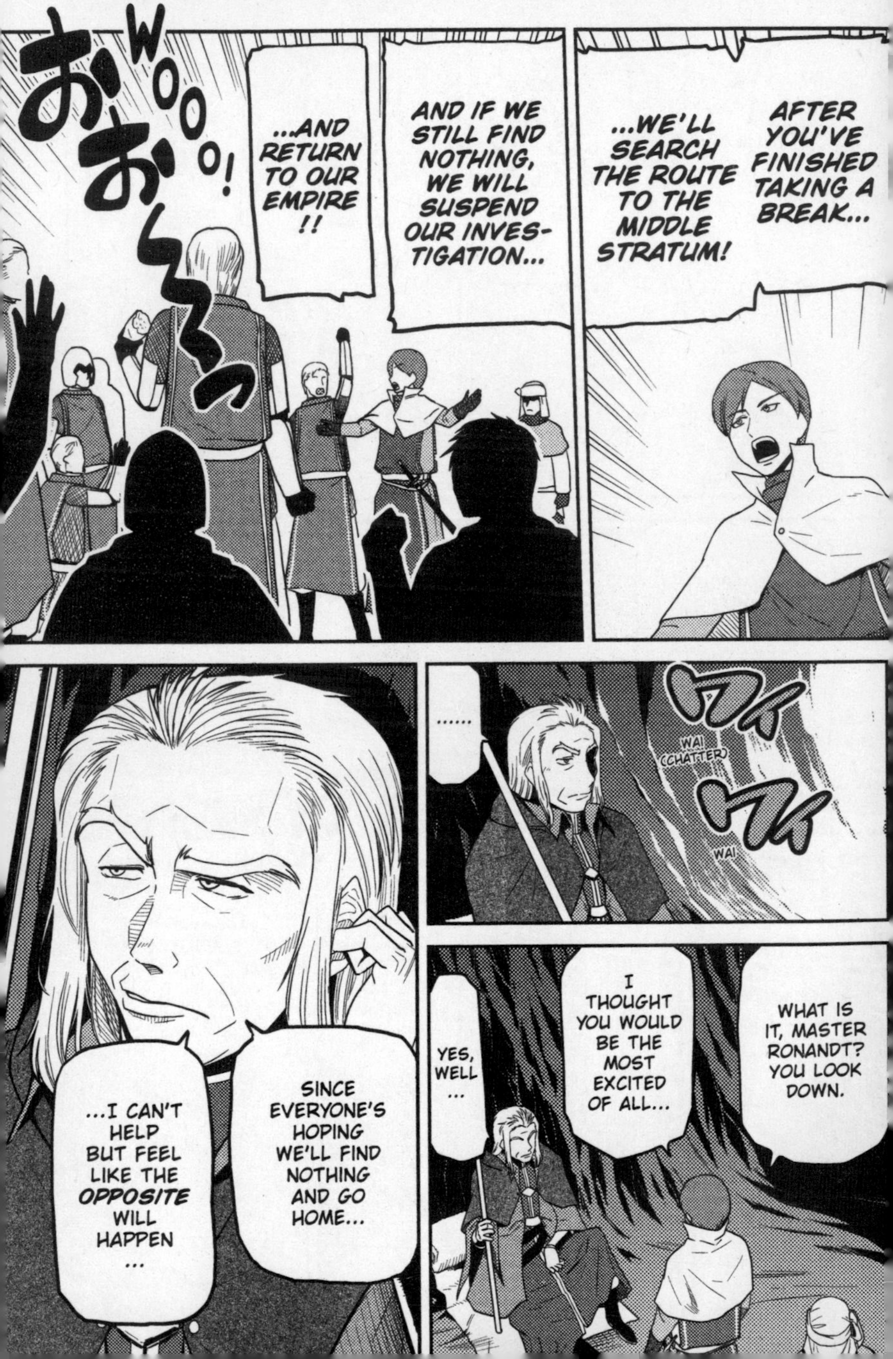
AFTER YOU'VE FINISHED TAKING A BREAK...
...WE'LL SEARCH THE ROUTE TO THE MIDDLE STRATUM!
AND IF WE STILL FIND NOTHING, WE WILL SUSPEND OUR INVES-TIGATION...
...AND RETURN TO OUR EMPIRE!!
WOOOO!
......
WAI (CHATTER)
WAI
WHAT IS IT, MASTER RONANDT? YOU LOOK DOWN.
I THOUGHT YOU WOULD BE THE MOST EXCITED OF ALL...
YES, WELL...
SINCE EVERYONE'S HOPING WE'LL FIND NOTHING AND GO HOME...
...I CAN'T HELP BUT FEEL LIKE THE *OPPOSITE* WILL HAPPEN...

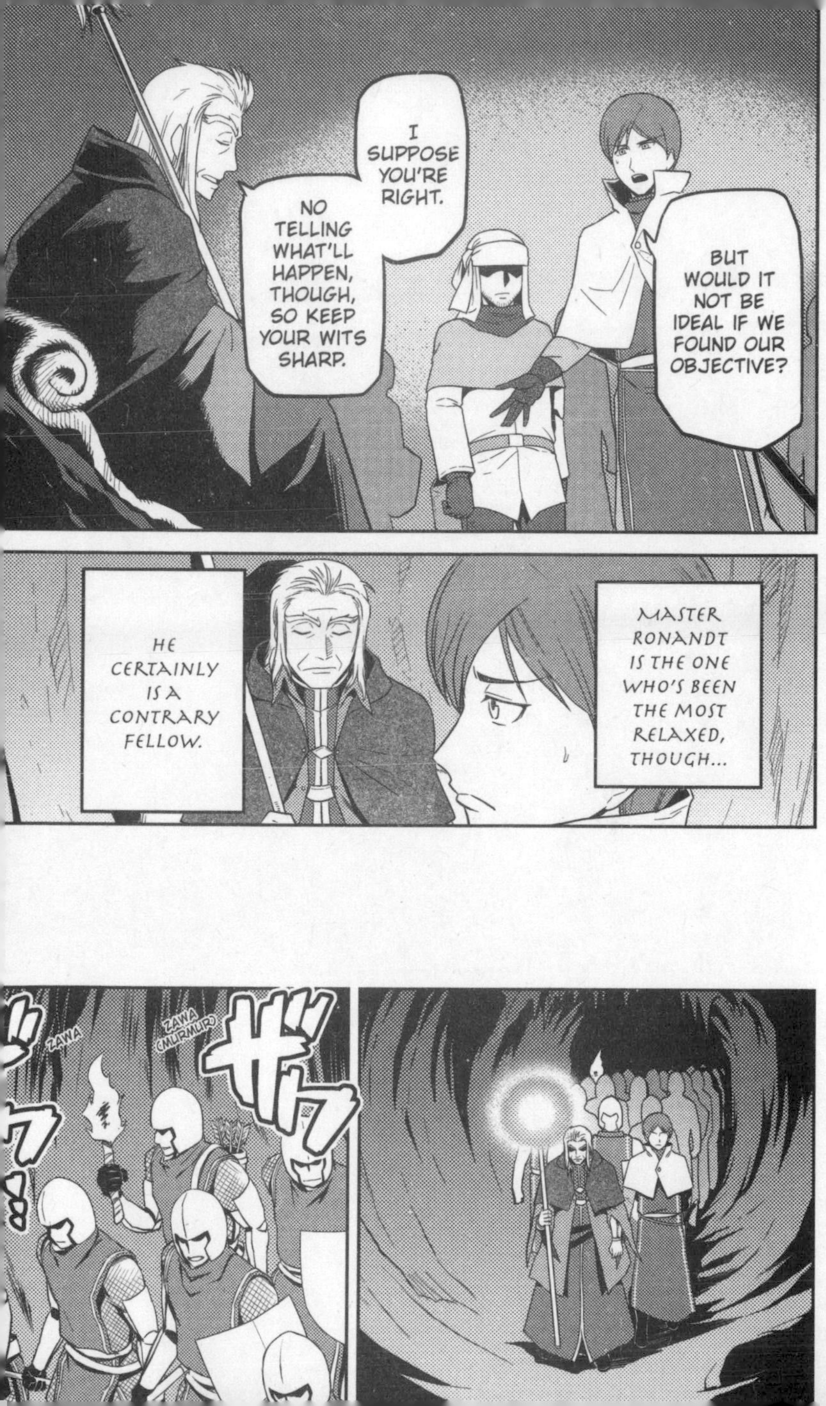
BUT WOULD IT NOT BE IDEAL IF WE FOUND OUR OBJECTIVE?
I SUPPOSE YOU'RE RIGHT.
NO TELLING WHAT'LL HAPPEN, THOUGH, SO KEEP YOUR WITS SHARP.
MASTER RONANDT IS THE ONE WHO'S BEEN THE MOST RELAXED, THOUGH...
HE CERTAINLY IS A CONTRARY FELLOW.
ZAWA (MURMUR)
ZAWA

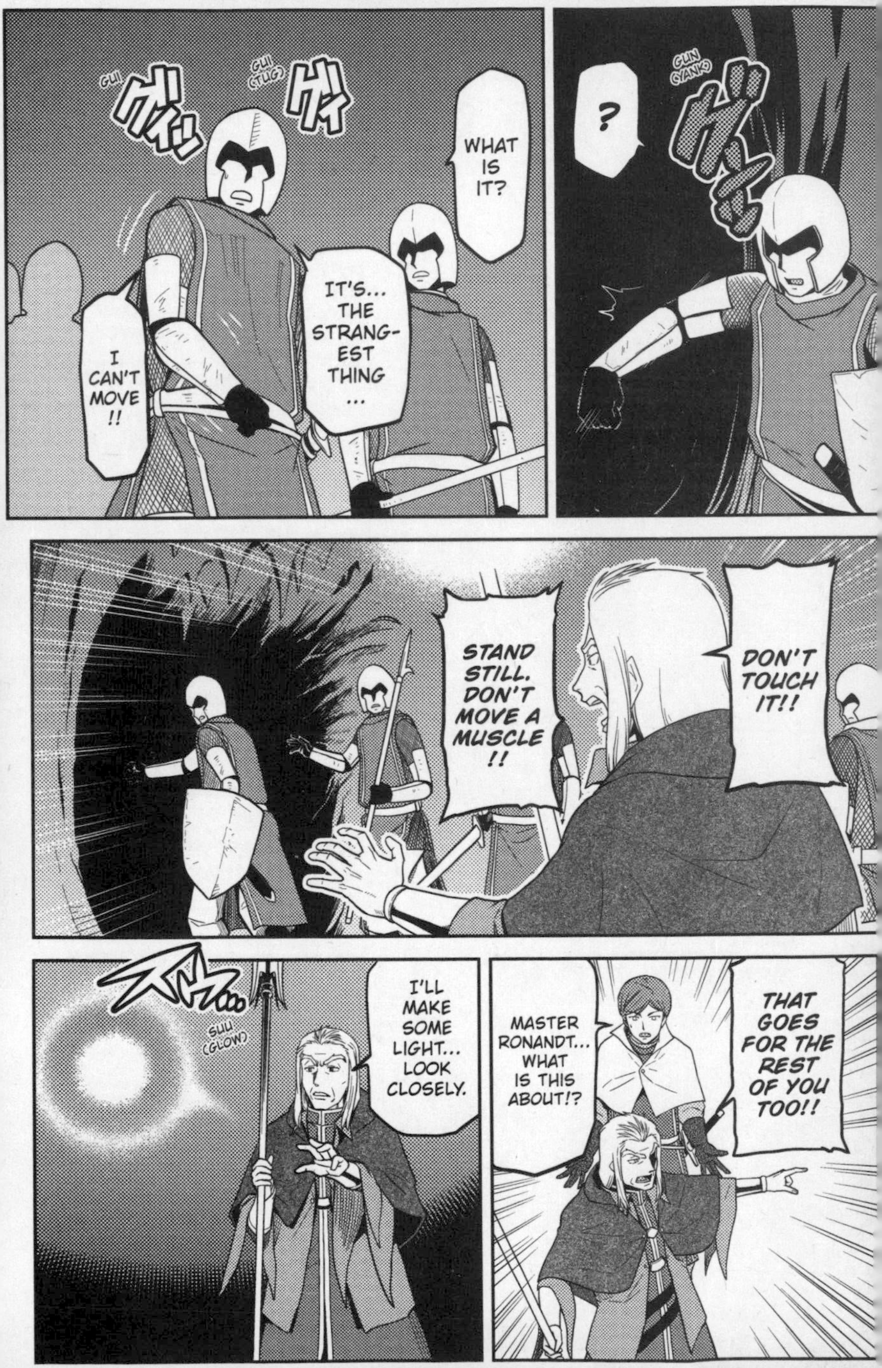
?
GUN (YANK)
WHAT IS IT?
GUI (TUG)
GUI
IT'S... THE STRANGEST THING...
I CAN'T MOVE!!
DON'T TOUCH IT!!
STAND STILL. DON'T MOVE A MUSCLE!!
THAT GOES FOR THE REST OF YOU TOO!!
MASTER RONANDT... WHAT IS THIS ABOUT!?
I'LL MAKE SOME LIGHT... LOOK CLOSELY.
SUU (GLOW)

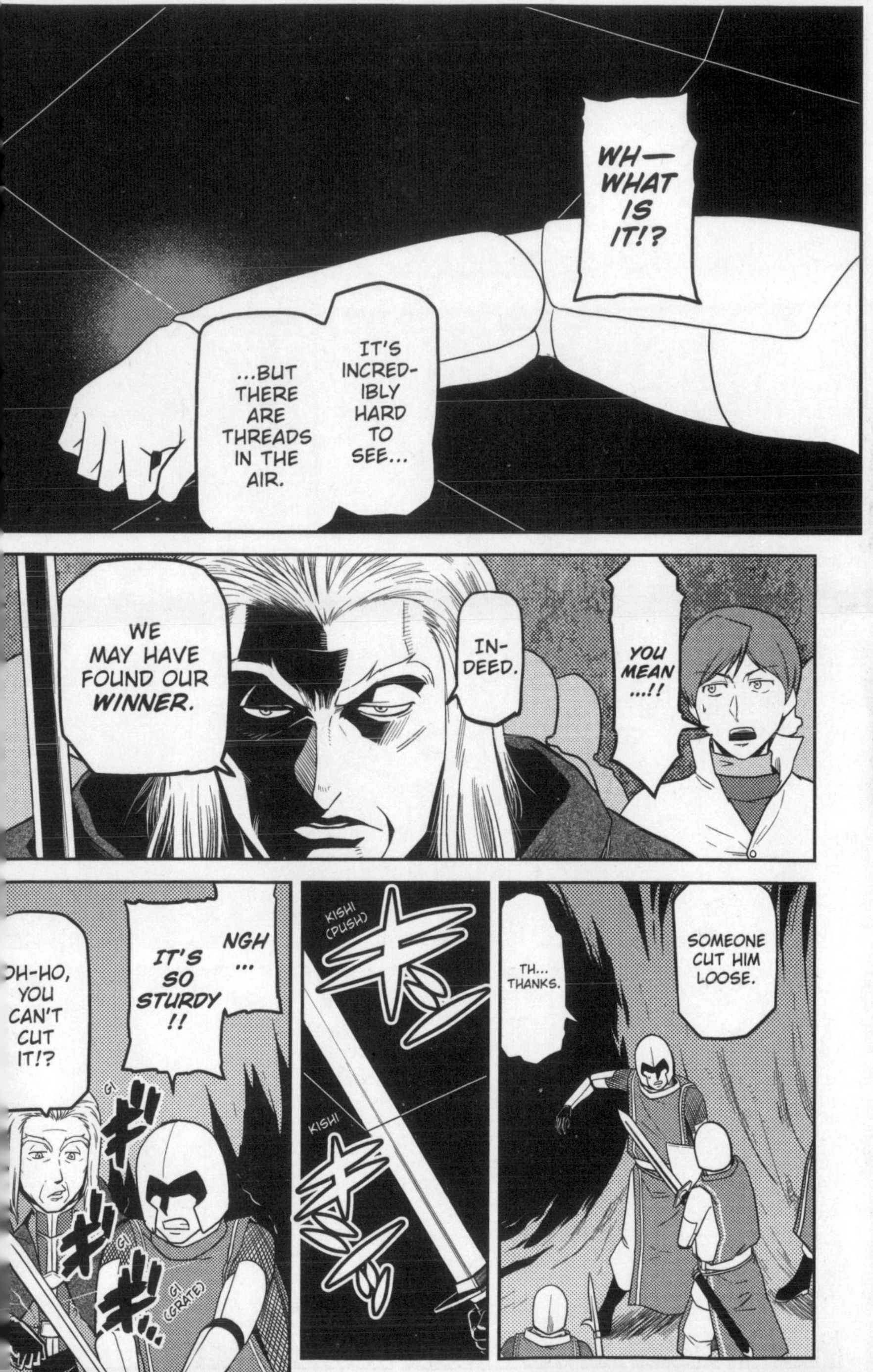
WH— WHAT IS IT!?
IT'S INCRED-IBLY HARD TO SEE...
...BUT THERE ARE THREADS IN THE AIR.
YOU MEAN ...!!
IN-DEED.
WE MAY HAVE FOUND OUR WINNER.
SOMEONE CUT HIM LOOSE.
TH... THANKS.
KISHI (PUSH)
KISHI
NGH ...
IT'S SO STURDY !!
OH-HO, YOU CAN'T CUT IT!?
G (GRATE)

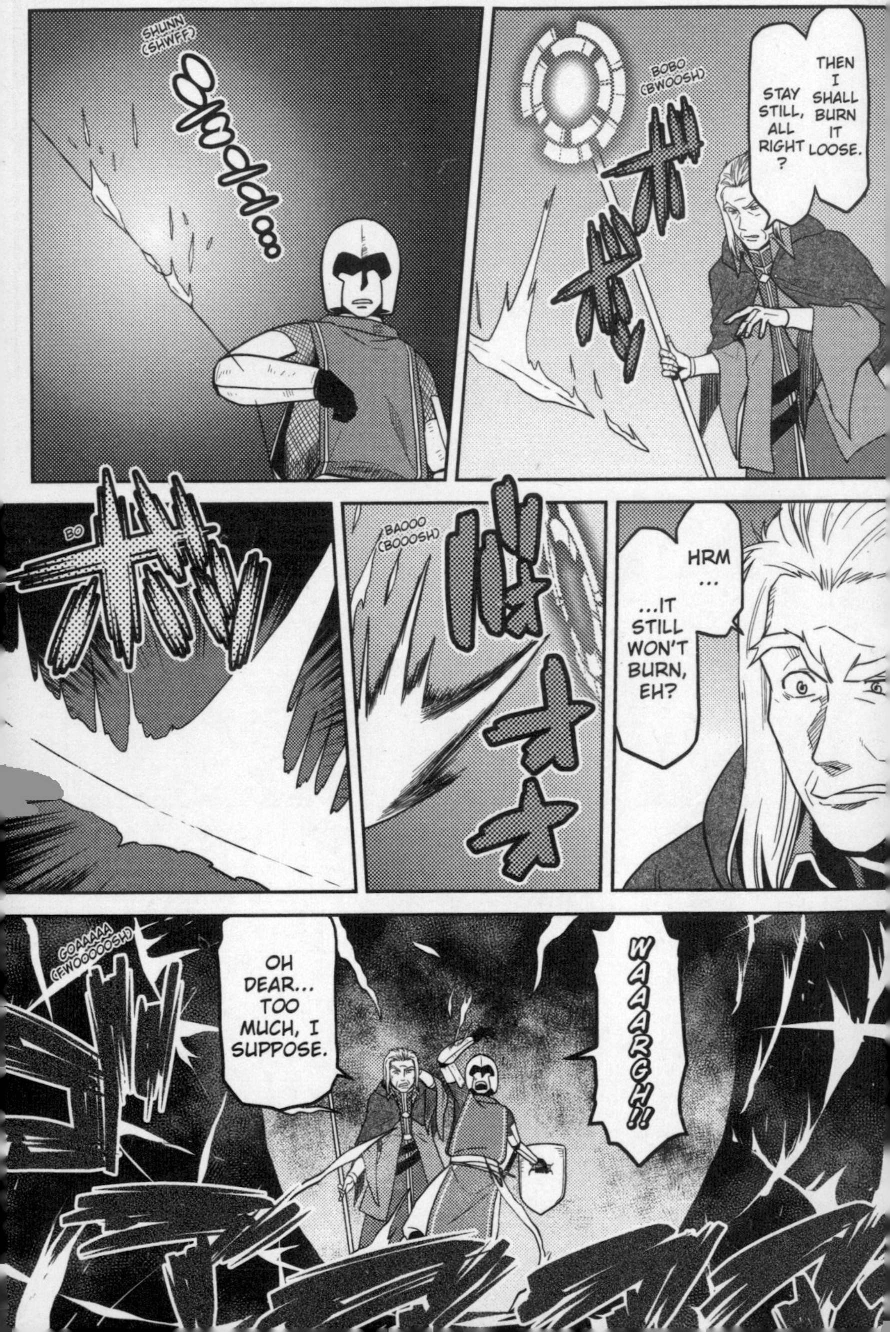
THEN I SHALL BURN IT LOOSE.
STAY STILL, ALL RIGHT?
BOBO (BWOOSH)
SHUNN (SHWFF)
HRM...
...IT STILL WON'T BURN, EH?
BAOOO (BOOOSH)
BO
WAAAARGH!!
OH DEAR... TOO MUCH, I SUPPOSE.
GOAAAAA (FWOOOOOSH)

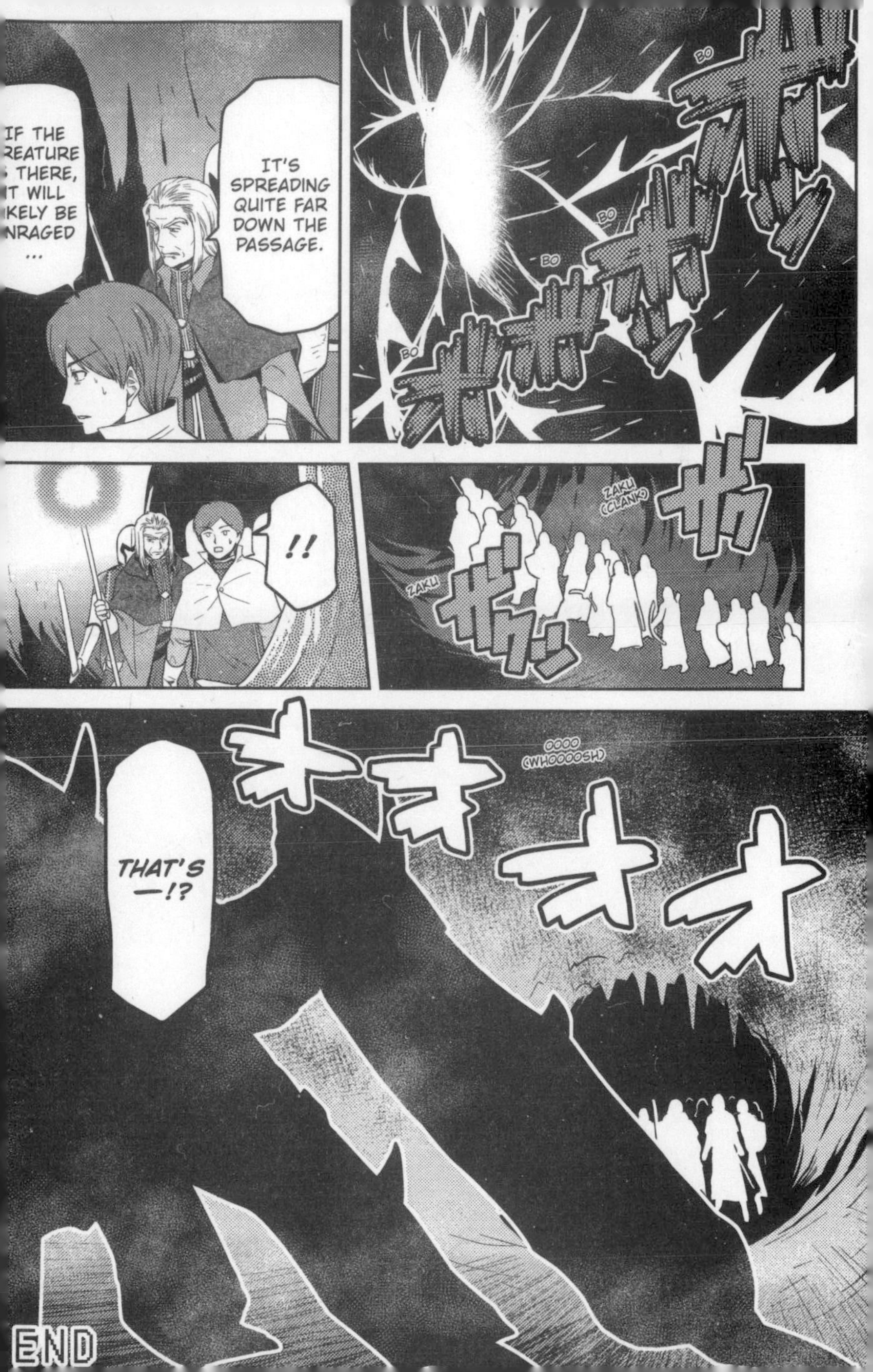
BO
BO
BO
BO
IT'S SPREADING QUITE FAR DOWN THE PASSAGE.
IF THE REATURE S THERE, T WILL KELY BE NRAGED ...
ZAKU (CLANK)
ZAKU
!!
OOOO (WHOOOOSH)
THAT'S —!?
END

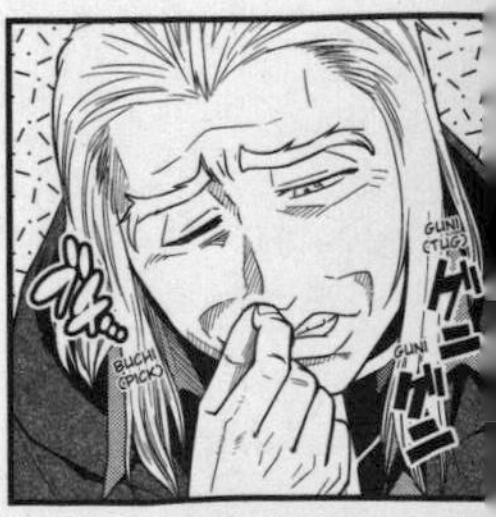
GUNI (TUG)
GUNI
BUCHI (PICK)

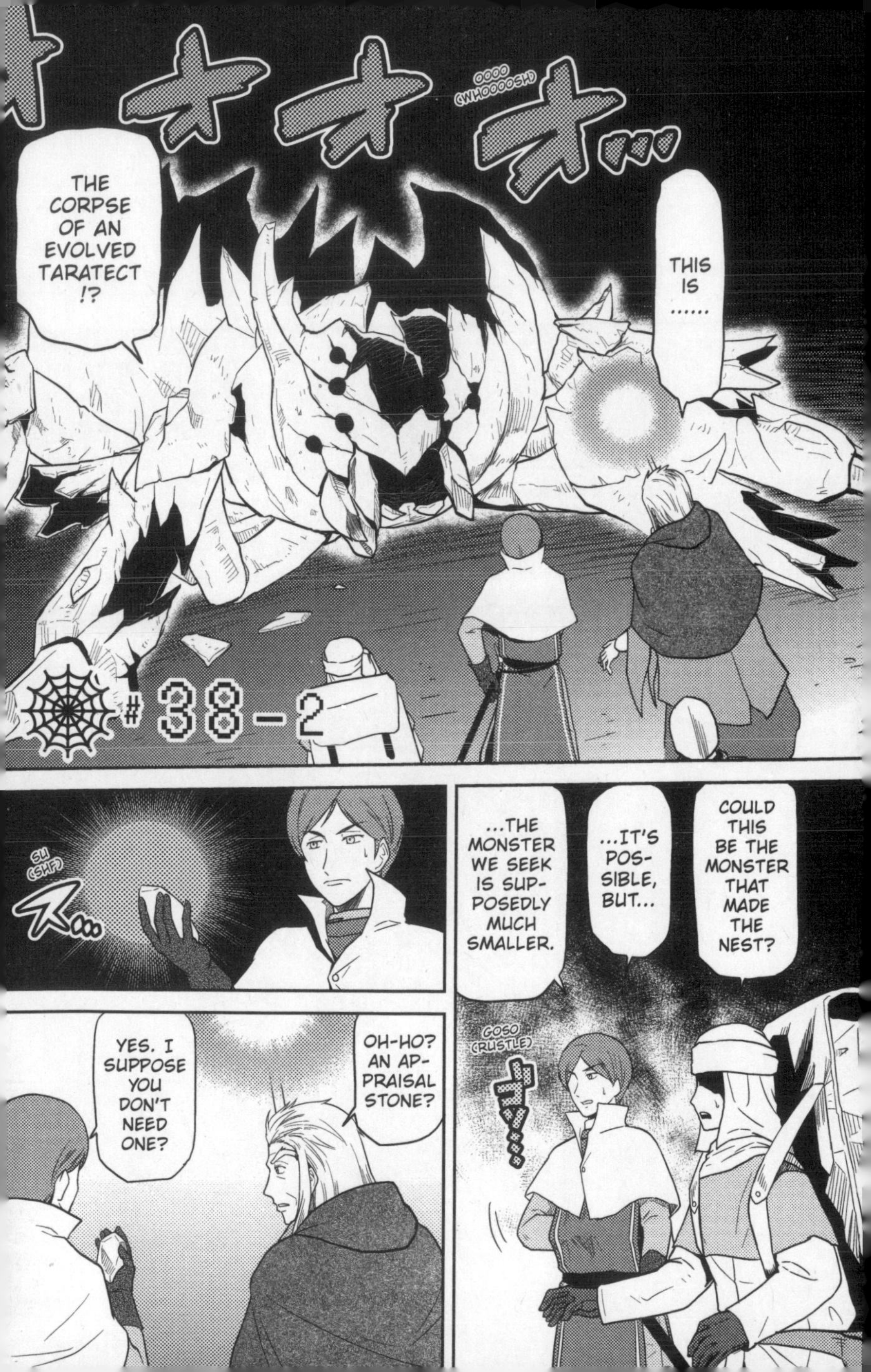
OOOO (WHOOOOSH)
THIS IS ......
THE CORPSE OF AN EVOLVED TARATECT!?
#38-2
COULD THIS BE THE MONSTER THAT MADE THE NEST?
...IT'S POSSIBLE, BUT...
...THE MONSTER WE SEEK IS SUPPOSEDLY MUCH SMALLER.
GOSO (RUSTLE)
SU (SHF)
OH-HO? AN APPRAISAL STONE?
YES. I SUPPOSE YOU DON'T NEED ONE?

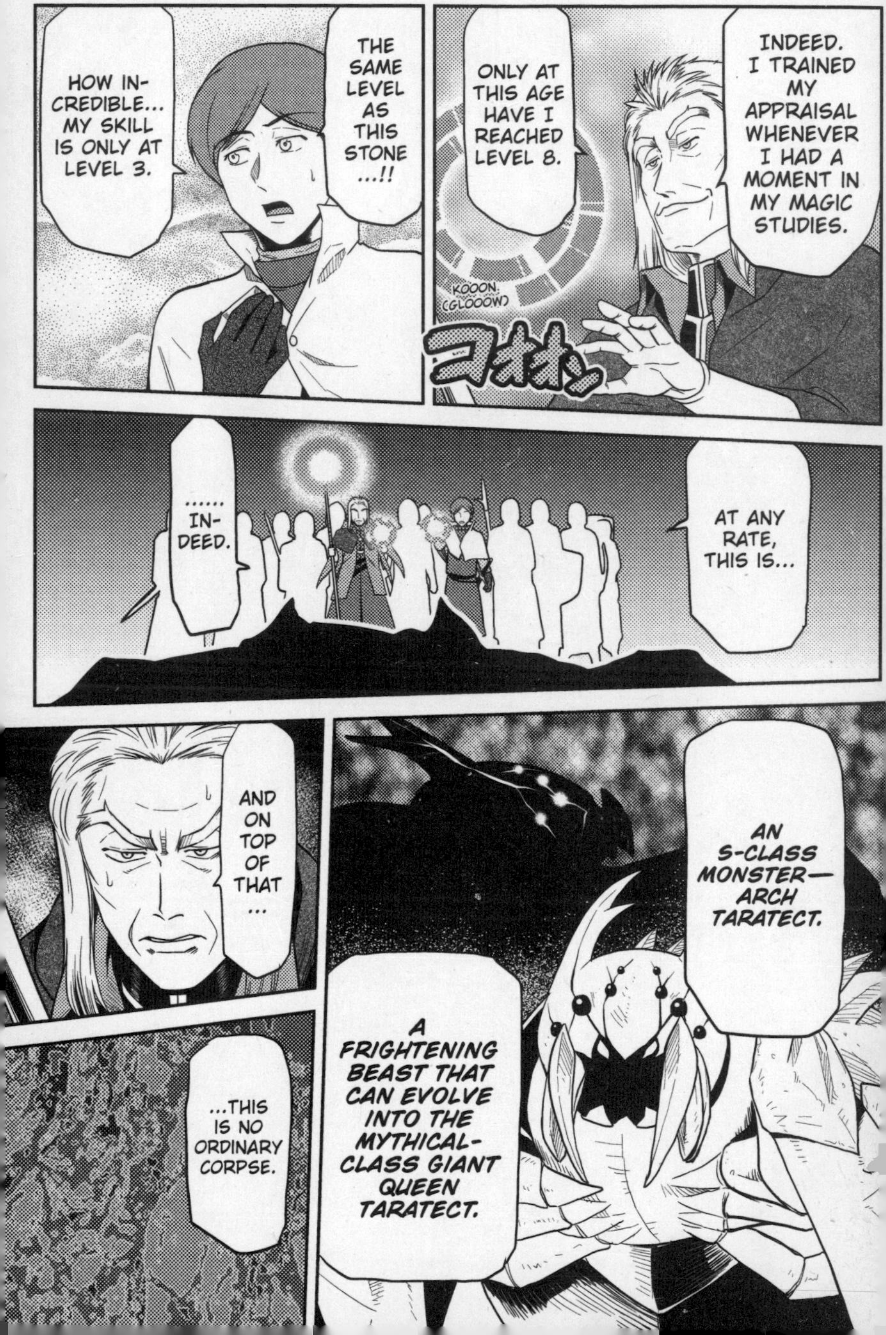
INDEED. I TRAINED MY APPRAISAL WHENEVER I HAD A MOMENT IN MY MAGIC STUDIES.
ONLY AT THIS AGE HAVE I REACHED LEVEL 8.
KOOON (GLOOOW)
THE SAME LEVEL AS THIS STONE ...!!
HOW IN-CREDIBLE... MY SKILL IS ONLY AT LEVEL 3.
AT ANY RATE, THIS IS...
...... IN-DEED.
AN S-CLASS MONSTER— ARCH TARATECT.
A FRIGHTENING BEAST THAT CAN EVOLVE INTO THE MYTHICAL-CLASS GIANT QUEEN TARATECT.
AND ON TOP OF THAT ...
...THIS IS NO ORDINARY CORPSE.

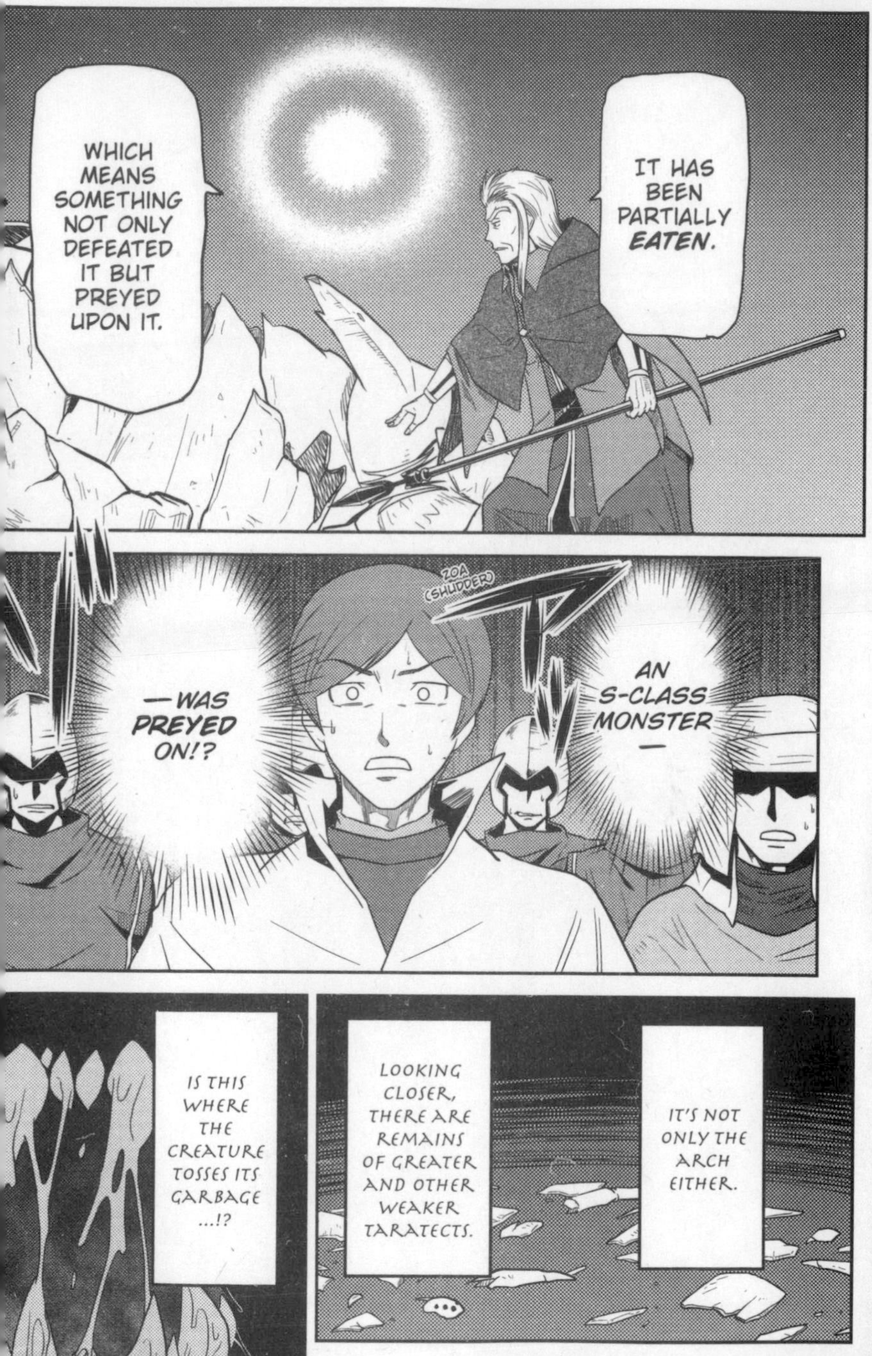
IT HAS BEEN PARTIALLY EATEN.
WHICH MEANS SOMETHING NOT ONLY DEFEATED IT BUT PREYED UPON IT.
ZOA (SHUDDER)
AN S-CLASS MONSTER —
—WAS PREYED ON!?
IT'S NOT ONLY THE ARCH EITHER.
LOOKING CLOSER, THERE ARE REMAINS OF GREATER AND OTHER WEAKER TARATECTS.
IS THIS WHERE THE CREATURE TOSSES ITS GARBAGE ...!?

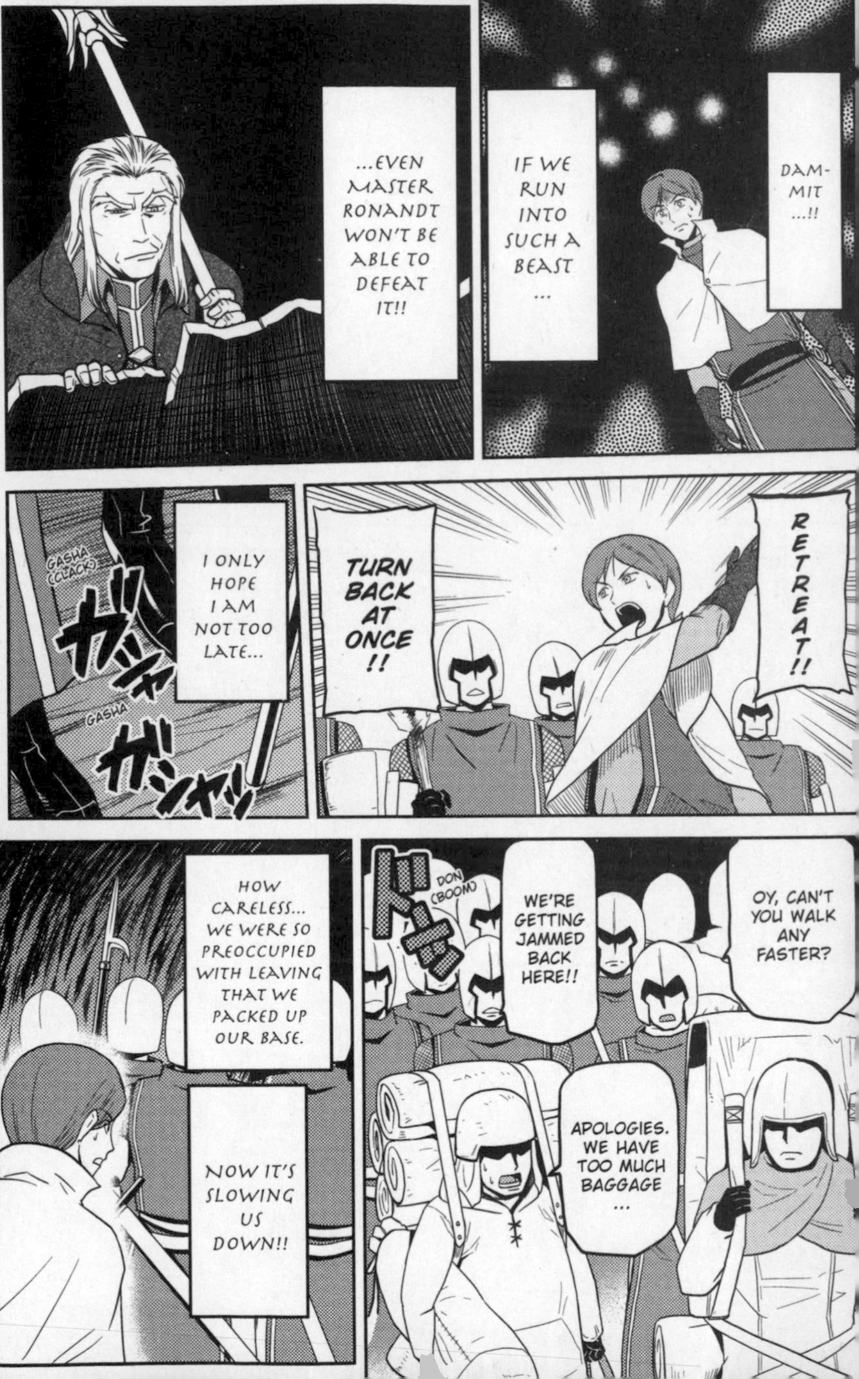
DAM-MIT ...!!
IF WE RUN INTO SUCH A BEAST ...
...EVEN MASTER RONANDT WON'T BE ABLE TO DEFEAT IT!!
RETREAT!!
TURN BACK AT ONCE!!
GASHA (CLACK)
GASHA
I ONLY HOPE I AM NOT TOO LATE...
OY, CAN'T YOU WALK ANY FASTER?
WE'RE GETTING JAMMED BACK HERE!!
DON (BOOM)
APOLOGIES. WE HAVE TOO MUCH BAGGAGE ...
HOW CARELESS... WE WERE SO PREOCCUPIED WITH LEAVING THAT WE PACKED UP OUR BASE.
NOW IT'S SLOWING US DOWN!!

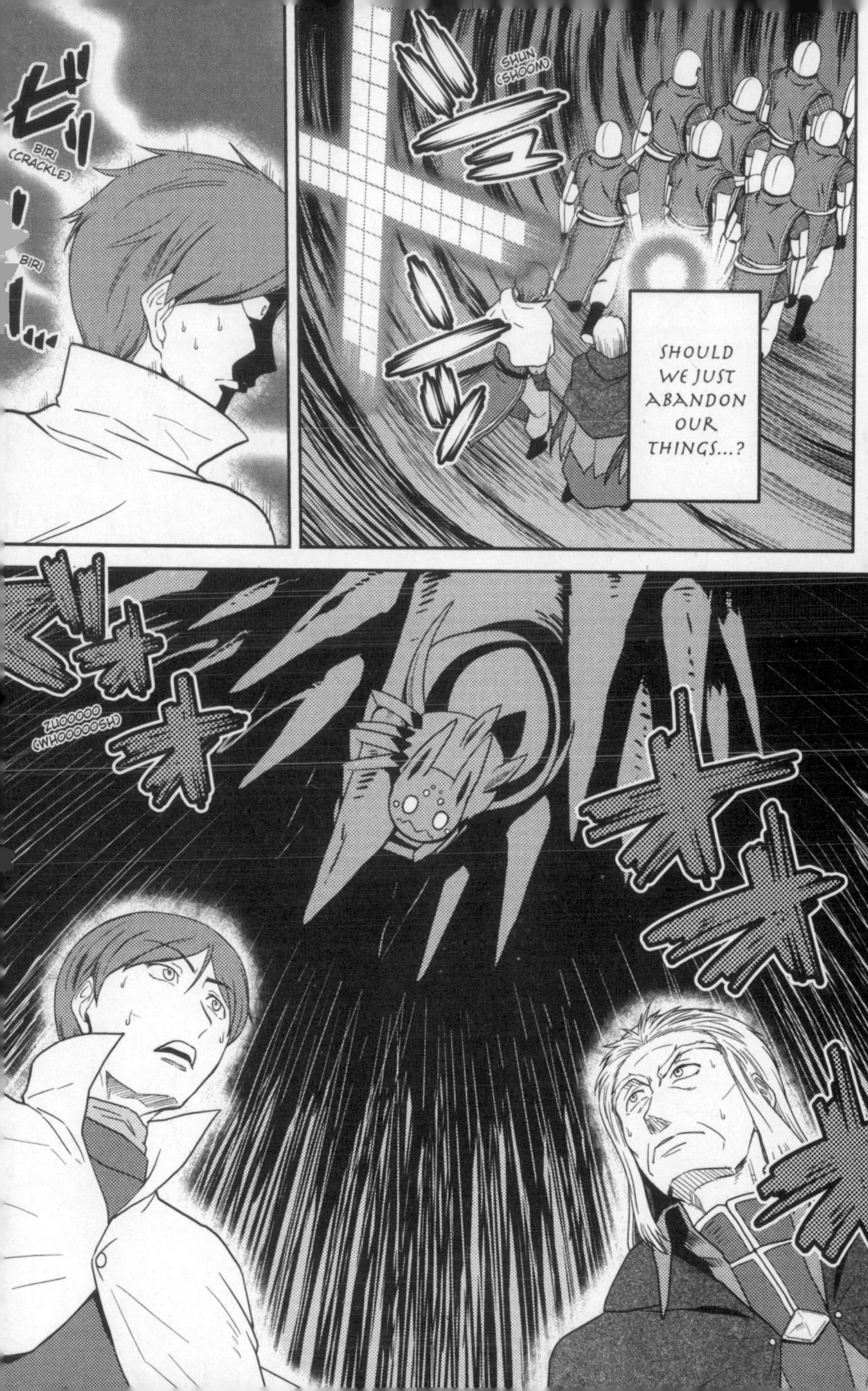
SHUN (SHOOM)
SHOULD WE JUST ABANDON OUR THINGS...?
BIRI (CRACKLE)
BIRI
ZUOOOOO (WHOOOOOSH)

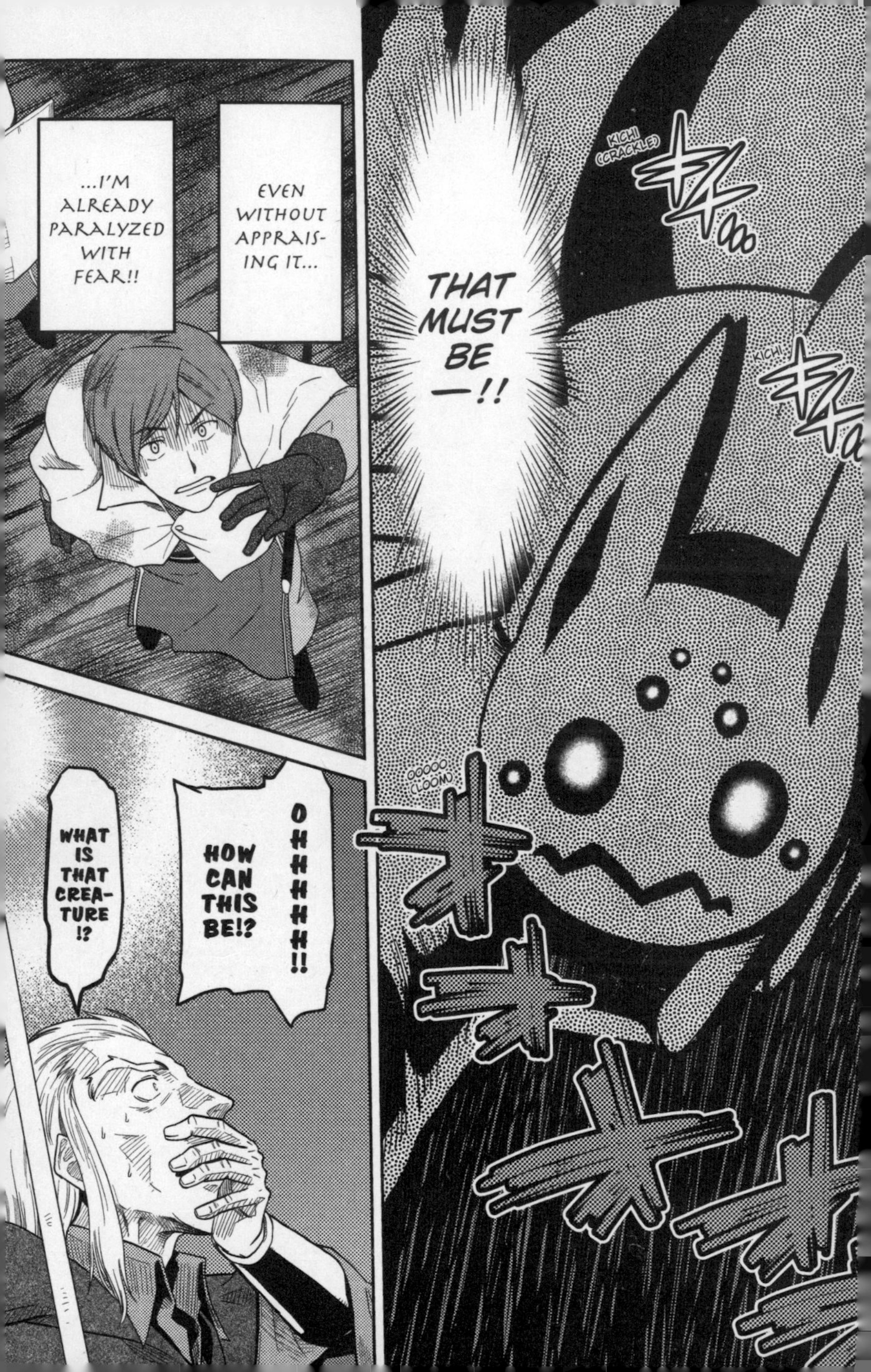
KICHI (CRACKLE)
THAT MUST BE—!!
KICHI
OOOOO (LOOM)
EVEN WITHOUT APPRAISING IT...
...I'M ALREADY PARALYZED WITH FEAR!!
OHHHHHH!!
HOW CAN THIS BE!?
WHAT IS THAT CREATURE!?

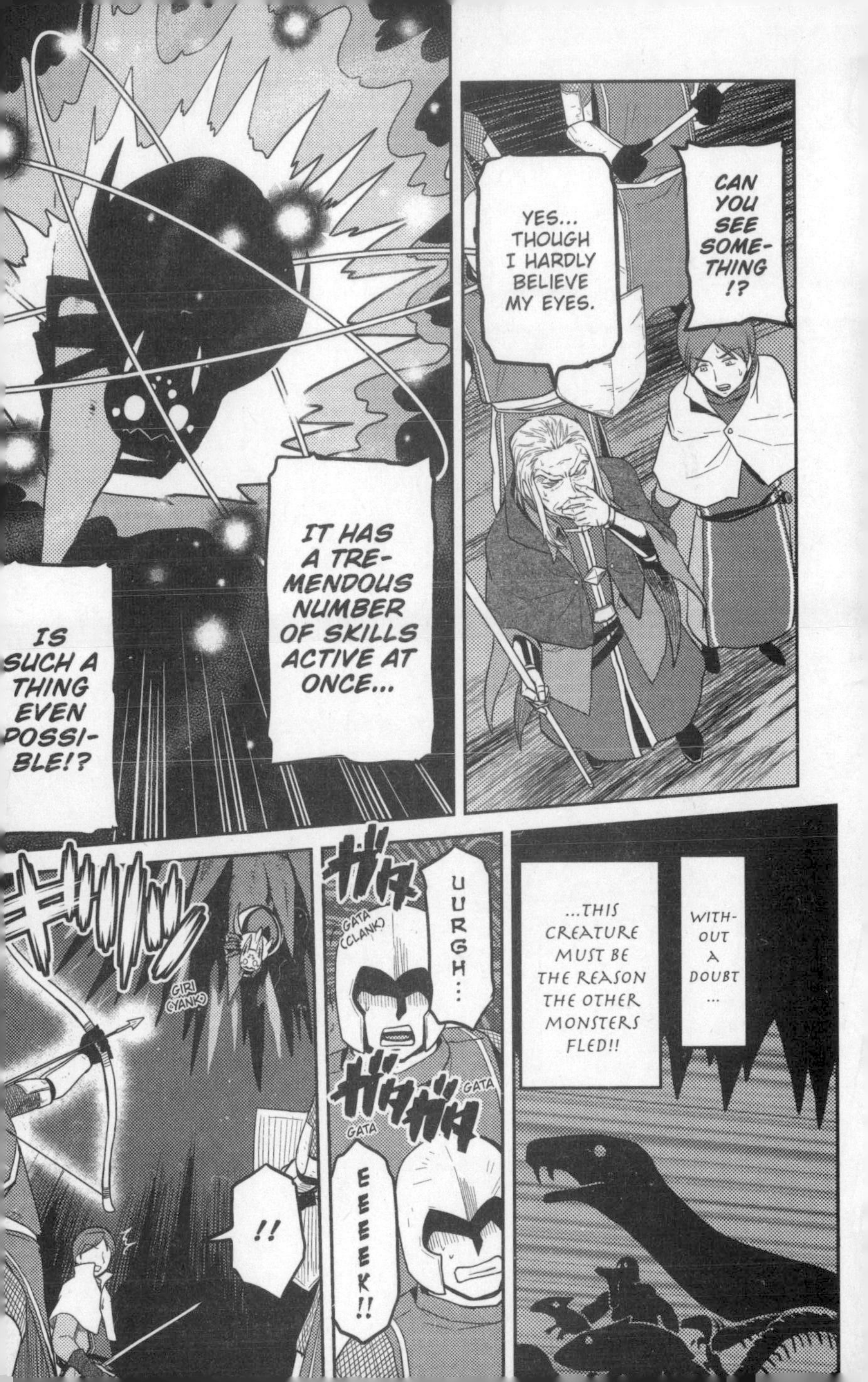
CAN YOU SEE SOME-THING!?
YES... THOUGH I HARDLY BELIEVE MY EYES.
IT HAS A TRE-MENDOUS NUMBER OF SKILLS ACTIVE AT ONCE...
IS SUCH A THING EVEN POSSI-BLE!?
WITH-OUT A DOUBT...
...THIS CREATURE MUST BE THE REASON THE OTHER MONSTERS FLED!!
ガタ
GATA (CLANK)
UURGH...
ガタガタ
GATA GATA
EEEEEK!!
GIRI (YANK)
!!

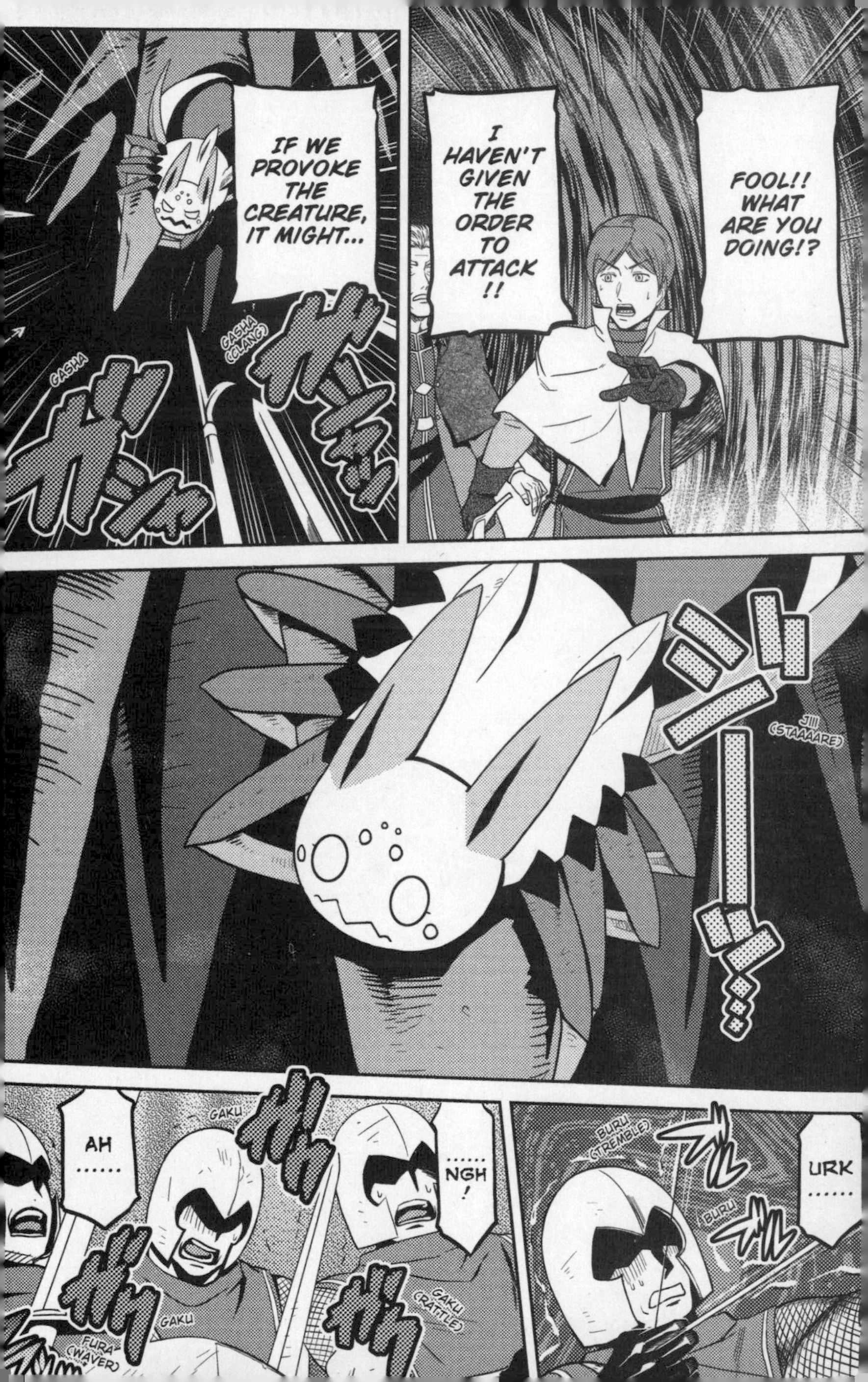
FOOL!! WHAT ARE YOU DOING!?
I HAVEN'T GIVEN THE ORDER TO ATTACK!!
IF WE PROVOKE THE CREATURE, IT MIGHT...
GASHA (CLANG)
GASHA
JIII (STAAAARE)
URK ......
BURU (TREMBLE)
BURU
...... NGH!
GAKU
AH ......
GAKU (RATTLE)
GAKU
FURA (WAVER)

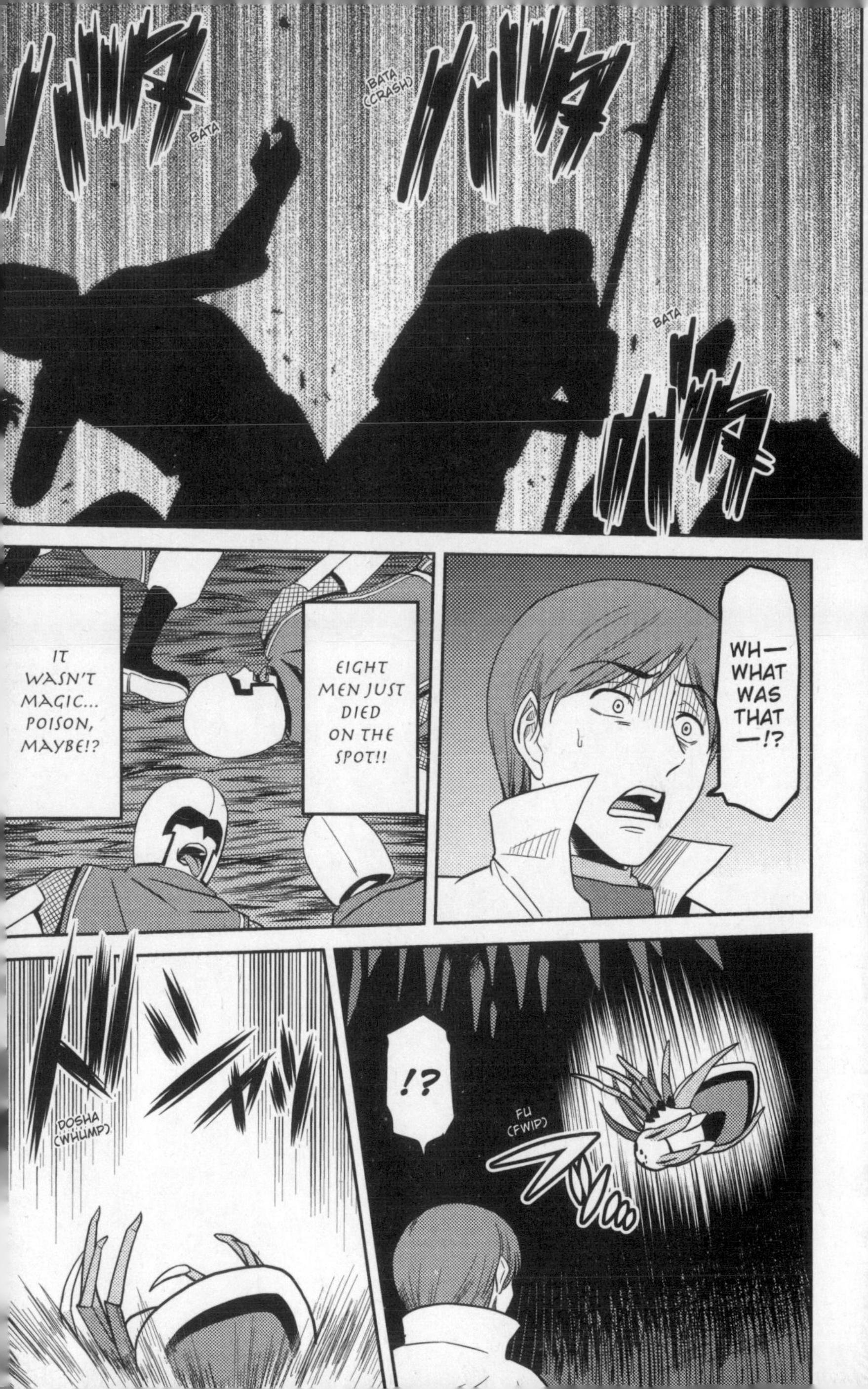
BATA (CRASH)
BATA
BATA
WH— WHAT WAS THAT —!?
EIGHT MEN JUST DIED ON THE SPOT!!
IT WASN'T MAGIC... POISON, MAYBE!?
!?
FU (FWIP)
DOSHA (WHUMP)

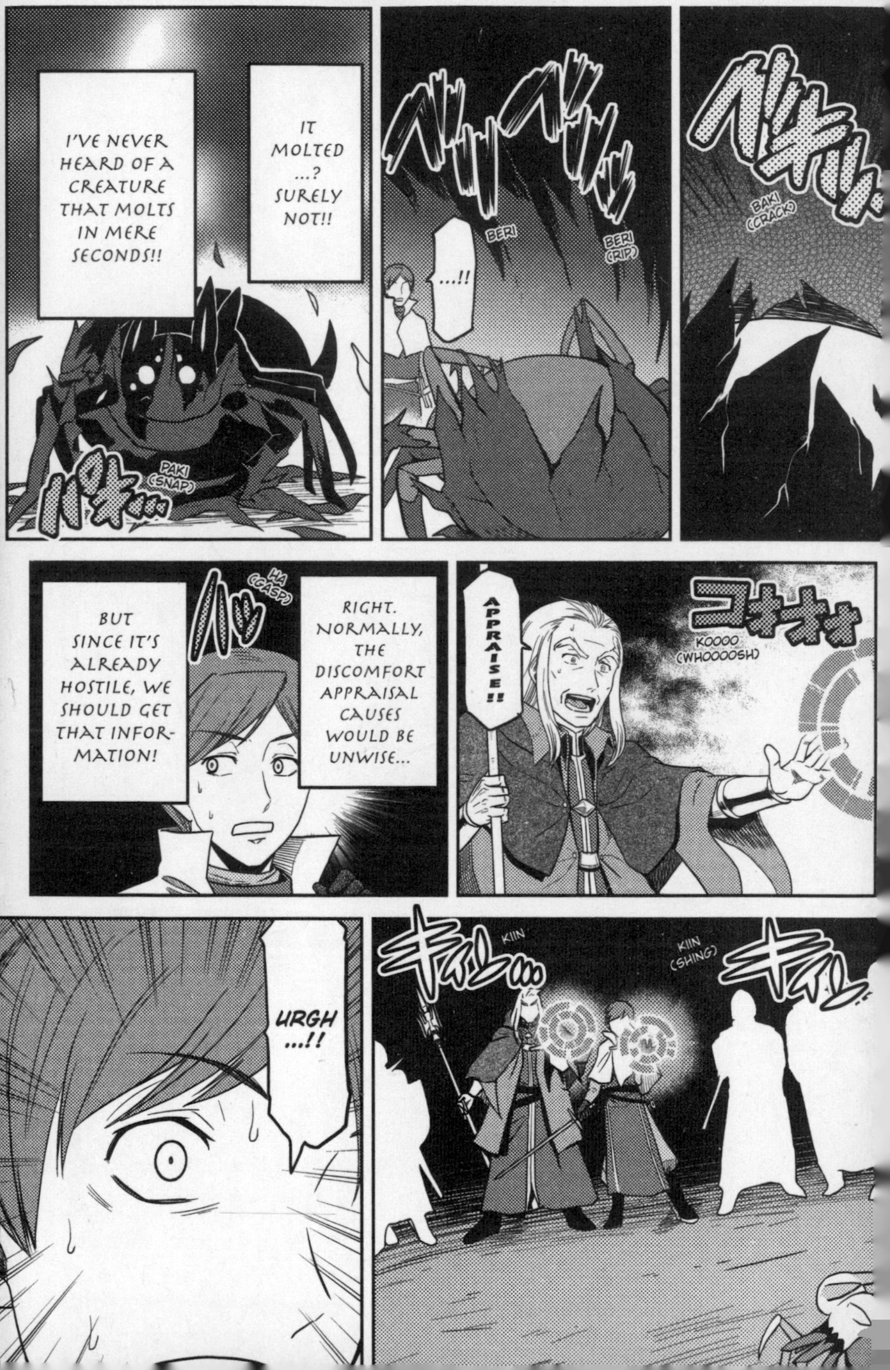
BAKI (CRACK)
BERI
BERI (RIP)
...!!
IT MOLTED ...? SURELY NOT!!
I'VE NEVER HEARD OF A CREATURE THAT MOLTS IN MERE SECONDS!!
PAKI (SNAP)
KOOOO (WHOOOOSH)
APPRAISE!!
HA (GASP)
RIGHT. NORMALLY, THE DISCOMFORT APPRAISAL CAUSES WOULD BE UNWISE...
BUT SINCE IT'S ALREADY HOSTILE, WE SHOULD GET THAT INFORMATION!
KIIN (SHING)
KIIN
URGH ...!!

[Rapid Recovery LV 7]

[Power Conferment LV 7]

[...ction Enhancement LV 6]

[...y Conferment LV 5]

[...ttack LV 4]

[...cine Synthesis LV 7]

[...nesis LV 1]

[...aneuvering LV 8]

[...rocessing LV 6]

[...d LV 7]

[... 8]

[... 10]

[Height of Occultism]

[SP Rapid Recovery LV 1]

[Cutting Enhancement LV 8]

[Dragon Power LV 7]

[Heretic Attack LV 6]

[Utility Thread LV 6]

[Throw LV 10]

[Concentration LV 10]

[Hit LV 8]

[St...

[...byss Magic LV 10]

[...rath LV 2]

[Magic Divinity LV 2]

[SP Minimized Consumption LV 1]

[Status Condition Super-Enhancement LV 1]

[Deadly Poison Attack LV 6]

[Poison Synthesis LV 10]

[Thread Control LV 10]

[Expel LV 2]

[Parallel Minds LV 7]

[Evasion LV 10]

[Camouflage LV 1]

[Conviction]

[Heretic Magic LV 10]

[Black Magic LV 2]

[Spatial Magic LV 10]

[Perseverance]

[Satiation LV 7]

[...estruction Resistance LV 5]

[...esistance LV 2]

[...istan...

[... ltifi...

[...oyan...

[...epellent]

[Perceptio...

[Ultimate...

[Fortitude...

[...st ...ance L... 5]

[Super... ...istance L... 3]

[Resistance LV 5]

[...uper-Mitigation LV 5]

[...vil Eye LV 6]

[...lating Evil Eye LV 3]

[...ty Expansion LV 6]

[...t Body LV 7]

[...hold LV 2]

[...esistance LV 5]

[...ance LV 6]

[...stance LV 9]

[Nigh... ...on LV 10]

[Inert Evil Eye LV 5]

[Five Senses Super-Enhancement LV 1]

[Celestial Power]

[Endurance LV 7]

[Skanda LV 7]

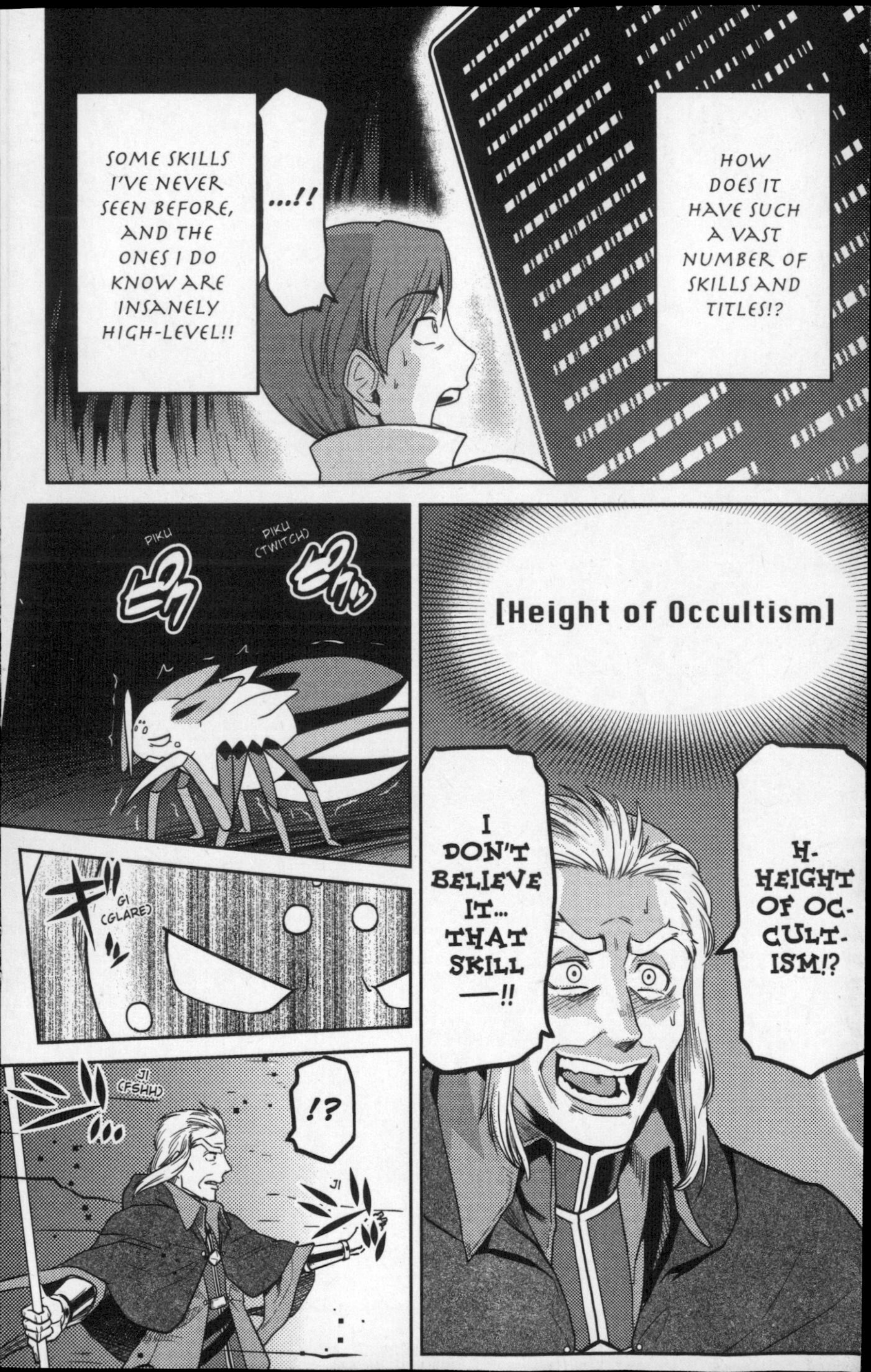
HOW DOES IT HAVE SUCH A VAST NUMBER OF SKILLS AND TITLES!?
...!!
SOME SKILLS I'VE NEVER SEEN BEFORE, AND THE ONES I DO KNOW ARE INSANELY HIGH-LEVEL!!
[Height of Occultism]
H-HEIGHT OF OC-CULT-ISM!?
I DON'T BELIEVE IT... THAT SKILL—!!
PIKU (TWITCH)
PIKU
GI (GLARE)
JI (FSHH)
!?
JI

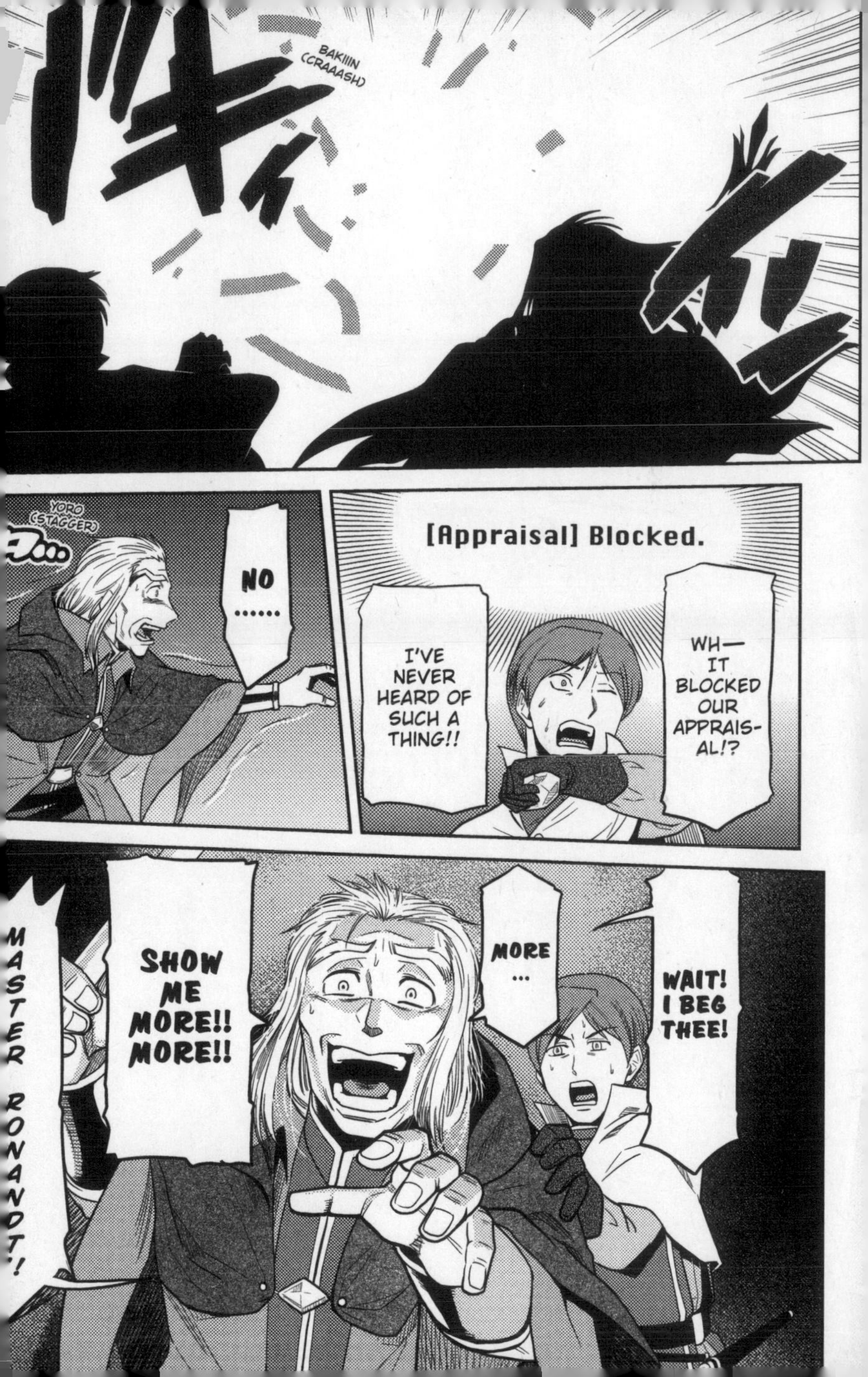
BAKIIN (CRAAASH)
[Appraisal] Blocked.
WH— IT BLOCKED OUR APPRAIS-AL!?
I'VE NEVER HEARD OF SUCH A THING!!
YORO (STAGGER)
NO ......
WAIT! I BEG THEE!
MORE ...
SHOW ME MORE!! MORE!!
MASTER RONANDT!

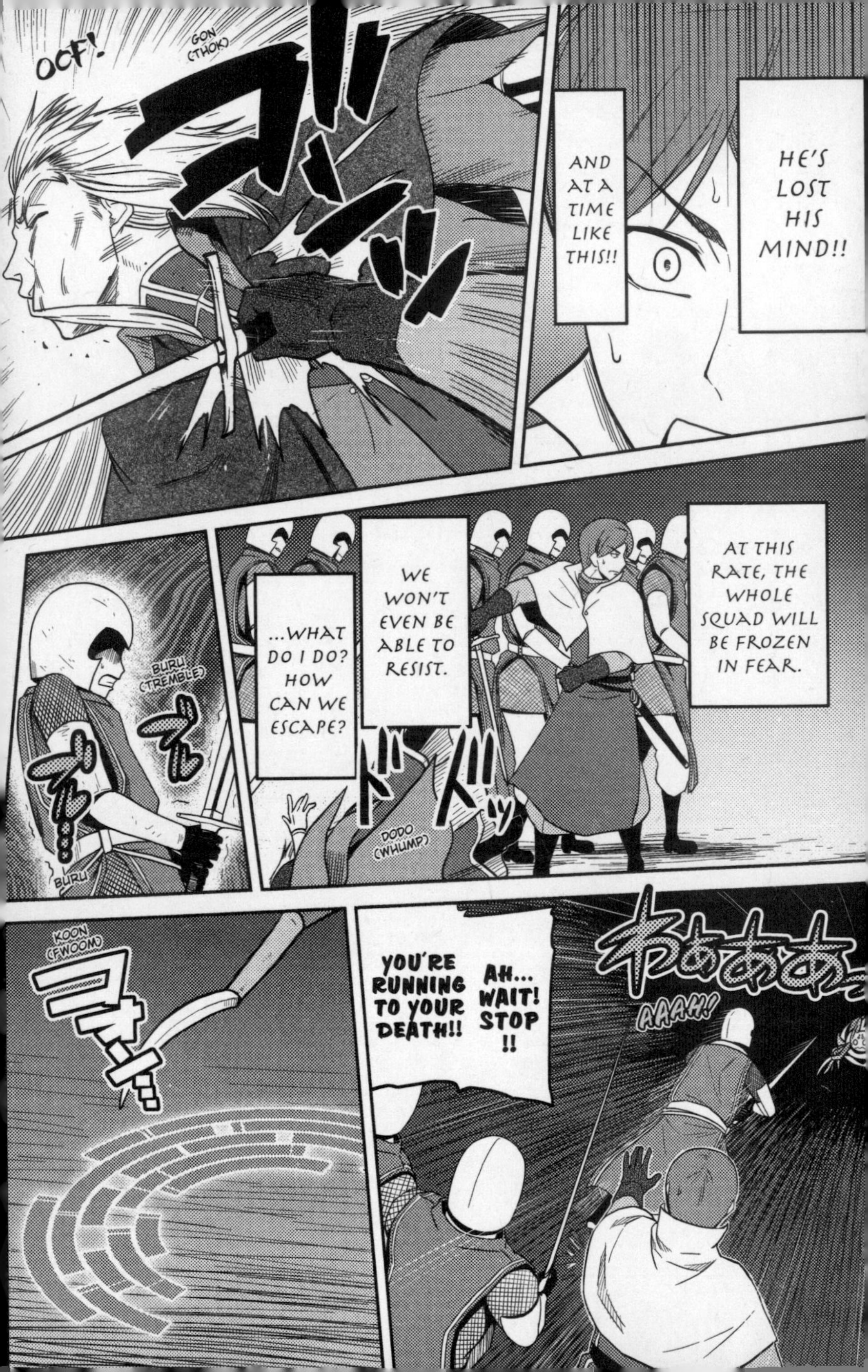
HE'S LOST HIS MIND!!
AND AT A TIME LIKE THIS!!
GON (THOK)
OCF!
AT THIS RATE, THE WHOLE SQUAD WILL BE FROZEN IN FEAR.
WE WON'T EVEN BE ABLE TO RESIST.
...WHAT DO I DO? HOW CAN WE ESCAPE?
DODO (WHUMP)
BURU (TREMBLE)
BURU
AH... WAIT! STOP !!
YOU'RE RUNNING TO YOUR DEATH!!
AAAH!
KOON (FWOOM)

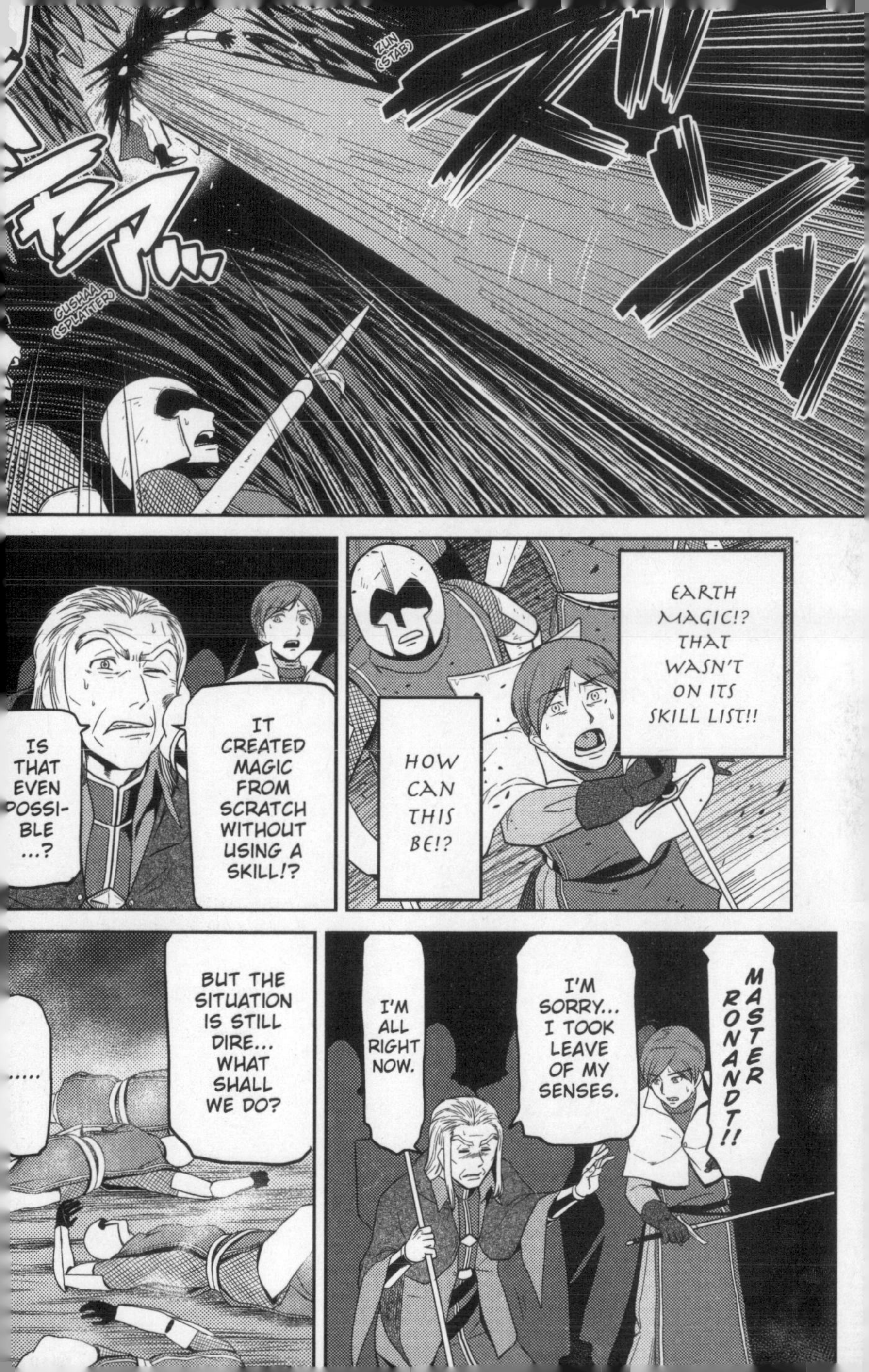
ZUN (STAB)
GUSHAA (SPLATTER)
EARTH MAGIC!? THAT WASN'T ON ITS SKILL LIST!!
HOW CAN THIS BE!?
IT CREATED MAGIC FROM SCRATCH WITHOUT USING A SKILL!?
IS THAT EVEN POSSI-BLE ...?
MASTER RONANDT!!
I'M SORRY... I TOOK LEAVE OF MY SENSES.
I'M ALL RIGHT NOW.
BUT THE SITUATION IS STILL DIRE... WHAT SHALL WE DO?
......

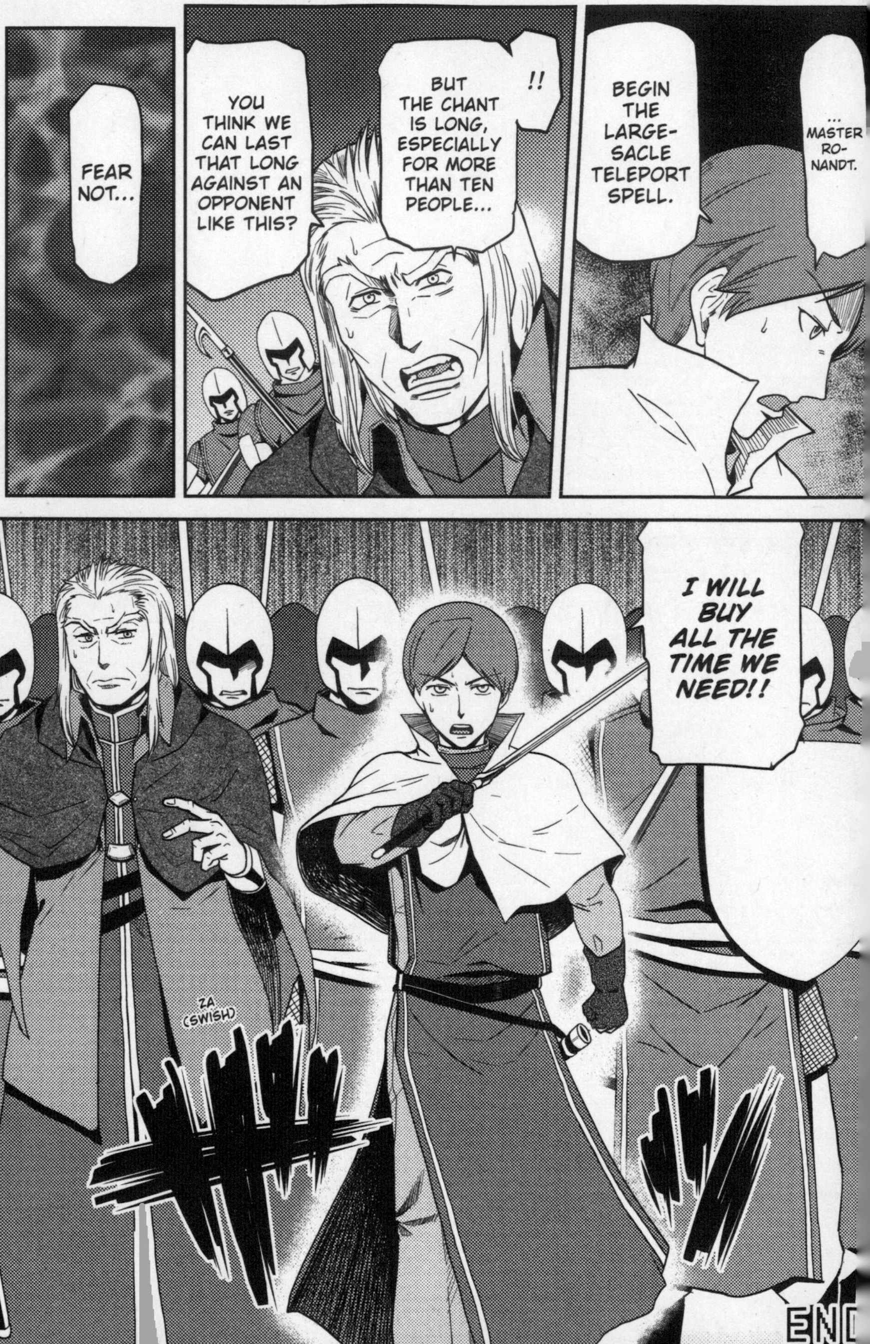

... MASTER RONANDT.
BEGIN THE LARGE-SACLE TELEPORT SPELL.
!!
BUT THE CHANT IS LONG, ESPECIALLY FOR MORE THAN TEN PEOPLE...
YOU THINK WE CAN LAST THAT LONG AGAINST AN OPPONENT LIKE THIS?
FEAR NOT...
I WILL BUY ALL THE TIME WE NEED!!
ZA (SWISH)
END

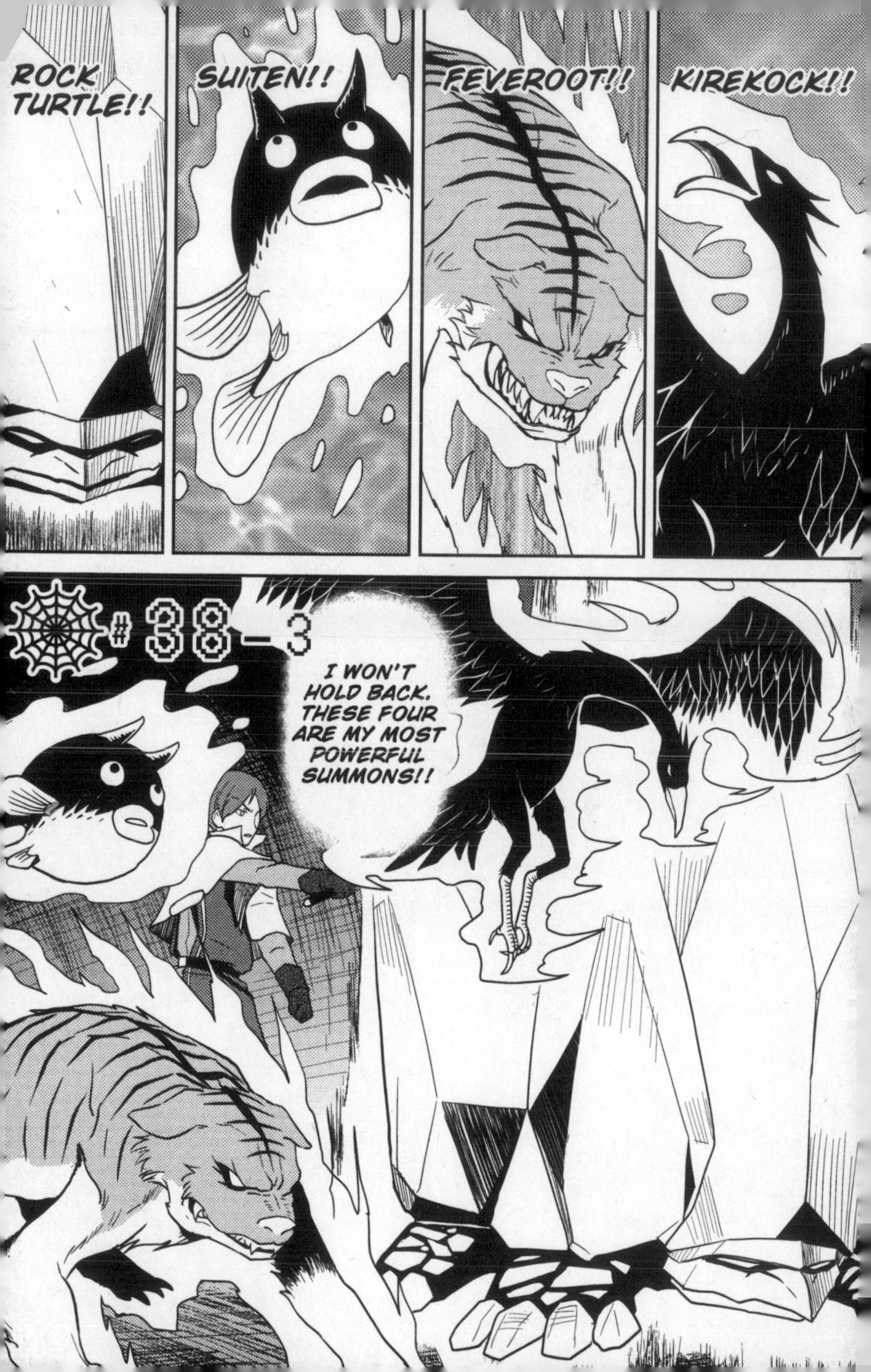
KIREKOCK!!
FEVEROOT!!
SUITEN!!
ROCK TURTLE!!
I WON'T HOLD BACK. THESE FOUR ARE MY MOST POWERFUL SUMMONS!!
#38-3

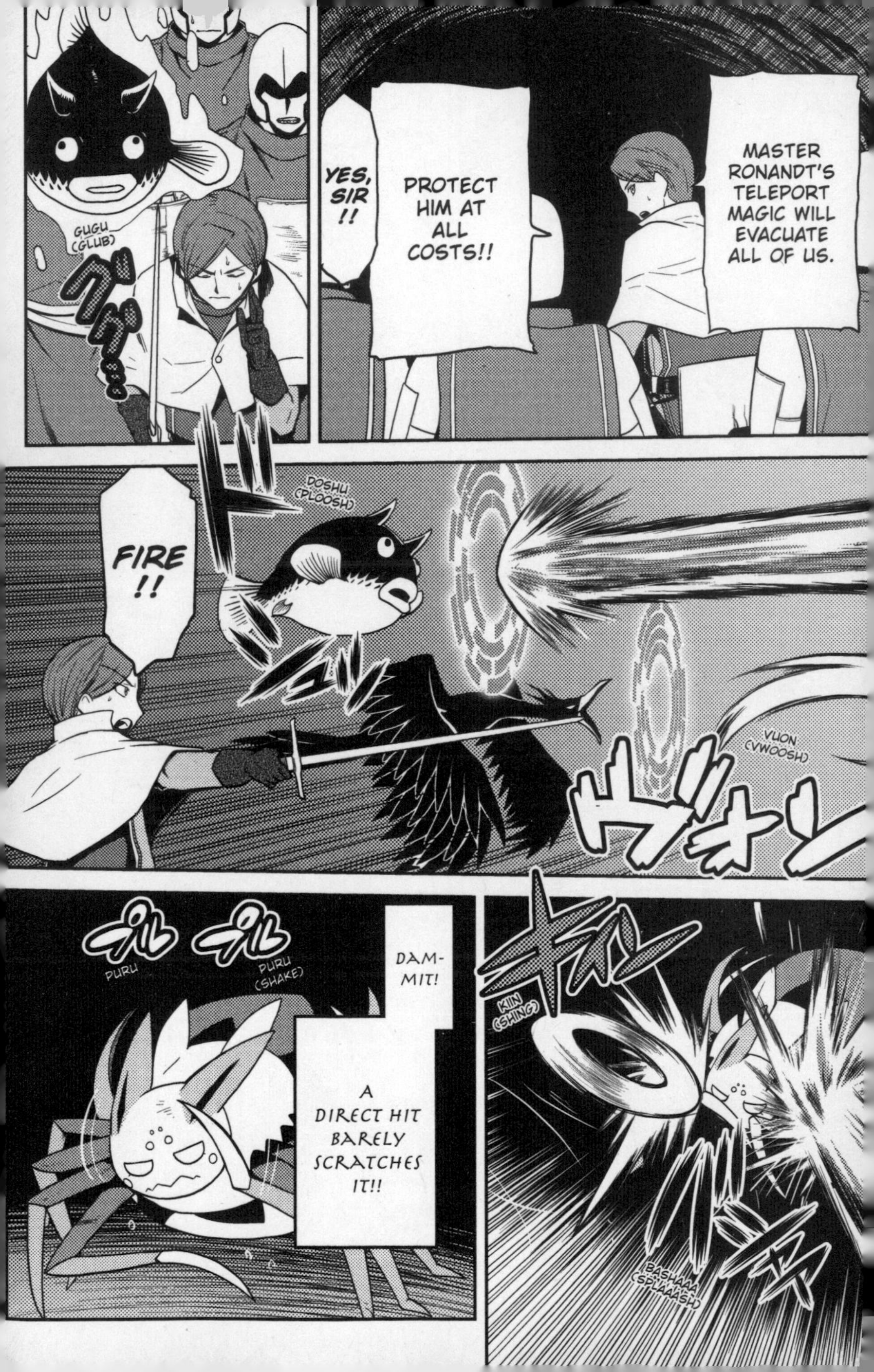
MASTER RONANDT'S TELEPORT MAGIC WILL EVACUATE ALL OF US.
PROTECT HIM AT ALL COSTS!!
YES, SIR!!
GUGU (GLUB)
DOSHU (PLOOSH)
FIRE!!
VUON (VWOOSH)
KIN (SHING)
BASHAAA (SPLAAASH)
DAM-MIT!
A DIRECT HIT BARELY SCRATCHES IT!!
PURU PURU (SHAKE)

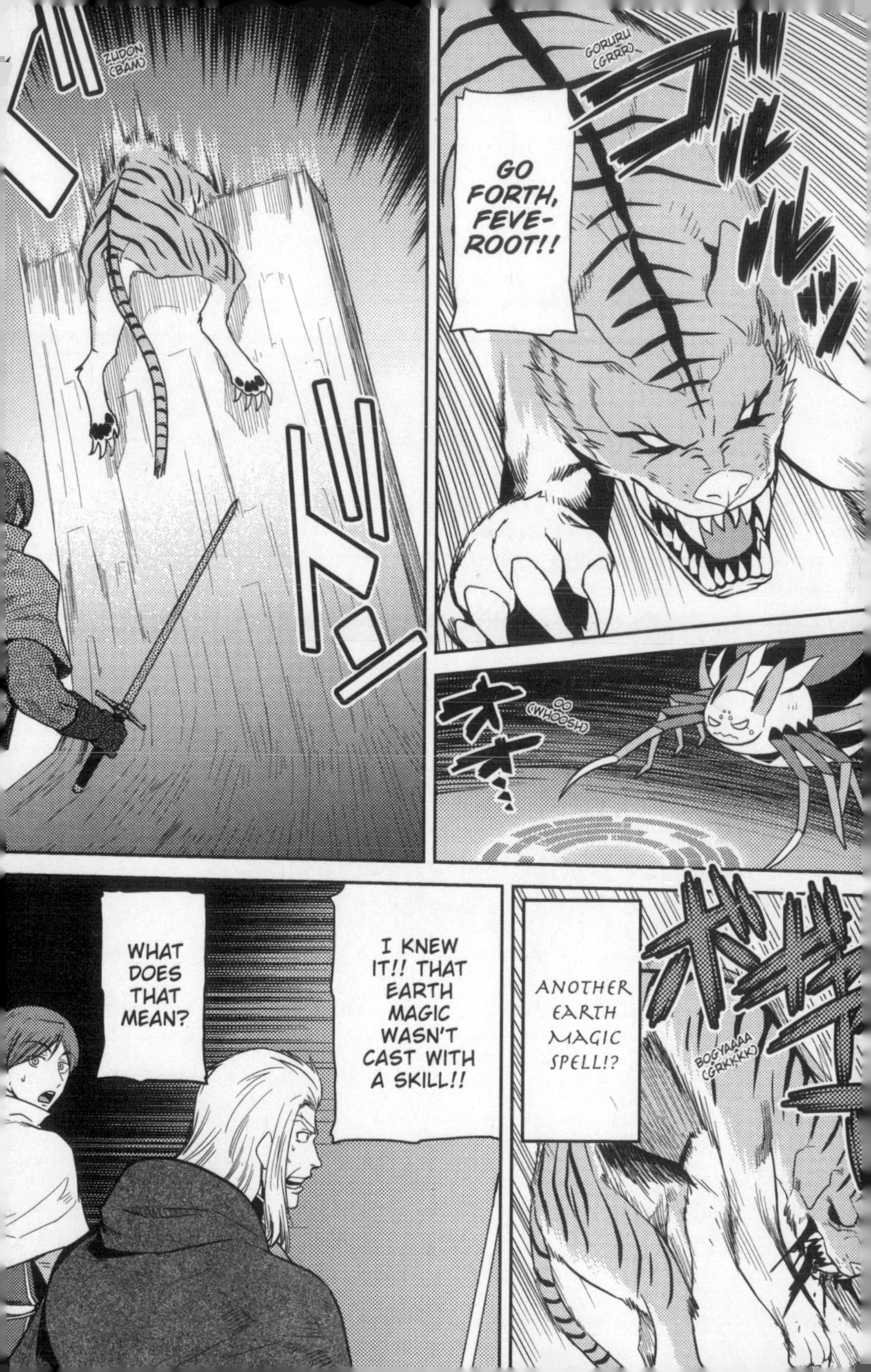
GORURU (GRRR)
GO FORTH, FEVE-ROOT!!
OO (WHOOSH)
ZUDON (BAM)
ANOTHER EARTH MAGIC SPELL!?
BOGYAAAA (GRKKKK)
I KNEW IT!! THAT EARTH MAGIC WASN'T CAST WITH A SKILL!!
WHAT DOES THAT MEAN?

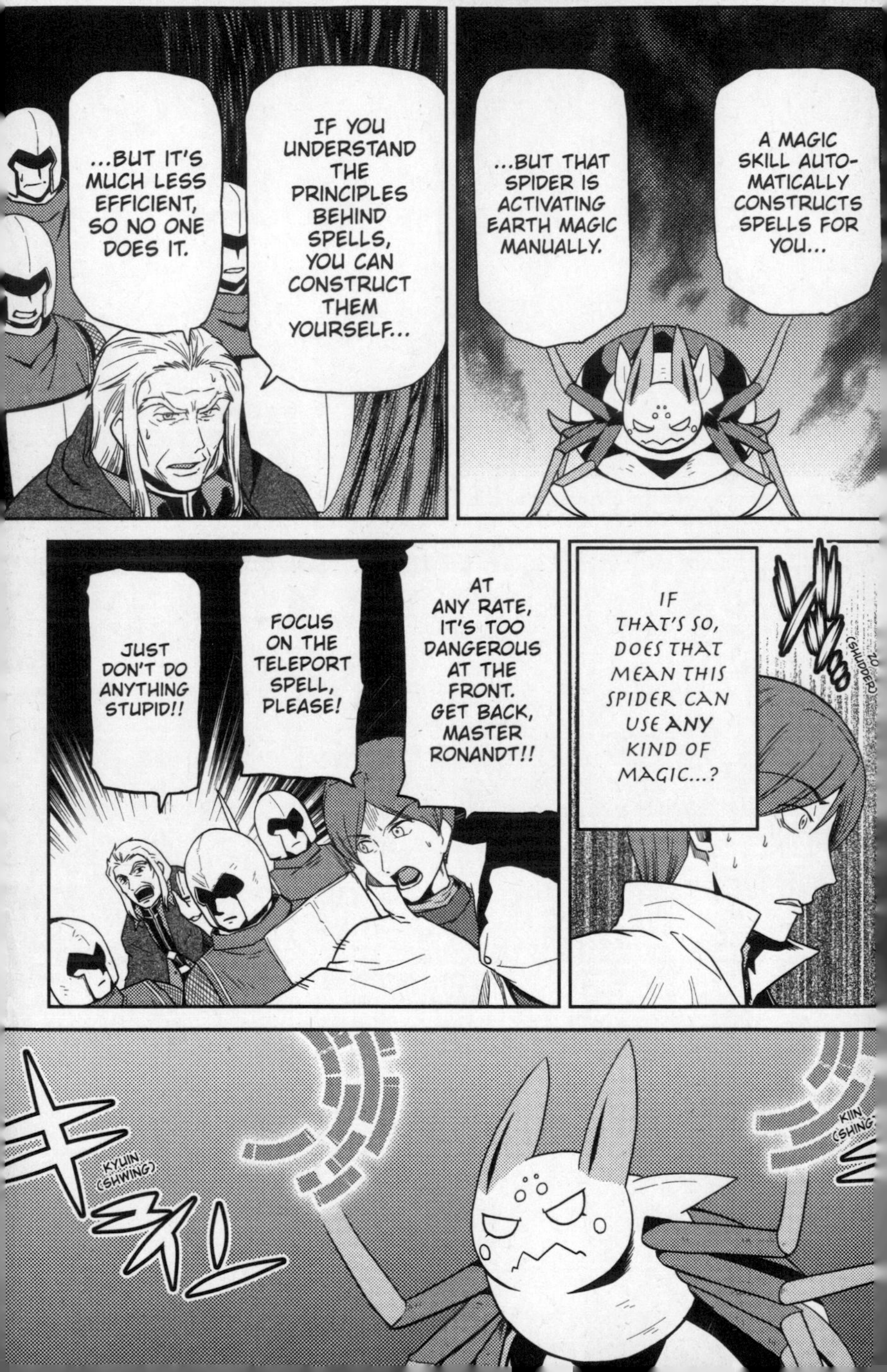
A MAGIC SKILL AUTO-MATICALLY CONSTRUCTS SPELLS FOR YOU...
...BUT THAT SPIDER IS ACTIVATING EARTH MAGIC MANUALLY.
IF YOU UNDERSTAND THE PRINCIPLES BEHIND SPELLS, YOU CAN CONSTRUCT THEM YOURSELF...
...BUT IT'S MUCH LESS EFFICIENT, SO NO ONE DOES IT.
ZO (SHUDDER)
IF THAT'S SO, DOES THAT MEAN THIS SPIDER CAN USE ANY KIND OF MAGIC...?
AT ANY RATE, IT'S TOO DANGEROUS AT THE FRONT. GET BACK, MASTER RONANDT!!
FOCUS ON THE TELEPORT SPELL, PLEASE!
JUST DON'T DO ANYTHING STUPID!!
KIIN (SHING)
KYUIN (SHWING)

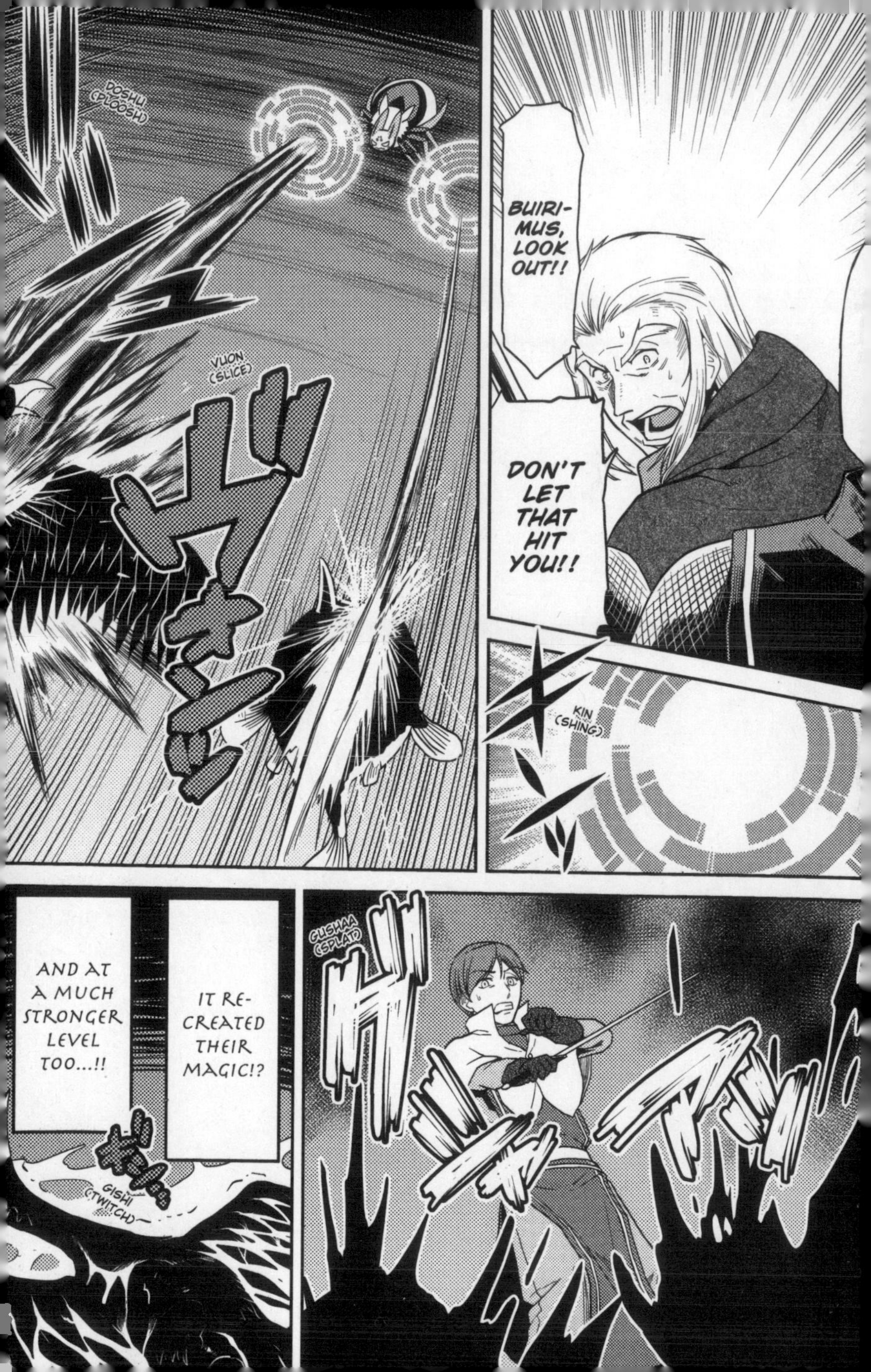
BUIRI-MUS, LOOK OUT!!
DON'T LET THAT HIT YOU!!
KIN (SHING)
DOSHU (PLOOSH)
VUON (SLICE)
GUSHAA (SPLAT)
IT RE-CREATED THEIR MAGIC!?
AND AT A MUCH STRONGER LEVEL TOO...!!
GISHI (TWITCH)

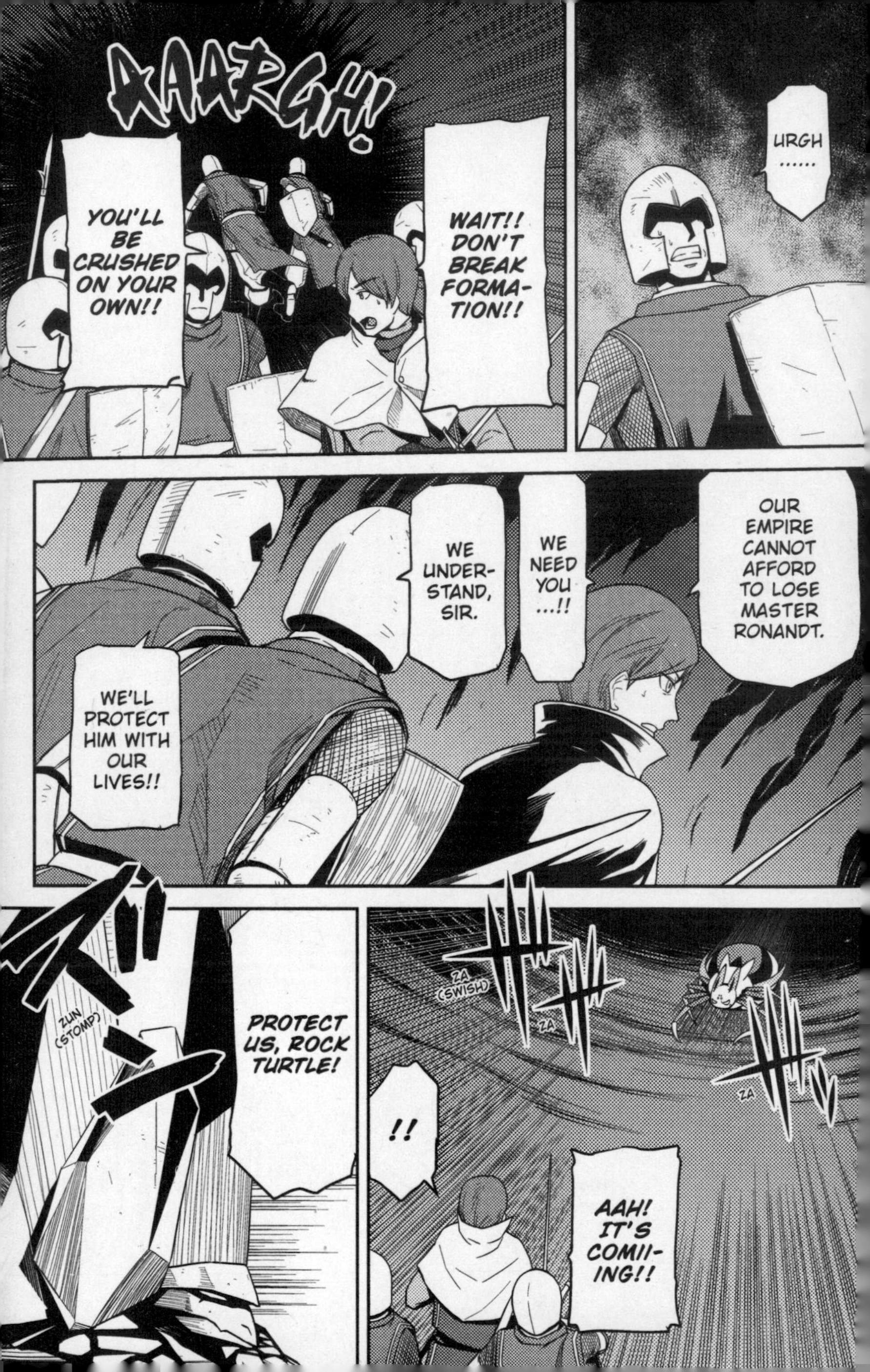
URGH ......
AAARGH!
WAIT!! DON'T BREAK FORMA-TION!!
YOU'LL BE CRUSHED ON YOUR OWN!!
OUR EMPIRE CANNOT AFFORD TO LOSE MASTER RONANDT.
WE NEED YOU ...!!
WE UNDER-STAND, SIR.
WE'LL PROTECT HIM WITH OUR LIVES!!
ZA (SWISH)
ZA
ZA
!!
AAH! IT'S COMI-ING!!
ZUN (STOMP)
PROTECT US, ROCK TURTLE!

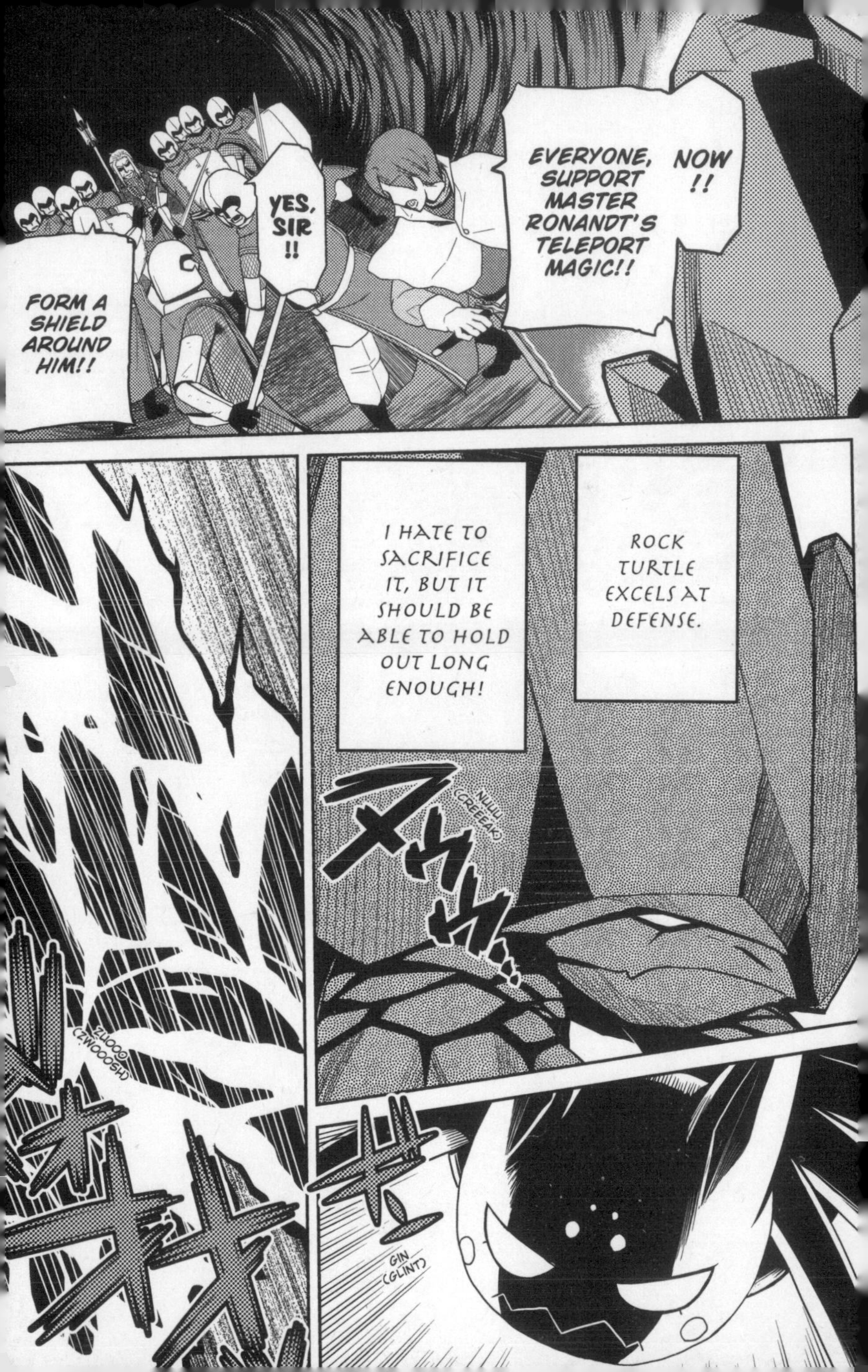
NOW!!
EVERYONE, SUPPORT MASTER RONANDT'S TELEPORT MAGIC!!
YES, SIR!!
FORM A SHIELD AROUND HIM!!
ROCK TURTLE EXCELS AT DEFENSE.
I HATE TO SACRIFICE IT, BUT IT SHOULD BE ABLE TO HOLD OUT LONG ENOUGH!
NUUU (CREEEAK)
GIN (GLINT)
(ZWOOOSH)

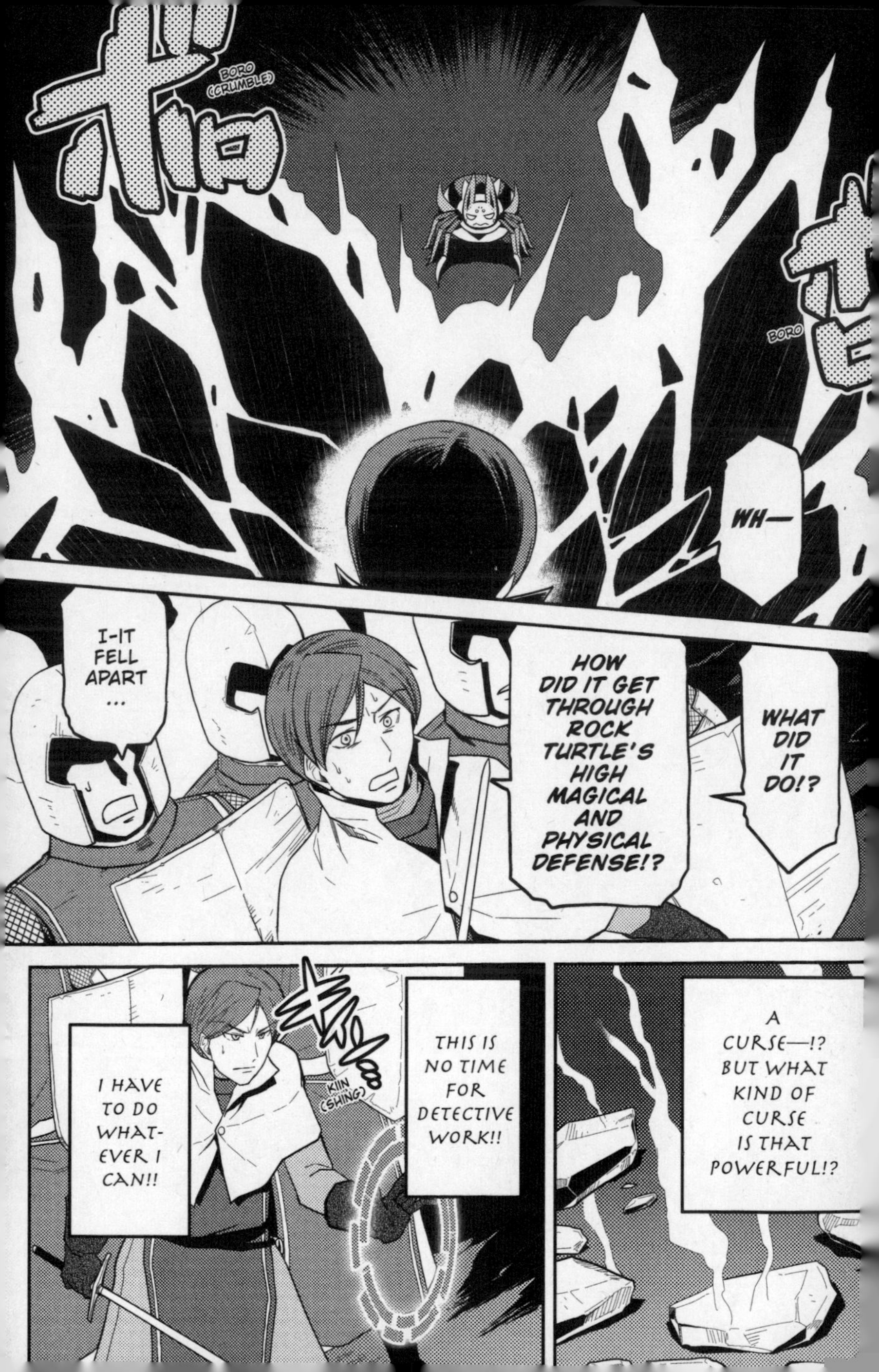
BORO (CRUMBLE)
BORO
WH—
WHAT DID IT DO!?
HOW DID IT GET THROUGH ROCK TURTLE'S HIGH MAGICAL AND PHYSICAL DEFENSE!?
I-IT FELL APART...
A CURSE—!? BUT WHAT KIND OF CURSE IS THAT POWERFUL!?
THIS IS NO TIME FOR DETECTIVE WORK!!
KIIN (SHING)
I HAVE TO DO WHAT-EVER I CAN!!

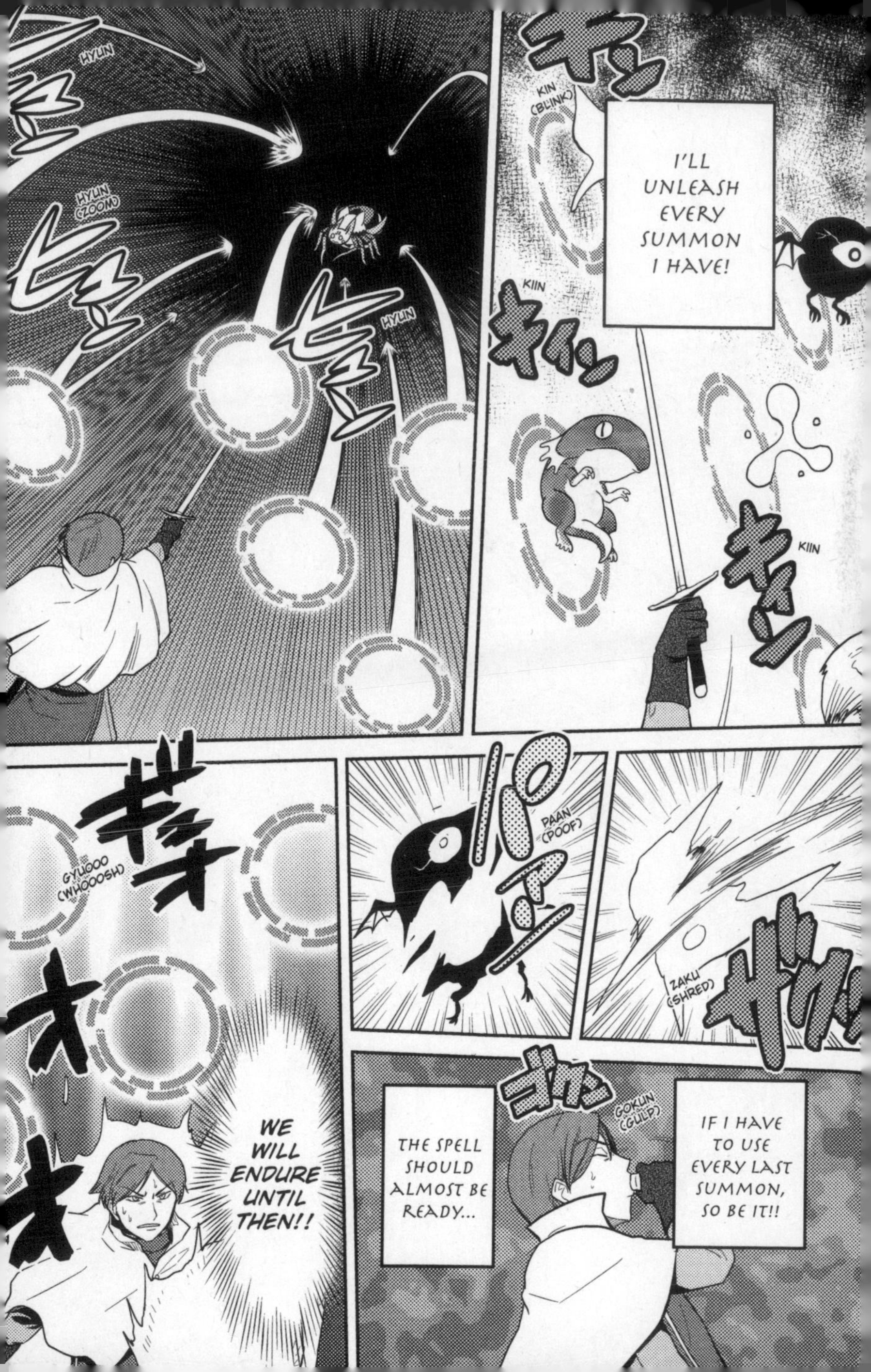

KIN (BLINK)
I'LL UNLEASH EVERY SUMMON I HAVE!
KIIN
KIIN
HYUN
HYUN (ZOOM)
HYUN
ZAKU (SHRED)
PAAN (POOF)
IF I HAVE TO USE EVERY LAST SUMMON, SO BE IT!!
GOKUN (GULP)
THE SPELL SHOULD ALMOST BE READY...
GYUOOO (WHOOOSH)
WE WILL ENDURE UNTIL THEN!!

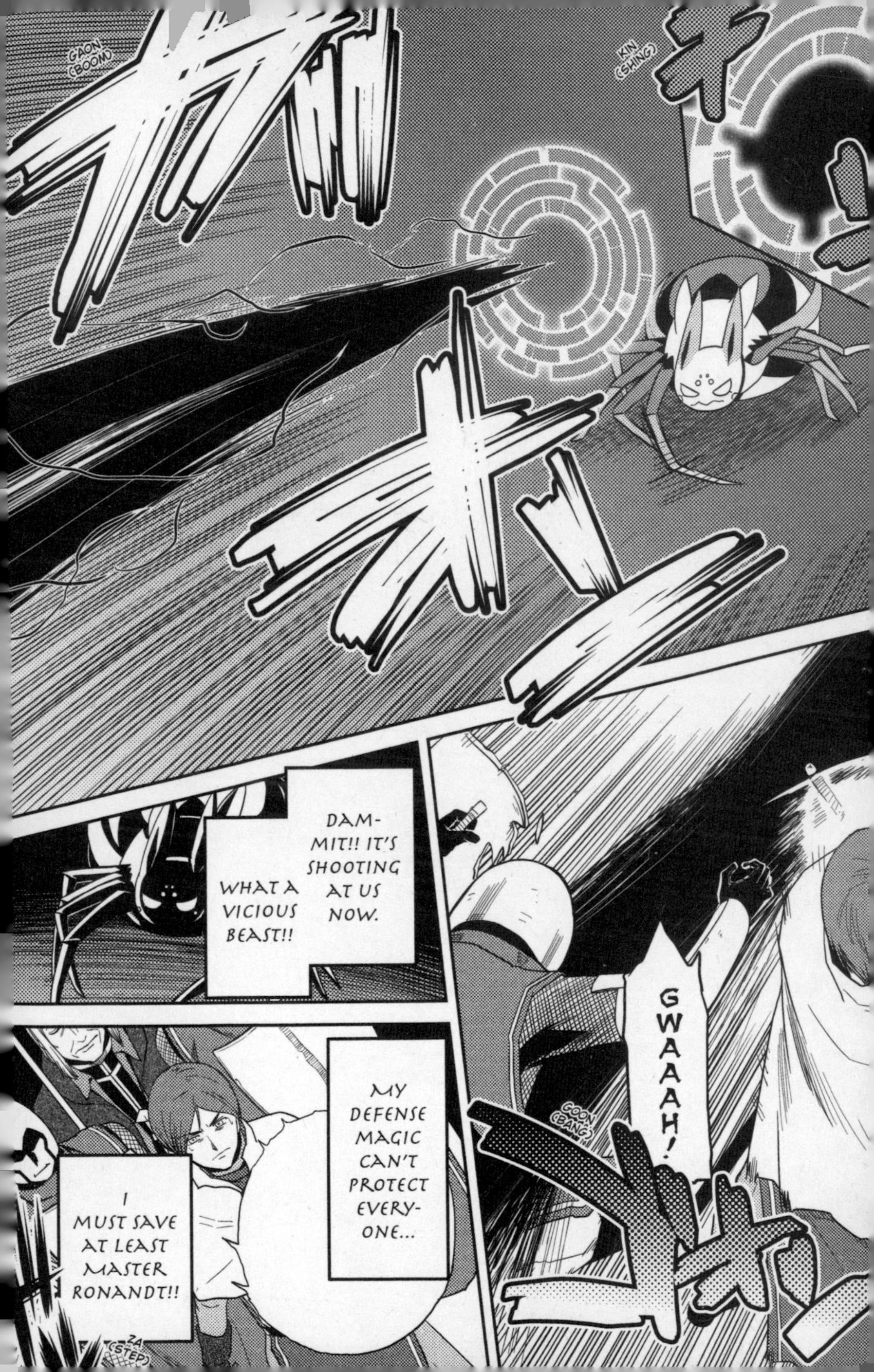
KIN (SHING)
GAON (BOOM)
GWAAAH!
GOON (BANG)
DAMMIT!! IT'S SHOOTING AT US NOW.
WHAT A VICIOUS BEAST!!
MY DEFENSE MAGIC CAN'T PROTECT EVERYONE...
I MUST SAVE AT LEAST MASTER RONANDT!!
ZA (STEP)

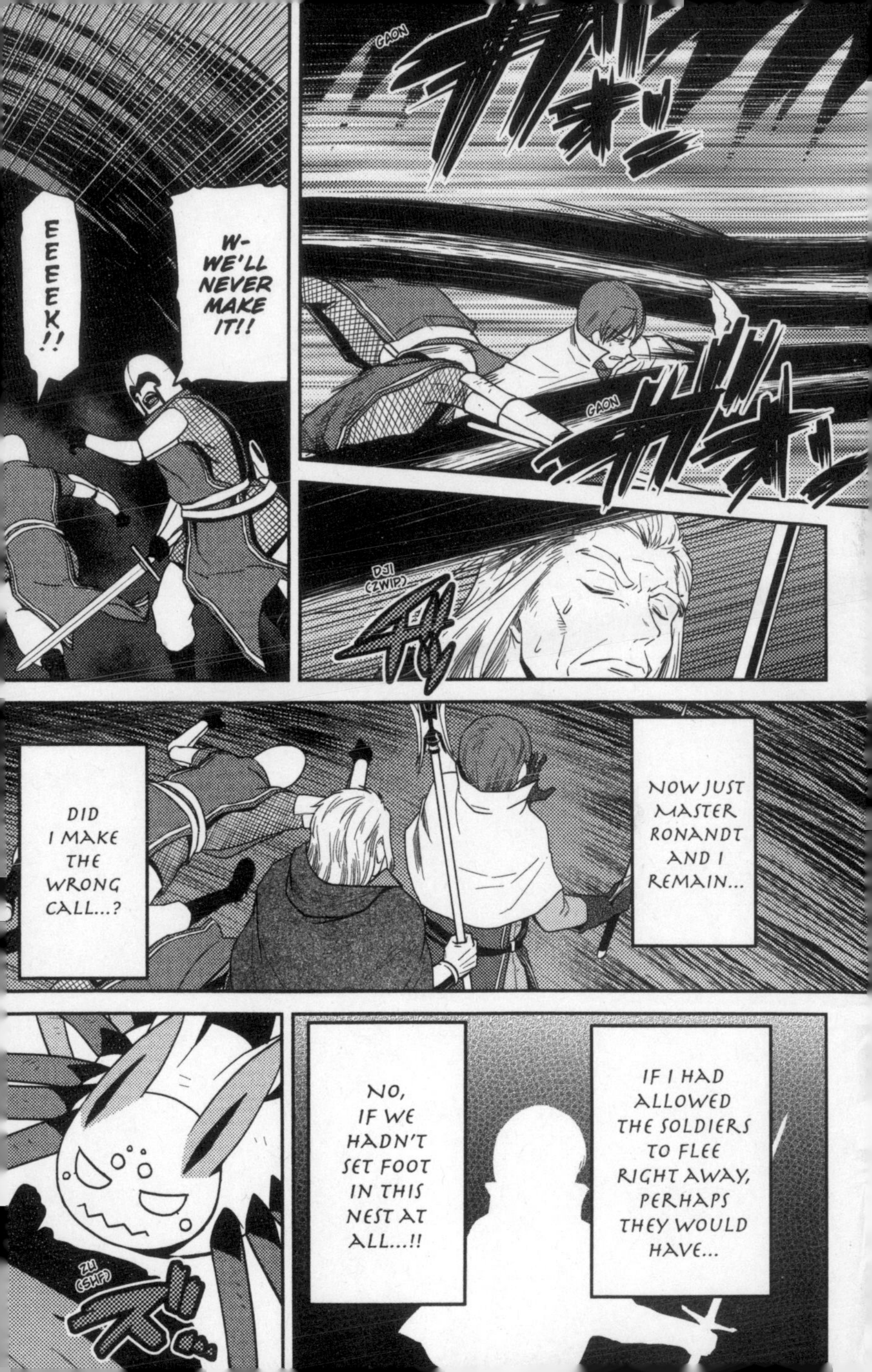
GAON
GAON
DJI (ZWIP)
W-WE'LL NEVER MAKE IT!!
EEEEEK!!
NOW JUST MASTER RONANDT AND I REMAIN...
DID I MAKE THE WRONG CALL...?
IF I HAD ALLOWED THE SOLDIERS TO FLEE RIGHT AWAY, PERHAPS THEY WOULD HAVE...
NO, IF WE HADN'T SET FOOT IN THIS NEST AT ALL...!!
ZU (SHF)

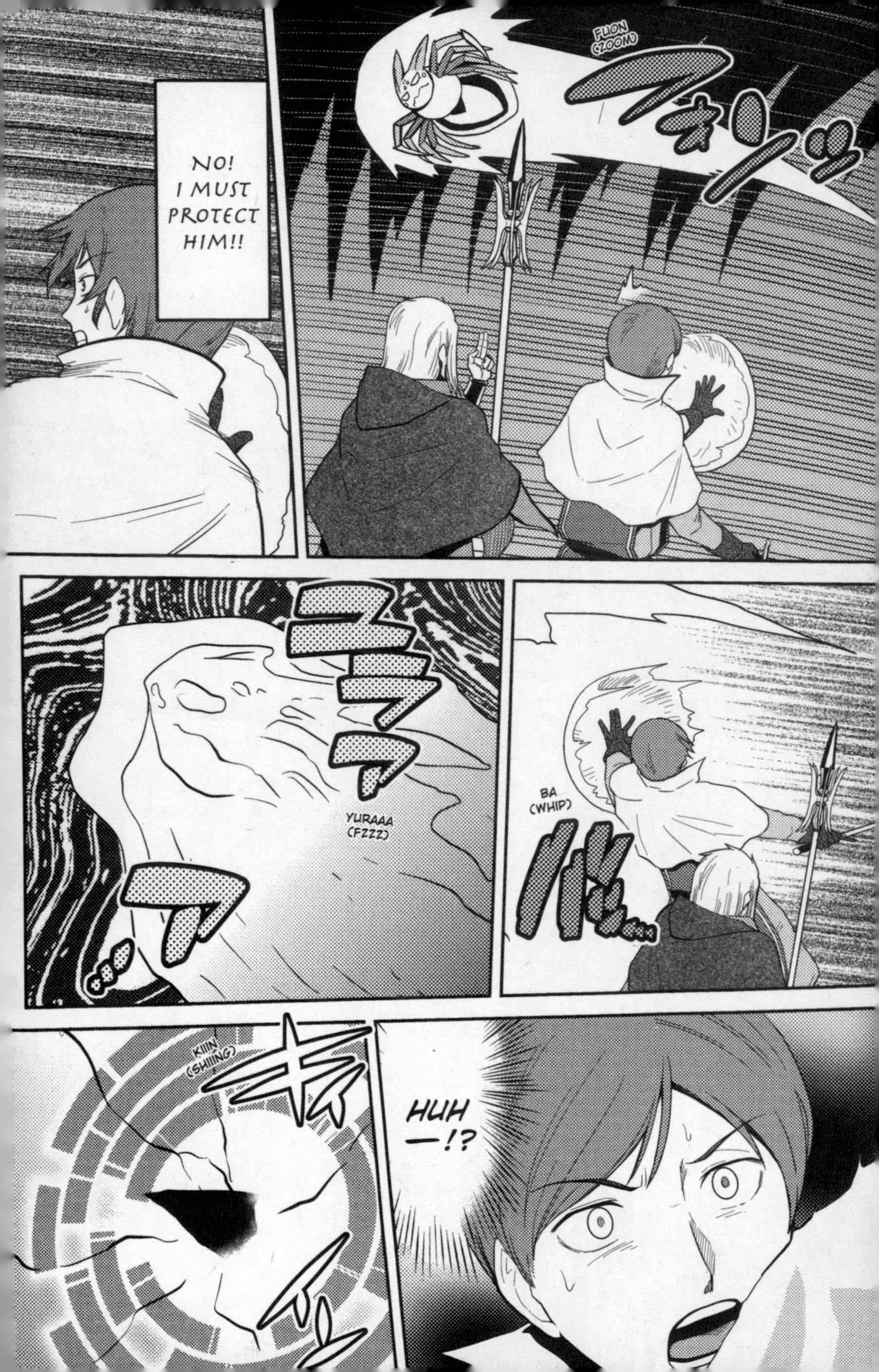
FUON (ZOOM)
NO! I MUST PROTECT HIM!!
BA (WHIP)
YURAAA (FZZZ)
HUH—!?
KIIN (SHIIING)

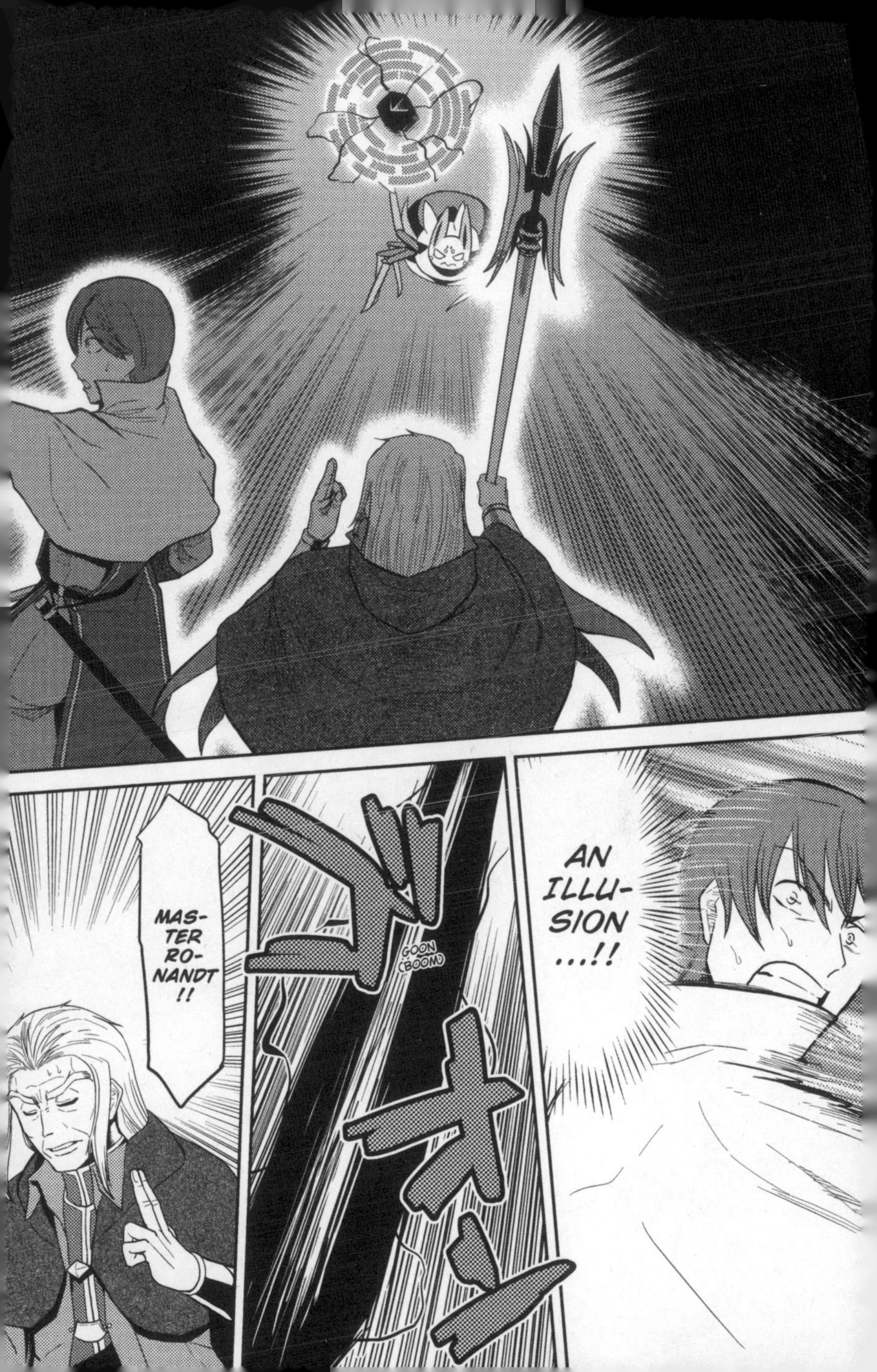
AN ILLUSION...!!
GOON (BOOM)
MASTER RONANDT!!

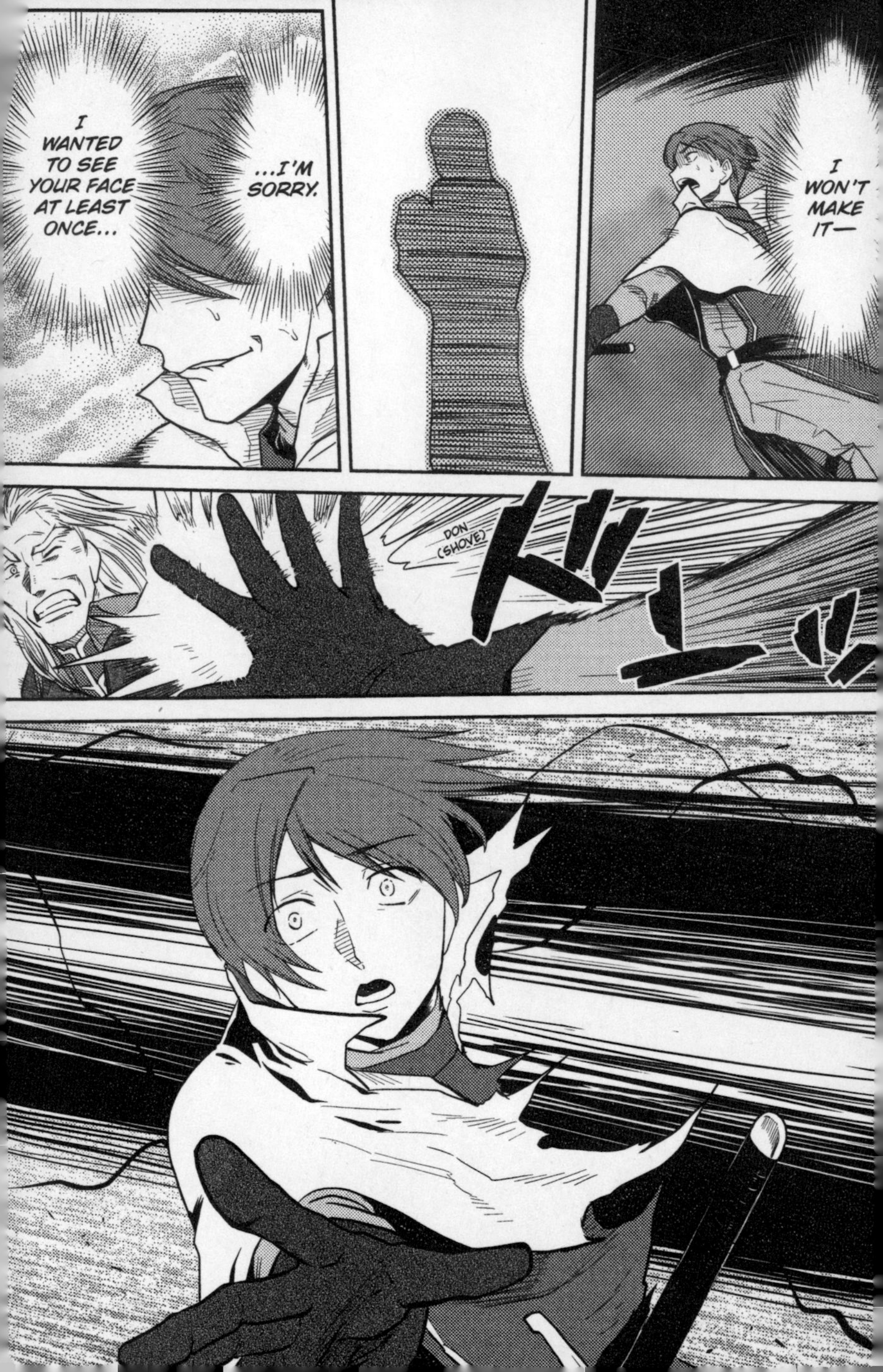
I WON'T MAKE IT—
...I'M SORRY.
I WANTED TO SEE YOUR FACE AT LEAST ONCE...
DON (SHOVE)

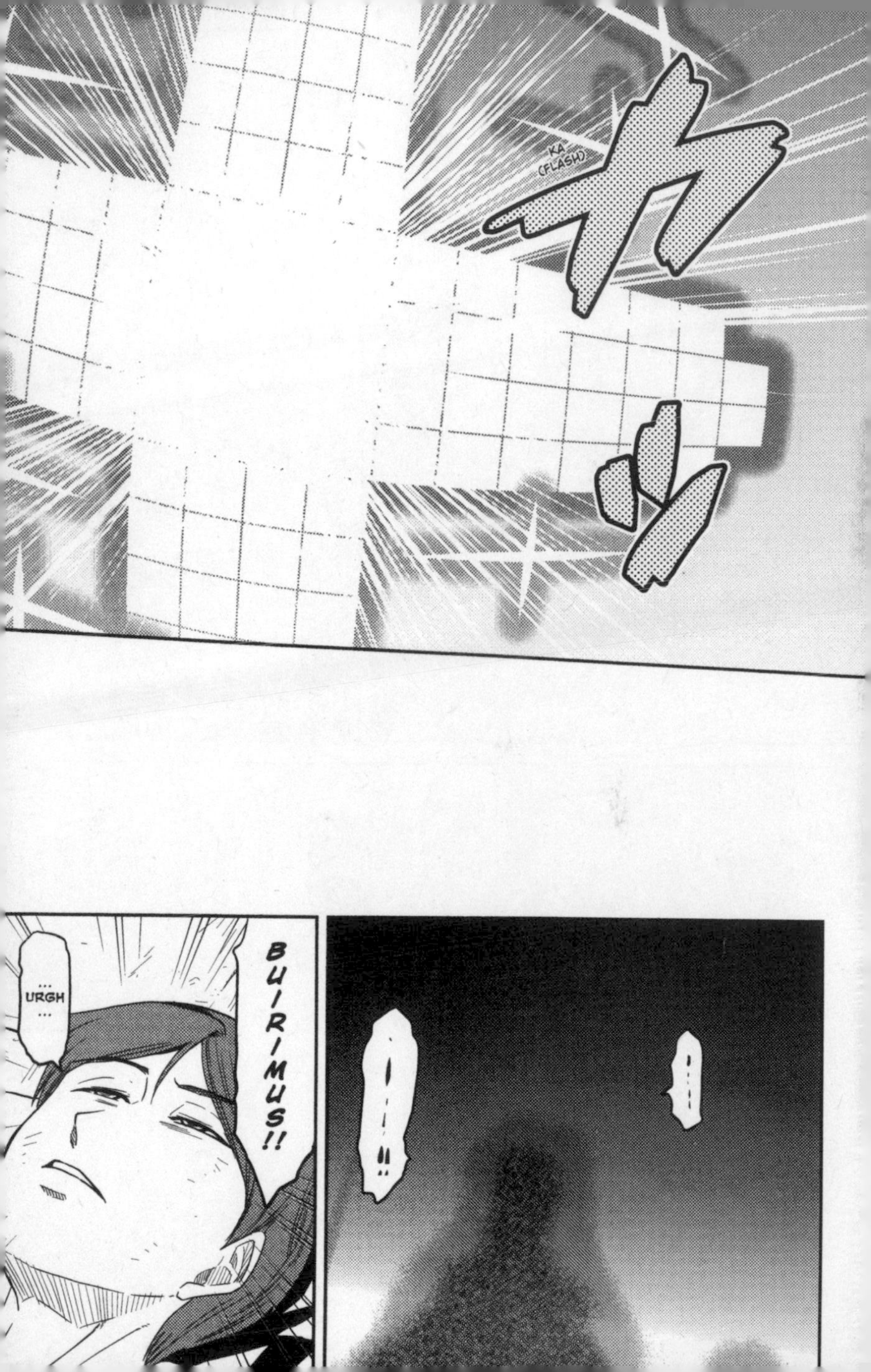
KA
(FLASH)
!...
!...!!
BUIRIMUS!!
...URGH...

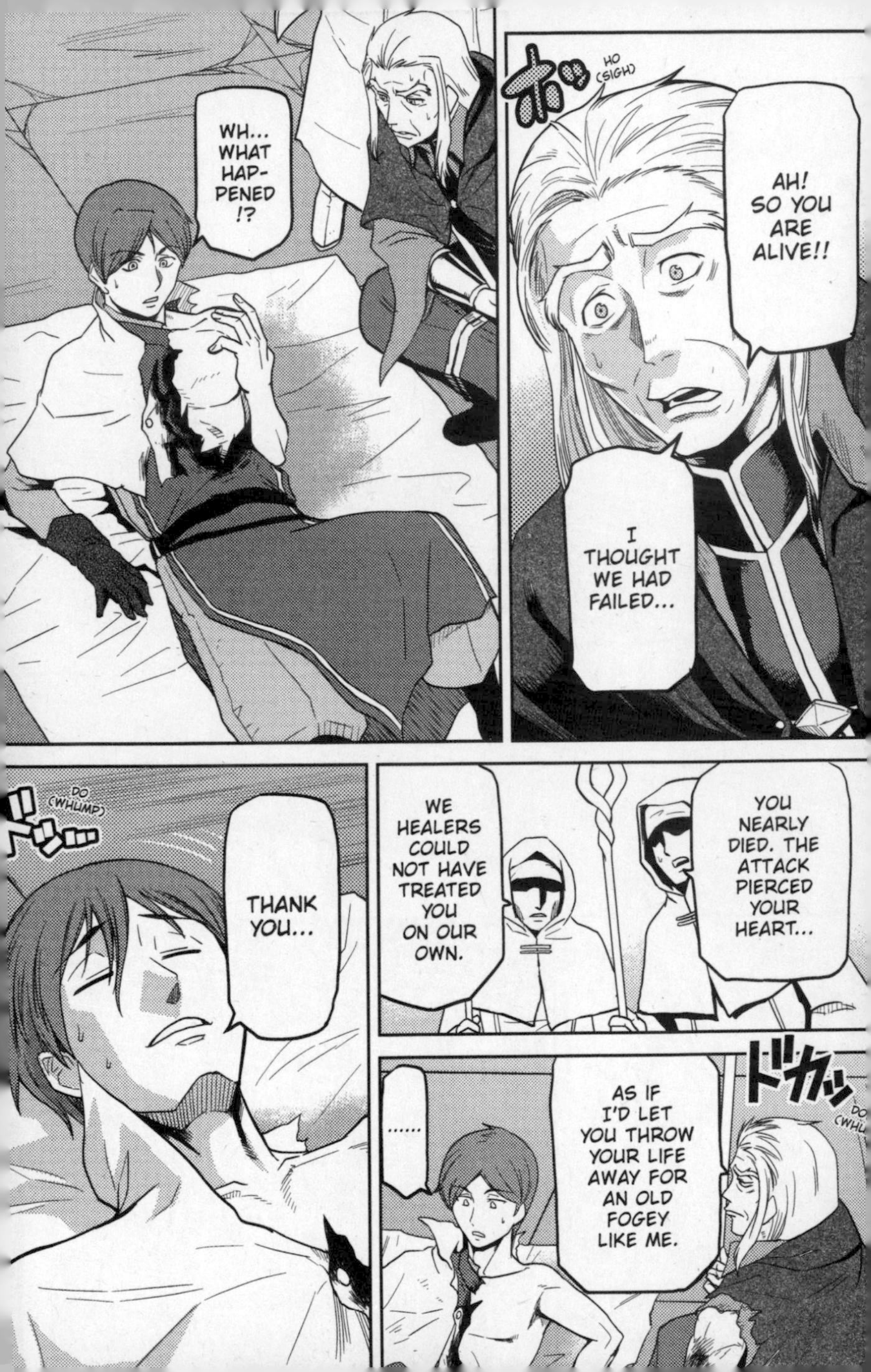
HO (SIGH)
AH! SO YOU ARE ALIVE!!
I THOUGHT WE HAD FAILED...
WH... WHAT HAP-PENED!?
YOU NEARLY DIED. THE ATTACK PIERCED YOUR HEART...
WE HEALERS COULD NOT HAVE TREATED YOU ON OUR OWN.
DO (WHU
AS IF I'D LET YOU THROW YOUR LIFE AWAY FOR AN OLD FOGEY LIKE ME.
......
DO (WHUMP)
THANK YOU...

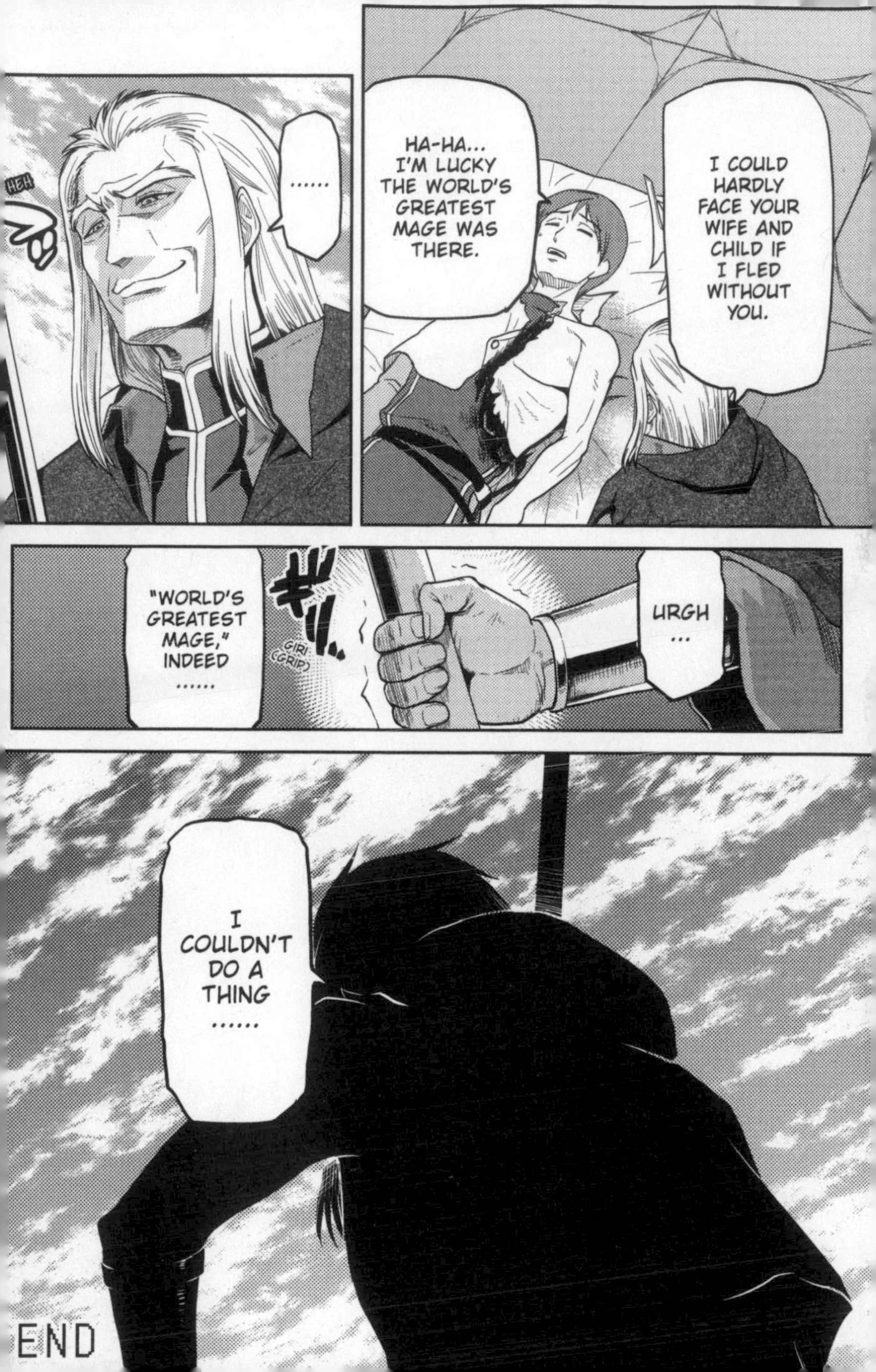
I COULD HARDLY FACE YOUR WIFE AND CHILD IF I FLED WITHOUT YOU.
HA-HA... I'M LUCKY THE WORLD'S GREATEST MAGE WAS THERE.
......
HEH
URGH ...
GIRI (GRIP)
"WORLD'S GREATEST MAGE," INDEED ......
I COULDN'T DO A THING ......
END

AFTERWORD

ORIGINAL CREATOR: OKINA BABA

WAIT—I BEG THEE! I'M OKINA BABA, THE ORIGINAL CREATOR!

THAT BELOVED MAIN HEROINE (THE OLD MAN) HAS FINALLY APPEARED!

HE'S SPOKEN THAT NONSENSICAL PHRASE AT LAST!

IT'S MOVING TO THINK THAT THIS IS WHERE THE MAIN HEROINE (THE OLD MAN) GOT HIS HUMBLE START.

IT'S HARD TO BELIEVE, BUT I FIRST CONCEIVED OF THE MAIN HEROINE (THE OLD MAN) AS JUST A REGULAR MINOR CHARACTER.

BUT WHEN HE SHOUTED "WAIT! SHOW ME MORE!!" HIS CHARACTER BECAME MUCH DEEPER. THEN, BEFORE I KNEW IT, HE STARTED SHOWING UP SO MUCH THAT HE'S BECOMING A REALLY IMPORTANT CHARACTER...

ANYWAY, THAT MAIN HEROINE (THE OLD MAN) GETS A LOT OF SCREEN TIME IN THIS VOLUME!

WHEN YOU SEE HIS BACK IN THAT LAST PANEL, HIS FEELINGS ARE EXPRESSED IN A WAY THAT CAN'T BE PUT INTO WORDS.

IT REALLY DRIVES HOME THE DIFFERENCE BETWEEN NOVELS— WHICH ONLY USE WORDS— AND COMICS.

THAT'S DEFINITELY THE HIGHLIGHT OF THIS VOLUME.

BY THE WAY, THIS VOLUME'S CONTENTS ARE FROM THE THIRD VOLUME OF THE NOVEL VERSION, WHICH SHOULD BE COMING OUT ON THE SAME DAY AS THIS VOLUME OF THE MANGA.

THAT'S ALSO PRETTY MOVING TO THINK ABOUT.

ANYWAY, IN THE AFTERWORD OF THE THIRD VOLUME OF THE NOVEL, I WROTE: "WE'RE BASICALLY JUST WRAPPING UP THE OPENING ACT NOW."

IN OTHER WORDS, KAKASHI-SENSEI'S BATTLE HAS ONLY JUST BEGUN!

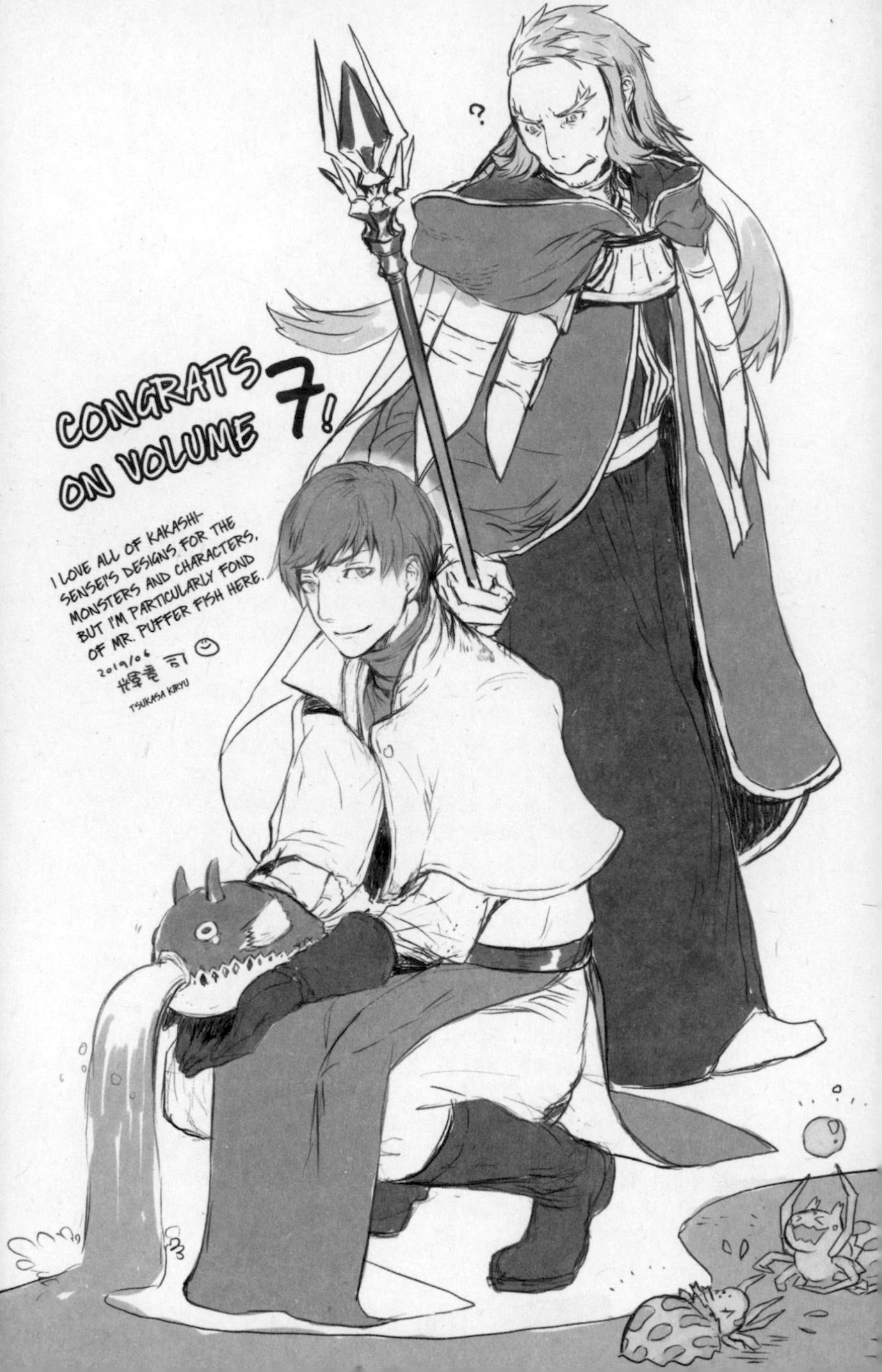
?
CONGRATS ON VOLUME 7!
I LOVE ALL OF KAKASHI-SENSEI'S DESIGNS FOR THE MONSTERS AND CHARACTERS, BUT I'M PARTICULARLY FOND OF MR. PUFFER FISH HERE.
2019/06
TSUKASA KIRYU

STAFF LIST

The author

ASAHIRO KAKASHI

Assistant

TERUO HATANAKA

Design

R design studio

(Shinji Yamaguchi)

You're reading
the wrong way!
Turn the page to read
a bonus short story by
So I'm a Spider, So What?
original creator,
Okina Baba!

stats and skills, you still never know if you're gonna win.

But I've done a lotta preparation.

Guess I better get moving.

[The end]

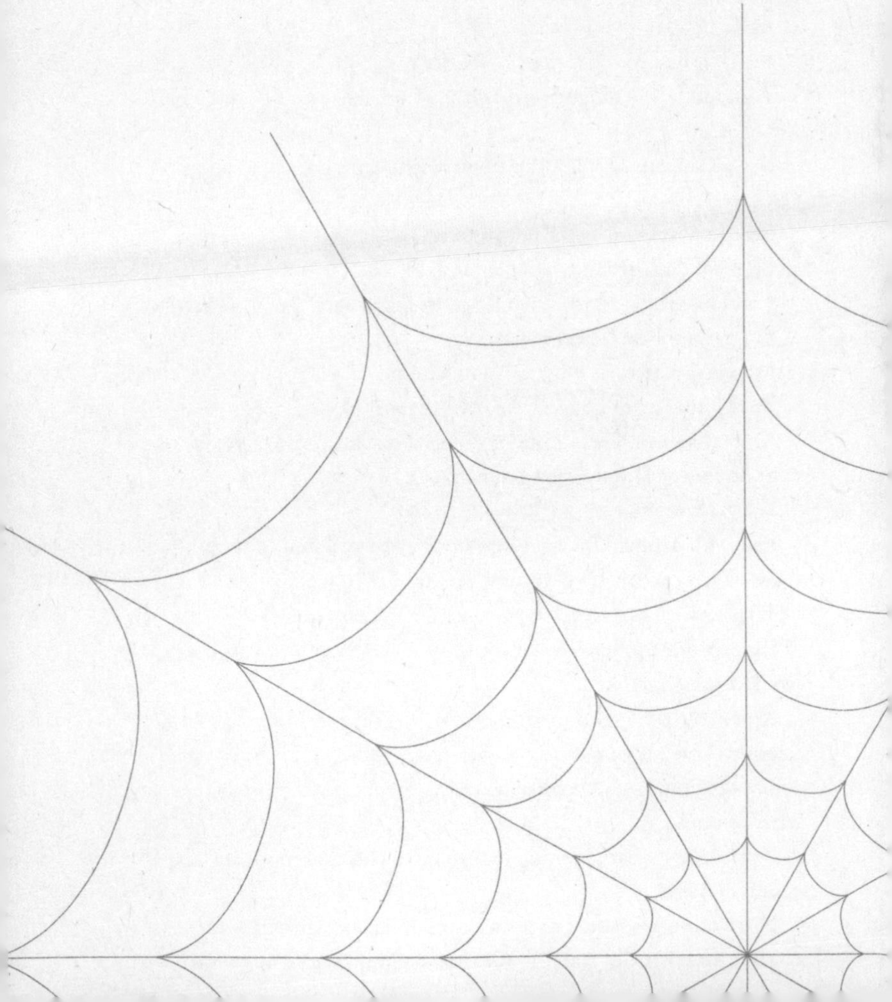

You mighta guessed it, but it generally uses those skills for a straightforward body slam that's s'posed to stab through its opponent. Sounds simple, right? But it could also become a one-hit kill.

If I hadn't figured it out with Appraisal and bolted outta there, I might have a giant stick-size air hole in my body right now.

Look, Appraise, bolt—then the next moment, the thing charged through where I'd been, like, a second earlier.

Just like that, I tell ya.

Eek! If spiders could sweat, I woulda been drenched.

I mean, obviously, I dodged it, but it's pretty hard to do stuff like that the first time you see it.

And if it hits you, you're probably dead.

Wonder if you could survive without a defense as high as an earth dragon's...

But all the monsters in the Lower Stratum have secret tricks like that.

See? I tell ya, they're all cowards!

Huh? Whaddaya mean, I'm a monster, too?

And I have tons of sneaky hidden tricks as well?

La, la, laaa. I can't hear you~...

It doesn't matter as long as I win, okay?!

But I guess that's how all the other monsters see it, too.

After all, every day is a life-and-death battle for monsters, so they can't be choosy about how they win.

I'm the same way.

At first, I scraped by with just my thread and poison fangs, but I had to keep coming up with new techniques to survive.

That's why I picked up so many skills to defeat enemies.

Especially Appraisal—so I could see what techniques my enemies would use against *me*.

Know thyself and know thine enemy, as they say—that way you'll never lose even if you fight a hundred battles.

Those kill-on-sight techniques only work if the victim doesn't know what's coming.

If you know what's coming beforehand, you can figure out how to counteract it.

None of my enemies has seen my techniques beforehand.

...But what's really scary about this world is that, in spite of all the

So I'm a Spider, So What?
Might Makes Right
Okina Baba

I feel like I can say this, 'cause I've seen a lotta different monsters here in the Great Elroe Labyrinth, so here goes:

Monsters are cowards!

I mean, just think about it. Normally, those guys'll kill you as soon as they see you, right?

That's all well and good in a game where you have infinite lives, but, dude, we've got only one life in this one.

If you die, that's it.

But these guys have no problem coming after you with all these one-hit kills and combos and stuff.

How is that not cowardly?!

Even the weak monsters in the Upper Stratum—like the centipedes—attack in swarms, using their fangs to paralyze their prey before tormenting them with slow and painful deaths.

And in the Middle Stratum, without Fire Resistance, you can't have a fair fight with any of those monsters.

The Lower Stratum?

All the monsters in that pit are cowards, too!

Even though I'm much stronger now, I mighta fallen for some dirty tricks down there if I didn't have Appraisal.

All hail Appraisal!

If you can see your opponent's skills, you can usually tell what they're gonna do.

Even then, I've still gotten myself in quite a few tight spots.

Like, there's this one monster that looks like a stick with arms and legs, but it's got wicked-high speed stats, and its skills specialize in Piercing attacks.

So I'm a Spider, So What?

7

Art: **Asahiro Kakashi**

Original Story: **Okina Baba**

Character Design: **Tsukasa Kiryu**

Translation: Jenny McKeon · Lettering: Bianca Pistillo

Kumo desuga, nanika? Volume 7
© Asahiro Kakashi 2019
© Okina Baba, Tsukasa Kiryu 2019
First published in Japan in 2019 by KADOKAWA CORPORATION, Tokyo.
English translation rights arranged with KADOKAWA CORPORATION, Tokyo,
through TUTTLE-MORI AGENCY, INC.

English translation © 2020 by Yen Press, LLC

Yen Press
150 West 30th Street, 19th Floor
New York, NY 10001

Visit us at yenpress.com
facebook.com/yenpress
twitter.com/yenpress
yenpress.tumblr.com
instagram.com/yenpress

First Yen Press Edition: March 2020

Yen Press is an imprint of Yen Press, LLC.
The Yen Press name and logo are trademarks of Yen Press, LLC.

Printed in the United States of America